M A R K E R

MARKER

LOWELL CAUFFIEL

ST. MARTIN'S PRESS ≋ NEW YORK

Library of Congress Cataloging-in-Publication Data

Cauffiel, Lowell.
    Marker / Lowell Cauffiel.
        p.   cm.
    ISBN 0-312-15583-2
    I. Title.
    PS3553.A938M37   1997
    813'.54—dc21   97-9111
                                                          CIP

Book design by Julie Duquet

First Edition: July 1997

10   9   8   7   6   5   4   3   2   1

*For Richard, Al, Don, and the many
others who first showed me
how it works.*

MARKER

CHAPTER 1

THE WORD WAS *proactive*. Lawrence Gary decided he needed to go *proactive*, the revelation coming the day he asked Tino Dentz if he knew the thinking behind those two signs hanging in the mess hall—two giant smiley faces with HAVE A NICE DAY! Right there in the State Prison of Southern Michigan.

"I'm down with you, man," Dentz said. He dipped his spoon into red beans and rice. "Maybe they gonna cook us Big Macs in here one day."

Gary pointed with his fork, staying with the subject. "No, Tino, I'll give you a clue. Those signs do dictate the mood in here, but not in a way you might think."

Dentz looked up, seeing now what Gary saw: One sign on the east wall, the other on the north. Both four by four feet, black outline on chalk white, no yellow fill-in on the smiley face. Both in six-inch-deep frames, bolted to white cement block, a good ten feet above three hundred level-four prisoners eating at small square tables, another fifty cons still in line.

"You saying they really one-way glass?" Dentz asked. "Like in the county?"

Gary pointed over his shoulder. "No, dig, Tino. Behind me. That sky-box with the slits. That's where they're checking you out."

Dentz glanced up, seeing the gun turret.

Gary said, "Guy on my rock says they've got a correction officer in there with a thirty-aught-six while we chow."

"It's prison, ain't it?" Dentz said. "So what?"

"So, I'm saying the gun, the skybox, the smiley faces, they're all part of the same thing. They all go *together*. Can't you see it?"

Dentz pushed his stainless-steel tray to the center of the table. He thought about what Gary was saying for a good half minute, his tongue searching for bean skins in his teeth.

"People who run this place put the signs up there to fuck with us, Gary," Dentz finally said. "That's all those signs are for. To fuck with us. *Every time we eat.*"

"You sweethearts always chow down alone?"

Gary looked up. The lifer was standing over them, his hands squeezing his tray. His chest and arms looked as if they still had a good pump from the weight pen in Building 19.

Gary motioned. The lifer sat down between them. Gary watched him carefully open his milk carton, his closely trimmed nails and stubby fingers struggling a little with the seal. He saw two tattoos: A winged Harley wheel on his left forearm, a burning cross on the right, on Tino Dentz's side.

Tino Dentz waited until the man put the milk to his lips, then stood up slowly, rising six feet in his black prison shoes, the corrugated Vibram soles giving him the final inch. Dentz reached down and scratched his balls, making sure the lifer had an eye-level view.

When Dentz sat back down, the lifer said, "So what you sweethearts in for?"

"Armed robbery," Gary said. "Plus, a mandatory two."

Dentz folded his arms, his eyes on something distant, his tongue back to work in the crevices in his teeth.

The lifer motioned with his head at Dentz. "What about your boyfriend here?"

"We came in together," Gary said.

"Same case?"

Gary nodded.

"Same bit?"

"That's what the man said, didn't he?" Dentz said, still staring off into space. "And he ain't my fucking boyfriend, you dig?"

The lifer looked over, shrugging as if it didn't matter. "So what you rip?" he asked.

"A Knights of Columbus hall," Gary said.

The lifer squinted. "Man, they don't keep a fucking thing in those."

Gary, lifting his eyebrows, said, "When there's a big wedding inside they do."

The lifer thought about it, nodding a couple times, as if to say, Yeah, that wasn't a bad idea.

He began eating his rice.

This, Gary later decided, was an important juncture. If he'd been proactive—if he, as the *Webster's* defined it, had been "serving to prepare for, intervene in or control an expected occurrence or situation"—he would have changed the subject right then and there.

But he didn't.

He turned to Dentz and said, "And there was supposed to be a big wedding in there that night."

Dentz said, "Don't you fucking look at me. You should have checked it out for yourself, Gary. *Before* me and Bobby hit the door."

The lifer glanced up from his tray.

Gary thought about the smiley faces. He was thinking that maybe Tino Dentz just didn't have the cognitive ability to interpret detail, see it as part of a larger scheme.

"You know I've been thinking," Gary said. "Did you happen to notice all those sweaters when you and Bobby got inside."

"Sweaters?" Dentz said.

"There were what, a hundred men in the hall?"

"Maybe a hundred. Maybe a hundred and fifty. So what?"

"Maybe half them were wearing sweaters, right?"

The lifer chewed, his eyes were following their words.

"I wasn't looking for sweaters, Gary," Dentz said. "I was looking for the wall you wanted us to find."

The way Lawrence Gary remembered the job, he wanted Tino Dentz and Bobby Tank to find quite a bit more than that. He'd cased the hall three straight weekends. Observed three wedding receptions, taking his cameras into the last one, moving easily through the crowd. He'd photographed the general layout and the exits and the little stage. He'd shot damn near everything, even the bride and groom. Then he showed Tino and Bobby all the views, emphasizing the wall where they could line everybody up and pass the trash bag. And since it was a wedding, Gary remembered telling them, You search the groom. You check between the bride's tits, a move that intrigued Dentz from the start. Gary waited in the car. He'd always waited. And he never left the crew, even on that Saturday night.

Gary said, "Let me put it this way. Did you see a tux?"

Dentz blinked.

"Did you see one woman in a white dress or any bitches in matching gowns?"

Dentz still was unaware of where Gary was going, but the lifer was catching his drift.

"You see a lot of guys in sweaters," Gary continued. "Maybe a few in sport coats. But no formal wear. Doesn't that tell you something, my man?"

The lifer's eyebrows went up.

"I was inside," Dentz said. "You were *outside*. At the time, the party looked real fresh. The way I was seeing it at least."

"All right," Gary said. "That's fair. So fucking tell me exactly what you did see, Tino. I'd like to know."

Dentz began going over it for himself now, as if he was there again. ". . . So we hit the door. We're not showing them anything. Not right away. We're checking it out. I'm checking out the deejay. Bobby, checking the exits. Like we agreed. I see the wall. The bar's on the right, just like you showed us in the pictures. And most the guys were at the bar. I mean lined up, thick."

"Then?" Gary asked.

"Bobby says, 'Let's do it.' Once we open our coats, we are committed. You pull out a twelve in a situation like that, *you are committed*, Gary."

The lifer looked up, saying, "I'd have to agree with the man on that."

Dentz ignored the lifer.

Gary nodded. "So, you *did* look around? That's good."

"Yeah, I looked around. I can't speak for Bobby. But I fucking looked around."

"And you said you saw a deejay."

"Saw his sign, too."

"A *sign*?"

"Yeah, big one."

"You never said anything about a sign before. What sign was that?"

4

"Hanging behind him on the stage."

"You mean a banner?"

"Like I said, a sign. Deejay had a fucked-up name."

"Fucked up how?"

"Wayne Fope."

"What?"

"Wayne *Fope.*"

"Spell it."

"F–O–P. Fope. 'Cause I remembering thinking before I pulled the twelve out of my coat, That gotta be the most wack deejay name I ever seen."

"Wack?" the lifer asked.

"Yeah, fucked-up," Dentz said.

The lifer began laughing, the bald spot on his head turning a freckled red.

"Yo, what you laughing at, motherfucker?" Dentz asked, reaching for his tray to leave.

The lifer caught his breath. "*Wayne* is Wayne County. You stupid fucking nigger, F–O–P is the Fraternal Order of Police."

Gary later thought what Tino Dentz did next was like the trick where a guy pulls a tablecloth out from under china and candelabra. He thought that because when Dentz removed the tray, his plate and utensils stayed on the table. One smooth move, coming up and over with both hands, putting his body into it.

The tray slammed hard into the lifer's face.

The lifer on his feet now, but blinking like somebody with sand thrown in his eyes.

Gary jumped up and backpedaled.

Dentz up now, swinging the tray again, finishing off the lifer, then turning the tray sideways and landing it just under the chin of a con who charged from the adjacent table. The con on the floor. The other table, Gary later realized, manned by the lifer's block crew.

Another con on his feet now, juking a little.

"Yo, motherfucker, you want some?" Dentz barked. "I got plenty to go around."

The entire mess hall up now, yelling.

But not long. The third and final shot from the thirty-aught-six in the gun turret was followed by dead silence. Jesus, Gary thought, that fucking rifle was loud.

His eyes went to the east wall, the debris floating down from HAVE A NICE DAY. Three chunks blown out of the smile, simply confirming what he was trying get Tino Dentz to see, the smiley faces being bullet backstops.

Later, Gary decided it would be fruitless to try to explain. At his disciplinary hearing, he simply maintained that he was not the source of the trouble. He just happened to be around it. The story of his life, really. But the hearing officer didn't see it that way. Everyone who left a table got ninety days in administrative segregation.

That's where going proactive came in. In the hole, Lawrence Gary began thinking about all those signs nobody was reading. He told himself, shit, if he was taking the rap anyway, maybe he ought to be calling the moves.

As far as he was concerned, the writing was on the wall.

THEY DID MOST their time in Eleven Block at SMPC. Few people called the prison SMPC. They called it Jackson, the name of the Michigan city where it was located. Or Jacktown. Gary learned that Jackson was the largest walled correctional facility in the world. And it had that Cagney flick look. Built in the twenties. A dozen five-tier housing units on fifty-seven acres, the place shaped liked the Pentagon, with industrial buildings, guard towers, the whole ball of wax.

Gary consoled himself with that at first, looked forward to being able to say it when he got out. Lawrence Gary, twenty-eight, doing three to five, his first bit, at the biggest walled prison on earth. Two years mandatory, for use of the firearm. They'd stuck Gary with that, too, being they'd found Tino Dentz's Ruger under his car seat the night all those sweaters charged out of the Knights of Columbus hall, their sidearms drawn.

But in the final analysis, Lawrence Gary would have to say Jackson fell short of his expectations. He'd heard before going in that the tiers in the housing units were painted different colors, that the warden believed pastels kept prisoners calm. Instead, there was a new warden, and the entire block was painted sandstone. The warden's staff claimed it was beige. But Gary knew his colors, and it was fucking sandstone. Sandstone, black-and-white TVs, and noise, all the six-by-nines with open bars. No doors like the new prisons. Niggers yelling and talking trash *twenty-four hours a day*. And Gary, being a former student of the fine arts, had trouble tuning it out. The right side of his brain, the creative side, was hardwired, he believed. The noise. The lack of color. His brain. The combination sometimes made him feel as if he was doing time on bad acid laced with speed.

In the county, he'd also heard that Jacktown had a prison newspaper, complete with a full photo lab, and an art deco auditorium for theater productions and guest acts like B. B. King. That was gone, too, the auditorium gutted after a woman guard was raped and murdered under the stage. The *Spectator* was still there, but the warden had ordered the photo lab removed. The newspaper staff no longer had run of the prison, but had to obtain a call-out to put a story together, the bulls watching them everywhere they went.

Tino Dentz snagged a job first, in the sign factory, making $2.62 a day, toting around the silkscreens and metal signs.

"What kind of signs?" Gary asked.

"Freeway signs and those little ones that go up in neighborhoods."

"Stop signs?"

"No, the ones that say, 'This area protected by Neighborhood Watch.'"

Gary thought that was a good job for Dentz, that it might do something for his power of observation. Dentz thought it was sweet, too, until they ganged him up for an outside work detail. The gang spent a day putting up street signs at a place called Cherry Hill.

"You know what that is, Gary?"

The editor of the *Spectator* had already told Gary. "That's where they bury the cons that don't get out of here. If the family don't claim 'em. Six hundred and fifty-seven in there at last count."

Dentz said he'd received a letter from his mother. That she had something going for him outside when he got out. But if he fucked up again . . . "She disowning me," he said.

"So," Gary said. "You spend a lot of time with your mother?"

"That's not the point," Dentz said. "The point is I ain't fucking ending up out there."

Gary thought about the glossy he'd seen of the cemetery in the *Spectator* photo file. A bunch of stones the size of paperbacks lined up in rows. It reminded him of Arlington National Cemetery, on a tiny scale. Shit, he didn't think it looked that bad.

Lawrence Gary didn't get his bearings in Jackson until the day he came across a book in the library called *The Art of Negotiation*. In fact, reading that little book was a brain-balancing experience. The author laid out all the angles, his underlying premise being that negotiation was both gratifying and rewarding for opposing parties, not something to be feared, the way most people did on a car lot. The book fed right into his new proactive philosophy. He politely declined a two-buck job in the shoe factory, easily negotiating his way down to an assignment most of the cons considered chump change. He took Polaroids of inmates and their visitors, which only paid $1.26, but got him called out of Eleven Block at least three or four times a day. Soon, he was shooting for the *Spectator*. Then, he slid into a second position in the law library, clerking books and periodicals like *Lawyers Weekly* two days a week. The mobility of one job and the content of the other married into his own gig. He started a clipping service for inmates doing major time. The *Detroit Legal News* reported some appellate decisions long before many of the cons' court-appointed attorneys ever did. So he kept the cons in xeroxed copies, negotiating various favors—Kools for himself, other favors for Tino, mainly—in return for keeping them well informed.

Still, Gary thought Bobby Tank got the best deal. Two years mandatory, simply for coughing up a written statement for the prosecutor about the K of C heist. They sent Bobby to the Gus Harrison Regional Facility, which Gary heard looked like a community college with razor wire.

"Bobby out and back in Detroit," Dentz said one day. "That's what a guy who just transferred over from Gus said. He didn't go back to West Virginia."

Gary didn't think Bobby Tank would ever go back, not the way he used to talk about Marshall County, saying all it had was pussy that bore a family resemblance, and coal.

Tino Dentz said he was lucky RGC hadn't shipped him to Marquette, a Level 5 and 6 prison for violent offenders. But one of the paralegals in the library told Gary luck had nothing to do with it, though Dentz claimed he had a long juvenile record in Detroit. He started running scag for Young Boys Incorporated at thirteen. Ten-dollar packs, with names like ".44 Magnum" stamped on them, a marketing breakthrough in its day. By sixteen, he'd moved up to the YBI wrecking crew. Gary thought the whole chronology might be a story, until one of the paralegals said that the juvie file didn't follow you into the adult system. That was the genius of YBI, Gary decided. The brains never handled the powder, or did the heavy work. They made decisions. And at eighteen, the youngsters were free to move on to bigger and better things with a clean sheet.

Lawrence Gary and Torino Dentz and Bobby Tank. Dentz liked "Tino," complaining his mother named him after a fucking Ford. Bobby was Bobby, even on his birth certificate. Gary insisted on Lawrence, or Gary. Never Larry, because of the rhyme problem.

They all were first offenders—on paper, at least. They'd pulled some good jobs before the hall, businesses most people in the life overlooked, places Gary came up with from his dealing days, all the talking his upscale customers did once they got his good shit up their noses. A suburban clinic, which really was a script mill. A bar moving some rock. A lingerie shop in Utica where models cavorted around in teddies in private viewing rooms. Tino was always wanting to do those. "We got to lay off on the jack-off parlors," Gary told him one time. "You do the same jobs, pretty soon they're looking at a modus, and that's what draws the heat."

Lawrence Gary's rips had a theme, not an MO. The theme was: hit businesses that had something to hide. That way a mark wouldn't be down at the detective bureau every day, riding cops to close the case. That's where he'd erred on the K of C hall, Gary ultimately decided. Shooting the photos was easy, but he'd deviated from his basic theme. He'd not been *proactive* when Bobby Tank spotted the place, then insisted they hit it.

When they got their out-dates, Tino Dentz began making plans. Dentz had hooked up with a con on fourth tier, the man telling Tino before he went to dress-out, that he had a line on some quality crank back in Detroit.

Gary said, "Tino, I've been doing a lot of thinking. And the word that keeps coming to me is 'exposure.' "

"You talking pictures?" Dentz said.

"I'm talking exposure to things you can't negotiate."

Mandatory time on amounts over sixteen grams, he said, up to life for a pound. And now more mandatory time on a second firearm offense. Five years, if the judge wanted to be a prick. He'd read about it in the *Legal News.*

"We need to reduce our exposure," Gary said. "Especially if you're still worried about that cemetery out there."

He'd been thinking a lot in those terms in his last days on third tier, trying to wash out the noise in Eleven Block at night. Trying to put the left side and the right side together. Browsing through mental snapshots. Come up with a good theme, then go proactive. Put it all in motion. Go beyond crime.

Shit, make it performance art.

"Show me something," Tino Dentz said. "Maybe I'll be there."

THEY RELEASED DENTZ two days ahead of Gary. His mother was waiting for him in the parking lot in front of Central Complex. She brought along somebody from her church, Dentz told Gary.

"That's worse than the bus," Gary said. He was on the pay phone in the yard. "You got wheels yet?"

"I will tomorrow. Gonna have my own place, too."

Gary didn't ask for the details. He'd get that later, after he got out tomorrow.

"I need you to pick me up in the morning," Gary said.

"I got an appointment."

"What kind of appointment? Your PO?"

"My hair."

Gary decided not to even try it. He'd heard the complaints for three years, Tino always wondering how Gary got his retro waterfall, then bitching, "Yo, Gary, how come you can't *negotiate* some good hair products for me in here?"

Gary asked, "How about later?"

Maybe at the Detroit bus station, Dentz said—not the prison, adding, "Even then, you know they can violate you right there for that."

"You think your PO's going to be at the blue goose?"

"That's not what I'm saying."

"Then, you're saying you're gonna be there."

"Probably."

"There can't be no 'probably' about it. Either you're going to be there, or you aren't."

"Depends on the time."

"What time's your appointment?"

"Nine."

"Then I'll see you at the bus station at noon."

Gary hung up, but lingered at the phone, thinking. He'd kept Tino Dentz's loyalty, and bought his protection with certain favors, not to mention the reefer and issues of *Hustler* and *Chic*, his payments from the lifers. He suspected he'd have to keep the goodies coming, if he wanted Tino Dentz's loyalty to remain very deep.

A half hour later, he was in the rotunda in Central, the corrections bureaucrat saying, "Mr. Gary, I'm ready for you now." She was a fat gal with rose glasses, calling from the doorway of the interview room near the control center.

Inside, there was a table, two chairs, and a manila folder with his name and corrections number on the tab. She pulled out something called a "Certificate of Parole."

"Now, Mr. Gary, I am required to read this to you so you are fully aware of the terms. Then I'm going to ask you to sign it, signifying you understand those terms."

Gary said, "Of course."

Her nose still in his paperwork, she said, "I see this is your first parole." Looking up, she said, "Maybe we better review some of the particulars."

Gary smiled, wanting her to feel that he appreciated she was doing that.

She ignored the overture. "I see you will be released tomorrow, August first, and take up residence with your mother, Tula Gary, in Detroit, is that correct?"

Gary nodded, still smiling.

She went back to the papers. "Now, let's review your parole conditions."

He folded his hands in front of him as she began.

" 'You must contact your parole field agent as instructed no later than the first business day following release. Thereafter, you must report, *truthfully*, as often as the field agent requires. You must report any arrest or police contact, loss of employment, or change of residence to the field agent within twenty-four hours, weekends and holidays excepted.' Do you understand, Mr. Gary?"

"Fully," he said.

She slid a paper toward him, saying, "Here is the address and phone of the Detroit Metro office. Do you need directions to this office?"

He glanced at it and said, "No, thank you. I believe I can find it just fine."

"Okay," she said, reading again, " 'You must not leave the state without prior written permission.' "

"Of course not."

" 'You must not engage in any behavior that constitutes a violation of any criminal law of any unit of government. You must not engage in assaultive, abusive, threatening or intimidating behavior. You must not use or possess controlled substances or drug paraphernalia or be with anyone you know to possess these items.' "

She looked up.

Gary nodded, gave her another smile.

"You have to say yes," she said.

"Yes."

" 'You must not associate with anyone you know to have a felony record without permission of the field agent. You must not associate with anyone you know to be engaged in any behavior that constitutes a violation of any criminal law in any unit of government.' "

"Yes."

She looked over the glasses with scolding eyes. "That includes this facility, Mr. Gary. You are not to visit or have phone contact with inmates."

"That's not in my plans," Gary said.

Reading again. " 'You must not use any object as a weapon. You must not own or possess a weapon. . . . ' "

She continued for five minutes, detailing special conditions set by the parole board, including his promise that he planned to seek work and report his progress on a regular basis to his PO.

When she was done, she said, "Now, Mr. Gary, will your mother, or someone else, be picking you up here at Central?"

"No," he said. "She has a sitting tomorrow."

The woman looked over her glasses, making eye contact for the first time. "A sitting?"

"A sitting."

Her eyes wanted an explanation.

"She's a painter," he said. "You know, she paints portraits."

"Really," she said, drawing the word out. "For a living?"

He smiled again.

"I'm taking a class at JCC this summer in oils," she said. "I took watercolors last term."

"Really?"

"Hearing about somebody making a living at it," she said, smiling, "that's really neat."

Neat, Gary thought. His mother didn't make a living. She cashed alimony checks and picked up maybe five hundred a month with her half-ass renderings. For twenty years she'd been stinking up the house with turpentine and oils, the curtains closed, completely oblivious to the neighborhood going to hell. That's what drew him to photography. It didn't smell.

"She's *quite* good," he said.

"Well, you're taking the bus, then?"

"I guess I am."

"Do you have money for the bus?"

"I've saved up more than six hundred in my account."

"Very good," she said.

The fat bureaucrat was looking at him differently now. Not like a con, but like he had something going for him.

"Well, there's nothing about that here in my paperwork. I'll arrange that a corrections officer drive you over to the Greyhound in downtown Jackson."

"You don't need to do anything special."

"It's procedure, really. But I'll make sure you don't have to wait."

She was going through his entire Department of Corrections folder now, checking out everything about him. When she was done reading she said, "It says here you want to pursue opportunities in the fine-arts field, Mr. Gary."

"That's right," he said.

"So what are you planning on doing, Mr. Gary? Do you want to be a painter, too?"

She handed him the certificate.

"No, photography," he said, signing the paper *"Gary"* with a certain flair.

He slid the paper to her across the table.

She glanced at his signature momentarily, then leaned forward, resting her fingers under her chin.

"So, you're going to be shooting pictures, then?" she asked, smiling again.

"Yeah—lots of them," he said.

CHAPTER 2

WHEN OZZIE SAW all the eight-by-tens hanging in the Anchor Bar he asked Connor, "Who are those guys?"

Pointing, Connor said, "That's the former mayor. And over there, that's Doc, the old *News* columnist. And there, that guy with the hat, that's Chickie. He was a bookie."

There were a couple dozen photos in all, mostly black-and-whites taken in the fifties and sixties, suspended in plain black frames above the mirror, over the liquor bottles. Connor knew some of the politicians and the judges, a good number of them being Irish. He didn't know the old newspapermen, though a city editor in a white shirt and vest looked vaguely familiar. His sleeves rolled up, a pencil in his ear, he looked like he'd come from central casting. Most of them did.

But that's not what Ozzie said he was saying.

"What I'm asking," Ozzie said, "is when is your picture going up there?"

"I'm in no hurry," Connor quipped. "Those are the dead drunks—looking down at the live drunks."

Ozzie saw a half dozen regulars at the bar rail. "So you have to be a customer, *and* you have to be deceased?"

Connor said, "Yeah, and some days in here, it's a little hard to tell the difference between the two."

The Anchor had no nautical motif, no view of the Detroit River. In fact, it had no view at all. There were only the photos of the dead luminaries, cheap drinks, and a downtown clientele who came in for the former, while trying not to become the latter.

Nelson Connor liked the place.

He liked the Anchor because the bar refused to surrender while everything else attached to it had decayed. It was in the Pick-Fort Shelby, an old high-rise hotel closed for twenty years or more. For sale with no buyers. Seventeen floors of dark, gutted singles, doubles, and suites. The Anchor had its own street entrance, the only hint of inside activity the hum of its exhaust fan blowing burger fumes onto Lafayette. He'd discovered the bar during his first law practice. It used to be a newspaper bar, the *Detroit News* and the *Free Press* a short walk away. Connor used to sit with the writers, soaking up bourbon and a certain reckless intelligence some of them had. The older ones were on the wall now. The new breed wore power ties and suspenders. They didn't cover trials and the courts much, and they hardly drank. A few hunted for scandals. But most were occupied saving readers from themselves, writing stories about cigarettes and high-fat foods. He didn't see reporters he knew at the Anchor anymore. If he did, he would have never suggested to Ozzie they meet at the Anchor Bar.

In fact, Nelson Connor rarely came to the Anchor to drink with anyone, not the workers from the Federal Building or the bank secretaries who dropped by on paydays. He came because he didn't see lawyers there. He saw lawyers all day at work. The Anchor was too far to walk from the City County Building or the Frank Murphy Hall of Justice. Connor drove over, parking on Lafayette, feeding the meter two quarters every hour. He ran a bar tab of about a hundred a week. Took a check from home and tucked it in his billfold every Monday so he could pay it off on Wednesday. Always got a free double, Jim Beam, usually, when he paid. He'd simply decided a couple years ago he was better off in the Anchor than sitting on a packed freeway. And he didn't worry about drinking. He'd made a deal with himself. He'd worry the day he found himself sitting under those pictures above the bar.

They took a couple of Beams to the table in the back, near the pool table. It was after lunch, Connor already dispensing with all his business in court on a slow Monday, Ozzie showing in a pair of chalk twills and a bright Tommy Hilfiger sport top.

"My sales look," Ozzie said.

"One of many throughout the years," Connor said.

Ozzie grinned. "Remember when we took over the university? After Kent State?"

He remembered the president of Wayne State suspending classes, and telling Connor, who was on the strike committee, "Then, goddamn it, you people run it." The campus Catholics gave them the Newman Center in the SCB. They hung out in the chapel for three days, mainly getting stoned on Ozzie's weed.

"I finally came up with a word for what we were doing," Connor said.

"Not 'revolutionaries.' "

"Two words, actually. 'Situational radicals.' "

Connor drained his Beam-and-soda. Ozzie went to the bar for two more. When he returned, Ozzie dropped the small talk.

"So, my situation," he said. "How do you think it looks?"

Connor stirred the twist of lemon in the ice with his finger, then lit a Camel Light.

"Tell me about the girl," Connor said.

"You mean Kelly?"

"I thought she had another name."

"You mean Taylor. But she only uses that when she works."

"All right, then tell me about Kelly. We'll get to Taylor later."

"What do you want to know?"

"You were truthful with the court aide, weren't you?"

Ozzie nodded.

"It was this Kelly who set you up with the undercover guy?" Connor asked.

Ozzie hunched forward. "Connor, you know me. I've never been into anything big. It was strictly for personal use. Until this guy showed. I only did it for her."

"What exactly does this girl do?"

"Things you would not believe," Ozzie said, grinning. "I've been seeing her almost a year."

Connor rolled his eyes. "No, what I'm asking is: The AOI said she was a dancer."

"AOI?"

"Arraignment on the information. When you were arraigned in circuit court. What kind of dancer?"

"She works at several places. She's freelance."

"So we're talking topless?"

Ozzie held up his hands. "I know what you're thinking. But it's different now. All top-of-the-line. Not those dives like you and I used to hit on Eight Mile Road."

"Worth leaving your wife for?"

"I couldn't handle doing them both," Ozzie said.

Connor thought about it. He'd seen a few colleagues go that route, few with good results. "How did you do it at all?" he asked.

"You learn to lie," Ozzie said. "It's almost scary the shit you come up with." He hunched forward. "You know the secret to telling a good lie, don't you?"

"No, but I believe you're going to tell me."

"Well, like the first time we got it on. She used to wear this perfume. I took three showers, and I'm still smelling it on the ride home. So I crawl into bed, and the wife says, 'You smell like perfume.' So you know what I say?"

"You were looking at perfume for her at Hudson's?"

"At two in the morning? No, I say, 'You're right, honey. I was at the Maverick. Got a lap dance from one of the girls.' "

"Lap dance?"

"That's where they get right on top of you. Like I said, Connor, it's changed."

"So you told her about that?"

Ozzie nodded. "Which was absolutely true. The lie was based in truth. That's the secret. That way, the wife gets to raise some hell. I look guilty. But I'm covered on the big one, the fact that I was screwing her, too."

"You don't leave your wife unless you're serious," Connor said. "This girl must be more than a screw."

"She's sharp. That's why I trusted her on this thing."

"You still trust her? She wasn't arrested."

"Absolutely. In fact, she saved my ass. Maybe yours, too."

Connor leaned forward, lowering his voice. "Saved my ass?"

"Well, after I got popped, got the one phone call, I called her. She got my phone book. I was worried if the undercover guy got his hands on that, he'd be hassling a lot of people."

"My phone number was in there?"

Ozzie raised his eyebrows. "Both of them," he said.

Connor thought about the implications. It had been years since he'd bought anything from Jimmy Osborne, some weed back in law school. They'd shared a couple joints over the years. But he appreciated the gesture nonetheless.

Connor turned the subject back to Jimmy Osborne's upcoming sentencing.

"You should have picked a different judge," Connor said.

"I'll take my chances."

"I should have told you that."

Ozzie had pled guilty to the lesser charge, as Connor had suggested when he called for legal advice four weeks ago. Ozzie had picked the judge of his choice for sentencing. That was entirely within the rules.

"So," Ozzie said. "You think I'm in big trouble?"

Connor finished off the glass, feeling the bourbon-and-soda dance down his throat. "Most judges base their sentences on what the presentence report says," he said. "That's why it's important to be truthful to the court aide."

"I was."

"Then I wouldn't lose sleep over it. Not on a first offense."

Ozzie seemed satisfied with the answer. Nelson Connor wanted to change the subject. He'd have a few more drinks, then he'd tell Ozzie he really couldn't have anything more to do with his case. After all, certain rules of conduct were involved.

They drank bourbon for an hour and told stories, stuff popping into both their minds. They'd essentially gone their separate ways, but always kept in touch, meeting two or three times a year in obscure watering holes. That suited Connor, considering the rules that governed his profession, considering some of the things Ozzie was into on the side.

The story came up. It always did when they were drinking hard.

"You remember that guy from Brightmore?" Ozzie asked. "The day you saw me?"

"You mean when I saw both of you?"

Twenty years ago, Connor coming out of a brief coma induced by a twelve-ounce glove, Ozzie over him, in pairs. Connor was trying out for the Wayne State boxing team when this middleweight hit him with an upper cut he never saw coming, ending any plans he had for a collegiate career.

"You sure that middleweight was from Brightmore?" Connor asked.

"I think he's in a biker gang now."

Ozzie, also from Brightmore, was overachieving as a premed student, thinking that also meant hanging around the Walter P. Matthaie gym as a cut man. Ozzie brought Connor back with the salts, then bought him Stroh's all night at the Traffic Jam.

Both of them were from tough neighborhoods, which, among other things, was probably the basis of their rapport.

"How did we ever get through school?" Connor asked.

"I didn't, remember?" Ozzie said.

"You got talent, Oz, you just need to get focused."

"I'm trying," he said, gesturing with his glass. "Hell, I'm only forty-four."

He hardly looked thirty-five, Connor thought, as he watched Jimmy Osborne get up, stretch, then stroll off to the john.

When Ozzie didn't return right away, Connor went to the bar and got a couple more drinks. Back at the table, he knew he was well under way. He could feel his own face, his jaw heavy. Still, he wasn't where he wanted to be.

He was still thinking about it when Ozzie got back.

"You know, back then, it was easy to get that click," Connor said. "You get older, it's not so easy anymore."

Ozzie studied him momentarily. "What click is that?"

"That feeling," Nelson Connor said, lifting his glass. "That feeling that *clicks* in."

"You mean getting shit-faced?"

"No," Connor said. "That's definitely not what I mean."

Drunk covered mental and physical acumen, Connor tried to explain. Drunk was sitting at the bar rail, barely able to stand. The click was a state of mind.

"I still don't understand," Ozzie said.

Connor looked at his old friend, tapping his fingers on the table like they were bongos, working with the Stones' "Start Me Up" on the juke-box. Ozzie ought to understand, he thought. Shit, Ozzie was there.

Connor asked, "Look, you ever see that movie with Paul Newman and Elizabeth Taylor, *Cat on a Hot Tin Roof?*"

Ozzie nodded, his head picking up the beat of his hands.

"Well, remember that scene in Liz Taylor's bedroom? Christ, she's walking around in this slip, looking real hot. Her and Paul Newman spending the whole day in there. Newman, he's been hitting Old Grand-dad out of pint bottles, remember? Then, all of a sudden, Big Daddy, Burl Ives, comes in."

"Yeah," Ozzie said. "I think I remember that."

"Well, remember what Big Daddy says?"

"I can't say I do, Connor."

"He says, *'Son, when you going to stop drinking? You been drinking all goddamn day.'* " Connor trying to do his best Burl Ives. "And New-man says, *'And I'm gonna keep drinkin', Big Daddy. 'Cause I ain't found that click yet.'* "

His hands still now, Ozzie just looked at him.

"That's the click I'm talking about," Connor said. He added, "Of course, during the movie, I'm not sure he ever finds it. But that's another story altogether."

Ozzie stood up. "C'mon, Connor," he said.

"Where we going?" Connor asked, looking up.

"Out to my car."

"We going someplace else?" He didn't want to move. He didn't feel like moving. They'd been drinking all afternoon.

"Not necessarily," Ozzie answered.

"Then why?"

"I got something I want you to try."

"Like what?"

Ozzie brushed a dead ash off of Connor's Brooks Brothers lapel and said, "Something that's going to help you find that click."

TWO HOURS LATER, Connor set down his drink, stuck a Camel Light in his mouth and dropped two more quarters into Q-Bert. This was his special spot, like the one Carlos Castaneda wrote about in the *The Teachings of Don Juan*, standing at the arcade game around the corner from the barmaid's station, out of sight.

Ozzie gone now.

The machine gave up a jingle and a quick game preview. The idea was to move Q-Bert up and down a pyramid of cubes, changing their colors as snakes chased him. Change all the cubes, you scored and moved to the next level. Make a bad move, or don't get all the colors changed, the bad guys got you.

Nelson Connor knew the game well. Probably too well. He fed it at least twenty-five bucks in quarters a week.

On the fifth level, he heard his name announced at the barmaid's station.

"Nelson Connor."

He stuck with the joystick. He hated the way she did that, sounding like a bailiff trying to conjure a defendant in a packed courtroom on arraignment day.

"Nelson Connor!"

He didn't like the barmaid's voice. He liked the way she wore jeans and tank tops, her breasts pushed up with a Wonderbra. She'd never given him anything but liquor and change, but he found her chill seductive, a strange effect, considering the same from his wife Katherine produced the opposite result.

"Nelson Connor!"

Almost to the next level now.

He yelled, *"In a minute."*

The Camel's secondhand smoke reached his nostril, watering his eye. He jerked the butt away from his face with his left hand, keeping his right on the joystick.

"Damn," he said, whacking the controller with his palm, rattling it.

He finished the Beam-and-soda as he walked away from the machine. He handed the barmaid his empty glass as he passed her, asking her for another. The phone was waiting for him near the men's-room door, the receiver hanging by its cord. He remembered telling himself after his last trip to the john he'd have one more—one more drink, one more game—and be home by seven. He glanced at his watch.

He hadn't made it.

Katherine said, "Nelson, what are you doing?"

She called him Connor usually, but recently she'd been calling him Nelson. They called each other all kinds of names. Early on he called her KC. Somehow in their fifteen years together that evolved into Kace.

"I had a matter to attend to, Kace," he said.

"In the bar?"

"Well, I stopped off for a couple."

"I didn't know they had twenty-ounce glasses there."

He let it go. "Did you save dinner? I was just leaving."

She didn't answer for a couple seconds. An old Boy George tune filled the space. He wished the jukebox wasn't so loud.

"We got pizza," she said, finally. "The *vet* appointment took an hour and a half."

The way she said it made him remember. Yes, he had offered to take the monkey to the vet. "You bought it," she'd told him that morning. "You should deal with it."

"So what's the story?" Connor asked, deciding to ignore the oversight entirely. "Tell me something good. Tell me the little bastard is going to die."

Another pause. Then she said, "John must have fed him something. But monkeys do that, the vet says. He says they mark territory."

"By what, cutting loose all over the house?"

She didn't answer.

"So what did he suggest?"

"He suggested diapers."

"That's it?"

"Seventy-five dollars," she said.

"For the diapers, or to tell you monkeys like to take a shit?"

"No, for the tests," she said.

He added it up. He had somewhere near a thousand in the animal now. A squirrel monkey. A momentary lapse in judgment on a Saturday morning. Hung over, he'd taken his boy to the pet store, looking for a blond lab, but walked out with the monkey.

"So, did you talk to John, about feeding him junk?"

"Why don't *you* talk to him?" Katherine asked.

He waited, expecting to hear his son's voice.

"Hey," he yelled to the barmaid, motioning with his drink at the jukebox. "Can you turn that goddamn thing down?"

Then Nelson Connor heard a dial tone.

He stood there for a while, holding the receiver like he had a connection, studying the color of his drink, the way it looked over the cracked ice. Then he walked into the men's room, closing the stall door behind him and sitting on the toilet, never undoing his belt.

The little vial Ozzie had given him was in his suit pocket. He'd told Ozzie in the car that he didn't see what the big deal was. "I can get the same buzz off black coffee," he said. Then they'd spent two more hours drinking, playing the Q-Bert game, and snorting a couple hundred bucks' worth of cocaine, Ozzie leaving him with another gram when he hit the road. Ozzie didn't want him to pay, but Connor insisted. He owed him three hundred. He wasn't comfortable owing Ozzie a dime.

He sat on the toilet and waited, until he could taste the coke in the back of this throat, until it negated the effect of the countless drinks he'd had. He waited for the click.

Outside, the barmaid with the Wonderbra was standing at the waitress station, filling another order. A couple of regulars nearby were talking trash to her, but she ignored them.

Connor touched a glass of ice to her bare shoulder.

"Could you bring me another one back by the machine?"

His eyes went to her chest, catching an angle, a look deeper. He wondered what this gal, Kelly, of Ozzie's looked like. Then he thought of Kace, all pissed off at home.

"On your tab?" the waitress asked, turning, taking his glass.

"Right," he said. "And bring me ten bucks in quarters, too."

THE DAY THE real-estate salesman showed them the house in Northville, five years ago, he told Nelson and Katherine Connor that the Jeffries Freeway was probably the best commute out of Detroit, saying, "A straight shot, a half hour from downtown Detroit, max." The realtor, who wore a blue jacket that matched his sales sign, added, "*And*, you save time being close to the village. Heck, you can walk to the village from the house."

Nelson Connor thought about that realtor on the freeway a lot. He figured his time share once. Used a calculator. If you spent an hour and a half both ways, counting parking the car in the structure and going up and down the CCB elevators, you spent 437 days across twenty-five years of commuting. Damn near a year and a quarter of your life, doing nothing but following a goddamn line up and down the road.

They had a townhouse near Corktown, a five-minute drive to work. But Katherine wanted their son in a safe public school system and, with her graphics business growing, she said they had to face it: They were running out of room.

He'd always liked the city. Felt like he earned his place there. He didn't fear Detroit like the suburbanites who hadn't been downtown since '67. He grew up on the West Side, saw the flames light up the sky that year, his father vowing that no goddamn riot was going to push him out. When he started at McKenzie High, the old man signed him up with the Kronk gym. He learned to jab, cross, and take a heavy shot. Picked up only a couple junior trophies, but learned the proper attitude. That's what protected him in the hood. Word got around at McKenzie: That white boy Nelson was quick, and a crazy motherfucker, too.

"What are you suggesting, Connor?" Katherine had asked. "We start training a seven-year-old for the Golden Gloves?"

So, he told her go ahead, handle it. This is what he liked about her. She didn't need hand-holding and she knew him. She knew he hated one-story suburbs and subdivisions and ranch houses. So she started looking thirty miles out.

He saw the location for the first time on a Saturday morning. They met the realtor for Bloody Marys at a bar called the Hole in the Wall, just a couple blocks from Northville Downs. The realtor said Northville Downs was a fine harness track, adding, "People *love* the sight of those horse trailers coming into town." The realtor said Northville was the ideal community, that people still left their doors unlocked and their keys in the cars, something Katherine did frequently after they moved.

The realtor kept pumping the location as a "New England–like village," and Connor had to give him that. Studios and specialty shops and restaurants occupied the two-story brick village storefronts. "Northville has everything a family could want," the realtor said. If you had the money. They needed Kace's income to swing it. She dropped some downtown Detroit accounts, but picked up the slack with local brochures and ad layouts.

"And, you can walk to the village," the realtor kept saying.

"Well, then, let's walk," Katherine said.

They walked to a two-story restored Victorian, with a carriage house out back. She took him there first. It had two sets of large carriage doors in front. The realtor said they could easily rip those off and install electric garage doors, but Connor could tell by the look on Katherine's face, those doors were staying. She took Connor up the narrow steps to a small apartment that looked out over the yard and street. She wanted to install skylights and make it her studio. He saw her eyes and he knew they were buying it before he ever toured the interior of the house.

It needed little work. There was a cherry banister, leading to three large bedrooms upstairs. On the first floor, there were a half dozen rooms, all with hardwood floors. The kitchen was expansive, in the back of the house, with a breakfast nook that had a southern exposure. There was a library, with two sliding doors and enough built-in maple bookcases to take all the law books Connor could cart in and more. She hung white-on-white embroidered curtains on the first floor, keeping with the Queen Anne look. He saw them for the first time on a warm, windy day. She'd opened all the double-sash windows, the draperies moving like white flags in slow motion. "I surrender," he said. She had outdone herself, he decided, especially considering his peculiar needs.

Now, the squirrel monkey had ruined three sets of the white curtains in three weeks. Scampered up, hung by one hand from the curtain rod, swinging. Made a defiant gesture at Connor when he tried to control him, then ripped his way down, taking the entire window treatment with him. The monkey was fine for the first two months. A little smart-ass, maybe, but generally cute at first, making everybody laugh. Older now, more seasoned in his surroundings, now the monkey produced only belligerent chaos, or he slept.

Driving on the freeway, Connor wondered what he found more torturous, the squirrel monkey or the drive home. Recently, he'd confessed to Katherine that maybe the monkey had nothing to do with his attitude. He'd been thinking that he just wasn't comfortable living in total safety. He found Mondays the worst. And he'd come to hate Sunday nights, when the Detroit newscasts ran a lot of crime stories. "On Mondays, I feel like I'm heading back to a theme park dedicated to urban violence," he said.

"Connor, your reasoning makes no sense," she said.

He explained, he used to be oblivious to it. Hell, he saw perpetrators and victims every day in court. But maybe, he explained, when you live in the city, the violence is like a jackhammer. "You know, you don't notice it when it's outside your window all the time." He was *aware* of it now. Maybe, he told her, this was the cause of what he could only describe as a free-floating bad attitude, one that seemed only to be relieved in his special spot at the Anchor Bar.

Kace said, "I've got to give it to you for creativity, but that's about the biggest line of shit I've ever heard."

So Mondays tended to begin, or end, like that. When he got home he often found her in front of the little Sony in the breakfast nook, aiming only a cheek at him for a kiss. She liked to watch *Cops* at seven-thirty; the squirrel monkey perched on the windowsill, nervously munching on something, watching her, then him.

"Why do you watch that show?" he asked her one time, the cops separating a brawling couple on a domestic call.

"It makes me feel good I'm not living that way—at least not yet," she said.

CONNOR WAS THINKING about the realtor's freeway again when rubber construction barrels and blinking lights began squeezing four lanes of Jeffries traffic into one crawl. He rolled down his window, letting the August air hit his face.

A hundred yards farther down the road, the sound of the generator engine on a blinking merge arrow invaded the Buick's leather interior. Connor tossed the butt of his Camel into its yellow lights, sparks flying. He closed the window and reached down between his legs.

The bourbon tasted good, even from a Styrofoam cup.

When the freeway opened up, Connor didn't push the Buick past sixty. Leaving the near suburbs, the overhead lighting disappeared and the expressway became a trail of broken white lines. He squinted, then closed one eye. First the left. Then the right. The left eye open, the right eye closed. That was the best combination. Now double lines were one.

The going became tougher off the freeway: the center line faded on the two-lane leading into Northville. Ahead, the track lights of Northville Downs painted a halo over the village limits. When Connor reached the crossroads at the harness track, the intersection was vacant, the signal red.

Connor glided to a stop, looking around. The gamblers were all inside, he guessed, waiting for the last races to send them home on a high note.

He reached into his breast pocket for the vial. There was hardly a hit left, but he tapped it out, finishing it off from his thumbnail, after checking his mirror.

As he waited for the light, he found himself looking through a small gap under the track's fence. He saw a trailing horse and driver go by. Above the fence, he saw the driver's whip, it cracking once, the jockey driving the horse hard into the turn.

He looked up and saw the signal. Green now.

He looked right, checking the crossroad. He looked left, driving defensively.

A patrol car sitting next to him on the left.

A woman cop inside.

A minute later, she said, "Judge Connor, I'm going to have to ask you to step out of your car."

CHAPTER 3

TINO DENTZ WAS waiting for Lawrence Gary outside the Detroit Grey-hound station, sitting behind the wheel of a brand-new Chrysler van, royal purple, with a little metal flake that made the color snap.

Getting in, Gary said, "Whatup? Where did you steal it?"

The van lurched away from the station, Dentz looking straight ahead, playing coy.

"Talk to me," Gary said, getting a good whiff of the new interior.

"Check out the phone," Dentz said.

He'd already seen it. Not a cheap bag model, but a nice hand-held cellular with a car cradle.

"You lift that separate, or did that come with it?"

"I didn't lift it."

Gary put up his hands. "I'm sorry. I wasn't thinking. You walked into Chrysler World Headquarters and Lido Fucking Iaccoca dropped by, saw you in the lobby, and said, 'Yo, somebody give that fine-lookin' spade over there a brand-new car.'" Gary twisted the mirror to his side, checked his hair, then added, "'And give the man a cell phone, too.'"

"I didn't steal it, man." Dentz sped down the freeway ramp. "My mother's church gave it to me."

"They *gave* it to you?"

Dentz nodded. "Gave me a job and a place to stay, too."

Gary shook his head. "Church don't have that kind of money."

"This church does."

"So, where is this church?" Gary asked, curious now.

"On Woodward. Gotta be a thousand people in there on Sunday, all styled out in pearls and fine dresses and shit."

"What else this church got?"

"Pastor's got his own UHF show. *Pastor H. Roy Butler,*" he said slowly, pronouncing each component of his name. "Got a radio gig, too. Got a movie theater in the church building. A movie theater for all ages, that's what his yellow-pages ad say. And a singles club. Got one of them, and a ministry in Haiti. I'm not talking about some storefront, now."

"And they gave you a new van because you *served* your time," Gary said sarcastically.

"Something like that," Tino said.

Gary thought about it for a few seconds, but couldn't find the angle. He was looking at Tino Dentz, the certain charm the young man had. New GeriCurl. Had himself some new linen pants and an Evan Picone shirt, shooting for that *GQ* look. This made Gary want to hit Harry's Army Surplus, pick up something for himself. A French infantry shirt, some Doc Martens. Some decent shades. The light, all that chrome and hot pavement ahead, hurt his eyes.

Gary said, "Okay. The pastor *gave* you the van."

Dentz looked at him now. "Actually, he didn't give it. But I got it. It's the church bus. I'm driving the church bus. They *gave* me that job. Remember, I told you she was lining me up with her church."

"Who?" Gary didn't listen to half the shit Tino talked in yard.

"My mother. She and the Reverend Roy real tight."

"Where you drive this church bus to?"

"I pick up kids in the morning for something they call mini Bible school. Drop 'em off in the afternoon. Pick up some on Saturday for some kind of children's workshop. Drop them off, too."

Gary laughed. "They are letting you drive around children?"

Tino said, "Yeah, but the rest of the time, it's mine. And like I said, they gave me a place to live."

"At the church?"

"No, the Reverend Roy's got a mansion in Palmer Woods. He gave me a room above the garage. Nice one, too."

Gary thought Dentz should get it straight. "You mean a carriage house, Tino. Over there, in Palmer Woods, it's called a carriage house. Over there, you want to get your nomenclature right."

"My what?"

"Forget it." Gary reached for a cigarette.

"You can't smoke in here," Dentz said.

Gary lit it anyway and brooded. He didn't like the way Dentz had fallen into something like this, not unless he could get a piece.

"And the phone?" Gary asked.

"What about it?"

"What the pastor say you need the phone for?"

Dentz leaned on the armrest, driving with one hand now, obviously enjoying that Gary was asking him about all the toys.

"I'm on call, man. In case the Reverend Roy needs it or something. Sometimes I gotta take people downtown for political meetings at city hall and shit like that."

Dentz reached down to his belt and handed something to Gary, saying, "Got one of these, too."

Gary examined the pager, a digital model that gave the phone number of the caller.

Dentz pointed. "Call it, Lawrence."

Gary was checking it out, trying to decide if it was ergonomic or just a bad-looking design.

"Call it," Dentz said again, looking.

"Don't do that," Gary said.

"Do what?"

"Don't look at me while you're driving. You know how I feel about that."

Dentz looked back at the road. "Gary, just call the fucking pager on the car phone, man."

"What's the number?" Gary asked, thinking, Shit, you'd think he'd never seen a pager before.

Gary called the number Dentz gave him, then entered the car phone's. A minute later, the pager began vibrating.

"They call that a 'silent page,' " Dentz said.

"Really," Gary said, thinking, What else is new?

Dentz looked over again, grinning. "I plan on wearing it right next to my dick," he said.

They got off on Eight Mile. Tino Dentz pulled into a Picway Self-Serve Shoe Mart, put the van in park and turned off the key.

Gary asked, "What are you doing? I want to get this thing with my old lady over with."

Dentz said, "I want to check this store out. They got more in here than you think."

Gary remembered hitting a Picway. It was their first lift, back when he was checking out the kind of moves Tino Dentz and Bobby Tank had. Gary thought, Two or three bills in the register, max. In this neighborhood, maybe less than that.

"I'm not going inside," Gary said.

"Why not?"

"I'm not doing this anymore. I told you that in Jackson."

Gary looked around, checking to see what other businesses were around, listening to the drone of six lanes on Eight Mile. Party store next door, probably run by Chaldeans. Those guys packed semiautos, usually, but they didn't like to venture outside the Plexiglas unless somebody took *their* Twinkies.

Gary added, "But, I do admit, it feels good."

Dentz said, "Feels good to be out."

Lawrence Gary liked casing. He liked it more than the act itself. A good eye. A good ear. An ability to see the whole canvas, put it all together.

He'd put his little crew together after he got out of the dope business. He'd started with Buddha sticks and other exotics, then moved into quality cocaine in his last days in art school at the Center for Creative Studies, or CCS. But it got to be like Amway. Moving two pounds a week, delivering ounces in the suburbs mainly. Mostly upscale types: Artists. Lawyers. Stockbrokers. Salesmen. Even had a local sportscaster for a customer. Taught them all how to step on the blow with mannitol, then move diluted grams to their friends. They tried not to be their own best customers, but they always were in the hole. The credit situation became a real burden. One day, Gary decided if he was going to be putting up with all this shit, he might as well be shopping for suits at Sears and working in a collections office, covered by a company health insurance policy. He squared his biggest accounts in one week, telling customers with markers, "Look, my people want their money. They want names and addresses for this guy they're sending in from Tampa on a plane." That took care of most. He built a darkroom with the profits. Bought a real nice Canon system, two camera bodies with auto exposure and shutter, one a motor drive, and a set of lenses ranging from a 21mm wide angle to a 1,000mm telephoto, which was a 10× magnification. That's what got him into casing jobs. Those crisp Canon lenses.

Tino Dentz, actually, inspired the idea, the night he met him at a rave in Greektown, in an old warehouse on Broadway. He first saw Dentz in the chill-out room, surrounded by all these E-bunnies, all wanting him to touch them. They said with his GeriCurl he looked like some kind of Greek god. Gary could tell he was no Greek, or Italian, just a spade with a lot of ivory in his tree. He moved in to do some close-ups of Tino and those girls tripping on Ecstasy. Afterward, they went back to his place, where Tino confided when he peaked that he was looking to get into something new. He and Bobby Tank were almost taken out the night before by an Iraqi who came up from behind the counter with a Browning .45.

Gary told him, "You need to employ a little previsualization." That's where the photos came in. Gary said he could shoot the jobs first, using various ruses. Give the crew some nice black-and-white glossies, no color, pointing out that people grasp details better in two tones. Tino brought Bobby aboard, and Lawrence Gary was in the armed-robbery business just like that.

Now, Tino Dentz was talking about going back.

"I like the traffic on Eight Mile," Gary said. "Easy to lose the ride, even this Pope-mobile."

"Yo, Gary, I think you got it all wrong."

"No, I got nothing wrong."

Gary looked at the shoe store again, a big white banner announcing, SALE! SALE! SALE! He could see a young cashier at the register and a high-school kid stocking a row with those discount shoes. He could use the money. Use it as a security deposit so he wouldn't have to smell all that raw sienna his mother liked to use.

"This neighborhood," Gary said. "You know they got an alarm." He was wondering now where Dentz picked up a piece, where he was keeping it, and why he didn't tell him about it.

"I'm not worried about an alarm," said Dentz.

"Well you ought to be. But I wouldn't worry about it too much. If we sit here any longer, they'll be taking notes."

No, Gary decided it was no good. Shit, the van was *purple.* And the van had a plate, too.

He turned to Dentz, who was leaning against his door. Gary looked back at the dash, putting his hands together in front of him. Save the Kool hanging from his mouth, he might have looked like he was praying.

"Sometimes I wonder if you really hear what I'm saying," Gary said.

"I hear you. I hear you just fine, man."

"Did our time together. Same block, right?"

Dentz nodded.

"And I *do* feel responsible, somewhat, for that. I've been thinking that maybe you were right. I should have checked out that hall myself."

"You already know how I feel about that," Dentz said.

"And I've been thinking I'm going to make it up to you. I'm not going to make it up to Bobby, because he coughed up that statement. But I can't make up anything if we do this."

"Do what?"

"No more robberies. No more guns, you understand what I'm saying?"

"So what you got in mind?"

"Something where we can apply all these new resources," Gary said, pointing to the cell phone. "Something that carries no fucking mandatory time."

Dentz opened the door. Started to get out.

Gary grabbed his shirt, asking, "Hey, where you going? I thought you said you heard me."

"I did," Dentz said.

Gary pointed to the Picway. "Then what the fuck are you doing?"

Tino Dentz removed Gary's hand from his shirtsleeve, spun in his seat, and put his corrugated prison sole in Lawrence Gary's face.

"Gary," he said. "I just want to get some fucking shoes."

TULA GARY HELD the pallet and brush away from the front of her body, out to her sides, and turned her cheek so he could lean in and kiss her, saying, "Stay away from the paint."

"Don't worry," Lawrence Gary said.

Later, she took the Pall Mall out of her mouth.

Some things in his room were unchanged. There was the single bed, the same slipcover he'd used in high school, but it was yellowed by three years of dust and nicotine. And the walls of his room were lined with paintings she hadn't sold. Not hanging, stacked along the floor. Still lifes. Landscapes. Bad moderns. He dragged his prison locker inside, leaving it next to the bed. He'd had more space in his cell.

Gary went to the basement, jogging down the steps. At the bottom, reaching above him, he palmed the third-floor joist, finding the key where he'd hung it. Then he unlatched the Masterlock and opened the darkroom door.

Inside, the darkroom had remained spotless, Gary going to great lengths to make the ten-by-ten dust-free when he built it. The Bogen enlarger. His timer. His trays. The chemicals. He'd have to replace some of the chemicals, which now were beyond their expiration dates. That would run a hundred. With that, and a few other purchases, he knew the six hundred from Jackson would disappear pretty quick.

Gary pulled out a trunk under the development table. He heard footsteps on the stairs.

"How long you expect me to wait out there?" Dentz asked, walking in.

"I'm getting my cameras."

Gary fit one camera body with a macro zoom, another, which was a motor drive, with a three hundred. He liked carrying two, not only for versatility; two imparted a certain status.

"Why you want those?" Dentz asked.

"You never know when you're going to get lucky in this town," Gary said. "See a bunch of people get wasted. Grab a Pulitzer prize–winning shot."

BOTH BODIES WERE on his shoulder when they walked into the Maverick a half hour later, a topless club just inside the Detroit city limits, Gary agreeing when Tino Dentz said they ought to take some time to celebrate their release. At first, the bouncer said there was no fucking way those cameras were coming in. Gary opened both bodies, showing there was no film.

Then he asked for the manager. "With all due respect to your valet out there," he explained, "these cameras are very expensive, and I just don't feel comfortable leaving them in the car."

They got a corner booth, Gary laying his equipment on the table.

Dentz's eyes were on the stage. About thirty girls up there. Hardly moving, just stretching, still early in their shift.

Gary felt comfortable. He liked dark places. In fact, people sometimes said he didn't get enough sunlight. "Your skin was any whiter," the editor of the *Spectator* told him once, "they could put you in the World Book as one of those anatomy shots."

Gary ordered a New York strip and a Heineken. Only six bucks for the steak, the businessman's lunch special. Dentz ordered the same, both of them wondering how they could sell it so cheap. After the steak came, the girls moved out among the tables, angling for lap dances. Gary turned away a half dozen, saying to the last one, What the fuck ever gave her the idea that he liked to eat food with her bare ass in his face?

When they finished, Dentz invited one of the lap whores into the booth, a platinum blonde with modest tits, but real.

"So, would you like a dance?" the blonde asked, snuggling up close to Dentz.

"How much?" he asked.

Gary pointed his knife at the table, where a little table sign read: $20 a Dance. Still chewing, he said, "Prices have gone up, Tino."

Dentz fed the lap whore a story about Gary being a working photographer. Gary ran with it, improvising as he went, saying they were considering putting together a businessman's guide to the best dancers in the metropolitan area, going into quite a bit of detail how it would look, how it would sell. After he framed her a couple of times in the macro, she jumped on Dentz, giving him a free ride.

After she left, Gary said, "I don't know how they can give you meat like that for six bucks."

Dentz said, "You said it's twenty for a dance."

"I'm talking about the steak," Gary said.

"They're making money."

"I guess so."

"It's different now," said Dentz. "They *pay* the bar to dance. *One hundred dollars* just to walk in the door. They keep the dance money. Even then, they make out good."

"How do you know all this shit?" Gary asked.

"Girl told me last night."

"You were in here yesterday?"

Dentz nodded.

Gary started calculating. This always took longer for him, being it involved the left side of his brain. Thirty girls, he estimated, times one hundred. Three grand. Times two shifts, six grand—a day. Times seven.

"Forty-three thousand dollars—*a week*, Tino. And that's not counting the drinks."

"Whatever," Dentz said. He had his eyes now on a girl working one of the brass poles to an AC/DC tune. She had a set, but Gary also spotted two scars the surgeon left behind.

Dentz clapping now, saying, "Do it, girl."

The idea of all that money coming into the Maverick agitated Lawrence Gary. Dentz and the dancer at the pole agitated him, her playing Tino like a trick, Dentz buying the entire illusion.

Later, he guessed it all must have agitated the right side of his brain.

Gary said, "No reason we couldn't do something like this."

"Do what?" said Dentz, his eyes still on the stage.

"Something like one of these bars."

Dentz glanced at him. "Shit, they ain't gonna give no ex-con a liquor license. I know. My uncle tried."

Gary wasn't thinking about liquor. He was thinking about *safe sex*, and article he saw in the prison library about the new safe-sex industry, right there on the *Detroit News* finance page. Safe sex *without* liquor, he was thinking. Liquor was a hassle anyway. And now he had a new wrinkle.

"Tino, you remember those parlors we hit?" he asked.

"How could I forget?"

"You check out the sports page lately?"

Dentz shook his head, his eyes were still captured.

Gary continued. "Oriental spas. Nude massage. Chat lines. Private lines. Private lingerie modeling, both in-call and out-call."

"I thought you said you don't want to do that no more," said Dentz.

"I'm not talking hitting them. I'm talking running them."

Gary went on to explain that lingerie was nice, but there probably was no place around with leather. If he was going to do something like that, he'd have both leather and lingerie, your choice. Maybe even S&M. Locate it near the airport, for guys on the road, staying in those airport hotels. Give customers a private room with a big overstuffed leather chair. All *completely* legal. No actual fucking allowed.

"That's the beauty of it," Gary concluded. "They can't bust you for handing out Kleenex."

Dentz said he was forgetting something. "Private rooms, you wouldn't know the girls were sticking with the program. You'd never know if they were turning tricks on the side until Vice came through the door."

"That's where you'd come in," Gary said.

Dentz turned, showing some genuine interest now.

"I'd bring you in incognito, like a customer. Give you money and you'd try to get them to go all the way. If you could fuck 'em, I'd have to fire 'em."

Dentz grinned. "You wouldn't have nobody working for you after a while"

"No," Gary said. "These girls would be paying to work there, just like here." That's where the new wrinkle came in. "Of course, after a while the models would get to know you. Then your job would be managing all the girls, deciding who we should hire."

Dentz wasn't looking at the dancer anymore. "How you gonna get those girls to pay?" he asked. "Like I was saying, they make good money here."

Gary leaned closer. "I'd do everything different. Do it . . . *creative*. Put up posters of the models all around the place. Light 'em with track lights. Make those whores think they were celebrities."

He was brainstorming now.

"Shit, man. Put out a magazine. They work at our place and they get to be in a magazine we hand out at the door. They all need portfolios.

They all need credits. Tino, they'd be lined up out there with hundred-dollar bills, waiting to get in and go to work."

Dentz gulped a mouthful of Heineken from the bottle. Laughed. Then looked back at the stage, saying, "Gary, where the fuck we gonna get the money to open a place like that?"

"Fifty thou," Gary said, picking an arbitrary figure. "That would cover it. Once we had a location, we could put Bobby Tank to work fixing it up. He knows how to do shit like that."

Dentz laughed again. "Fifty? Where we gonna get fifty?"

Gary saw the lap whore at the top of the pole, spiraling down now with her hand out. He hated when somebody sabotaged the creative process. That had always been a problem, finding people who would go with it, not fight it, like Torino Dentz. What did he expect from someone named after a fucking car?

He slumped in the booth, looking around now. A lot of guys in suits, stuffing twenties in the pants of those lap whores, probably writing the whole lunch off.

"A lot of motherfuckers still owe me money," he said.

"What you say?" Dentz said, his eyes following another dancer on the stage.

"People owe me fucking money." Louder now.

Dentz turned. "Those old dope markers of yours? That's no fifty grand, is it?

"I wasn't thinking that."

He was thinking about his bedroom, going back there, not having a crib of his own.

Dentz said, "Gary, you been doing time, remember? You ain't going to see those people ever again, unless you go looking for them."

Reaching for a Kool, Lawrence Gary said, "Then maybe the time has come to try."

CHAPTER 4

THAT MORNING, A uniformed officer took Nelson Connor from the small cell with the cement-slab bed to an interview room, Connor holding up his slacks as he walked, his belt gone.

"A detective will be in to see you shortly," the cop said.

And then he shut the door.

The interview room closed in on Connor in a way the cell never had. Space for only a table and two chairs. Heel marks on the walls. He wanted to pace, or find a distant corner. He wanted water, water to drink and water in a sink under a good mirror. He searched his pockets for a bottle of Visine he carried, but it was gone. They must have taken it with the belt. He didn't remember them taking anything, specifically. But he remembered the procedure. He'd represented clients detained on OUILs.

He went through the motions, buttoning his oxford, cinching his tie, running his hands through his wavy dark hair. He hoped he looked better than his suit jacket. He'd slept in it. Woke up with his head under a wool blanket. He wasn't hung over. Not yet. That would hit soon, if he didn't get a Bloody Mary, or at least a beer.

The door opened abruptly.

"Hi, Judge."

Connor did not look up at first, but he knew the voice belonged to a morning person, somebody who got a charge out of waking up. He smelled Mennen Skin Bracer and fresh coffee.

The detective closed the door with his hip, paperwork and a steaming cup in his hands.

"Want some coffee?" he said, still standing.

Connor knew him. From somewhere.

"No. Thanks." He was afraid coffee would make him shake.

"Anything?"

"Water?"

The cop set the cup and paperwork on the table, the printed side down. The coffee mug had an FOP emblem. Connor looked at the papers, but resisted the urge to touch them, his legal mind coming up with all the possibilities that could be written there.

The cop returned with a matching mug. Connor drank half the cup. He wanted to drink it all, but he didn't want to look desperate.

The cop sat across from him. About fifty. He was wearing a short-sleeved white shirt and a tie tacked with miniature handcuffs. When Connor looked in his eyes, he saw only routine.

"Sleep well?"

Connor cracked a slight grin, shaking his head in disbelief, as if that alone, like a room with a distant corner, could detach him from what had happened. He did not remember falling asleep. In fact, all he could remember was that he'd dropped Ozzie's vial in the crevice beneath the Reatta's seat.

"Did my wife come?" Connor said. "I mean, did she pick up my car?"

The cop turned over the paperwork, looking at the last page. "Silver Buick Reatta? I think I saw that in the back lot when I came in. *Nice car*, Judge."

The mental snapshots started coming. He remembered dropping a quarter into the pay phone, but he couldn't recall exactly what he'd told Katherine. They took him to the pay phone after he blew into the Breath-alyzer. Or was it before?

He forced himself to look at the detective.

"You don't remember me, do you, Judge Connor?"

He put out his hand, introducing himself, a detective sergeant. The name didn't ring any bells.

Connor said, "I'm just having a hard time placing. What was the case?" He was making a calculated guess. Cops sat all the time with prosecutors, assisting. In his courtroom.

"Six years ago."

The detective recalled all the details. A repeat offender, a rapist. Then Connor remembered the defendant, the way he'd more than maxed him out. Gave him one hundred and twenty-five years, but he was overturned, the appellate court saying he'd exceeded standard sentencing guidelines.

"Sure, I remember," Connor said. "The court of appeals reduced his sentence to twenty-five."

The detective said, "You can't say we didn't try." The cop looked down at the report, then back up.

Connor wished he would just get to it now. He made the request with his eyes.

The detective went to the last page first. "Well, let's see what we got here. Our patrolman, our patrol*person*, said she first spotted you driving erratically on Sheldon Road."

He read on to himself for a few moments.

"So, how many drinks did you have?"

Connor hesitated, his stomach turning. The Skin Bracer. The detective must have used a half a bottle. The lawyer inside him told him to say nothing. Something else told him to talk.

Don't lie. Cops hated liars. He hated being lied to on the bench as well.

"Too many," Connor said. "I got carried away downtown. I shouldn't have been on the road."

"I've been there myself," the detective said. "When I was young and foolish."

The detective looked back down at the paperwork, rubbing his forehead, not looking like a morning man now. "I've talked at length with the officer who picked you up last night. In fact, she's up the hall, waiting to finish her report so she can go home. But I got a few more questions, before I can let anybody go."

He pushed the paperwork aside. "Does anyone else in your family drive your car? A teenager, perhaps?"

Now Connor knew they'd found the vial.

"My wife always drives the Cherokee. My boy is only twelve."

"What about other individuals?"

He knew where the detective was going. Let him go there, he told himself, don't offer anything.

"What do you mean?" Connor asked. "It's my car."

"What I mean is, has anyone else had possession of it recently? Friends? Relatives?"

He looked into the detective's eyes. Thought he saw something, a cop wanting to give him a way out. He hesitated, then took it.

"Only the parking structure downtown. I got a deal where the guys wash it twice a week." Connor paused, then added, "Why, might I ask?"

Now he wished he hadn't said it.

The detective shifted in his seat. "Well, the night-side officer indicated to me this morning that she found some drug paraphernalia in the car after she searched it back here at the station."

"What do you mean, '*drug paraphernalia*'?"

"A small vial."

"A vial?"

"You know, the kind of thing they use. Apparently it had a remnant of a controlled substance. But hardly enough to test."

Connor's mind raced. The woman cop. Maybe she hadn't seen him. Maybe she just saw him weaving. Or, maybe the detective was just setting him up for the next question.

The detective broke the silence. "Do you have any idea how that might have gotten into your car?"

Connor decided that if he blamed the attendants, the detective would believe it was his. Cops just thought that way.

"No," Connor said. "I don't. And those guys in the structure, they seem pretty straight, as far as I can tell."

The detective leaned forward, contemplating his answer, Connor staying with his eyes. "But you never know, do you? Having a few too many, I can understand that. But, the other thing, I find it hard to believe that somebody in your position, somebody with your education and stature, would be so goddamn stupid to take a risk like that."

After five seconds of silence, Connor had to say something, or he was going to fly apart.

"What's the procedure here?" he asked. "What's next?"

The detective leaned back. "Well, do you have someone available to pick you up?"

"I can make a call."

He thought about Kace, the way she would be looking at him when he walked out of the station. He added, "But you said my car was out back."

The detective nodded. "Sure, you'll get your keys with the rest of your property."

"Am I being charged?"

The detective picked up the papers and tapped them on the table, squaring them up.

"I'm going to suggest careless driving. I'm not sure our patrolperson out there is going to like that. I'd watch your speed if I was you at night, especially on Sheldon Road."

The detective paused momentarily, letting it sink in, then said matter-of-factly, "I guess they had a little problem with the Breathalyzer. Seems the night shift forgot to calibrate it, and you know what a good lawyer can do with that. That's why I asked you about your wife."

"I don't understand."

"Well, we don't have an official blood-alcohol level on you from last night. But with an OUIL, we don't let someone just drive out of here. I mean, some people blow over the limit the next morning. So, if you want your keys *and* the car, then we're going to have to ask you to blow into it again."

Connor looked at him, at a loss for words.

The detective said, "What I'm saying, Judge, is the machine is calibrated just fine now."

Nelson Connor said, "Let me call my wife."

HE HELD THE silence in the Cherokee at bay by saying, Jesus, he had to get showered and changed and get downtown. Use her car. Maybe she could walk over to the police station later. Pick up his Buick. He had a jury trial and sentencings scheduled, lawyers showing up at nine-thirty A.M. One hell of a day.

She turned off the ignition in the driveway and rubbed her face with the palms of her hands.

"Connor," she said, looking over. "I know you don't want to hear this right now, but you can't just keep going on like this."

"We'll talk tonight," he said.

He was already upstairs in the bathroom when he heard the front door slam.

He sat for a long time on the toilet. On his lap he had an old issue of the *State Bar Review*, its varnished pages distorted with water stains. He'd opened to the page with the feature on the Michigan Judicial Tenure Commission, complete with a boxed list of seven canons from the Michigan Code of Judicial Conduct. The second caught his eye: *A Judge should avoid impropriety and the appearance of impropriety in all his activities.*

He thought, What about the impropriety of the cop? Hell, he hadn't asked for any favors.

Next to the canons were photos of the tenure commission, eight men and one woman with the power to discipline any sitting judge in the state. Connor's eyes stuck on the picture of Judge Michael Cooney, the commission's circuit representative. Cooney ran the courtroom above his in the CCB. Connor often found himself looking at Michael Cooney's picture, but not because of the commission. He started looking at it two months ago when he heard the governor had made a phone call, asking Michael Cooney to run for the Michigan Supreme Court. He hated that goddamn photo. Hated that same smug grin he saw in the halls of the CCB. Nelson Connor believed he had deserved the phone call from the governor, not Michael Cooney. He was the youngest judge ever elected to the Third Circuit, not Cooney. He'd cleaned up the felony docket. He'd served on the governor's task force. What had Cooney done? The commission busted a couple greedy district judges every year on ticket-fixing scams.

Connor tossed the magazine back into a pile of reading material near the bathtub, wondering why he kept it around. He lit a cigarette, exhaled, and began coughing. The cough became a retch, a dry one.

When it stopped, he remembered a funny story around the Anchor Bar about Doc, the old *News* columnist, about the time Doc quit drinking for a week.

Somebody asked Doc at the bar, the day he fell off the wagon, "So, what was it like, Doc?"

Doc said, "Hey, I never missed the booze."

Somebody said, "So why did you go back?"

Doc said, "I just couldn't live without starting my day by throwing up."

Connor started laughing, but this brought only more coughing, and a layer of sweat across his face. When he stopped, he thought about what had happened last night, this morning. How he'd gotten lucky.

Shit, he thought, he could still laugh. And it scared him half to death that he could.

CHAPTER 5

HE PLANNED TO go straight in, but on the Jeffries he felt his blood sugar dropping, his hands shaking, so he stopped off at a little bar he knew in Redford and slammed down two vodka-and-grapefruit, then hit the drugstore across the street for Visine. He was running only ten minutes late when he got to his courtroom, but his hands were steady.

Lewis was sitting in a dark corner of the clerical office behind the courtroom, playing solitaire on the computer, the screen's colors highlighted in his white hair. The bailiff had been with Nelson Connor all of his twelve years on the Third Circuit. Connor spotted Lewis's gun belt and pearl-handled Colt .45 on the desk of his clerk, Barbara. Barbara had been with him since the beginning, too.

Connor walked directly into his chambers, saying, "Where the hell is she?"

He heard a voice behind him. "I'm right here."

He turned and saw her through his open door, Barbara dropping an armful of files on her desk.

"Are both parties ready? Is the jury here?"

He put his suit coat on an oak hall tree, where his robe hung.

"Everyone is waiting for Lensley—and *you*, Your Honor."

"Don't call me that back here," Connor said.

He watched Barbara light a cigarette. She was nearly fifty and about twenty-five pounds overweight. She smoked Camels, switching to Connor's brand after she quit and started bumming. By statute, smoking was prohibited in the CCB. "I interpret the law in this courtroom," Connor planned on saying if anybody brought it up. But no one ever did.

Barbara plopped down in her chair, exhaled, and eyed the bailiff's gun on her desk.

"Jesus Christ, Lewis," she said. "Why is this goddamn cowboy rig here on my desk? Why do you do that?"

Connor pulled the robe over his head, letting it drop into place with its own weight.

"Do what?" Lewis said.

Barbara turned the holster in his direction. "Here, why don't you look down the barrel for a change?"

They bickered about the gun often. Lewis put it on her desk to irritate her. He only wore the weapon in the courtroom, locking it in Connor's chambers safe at night. The argument over the gun belt endured as a morning ritual, as if everyone needed a little conflict as a prep for what was waiting for them in the court.

Connor walked out, saying, "Come now, children."

He liked his staff, warts and all. He liked them because they had warts. He was feeling more comfortable. He always felt comfortable in his courtroom. He always felt comfortable in the robe.

"The prosecutor is predicting he'll rest before lunch," Barbara said. "So, I'm leaving the miscellaneous matters in place for the afternoon."

"Or we can handle them while the jury's out," said Connor.

"Trial might be over today?" Lewis asked.

Connor said, "This trial was over for Darryl Lensley at the voir dire."

It wasn't news, not in any courtroom in the CCB. Darryl Lensley unarguably was the worst defense attorney practicing criminal law in Wayne County. Yes, he looked the part, everyone agreed. Meticulously so. He had distinguished, prematurely gray hair and a small but fine collection of tailored blue suits. Generally, he grasped legal principles, but not beyond the letter of the law. The larger, strategic picture always eluded him, a horrific blind spot for a trial attorney. His befuddlements were so legendary, Darryl Lensley had earned the nickname *"Densely"* from the entire Third Circuit bench.

"All rise," Barbara said.

As Lewis brought the jury in, Connor surveyed his courtroom. Most of the rows were empty, except for two black couples and a half dozen of their kids, ages ranging from six to sixteen. He knew they were grand-children of the victim. Yesterday, he suspected, the jury had figured out who those kids were as well.

He turned to the jurors. "Good morning, ladies and gentlemen."

Most were smiling.

Nelson Connor knew that would soon change.

It had been a thing of beauty to watch. The assistant prosecutor had a dull delivery, but a calculating mind. Yesterday, he'd quietly taken the first twelve jurors in the voir dire, challenging no one, asking them only if they understood they were being asked to decide a sexual mis-conduct case. Darryl Lensley took the gambit, figuring he'd been lucky to get a largely white panel for his white defendant. He asked a couple of questions during the jury selection, but never the most important: Would you find the details of this case offensive?

In a quick-moving afternoon, the assistant prosecutor presented his case in reverse. He first called the officers brought to the scene.

"Were there signs of breaking and entering?" he'd asked.

"Yes, there were."

"Did you talk to the victim?"

"Yes."

"Was she upset?"

"Yes, she—"

"No, Officer, you don't have to tell us what she said."

The prosecutor called the doctor who'd examined the victim. The ER physician was clinical. The prosecutor wanted it that way.

"My examination showed an eighty-year-old white female who showed clear evidence of vaginal trauma, along with various abrasions and con-tusions about her body."

There were only six state witnesses in all yesterday, including a neigh-bor who saw the defendant running from the victim's house. Still, on the second day now, the jury hardly knew any details about the crime.

Today, Connor guessed, that was about to change. When the prose-cutor called the grandmother, she toddled into the courtroom, her hips crippled with arthritis.

As she was sworn, most of the jurors glanced at the defendant, a thirty-year-old repeat offender from the East Side. Clean-shaven, his hair slicked back with mousse, he was wearing an old blue suit Darryl Lensley had loaned him for the trial.

After she pointed out the defendant, the assistant prosecutor began to extract the details. It took nearly an hour. The grandmother testified she'd been raped repeatedly. Then she'd been tied up in a chair in her bedroom and left there to bleed to death.

"Where were you bleeding, ma'am?"

"From my vagina."

"How long were you bleeding?"

The grandmother was having a hard time with the words. "A very long time. Until I got free."

Darryl Lensley jumped up. "Objection. Vague and unresponsive."

Densely, Connor thought. "Sit down," he barked.

Connor casually looked over to the jury. Some eyes were on the victim, others on the grandchildren in the seats. One juror, a Teamster in the front row, was glaring at Densely and his client. Five minutes into the testimony, jurors were wiping tears from their eyes.

"So how were you able to free yourself and call police?" the assistant prosecutor asked.

"There was a nail file on my dresser."

"And how did you get it, being tied up, as you've already testified?"

"I got it between my toes. Then I got it in my hands somehow."

"And how long did it take you to file the ropes?"

"Three or four hours, I guess."

The assistant prosecutor turned to the jury, asking the next question. "Where is that nail file today?"

"I'm not sure."

"Is it still in the house?"

"I'm not sure."

"Why not?"

"I haven't been able to bring myself to go back there."

"And how long had you lived there, ma'am?"

The witness herself turned to the jury, nodding her head. "My late husband and I bought that house fifty-two years ago next month."

Densely attempted a cross-examination, but backed off not two minutes into it. He didn't like the way the jury was looking at him.

The closings and instructions moved quickly.

So did the jury. They came back in fifteen minutes; guilty as charged. It wasn't even lunch.

"Thank you, ladies and gentlemen," Connor said. "You can retire to the jury room now and I'll be back to talk to you in a few minutes."

They all filed out, except the Teamster. He remained at the railing, staring at the defendant. Later, in the back office, Lewis said he was sure the Teamster was going to come right out of the box.

Lewis also said, "You wouldn't believe what that idiot said to me on the way back to the lockup."

"Who?" Connor said. "Densely or his client?"

"The rapo. He shrugs and says, 'I don't give a fuck what Judge Connor gives me. I'll be out in ten years and still be able to fuck some more.'"

Connor said, "Did you remind him that he's still in *my courtroom*, that he's going to be sentenced here in a couple of weeks?"

"That's why I'm telling you," Lewis said. "I figure you'd want to do that yourself."

HE BOUGHT BARBARA and Lewis lunch at Jacoby's, drinking two Beck's with his sauerbraten, making them last and not chasing the beer with anything else.

"Christ," Connor said, feeling better than he had all day now. "Did you see the way Densely got sandbagged?"

"All day long," Barbara said, snuffing out a smoke.

"You want everybody in the jury box when we get back?" asked Lewis.

"What do we have on the docket?" Connor asked Barbara.

"Mixed bag. AOIs. A couple calendar conferences. Three sentencings. You read the presentence reports?"

"Not yet," he said.

"So where do you want them?" Lewis asked again. "All together or one at a time?"

"The usual," Connor said. "Pack in as many as you can."

He'd designed it that way. He wanted defendants who were being given the opportunity to plead out during the AOIs to be in the courtroom. He wanted them watching in belly chains. They could see for themselves how he sentenced other defendants who'd taken plea deals. They could also see how he threw the book at those who demanded full trials and lost.

"You're the only one who does it that way," Lewis said, adding he'd have to call another deputy over to assist.

Connor said, "But I'm the only one they call a czar."

Another judge had bestowed the title. Thirty-five judges sat on the Third Judicial Circuit. It operated differently than the much smaller circuit jurisdictions around the state. In other counties, circuit judges tried civil matters, domestic relations, and criminal felonies. In Wayne County, which included Detroit, the work was split between two benches. The Recorder's Court in the Frank Murphy Hall of Justice handled Detroit felonies. The Third Circuit in the CCB tried the out-county crimes. Then the system became strained, the Recorder's judges complaining the circuit judges should help carry an increasing Detroit docket load. So, five circuit judges were assigned on a rotating basis to try Recorder's cases in three-month stints.

And they did. More than six hundred violent repeat offenders a year. Rapists. Crackheads and carjackers. Armed robbers, people who wasted victims whether they gave up the goods or not. But the Recorder's docket did not shrink. It grew. Last year, they had five hundred cases pending for trial. That's when Nelson Connor made a suggestion in a joint bench meeting with Recorder's. "Give me those five hundred cases," he said. Hell, he'd clear their docket. Do the job. Force the deals ponderous judges were unable or unwilling to do.

"You mean, you'd be like a czar?" Leonard Talbot, one of the toughest judges on the bench asked.

Connor said, "I wouldn't necessarily call it that."

In fact, he liked the term. And it stuck.

Connor reduced the backlog by offering two different deals: He eliminated half the pending cases by telling defense attorneys that if they pled their clients out, they could name their sentencing judge. He cleaned out another quarter by offering a pick of any one of eight judges for a bench trial, avoiding time-consuming juries.

This put him right on the top of the hit parade, a list kept by the chief judge of the most efficient docket loads. But he'd also paid a price, the dealmakers flocking to his courtroom daily. Gone were the more cerebral civil trials, replaced by a procession of defendants in jail greens. His docket was booked with arraignments, calendar conferences, and sentencings—where the deals were struck—not to mention the occasional bench or jury trial. Once a week all summer, he'd also driven to Lansing, serving on a governor's task force studying the decriminalization of drugs.

"You going to have another one?" Barbara asked, lighting another cigarette.

"I'm thinking we ought to get back," Connor said.

As they walked down Congress back to the CCB, he was thinking about Katherine, how she should come down and watch him for a day, instead of that cop show. He sentenced people with real problems. Ordered people to attend AA and NA meetings. Gave prison terms to drunks for vehicular manslaughter. His work had never suffered. He was never out of it, like Darryl Lensley.

He'd been momentarily stupid, that's all, buying that stuff from Ozzie. When you worked too hard, he told himself, you play too hard. But, hell, he was no *alcoholic*.

They'd never make a drunk the czar.

He turned to Barbara. "What are we looking at, anyway?"

"We're looking down Congress," she said. "Up there to your right is the Penobscot Building, and to your left, Cobo Hall."

"The sentencings, Barbara," he said.

"A drug case. Manslaughter with a vehicle. Couple of auto thefts. The usual crap."

"We have the presentence reports?"

"I asked you, remember? They're on your desk."

"The drug case?"

"Yes, the drug case. Don't you remember it, either?"

"I remember."

He'd been anticipating the drug case for days.

———

BACK IN CHAMBERS, he closed his door, reading the presentence report prepared by his court aide, Lori Eisenberg. He knew she would do anything within reason for him, not to mention the arduous task of interviewing defendants, checking their backgrounds, and recommending their sentences at a rate of a dozen a week. She prepared the reports by day, attended Detroit College of Law by night, and probably slept dreaming of one day practicing in his court. He could have asked her to slant the report on the drug case, and she would have done it. But he hadn't. He'd put off reading the report until he had to. Now, he was going to make his decision based upon what she said.

The defendant was a forty-four-year-old, fully employed white male from Livonia who had taken the prosecutor's deal. He'd agreed to plead guilty to simple possession of less than sixteen grams of cocaine. The prosecutor would drop the charge of possession with intent to deliver, which carried a mandatory jail term, and the defendant would throw himself before the mercy of the court.

In the first part of the report, Connor sped through the basics of the bust, how the undercover Detroit narcotics officer had made the buy, an eighth of an ounce, meeting the defendant alone outside a Taco Bell. Then he skipped to his court aide's summary of her interview with the defendant.

It read, "The defendant stated that this is the first time he has ever been in trouble, that he was a 'recreational' user, and only sold the cocaine to said undercover officer because of the persistence of his girlfriend."

No, Connor thought, this was not the first time the defendant had ever been in trouble. This was the first time Jimmy Osborne had been caught.

Connor walked to the window, looking at the Detroit River disappearing into the industrial haze of the west horizon. The proper thing to do would be to disqualify himself. Put it on the record that he had a personal relationship with the defendant. But how would that look? He could hear the prosecutor asking him later in chambers, "Judge, how do you know that guy?"

Connor couldn't figure how it all happened now, his meeting Ozzie at the Anchor, fully intending to tell Ozzie that he had to call his attorney and, goddamn it, pick somebody else. A couple dozen drinks later, he walks out owing Ozzie three hundred bucks.

He sat down at his desk again, turning to the court aide's report. Lori Eisenberg was recommending five years' probation and enrollment in outpatient drug treatment.

He thought maybe he could toughen it. Make him do a community service. Make him drop urine every two weeks for six months. That would balance the scales of impropriety. Hell, Jimmy Osborne was one among thousands.

Nobody would ever know.

Barbara cracked his door, saying, "We're ready when you are."

He closed the probation report and took his robe off the hall tree, slipping it on. He felt tired now from the two beers at lunch. They ought to decriminalize, he thought, take the money out of dope, clear up the dockets and clear out the prisons. He'd said that on the task force, but he was the minority opinion.

When he came out of chambers, Lewis was wondering if he'd have to handle an inmate transfer.

"What about that drug case that bonded out?" he asked. "Should I call the jail?"

"I'm leaning toward probation."

"The arresting officer will like that."

Connor said, "He's here?"

"He's no longer under. He's in Homicide now."

"But he's here?"

"Said he was in the building on another matter. He will not be happy."

Connor said, "You know anybody in this business that is?"

Besides, it was his courtroom.

Barbara said, "All rise."

CHAPTER 6

BY LATE AFTERNOON, Lawrence Gary had compiled a list of names and written them on the back of a napkin. All the people who owed him money. Exactly how much, he couldn't recall.

"How you going to collect if you don't know?" Dentz asked. He was shooting a move on a girl, the lap whore sitting next to him close, whispering something in his ear.

"First we find them," Gary said. "The rest I'll improvise."

Gary had the waitress bring over a Detroit phone book. It had no suburban listings.

"Why you need the suburbs?" Dentz asked.

He did most of his business in the suburbs, he said. Met his customers in places like Jake's in Birmingham, adding, "I wasn't fucking hanging on corners, man, moving rock to passing cars."

Gary picked up his cameras and walked out.

Dentz caught up with him outside, complaining he was making progress inside, just getting something set up.

They sat in the van, not moving. Gary decided to run the names on his list by directory assistance on the cellular. He explained to the first operator he had three names, all residential listings, but no street addresses, sometimes not even the city, just a general area.

He gave the operator the first.

"What city did you say that was?"

He explained it all again, hoping she was fucking listening this time.

"Is that a business or a residence?"

He gave her the name again, adding, "Does that name sound like a business?"

"Well, it could be a restaurant, sir," she said.

"John Smith also could be a restaurant. But would you go there? Would you say, 'Let's go up to *John Smith* and get a fucking steak'?"

She transferred him to a supervisor. And before he finished explaining to her that he needed three names, all residences, she cut him off by saying, "Our policy is that we can provide listings for only two names."

He never got to the second name, because when she said, "Hold for the number," she turned him over to the automated equipment and he got a recording: *"At the customer's request, the number is unlisted."*

Dentz, watching him, said, "Man, whatup? You keep calling, the Reverend Roy ain't gonna like his phone bill."

So Gary told him to drive. They'd find some suburban phone books. He needed two directories, one for Northern Oakland County and another for Western Wayne County. Dentz drove west on Ford Road into Garden City, then Westland. They stopped at a half dozen pay phones. The shelves underneath were empty.

"Fucking thieves," Gary said.

"I do need to get the van back," Dentz finally said.

"One more," Gary said, looking out the window at gas stations and party stores, looking for a small blue sign with the shape of a telephone on it.

"Gary, I don't want to blow this deal with the Reverend Roy."

"You picking up kids or somethin'?"

Gary lit a Kool.

"No, mini Bible school is only twice a week."

"Then what's your hurry?" Gary said, his eyes scanning the storefronts.

"It don't look good."

"What don't?"

"Disappearing with the Reverend Roy's van."

"You're not disappearing," Gary said, pointing to his belt. "That's what your vibrator is for."

Gary was thinking now that maybe Tino Dentz just wanted to drop him off home and go back to the Maverick, work his angle.

"Why you go for that stuff, anyway?" Gary asked. "Those lap whores."

"They fine, and they ain't easy."

"I know they ain't easy. That's my point."

"Easy gets you in a lot of trouble. Pretty soon, easy is carrying your baby. Getting the welfare office involved. That don't happen with a no-pro."

"You know, I never looked at it that way," Gary said.

He spotted a phone. "Yo, Tino. Turn."

Dentz wheeled into a car wash, a self-serve with four bays and spray wands. Gary headed for the phone, saying, "Why don't you wash the church bus? That'll make a good impression on your Reverend Roy."

Gary pulled the phone book from its stainless-steel shelf, where it was attached with a steel cable not much larger than a strand of yarn. A directory, Gary thought, but no fucking place to open it. He propped the book up and started looking for names, a summer breeze curling the pages around his hand.

"Spit it out, motherfucker."

Gary turned around just in time to see the heel of one of Torino Dentz's Picway point oxfords driving hard into a bill-changing machine. Dentz kicked it again.

Seconds later, he was walking toward Gary, swinging his arms in an exaggerated way. "That motherfucking machine took my bill."

A guy at a nearby vacuum island jumped into his Volvo and sped off, leaving the machine running, not liking what he saw.

"Single, five, or ten?" Gary asked.

"Nickle," Dentz said.

"Then don't worry about it. Go listen to the radio or something."

And then Lawrence Gary decided he better step out of the way. He didn't really believe Tino Dentz was coming for him, but he did believe the look on his face demanded he give the nigger some space.

Dentz grabbed the phone book's weatherproof cover with both hands and pulled once—hard.

The cable held.

He came right back at it, as if he was doing a Nautilus rep. Not just pulling now, but throwing his body into it.

Two pulls. Then three.

Gary backed up farther, looking around. He decided he'd just start walking if he saw a blue-and-white.

Dentz, still yanking, saying, *"motherfucker"* every time, his GeriCurl vibrating when the cable stopped him. Gary thought they might be taking the entire rig. Then the cable snapped.

Dentz, out of breath, tossed it over. "Here's your phone book."

"Thank you," Gary said. But he thought he better get the young man laid.

ON THE WAY back to Detroit, Gary didn't look in the book, though it was sitting on his lap, two feet of cable hanging between his legs. He was thinking about what he saw at the pay phone, or in the prison mess hall, for that matter, how difficult that was to capture. He could have gone for the motor drive, but he still would have missed the image. No time to set an exposure, or get an angle. He thought, The only one who'd ever captured rage like that was Diane Arbus, that photo she did of the pissed-off little kid holding a toy grenade.

Gary felt he'd shared something intimate with Tino, and that was like getting it on with somebody. Afterward you just didn't want to say anything for a while. They were on the Southfield Freeway, billboards going by. New products Gary hadn't heard about in Jacktown. New brands of cigarettes. New drinks. Something called Zima.

Finally, Gary said, "So how heavy did the work get?"

"What work?"

"With YBI."

Dentz looked over. Gary had never asked him about this before. Dentz told him once in Eleven Block that he did respect Gary for that. Respected him for not wanting to hang just to hear a lot of stories. But now, Gary believed this was the appropriate moment to ask.

Dentz said, "You ever take somebody out, Gary?"

"Not that I know of."

"You ever hurt anybody?"

"Not directly, but I've been instrumental in people getting hurt."

Dentz nodded, putting his two fingers out. Gary lit a Kool and slid it between them.

"In Boys, you didn't just hurt people," Dentz said. "You had to say something."

"Say what?"

"Any nigger can kill somebody. You got the job on the Boys crew, because you could make a *statement*."

Gary said he liked that approach, adding, "So what's the best thing you ever said?"

Dentz laughed.

"What's so funny?"

"Just thinkin'."

"C'mon, Tino, don't pull that shit on me."

Dentz hit the Kool then looked over. "This ever goes anywhere, I will find you, you understand?" He wasn't laughing now.

"Hey, no problem," Gary said.

Tino looked over, checking him out. Gary didn't say anything this time about Dentz keeping his eyes on the road.

"You ever use cement nails, Gary?"

"No, I have never used a cement nail."

"Well, there's a right way and a wrong way to use cement nails. You can't just pound 'em in. You gotta start them through wood first, or they will not go into the cement."

"I did not know that," Gary said.

"I didn't, either. I learned about that on the Boys crew."

Gary gave him some space. He knew Dentz wanted to tell the story now.

"See, Boys was a big organization. Brothers helpin' brothers, everybody used to say. But man, there was *a lot* of brothers. I mean, we're talking some two hundred young people, selling that bad scag."

"So how did they keep track?" Gary asked.

"Polaroids, man. People at the top took Polaroids of everybody. So they knew who was a Boy, and who was not. You follow what I'm saying?"

Gary said he liked the idea of using pictures.

"Well, this Arab on the West Side makes the *miscalculation* that because Boys was big, he could find a seam. Put some young brothers on a street corner, dressed in Nikes like Boys, using the same names on the dope, figuring our people wouldn't notice. But because of those Polaroids, that wasn't gonna happen."

Gary said photos were good for a lot of things.

"So they call the crew, saying we should go talk to this rag. Actually, talking isn't the word they use. They say, 'We want you to do this guy. But we want it done in such a way that every motherfucker with a TV will know what happens if they try to move in on our corners.'"

Gary said, "This is where the statement comes in."

Dentz nodded, hitting the Kool again. "So, it just so happens that all this is going down on a Good Friday. The guy running the crew must have all kinds of old church shit swimming around in his head. Because he says, 'We gonna take that rag out like Jesus.'"

Gary said, "That would have real news value."

"So we bust into this sand nigger's house over on West Grand and I put a Ruger seven against his head. But nobody can decide whether we gonna do him live, or do him dead. I mean, nail him. I think we figure that depends on whether the guy gives us our due respect."

Gary said, "Makes sense to me."

"Well, right off, we run into problems. Not only is the rag talking shit, but you see, we have to take him to his basement, 'cause that's where he keeps his scale and stash. We want to nail him in the cellar, so the connection is real clear."

Gary said, "So you needed to use cement nails?"

"I'm getting to that," Dentz said, irritated.

Gary said, "Sorry, go ahead."

"Concrete everywhere. Brick walls. Concrete steps. Cement floor. But somebody comes out of the furnace room with a box of these nails. Thick little motherfuckers that don't bend."

Dentz tossed the Kool out the window. "So I start nailin' the rag's hand to the floor, three other guys holding him. He's screaming at us in Arab. You know how they do, talking like they're gettin' somethin' up from the back of their throat. But the nail, it ain't going in. Then, I hit my thumb. And the rag, he starts laughing. Can you believe that? Motherfucker laughing at me because I hit my thumb. That hurts, Lawrence."

"So what did you do?"

"I shot him in the head."

Gary hesitated, then said, "But I thought you said you made a statement."

Dentz nodded. "We did. Somebody reads the directions on the box.

Says you got to pound them into wood first, then cement. We took some trim off a door. Made a cross. Spiked the rag onto the wood, then into the cement floor. Heard later they had a bitch of a time getting that guy to the morgue."

Gary said, "I think I remember reading about that."

"How to use the nails?"

Gary, wishing he had a picture of it, said, "No, the rag you nailed to the floor."

GARY FOUND THE fifth name on his napkin list in the Western Wayne directory. Same city. Same street. The guy hadn't moved.

"Here we go," he said, ripping out the phone page.

Dentz pulled up to his mother's house, sliding the van in park.

"I gotta get the Reverend Roy's ride back."

"He lives about twenty from here," Gary said.

"Who?"

"Used to sell this guy weed mostly, but was fronting him some coke near the end. He always looked like he had money, but that was the problem. House and clothes took my money, and his nose took all my blow."

"How much?"

"Couple hundred. Four, five, maybe. Like I said, I don't know."

"You let *that* go?"

"It became a hassle."

"That kind of money, you just don't leave it."

"Sometimes you got to move on."

Dentz said, "Boys let nobody go. For five hundred, they sent a crew over and fucked you up real good." He said it like Gary couldn't get the job done because he'd let the marker ride.

"You gonna call him?" Dentz asked.

Gary could feel himself getting pissed all over again. Thought he'd cleared out that mental baggage with a couple of E trips, but he hadn't. Four years later, thinking about one marker, and the baggage was back, all the reasons he got out.

"No," Gary said. "I'm not going to call him." He imagined the guy living it up while Gary was in the world's largest walled prison, shooting Polaroids of inmates and families for $1.62 a day.

"Why not?" Dentz asked.

Gary folded the page, tucking it into his shirt pocket. He lifted the phone book by the cable and tossed it into the backseat.

"We're going to go see him. *Tonight.*"

"I can't," Dentz said.

"I thought you had this ride twenty-four hours a day."

"I do. I got plans."

Gary knew what he was saying now. "You're thinking about that dancer."

Dentz grinned.

Gary, stroking him a little, said, "Man, I'll bet that lap whore wants to fuck you right in half."

Dentz said she was getting off at one A.M.

Gary said, "You come back. I'll get the money. And I'll give you a hundred. Show the dancer a good time. Maybe take her to Greektown."

"Feed her?"

"You can't be treating her like no street whore, Tino. Shit, man, she works in a nice place."

Dentz was looking at Gary like maybe this wasn't such a bad idea.

"Besides," Gary said. "I might need your help."

"For what?"

"To talk to this guy."

Dentz thought about it, then said, "I guess I can work with that."

Gary got out, walking toward his mother's house, checking out a couple of home boys hanging on the corner.

Dentz rolled down his window, saying, "Hey, what's the guy's name?"

Gary turned around, walking backwards, his hands on his camera straps. "What does it matter?"

"You want me to talk to the guy. I can be thinking about what I'm going to say."

Gary was thinking he'd be doing the talking, but he told Dentz anyway. "His name is Jimmy," he said. "But I always called him 'the Oz.' "

CHAPTER 7

THE MESSAGE WAS waiting for him when he stepped off the bench. The chief judge wanted to see him. The chief judge was reading a motion to suppress when Nelson Connor walked into his chambers, two floors above.

"Have a seat," Judge Kaufmann said.

The chief judge looked up only long enough to toss the Metro section of the *Detroit News* to him across his desk. It was folded in half. Connor saw a column of news briefs, the first about a school millage, the second about a new sewer line. The third: CIRCUIT JUDGE DETAINED.

Connor read the type underneath, the item reporting that Northville Police had detained him for "driving erratically" last night. The one-paragraph story was full of holes. Connor hoped a reporter wasn't working a newsroom phone today, trying to fill them up.

"I wasn't sure you saw that," the chief judge said, his eyes remaining on the motion.

"I hadn't."

"Well, it couldn't have been too bad. At least not bad enough to keep you away today."

Connor eyed the chief judge. Chief Judge Nicholas R. Kaufmann, Sr., or simply "old man Kaufmann," as some called him, so as not to confuse him with his son, who was on the district bench. Names were important in their business. *Connor. Kaufmann.* Names like *O'Brien* and *Cahalan*. Generations of voters continued to pick those names on Wayne County ballots, not really knowing anything about them as individuals, even if they were related or not.

Old man Kaufmann was sixty-five, had white hair and half-frames, which, when he wasn't wearing them, hung at about midtie. He took his lunch every day at the University Club. Always ate cottage cheese with two peaches. Always ate light, so he didn't sleep on the bench, an occupational hazard. The court of appeals overturned a Third Circuit judge once because of a vertical nap.

Old man Kaufmann had no statutory power over Nelson Connor. Only the tenure commission and the voters of Wayne County had that. But neither was he a paperboy. He wouldn't have called him to chambers if he didn't have something to say.

"Nick?" Connor finally said.

Kaufmann, still reading the motion, said, "Can you goddamn believe this? Defense counsel here wants me to suppress evidence because a state police trooper at Metro did not have full custody when he pulled, I quote, 'a dozen latex condoms full of heroin out of the defendant's rectum.'"

"Some trooper," Connor said, trying for a line, but getting no laugh.

Kaufmann read farther, then added, "And listen to this. Prosecutor says in his answer that the defendant, I quote, 'expelled' the first condom. And, get this, it 'slid down the defendant's pants onto his shoe when the surveillance dog began sniffing the defendant in airport concourse.'"

Kaufmann laughed now, hard. "Sounds like plain view to me," he said.

He glanced up at Connor.

When his eyes went back to the brief, he was no longer laughing.

"You know, Nelson, we are all human," he said.

Connor let a couple seconds pass. He remembered what Ozzie said about lying. He thought, Admit it. Not all the way, just some of it, like he did with the cop.

"I had too much to drink," Connor said.

Kaufmann was still leafing through the motion. "You heard from these people today?"

"What people?"

"The newspaper."

Connor shook his head.

"Well, then, you probably won't. Nobody gives a damn anymore about this court. On the other hand, if they sniff some kind of judicial privilege, they're going to be all over your ass."

Connor said nothing for a few moments. Then tried to make a graceful transition back to the motion in Kaufmann's hands.

"How are you going to rule?" he asked.

"About what?"

Connor pointed to the brief, saying, "On the motion to suppress."

The chief judge was writing something on a legal pad. "*U.S. versus Sedillo.* Seems to me the evidence is either in plain view or it isn't. You shouldn't have to crawl up some guy's asshole to find it."

Kaufmann ripped off the sheet and handed it to Connor.

He saw a time and a room number in the City County Building, the rest of the long page was just empty lines.

"What's this?" Connor asked.

"It's a meeting."

"A meeting?"

"Alcoholics Anonymous. Run by Billy Schmanski. You remember him, don't you? Or was that before your time?"

Connor remembered. "No, I tried a personal injury case before him years ago." A slip and fall. Back then, every trial lawyer in town knew that if you had a matter before Billy Schmanski you wanted your best evidence in before noon. After lunch, Schmanski was slurring his words, if he bothered to come back at all. He had retired just before the tenure commission planned to remove him from the bench for a litany of indiscretions.

"I guess it's a good group," Kaufmann said. "All men. Mostly professionals. It's done wonders for Billy. I thought I should pass it along."

"Thanks," Connor said, not really meaning it.

Kaufmann said, "It's up to you, Nelson. Myself, I don't give a damn, one way or the other."

Connor took the paper, standing up now, feeling awkward, wanting out of there.

No, he didn't feel awkward. He felt humiliated.

Connor started to walk out, but Kaufmann stopped him, saying he'd walk with him to the elevators. Connor waited as he put on his suit coat.

"As I was saying, Nelson, we're all human. We all sin."

"That we do," Connor said, forcing a smile.

Old man Kaufmann looked up from his jacket. "But if we're going to sin on the Third Circuit, let us do so in private from now on."

CONNOR SAW THE same Metro section on the table in the breakfast nook, the house quiet. The kitchen clock told him it was five-thirty. He'd found the rush hour lighter than he ever remembered it. He didn't see the squirrel monkey around.

He poured a Jack Daniel's on the rocks and walked out the back door to the carriage house. His Reatta was in the driveway, the keys in the ignition. He was going to say something to Katherine about the keys, but decided he better just let that issue lay low for now.

He heard her call his name when he was halfway up the stairs. At the top, in the doorway, he stopped, looking at her. She wasn't at her drawing board, but was sitting on her overstuffed couch, her arms folded in front of her like she was cold, though it was in the mid-seventies. She was wearing a denim skirt and long-sleeved western shirt.

"How did you know it was me?" he asked.

"Nobody else clinks," she said, glancing at his drink.

"Where's John?"

"At baseball practice."

"Where's the monkey?"

"In his cage. Was he quiet?"

"I didn't hear him."

He looked away, walking toward her drawing table. He saw an ad layout for a local bookstore.

"This is nice," he said.

She didn't answer.

He looked back at her. He saw something he'd never seen before from her. Not anger. Not frustration. He would have expected that, but he didn't see it.

He saw pity. Not a compassionate kind. Pity with distance, like the way people looked at a bad car wreck.

Kace asked, "What'ya gonna do?" Not begging, just flat, matter-of-fact.

Connor wanted a sip of the Jack, but forced himself to cradle it, trying to look like he really didn't need it.

"What'ya gonna do?"

He sipped, then set the bourbon on the drawing table. She shook her head, meaning, *You don't put a drink near my work.* He knew that. He picked up the glass and walked over, finishing it fast, setting it on a shelf so he didn't have it in his hand.

As he sat on the armrest he put his hand on her shoulder. "This will all blow over. Shit, people have done worse."

He waited for a response, but received none.

He said, "I guess I've been in a rut. This goddamn docket thing. Maybe we ought to head up to the cottage for a couple weeks. I can change my schedule. What do you think?"

He was looking for some kind of input, trying to see where he stood. She was looking out the window now, not at him.

"Connor," she said. "What'ya gonna do?"

HE DROVE ALL the way back downtown in the Cherokee, not taking the Reatta, unable to shake a feeling now that the car was somehow bad luck. He parked the Jeep in a small lot just outside the CCB, using his city parking card to access spaces reserved for official business only during the day.

A guard with Pinkerton patches stopped him just inside the door.

"You have to sign in," he said.

A ledger was sitting on a wooden pedestal stand. It reminded him of the kind they used for visitor books in mortuaries. He considered this a strange thought at first, until he realized he would rather have been going to a wake.

"I'm Judge Connor," he said.

"Here for the meeting?" the guard said.

"My office is on seventeen."

"You still have to sign in," he said.

There was a page of names, all with "604" under the destination column, the same number old man Kaufmann had given him. He scanned some, seeing if he recognized any, but most of the signatures were indecipherable, and some just had a first name with an initial for the last.

He signed his full name, but wrote his courtroom number.

On the elevator, he pushed the button for the sixth floor. Room 604 was the old county commissioners' conference room. He'd been there before, but it had been years ago, back when he first ran for the bench. He was trying to get endorsements, trying to get a few commissioners to spread the word on the precinct level that sure, Nelson Connor was young, but he brought impeccable credentials and experience to the job. "And don't forget, young man," he remembered one of the old commissioners saying cheerfully, "everyone will think they're voting for your old man."

The door opened.

He wanted to press the Down arrow. Call the whole thing off. Go back home. But back home, Katherine was insisting he check himself into Brighton Hospital, where Detroit cops dried out. No, that was too rash. In Brighton, they kept records. So he'd compromised by offering to attend the meeting, believing it was *"anonymous,"* but figuring he was about to meet a group of people who were going to sit around making excuses for themselves.

He stepped off the elevator. He stepped off because he couldn't think of anything else to do.

Inside room 604, he saw maybe thirty or forty men. He expected to see a podium, maybe even a little PA system, but he saw only the sprawling commissioners' conference table, everyone sitting around. He recognized retired judge William Schmanski sitting at the head. He looked younger than Connor recalled him being when he was on the bench.

Somebody was sitting next to Schmanski, reading something, finishing up. " 'The only requirement for membership is a desire to quit drinking. . . . ' "

When the reader looked up, Connor stopped. It was Michael Cooney, tenure commission poster boy. What the hell was he doing here?

Cooney saw him now, standing there. Frozen. Anybody who wasn't looking, was looking now.

"Jesus Christ," Cooney said, drawing it out, grinning.

Cooney stood up, motioning. "Hey, everybody, say hello to Nelson. Have a seat, we've been expecting you."

"Expecting me?" Connor asked.

"Yeah, I always figured you'd show up here one day."

CONNOR SAT NEXT to a guy in his late fifties. He had a Florida tan and a thin blond Errol Flynn mustache, highlighted by the sun. He was wearing an open sport shirt, a fine gold chain around his neck, and two gold rings on his right hand, the design sculptured like raw nuggets. He didn't look like an attorney, but he was smoking Camels. When he offered Connor one, Connor took it.

Schmanski, still at the head of the table, was reading something else now.

The guy with all the gold got up and came back with a coffee, whispering, "Hope you drink it black, my friend. My name's Jack. Jack Crilly."

"Nelson," Connor said.

"I know," he said, glancing at Cooney, rolling his eyes in disapproval. "I heard."

On Connor's right was an attorney, his suit jacket draped behind him on the seat. Connor had watched him work a dozen times in his own court. Divorce attorney. Knew the law. Good on his feet. A real prick. A great lawyer.

When he looked, the attorney said, "Welcome, Judge."

Connor nodded, starting to take an inventory of the table now. He knew maybe a dozen of them. The rest were just faces, but different than he expected. He was expecting drunks from Michigan Avenue with shopping bags.

After the reading, there was chatter, but Schmanski brought the meeting back to order, just by saying, "Now, gentlemen."

He was looking at Connor now.

"Nelson, is this your first meeting?"

Shit, Connor thought. Here it comes. Twenty-five questions.

He nodded.

Schmanski looked away, "Okay, being that we have a newcomer here, gentlemen. I think we should stick to the first step. The first step is: 'We admitted we were powerless over alcohol and our lives have become unmanageable.'"

He looked back at Connor.

"Now, before we go around and hear from our esteemed gathering, let me be the first to officially salute Nelson here. Nelson, whether you realize it or not, you are the most important person sitting at this table. Whether you choose to come back here, or we never see you in here again, deciding to go back out to further experience the rigorous trials and tribulations that have no doubt brought you here, we all here will be enriched greatly by your presence. I don't mean to put you on the spot, young man, but our hats are off to you. Walking through that door is never easy."

Connor expected a short applause to follow, but none did. Most of the men weren't even looking at him. Connor had no idea what Schmanski, who now had to be pushing his mid-seventies, was talking about. But it sounded rather eloquent. Schmanski always had been verbose and eloquent, even when he was pie-eyed on the bench.

Connor glanced again at Michael Cooney.

Schmanski continued. "Now, the way this works, is all of us will share something. One at a time. And when we're done, if you wish to speak, Nelson, you may do so. But that is entirely up to you."

Schmanski turned to Cooney.

Here it comes, Connor thought. Cooney must be a guest speaker, brought in to pontificate on the workings of state disciplinary boards.

"Hello," Cooney said. "My name is Mike, and I'm an alcoholic."

Connor blinked several times.

"This is a great organization," Cooney said. "But the dues we pay to get here, are very high. Some of us pay with our families. Some of us with houses. Others with our jobs. Little by little. Sometimes all at once. Others lose none of those things. For me, I wasn't ready to get better until the booze took every bit of my self-respect."

Cooney talked about how he didn't drink every day, just weekends, but hit it really hard. He said he'd woken one Sunday morning and found his wife sleeping on the couch, her face all bruised up. Said he demanded to know who did it, ready to kill the son of a bitch. Then she had explained that it was him.

Connor looked around the table, a little nervous for Cooney, wondering who the guys he didn't know really were, wondering if there was anyone there that might put that kind of information in the wrong hands. Connor thought, Christ, man, you're running for the highest court in the state.

But for the next hour, they all incriminated themselves, going around the table, one at a time, just like Schmanski said. Most of them talked no more than a couple of minutes. Connor had never seen lawyers keep anything under a minute. Not in Jacoby's. Not in his court.

He heard about the way they drank and the ways they tried to quit. Guys switching back to beer from the hard stuff, sticking to wine, or moving from the dark liquors to clear ones.

A lawyer from Grosse Pointe said, "Then, I remember standing in front of a roaring fire. I gather the whole family in the room, my elbow on the mantel, and announce that it's all about the gin. Gin was my problem. There was something in the juniper berries that was doing it. They looked at me like I was fucking crazy. And you know what? I was. My problem is alcohol, in any form. When I drink alcohol, I just can't predict the results."

A process server talked about something called a Jellinek chart, a chart of alcoholic symptoms: lying, antisocial behavior, use of other drugs. A drunk worked his way down that Jellinek chart, he said, the symptoms getting worse with time. "Emotional outbursts. Family trouble. Hiding booze. Paranoia. Then those goddamn blackouts."

Connor interrupted, "What do you mean, a blackout?"

The server said, "Loss of memory. You start with a few minutes here and there. Names of people. Minor details. Pretty soon you're losing hours. Waking up, wondering where you are. Wondering who's that broad next to you. Wondering where's your car."

The process server said that if you had the disease, you couldn't stop the slide. At the end of the Jellinek chart were three ways out: Insanity. Death. Or recovery. "Or prison, too," he added. "Though you can always get spud juice in there."

Everyone laughed.

A software salesman talked about how he used to try to hide his drinking from his wife. "I was doing a thousand miles a week, repping a court-reporting system. Always worried about open liquor in the car. I liked to work on cars, too. Had this MGB in my garage. Always out there in the garage, tinkering with it, me and my bottle of Jim Beam. Worked all night. Then stumble in after the old lady went to bed.

"Well, I'm working on this B one night, working on the windshield washer, and I get this great idea. I had this Dodge. My sales car. I pop the hood on the Dodge and decide I'm going to reroute the washer tubes. Put new ones in, actually. Routed one right into the car through the air conditioner under the steering wheel. Filled up the reservoir with Jim Beam, you follow me? Press the washer and it pumps whiskey right into my cup. Worked great until my old lady takes the car to the drugstore one night. She hits the washer and gets a lapful of bourbon. I came in here shortly after that. But not for her. No, not for her. You gotta come in here for yourself."

The attorney next to him spoke, saying he was an alcoholic first, like they all had.

"I liked breaking the rules. Hey, I'm a lawyer. The rules are made for others, the people we represent. Not us. We're in the business of making them, then finding seams, which is just another way of breaking them. And laws, shit. That was for the riffraff. Not for me. As for my problems, I rationalized them. I just happened to be the unluckiest son of a bitch who had the misfortune every day of running into the biggest string of assholes known to man. But every night it was the same. Every night I drank, thinking, Tomorrow, I'm going to kick the shit out of the world. Not drink so much. But the next day, there I was, climbing into that same old squirrel cage again."

Billy Schmanski called on Connor.

"I'm Nelson," he said. "I'm just going to listen." He'd heard a couple others just say that.

"That's fine," Schmanski said. "We hope you come back and see us again."

Crilly, the man with the gold, was last.

"When I came in here, I was living the life," he said. "And, I thought that's the way I had to live it. I owed everybody. Owed the landlord.

Owed my ex-wife. Owed my bookie. Now things are different. I don't owe anybody. I got money. Got a condo in Naples. I got self-respect. This program taught me to take care of my old debts. Ninth step says you do that. You make restitution, so nobody's got anything on you, so you don't have to live like that."

He looked at Connor, then the rest of the table.

"You know, my first meeting I didn't know what I was doing here or what anybody was talking about. But the important thing was: *I came*. Now, I always say, Buy yourself some sobriety. Keep coming. Hit another meeting. One day at a time. Keep coming and stay sober, until all this shit starts to make sense."

He glanced at Michael Cooney, then back to Connor.

"My friend, I don't know if you got a drinking problem. That's up for you to decide. But if you are an alk, it's kind of like being on a down elevator. It's up to you how long you want to stay on it. It's going all the way to the basement. Join us, and you can get off on any floor."

He turned to Schmanski. "That's all I got, Judge. Glad to be here."

The meeting ended with the Lord's Prayer, everyone standing and holding hands as they said it. When Connor let go of the hand with the gold rings, he said, "So, what do you do?"

"Used cars," Jack Crilly said, grinning widely. Connor saw more gold, glistening from two crowns deep in his mouth.

"Really?"

Crilly took out his wallet. "I've got my own lot."

In the corner of his eye, Connor could see Michael Cooney. He was working his way over to them, one handshake at a time. Cooney, he thought, coming over to ask a lot of questions.

"No kidding," Connor said.

Crilly was writing something on a business card.

Connor said, "I've got a car."

Crilly handed him the card anyway. "I'm not selling you one. I've written a meeting on the back. Wednesday night at Sacred Heart, across from the old Stroh's brewery. My home number is also on here. If you think you're going to drink and don't want to, call me. Call me *before*, not after. It's good to have phone numbers. Especially in the beginning."

"I don't want to be bothering you," Connor said, his eye still on Cooney.

"You won't be," Crilly said. "Maybe I'll see you tomorrow at the meeting."

"Maybe," Connor said.

"Jack, how goes the battle?" Michael Cooney said, putting out his hand for Crilly.

If he moved now, Nelson Connor decided, he could make a clean getaway to the door.

CHAPTER 8

HE DROVE WEST on Lafayette, past the Anchor Bar, slowing, looking at it, but then driving on. It had been three hours since his last drink, the Jack Daniel's back in Northville. Already he was counting, but he also was thinking about what he'd heard.

One guy who had five years said, "One day at a time. You hear a lot of trite and hackneyed phrases in here. I thought a Big Ten coach came up with that one. But what it means is you don't try to stop for the rest of your life. You break it down. One hour at a time, if you have to. Get to a meeting, then get your ass home. Put your head on that pillow. And the next day, you wake up and do it again."

On the freeway, Connor was thinking how long it had been since he hadn't drank for one day. Stayed sober for no reason or not set a goal, like he did in Lent. Just did not drink. Because he didn't *want to*, or need to.

He couldn't remember ever doing that.

The stories around the table were too familiar. No, he'd never rigged his windshield washer. But he remembered when Katherine hid his liquor for a while last winter. So he hid his stash from her in the garage and found reasons to go there. Built an ice rink for his son that January. Went out there every night, spraying the ice with a garden hose, saying he had to build it up in layers. Came in looking like Dr. Zhivago, snot icicles frozen to his face.

Try it, he told himself. Like they said.

He passed a billboard for a wine cooler and found himself thinking about his basement, two bottles of vintage Bordeaux he had down there. He and Katherine had saved them from their wedding. They were planning to open one on their twenty-fifth anniversary, the second on the fiftieth, if they were still around.

If he quit drinking, Nelson Connor thought, they wouldn't be able to do that.

Ten years from now.

One hour at a time, the guy said, not years. He was beginning to see the strategy.

And he liked the guy Crilly, not afraid to say exactly what he did. Selling used cars, and proud of it. In fact, he had to hand it to Michael Cooney. It took balls to stand up there. There was something brash about the men in that room. Something selfish, going there not for their wives or their bosses, but for themselves.

He liked that.

Nelson Connor was thinking about what the used-car salesman said when he pulled off the freeway, after he saw the city-limits sign for Livonia. He'd been thinking all day about Jimmy Osborne. Thinking about the way that cop at the prosecutor's table kept his eye on him at the sentencing. The way he stood up and walked out when the word "probation" came out of Connor's mouth. Connor could live with the sentence. But he couldn't live with the three hundred dollars. How it looked. Defendant gets judge high. Defendant gets probation.

The car salesman was right. He had to take care of it now. Eliminate the worry, before he could even consider going to AA.

Connor pulled up to the pay phone outside a gas station, stretching the handset into his car.

He told Ozzie he had to see him.

"How about that bar in Redford?" Ozzie asked.

"This will just take a second," Connor said. "Maybe I'll just drop by."

A mile up the road, he stopped at an ATM, one with a small enclosure, doors that locked while it spit out cash. He put in his card and punched $300 into the keyboard.

The screen stated: UNABLE TO PROCESS THIS REQUEST.

Connor looked through receipts littered around the unit, checking amounts and times, making sure the ATM wasn't down. A guy in a UAW jacket and beard stood outside, watching him, a couple feet away. Connor glanced over. He guessed he was okay, but the guy made him nervous. He'd seen too many personal-injury cases. Tried too many felons. Saw the way seemingly innocent things suddenly reached out and took a bite. He found himself thinking that if the guy mugged him when he came out, and he sustained serious injury, that there was a personal-injury lawyer somewhere who would try to argue the bank hadn't provided adequate security.

You're paranoid, Connor told himself. Two days ago you had a routine. Then, a night in jail. A stupid move in court. Your wife all over your ass. Now an AA meeting. Two days of trouble, and now the wheels are coming off.

He punched in $300 again and waited for the sound of the bills being counted off inside. When the machine spit out his card, the receipt stated: INSUFFICIENT FUNDS TO PROCESS THIS REQUEST.

Goddamn checking account, he thought, Katherine always running down the register with entries, never totaling the balance.

When he came out, the guy with the jacket said, "Broken?"

"I don't know."

"Enough to drive you to drink, huh?" the guy said.

In the car now, thinking about that. A double of Jack Daniel's on the rocks. No, Wild Turkey. There was a bar a mile up the road. Just a bracer to clear his head.

This time, he took it further, thinking beyond the first drink, like somebody at the table said to do. Yes, he'd go into the bar for only one, but he would stay there, looking for that click. He'd have to drive down Sheldon Road and avoid more trouble from the woman cop, and later, Kace. He'd have to wake up the next morning and look at Michael Cooney's picture. And that would be far worse tomorrow, because now he knew Cooney could go one day without a drink. And he couldn't. Not one goddamn day.

Maybe he belonged in room 604.

Maybe Ozzie did, too.

Nelson Connor opened his wallet, looking for the car salesman's business card. Maybe Ozzie would go to the Wednesday meeting with him.

That's when he saw the blank check, the one he kept in his wallet for his Anchor tab.

WHAT LAWRENCE GARY had in mind was Tino Dentz dropping him
off at the guy's house. Send Tino up the street for an ice cream, letting
the Oz wonder how he even got there. If Jimmy Osborne couldn't come
up with some cash, then Gary would ask to use his telephone, calling
Tino on the cellular, and Tino would arrive in less than a minute, parking
the van up the street.

Gary said, "That should get his attention."

"What if it don't?" Dentz asked.

"Then you're going to get a chance to talk to the man," Gary said.

Except the house was dark and the driveway vacant. So they cruised
the address three times, a brick ranch in a sub, Gary saying, "The house-
shitter was definitely here." Everybody living out their little lives in their
backyards with their little decks and their big gas barbecues, Gary
thought. He liked the setup. It gave him a lot of latitude.

On the fourth pass, they saw a red Firebird in the driveway, and a
light on in the picture window. Gary took two cameras with him. Dentz
sped off toward the Dairy Queen they'd seen a mile up the road.

When the door opened, Gary grinned, putting out his arms.

"Oz, my brother, what is going on?"

Gary hugged him, slapping his back as if they were separated at birth.

"Lawrence," Jimmy Osborne said, checking the street behind him.
"What in the hell are you doing here?"

HE SAT RIGHT down on the guy's couch, framing him a couple times
in the macro zoom. Jimmy Osborne stood for a couple seconds just looking at him. Gary lowered the camera and smiled like he was the Pub-
lisher's Clearing House Prize Patrol showing up unannounced.

"Hey," Osborne finally said. "Let me get you a beer."

Gary checked his camera, moving the ASA to sixteen hundred.

Osborne's voice from the kitchen said, "Where have you been?"

"Jackson," Gary said.

Osborne returned with a Miller Ice. "Jackson prison?" he said, handing him the can.

Gary summarized his incarceration, not going into too much detail, but making sure to mention that firearms and a couple of other guys were involved.

When he finished his story, Gary sat forward, his elbows on his knees, the beer can in both hands. He popped the tab and checked him out, doing it in such a way that the Oz knew that he was looking. Saw his salon-highlighted hair, which cut ten years off his age. Saw the horse on his golf shirt, figuring sixty or seventy in the Ralph Lauren shop at Hudson's. Saw twills by Liz Claiborne. No fucking Dockers from J.C. Penny's for this man now.

And Cohan loafers. Shit, those were a hundred and fifty.

Still smiling, Gary said, "Fucking Oz. Still haven't changed, man. Still living out here in suburbia, playing it totally straight."

Osborne shrugged, looking a little uncomfortable now.

"Still working for that discount house?" Gary said. "Selling those stocks and IRAs?"

"Got out of that a couple years ago."

"Still selling?"

"I'm selling windows."

"Windows?"

"Yeah, replacement windows. Double pane, vinyl casings. Guy runs an ad in the TV guide. You seen it, probably. Man, they move windows. But it's slow now. People don't get in the mood to buy until they start feeling cold drafts."

"Jimmy Osborne," Gary said again, figuring now the man hadn't forgotten the marker, the Oz already trying to tell him that he had no cash. "We moved some shit, didn't we? Those were some days."

"You had the best."

"Quality sells itself," Gary said. He paused, then added, "You never did get flush, if I remember right."

"Look, Lawrence . . ." Osborne started to say.

Gary put up his hand, waving him off. "Don't even think about it, man," he said.

Gary lifted up the macro zoom, taking a couple of shots.

"What you doing?" Osborne asked.

"Photography," said Gary, and nothing else.

Gary was thinking the guy had some money, or access to it. You need cash flow to own a house, pay taxes and insurance. Pay for that red bird in the driveway.

Gary said, "Hey Oz, you got any E?"

Some Ecstasy would be nice, after he collected the money.

Osborne shook his head. "I'm pretty much out of doing shit like that. Take care of a few old friends once in a while. But right now, I couldn't even scrounge up a joint."

"I can," Gary said.

He reached into his shirt pocket, something he bought from the homies on his corner. Lawrence Gary wanted Jimmy Osborne good and high.

Gary lit it, not inhaling, then passed it over, saying, "So what do you mean, getting out?"

"No thanks," Jimmy said. "I may have to drop urine next week."

Gary held it out at arm's length, just looking at him. "That's next week. This is now."

The Oz took it. Hit it. Held it, saying in that restricted voice, "I got popped."

"*No,*" Gary said.

Exhaling, Osborne said, "Last year. Narc set up my girlfriend. Got probation, though. Probation and something called diversion. Just came from court today. The fucking lawyer cost me fifteen hundred."

Another reference, Gary thought. Maybe he was going to have to call Tino pretty soon.

Taking the joint back, Gary looked over his shoulder, down the hall to the bedrooms. "Girlfriend?" he said. "Where's that sweet little wife I'd never let you introduce me to?" When he was moving blow, he didn't want to meet anybody. Not family, not friends.

Osborne said, "We're divorced. She really tapped me, then split for L.A. I had to buy out her equity in the house."

Hitting the weed, holding it in himself now, Gary thought Jimmy Osborne was definitely overselling the point now. *The Art of Negotiation* talked about that. But Oz should already know not to do that, being in sales and all.

"Who's the new gal?" he asked, still holding the smoke.

"Somebody I met in a club."

Gary could feel the herb now, spreading out his field of vision, slowing everything down. He began looking around the room. Not just a living room, but a collection of individual items. Hardly any furniture, just a coffee table in front of him. An ashtray. Two empty Miller cans. An *Esquire*. Next to it, some papers, stapled. He recognized the courier font.

Picking it up, he said, "This what you got."

Jimmy nodded, holding in a toke, liking it now.

Gary reading the sheet, said, "I wish they'd have offered me something like this."

He saw the judge's name and signature. The name looked familiar. He remembered reading something about him in the *Legal News*.

"Diversion is a good deal," Gary said. "Stay clean, they won't give you a sheet." Gary looked into Osborne's bloodshot eyes and added, "But you ain't staying very clean."

They both laughed. Hard and long. Gary thinking those homies on the corner sold him some pretty good shit.

Gary took another picture, Osborne with a joint in one hand, the other wiping the tears of laughter from his eyes.

Osborne said, "A friend wants me to go to a fucking AA meeting. Can you believe that?"

"They had that in Jackson," Gary said, taking another picture.

Gary saw him in the frame. Jimmy Osborne just looking at him now, the laugh fit gone as quickly as it came. Gary imagined what he was thinking. The Oz thinking how very fucked up he was, wondering what he was doing in his house taking pictures, after not seeing him for nearly four long years.

Gary thought that was the way performance art was supposed to go.

"Lawrence," the Oz said. "How'd you get here, man?"

"My people," Gary said, letting Osborne define for himself who that might be.

When he lowered the camera he said, "That reminds me. Can I use your telephone?"

THEY TOOK HIM in the church van, Gary saying he wanted to buy him a Dairy Queen, the Oz with the munchies and ready to go. Gary drove, Tino sitting in the backseat on the passenger's side.

Gary laid it all on Tino, saying he owed Mr. Dentz here nearly a thousand, Tino saying nothing, just like Gary instructed him to do if he got the call.

Osborne said, "I don't have that kind of money, Lawrence. I thought you said things were cool."

"They are with me," Gary said. "But my man in the backseat here needs his money now."

Gary drove right past the Dairy Queen, not even slowing down. The Oz's head turned halfway around, following the sign with his eyes.

He turned to Gary and said, "Look, okay. I got maybe a couple hundred in the bank. We can go to a machine."

"A couple hundred?" Gary said, looking over at him, saying nothing more.

"And I got a check."

"What kind of check?" Gary asked.

"A personal check. Maybe I can cash it somewhere."

Gary saw a 7-Eleven. He pulled into the parking lot and parked. Then he put out his hand.

"What?" Osborne said.

"The check. Let me see it."

Osborne hesitated.

"Oz," Gary said. "Let me fucking see it."

It was late, he explained, but if it looked halfway official, maybe they could kite it at an Arab check-cashing store in Detroit.

Osborne pulled the paper from his lapel pocket.

Gary studied the check for a while, putting it all together.

"Damn, Oz," he finally said. He memorized the address, then handed it back.

Osborne was leaning away from him now, his back against the passenger door. Gary put a lot of stock in body language. He'd learned what a body could say in sculpture class.

Gary turned around and looked at Tino Dentz.

"The check looks real good," he said.

—————

THEY WORKED OUT a move in the van, while Osborne was pulling two hundred out of a cash machine at a Comerica branch. Gary said he wanted the check, but he didn't want to cash it. He wanted to do a little research first.

Dentz said, "You sure you want to do that?"

Gary said, "I wouldn't even be discussing it if I didn't."

Dentz's hand came up with a McDonald's coffee stir, its tip piled with powder. Gary saw the bag sitting in his lap.

"Where'd you get that?" he asked.

"Hooked up with that guy from my tier on the crank," Dentz said.

He watched Tino powder both sides.

"Want some?" Tino asked.

"Put that shit away," Gary said. He wanted him listening closely to what he had to say.

"You're going to get the money," Tino said.

"But the paper is worth more than the money," Gary said. "It has the man's name right on it. His fucking title, too." Then Gary added, "What kind of lame would give his man paper, anyway?"

Dentz said, "Yo, what if the man don't want to give up the paper?"

"That's where you come in," Gary said.

Back on the road, Gary told Jimmy Osborne they were taking a ride to Northville.

The Oz said, "Hey, what you guys gonna do?"

"I'd just like to know where the man lives," Gary said.

Lawrence Gary really wasn't surprised by the way it was all working out. First you come up with the vision. The vision is *always* first, coming out of the right side of the brain, bubbling up from the unconscious. Then the left side, the analytic side, finds the right moves to make it work.

Jimmy Osborne started nervously filling in the blanks. The closer they got to Northville, the more he talked, telling them that it wouldn't be very smart to mess with this man, being that he was a circuit judge and well connected. They certainly couldn't walk right up to his house. Ask *him* for money. Shit, he was a family man.

The last few miles were very historical, the Oz explaining how they'd gone to college together. He was just a regular guy who liked to party hard.

"He thinks drugs should be decriminalized," Osborne said. "Man, he's on our side."

When he ran out of material, Osborne asked, "So what you guys gonna do?"

On the first slow pass, Gary spotted the carriage house, saw the sky-lights on the roof and the doors with all the Queen Anne scroll work. Saw the Buick Reatta and the Jeep Cherokee in the driveway. Liked the color scheme on the house, too.

Gary saw just one light on in the back. He guessed that was probably the kitchen. He was familiar with homes from the period, not from the architecture class he dropped at CCS, but from a classic Victorian he'd ripped off in Indian Village once.

"I'm going around the block," Gary said.

Back again, he stopped, turning off the lights and the engine. Rolled down the window. He liked the way the neighborhood smelled. Fresh-cut grass, a hint of roses, and someone cooking something with chocolate somewhere. Not dog shit and exhaust and spilled motor oil like his old lady's street.

Gary said, "You know the thing about Victorians, is most people don't know what to do with them."

Jimmy Osborne sat with his back to the window, his eyes blinking.

Gary said, "Oz, I'm going to need the man's check."

Osborne's hands didn't move.

"Yeah, people repainted 'em all one color in the fifties," Gary continued. He glanced back at Tino Dentz, indicating he should be getting ready.

Tino had something on his lap.

Gary rolled his window back up, saying, "Man, some people actually covered them with aluminum siding. But *that*. *That's* somebody who knows Victorian color. Looks like a creme base. Burgundy cornice and sash. Kinda hard to tell, though, in this light."

Gary put out his hand, wanting the paper.

"What you guys gonna do?" Osborne asked again.

"I'm gonna take that check off your hands," Gary said. "Then I'm going to give it to the man in the backseat."

Jimmy Osborne glanced at the house, then said, "No fucking way."

"Why not?" Gary asked calmly.

Osborne spat, "Not to some nigger I don't know."

Later, Gary would think it was out of character for the Oz to get his back up like that, make that kind of stand.

When Tino Dentz came over the top of the headrest, the phone book was in his left hand, the tail of the cable in his right. The Oz slammed back hard into the headrest, his eyes bulging.

"Grab his feet," Dentz said, pulling.

Gary shouted, "What the fuck are you doing?"

Dentz reefed another inch from the garrote. "I said get the mother-fucker's legs."

The Oz kicking at the dash.

"Yo, Lawrence," Tino Dentz pleaded. "He's gonna fuck up the Reverend Roy's ride."

CHAPTER 9

HE SLEPT POORLY. He heard car doors and voices outside. He put a pillow between his legs, another over his head, deciding he was imagining the noises. His mind was clearly playing tricks on him. In the dark, he saw insects darting around in the darkness under his eyelids.

Katherine complained that he was thrashing. So he went downstairs to the couch and tossed some more. On the far end of the room, in a night shadow, the squirrel monkey slept. It woke once. He could hear the animal making deliberate movements, as if it were rearranging the contents of its cage. When it stilled, he saw its squirrelly eyes staring at him, its tiny hands gripping the cage's wiry bars.

Nelson Connor's eyes opened around half past seven, early for him. Somehow he'd found a couple hours. Katherine was already in the kitchen, sitting with coffee, watching *Good Morning America.*

He poured himself a cup. Filled the mug too high. As he walked over to the breakfast nook, he spilled some. His hands were shaking.

"Jesus, Kace," he said. "Where's my breakfast?"

He felt a sick hunger.

She turned from the TV now. "Since when did you start eating breakfast?"

He didn't answer.

She got up anyway, heading for the stove. "You always told me food slowed you down in the morning."

"Then slow me down with eggs and bacon. Orange juice. English muffins. And potatoes. Lots of potatoes."

He sat in the breakfast nook. The Irish needed potatoes. That's what his old man always said. Crossed the goddamn Atlantic because of potatoes, when the crop failed. He needed potatoes, or he felt like he was going to shake right apart.

When she had two pans sizzling, she said, "So, how was the meeting?"

Now he was up, heading for the cupboard to the left of the sink. He opened the doors. The warm morning light from the windows hit his liquor bottles, making the whiskey more amber, giving the vodkas an almost golden tone.

One day.

He began pulling them out, lining them up on the counter.

"What are you doing?" she said, looking back at him from the stove.

He spun off the caps and began pouring into the garbage disposal, the fumes wafting up. Smelling it now, but not wanting to. Smelling only the alcohol, not whiskey or gin or scotch.

When he was done, he sat back down, putting his hands between his knees, his shoulders collapsed inward. He decided that he must have looked like he was putting on an act for Kace, but he wasn't. Not this time. He felt as if somebody had a hand up inside him, tugging, right under his heart. One good pull and he'd implode.

Kace said, "I guess the meeting went pretty good."

HE GOT HALFWAY through the breakfast, scarfing all the potatoes. Then, when his hands stopped shaking, he didn't want another bite. The whites of the eggs repulsed him.

She was sitting across from him now. She'd turned off the television and was studying him.

He lit a cigarette. The Camel tasted dry. But the coffee had a tart taste that felt good on his tongue.

Kace said, "Why don't you take the day off?"

"I can't," he said.

He couldn't sit around all day. No way.

She got up, taking the dishes with her to the sink. He watched her from behind, studying her as she ran the water. He decided that even at forty, from this angle, she could pass for a twenty-year-old. She was wearing faded jeans and safari shirt, the sleeves rolled up to just below the elbows. Her sandy-red hair hung to her shoulders. He followed her body line to her bare ankle, just above her sandals, then back up her long legs up to her waist, her shirt cinched with a woven leather belt. He remembered she was dressed something like that when he first met her in the mall at Wayne law, her walking over from the art school to sketch a sculpture there. She asked him what his major was. He remembered thinking that this girl couldn't possibly be trying to pick him up, not with that tired old line. "Law," he said. And she said, "Do you know how you get an attorney out of a tree?"

Connor left his cigarette and walked up behind her, putting his arms around her waist. She kept washing, her hands in the water.

"What's wrong?" he said.

She turned around, stepping out of his grasp, picking up one of the five empty bottles he'd left near the sink. She looked at it momentarily, like a shopper checking for a price, then tossed it into the trash. She started dropping the others in.

"So how long this time, Connor? A couple days? A week?"

He tried to explain. "They say you gotta take it a day at a time."

Walking toward the door, she said, "I've got to get John up."

"You don't believe it, do you?" he said.

She was nearly to the stairs when he heard her answer, her voice fading.

"I believe you believe it. You always do, for a few days at least."

GARY SAID HE wanted to shoot some pictures. First the big house in Northville, just a couple of drive-bys, he said. Then head downtown to the Detroit library. Check that out. Said he wanted to find a good copy machine. "One with good definition, not something at the post office," Tino Dentz heard him say.

Tino was running late, but he could deal with it. He wasn't going to get all pressured, like he knew Gary would. Lawrence Gary—the man always had big plans. But Tino had to give him his due this time, he'd stumbled into something good.

When he pulled up to Gary's house the time was one-fifteen. Not noon, like Gary wanted. Gary came out with his cameras over his shoulders and a thick briefcase made of stainless in his hand. He looked like he was on his way to cover the fucking Super-Bowl, the way he walked from the front porch to the van.

Gary handed the briefcase to him through the window, saying, "Careful with that."

Tino asked, "What is it?"

"A long lens," Gary said. "Where the fuck you been?"

Tino knew Gary sometimes treated him like he was his house nigger. But mostly, he just overlooked it, because Gary had angles on things he wanted. The man did know how to shoot some good moves.

"I was tied up," Tino said.

Staying at the window, Gary said, "Called you. Paged you. I told you, *timing*. Timing is everything on a gig like this."

"Beeper was in the van. Van was in the paint shop. I was in the waiting room."

"Paint shop?"

"Like I told you last night, I had to take it over. They wanted to keep it *all day*."

"Touch-up don't take all morning, let alone all day."

Tino motioned with his index finger, directing Gary around the front of the van. He wanted him to see the gold letters across the hood:

BIG ROCK CHURCH

"You didn't say a sign painter," Gary said, looking. "You said a paint shop. This took all morning?"

Tino said, "Yo, check out the other side."

Lawrence Gary walked around, getting a full view of the passenger side now. More gold letters, in large Sans Serif, all the letters coming out at you three-dimensional, exploding out from a single point, taking up almost the entire length of the van.

Nice work, he thought. Nice scheme. Gold on royal purple.

It read:

HEAVEN!

Then, below that, centered:

MAKE YOUR RESERVATION
AT
"BIG ROCK CHURCH"

Gary wondered why the church was in quotes. Maybe to imply that a choir was singing the words. Otherwise, the quotes made no sense. The sign painter had started the pastor's name underneath, but had only completed THE REV. ROY. The entire job stenciled and airbrushed. Lacquer, Gary decided. Had to be. Fast-drying lacquer, or all that gold in heaven would run.

"Gonna paint the left side like the right side," Dentz was saying, Gary getting in. "Guy wasn't too happy, me taking off before it was done. Gave him a story about the Reverend Roy needing it, so I gotta get it back."

Gary asked, "What does the man look like, anyway?"

"Like a painter, man."

"No, I mean the pastor."

"The Reverend Roy? I've never seen the man up close. Seen only his picture. Check it out. The man has his picture in the yellow pages."

"Full page?"

Dentz nodded as he pulled away from the curb.

Lawrence Gary was thinking that maybe the pastor could be a mark one day, if the conditions were right. Maybe they'd found an entire new line of work. But right now, there were too many connections with the preacher. That was the beauty of what they had going now. It was unconnected, and unexpected. Once Gary went with it, fully accepting what he had to work with, it made him think of the guy who parachuted into the middle of the Holyfield-Bowe fight in Vegas, a wind machine strapped to his back. Stopped a championship bout cold in the late rounds, at the peak of the fight. It had to happen right *then*. Not in the early rounds, or afterward, or while the card girl was walking around in heels.

That's what elevated it to art.

At the interchange, Gary directed him east, toward Detroit.

"I thought you wanted to go back to the judge's house."

"I do," Gary said. "Later."

A matter of timing, Gary thought.

THAT MORNING, NELSON Connor heard a domestic matter, a piece of ongoing business on his civil docket for years: A suburban couple fighting over joint custody of two adolescent boys. He'd entered the original divorce settlement six years ago, but the parents kept coming back, both trying to get the last word. The two sides camped on each side of his courtroom, the husband's new wife shooting looks at his ex-wife's new husband, the new husband rolling his eyes when the ex-husband's attorney interjected a point he didn't like. Doing it as if Connor should take note, and adjust his rulings accordingly.

Connor just wanted to get through the day.

"Where's the Friend of the Court?" Connor said, shuffling through paperwork filed by counsel.

The husband muttered, "They're no friend."

"I'll have order here," Connor said, rapping his gavel once.

The gavel broke, the top rolling off his bench. It stopped at the foot of the ex-wife's lawyer. Lewis started to retrieve it, but Connor barked, "Leave it."

By late morning, the two attorneys were arguing for a decision. Connor toyed with the idea of making it on the basis of the gavel head's location. Instead, he broke thirty minutes early for lunch, leaving the ex-husband, the ex-wife and two lawyers angry because now they would have to hang around downtown for a long, two-hour lunch. He could hear them murmuring as he left.

He disappeared into his back offices, went directly into his chambers, closing the door behind him. Two minutes later, he could hear Lewis and Barbara bickering outside. Today, he felt like slapping them. Telling them to get a hold of themselves, or get a new job.

He opened his chambers door. Handed Barbara five bucks, saying, "Could you bring me something from the deli?"

She returned fifteen minutes later, knocking first. He opened his door only wide enough to take a white bag, grease bleeding through its paper. He tried to read a pending motion while he ate grilled pastrami. He got through one page and two bites.

He could feel that hand pulling in his chest again.

Connor walked over and opened his window. The air outside was heavy and moving, hitting his face like a blast of exhaust from a city bus. He rubbed his eyes, then looked at the people below in Hart Plaza. They were perched on benches, others around the Scott fountain. He remembered years ago, when he first joined the Third Circuit, meeting Kace there for lunch. Some great lunches, her bringing a wicker basket with tuna salad and fresh-cut melons.

And Bloody Marys, in a thermos.

He eyed his suit jacket on the hall tree. He was thinking about the Anchor Bar now. Not going there to drink. Just to play some Q-Bert. Work off the anxiety he'd been feeling all morning. Outrun the bad guys. Get to the next level.

One drink would take the edge off.

He forced the thought from his mind. He knew if he even started the debate, he'd lose it.

He took his wallet out, got a different debate going. Whether to make the call or not. He walked over to the window one more time, then back to the phone, staying on his feet as he dialed the number of the front of the business card.

He waited briefly on hold, listening to a classical-music station. A used-car lot with classical hold music, he thought. The *1812 Overture*. He wondered what kind of lot this guy Jack Crilly ran.

The line picked up on the second cannon blast.

"Crilly here."

Connor said, "This is Nelson."

"Who?"

"Connor."

A moment of silence, then, "Right, you wanted the gold Taurus. It's already prepped, my friend. You can drive it right out of here today."

"No. Last night. I sat next to you. You said I could call."

Crilly started laughing.

Connor felt foolish. He wished he hadn't called now. He wished he hadn't bothered the guy at work.

But Crilly said, "Brain damage. Plus, it's an anonymous program, right? Wait till you play in an AA golf tournament. You look up at the leader board, and it doesn't tell you a goddamn thing."

Connor told him he was having some real trouble getting through the day.

Crilly said, "A couple blocks up Congress, then turn on Griswald. There's a little candy shop across from Kennedy Square. You know where it is?"

Connor knew.

"Meet me there in fifteen minutes," Crilly said.

THE SMELL OF hot sugar hit Connor's nostrils at the door. Hot fudge and strawberries and pineapple syrup and chocolates. All blended together into one overwhelming confection. The used-car salesman was waiting for him at the counter, a banana split in front of him, spoon in hand, into his third or fourth bite.

"Buy you a sundae?" he said, motioning for the girl behind the counter with his free hand.

"No thanks," Connor said, waving her off as he took a stool.

"Coffee?" Crilly said, motioning her back.

"That just makes me shake. I don't know how you guys drink it all the time."

"That's why I suggested a sundae."

"I don't eat desserts."

"Either did I," Crilly said. "Used to be real proud of that. Everybody ordering desserts after dinner. Not me. Had a couple more drinks, though. Later I found out two fingers of scotch has the same carbs as one of these things."

Crilly picked up a napkin and carefully wiped a wisp of whipped cream from his mustache.

"You called," he said. "That's good. And that means you haven't drank, right? But you're thinking about it. What's it been? How long?"

"Twenty-four hours—at six tonight."

Connor was pulling packets of sugar from the bowl in front of him, arranging them in a neat stack.

"Well," Crilly said. "About now you should be feeling like warmed-over shit."

"Worse."

"You sent out for lunch. Afraid to go out, right?"

"How did you know that?"

"Just a hunch."

"But you couldn't eat."

"Something like that."

"And you're worried about driving home tonight."

Connor turned, looking at him. "A little."

"No, not a little. You've been thinking about that drive all goddamn morning. Probably five or six bars you can hit. Or, maybe, when you were in your office, you looked out the window. You know a little place up the street where you can step in for a quick one. Settle your nerves. Of course, you probably wouldn't want to go there today. You'd probably go to another bar, one with sufficient distance. The place you go after work. So you don't see anybody from the office. Hell, who would know, right? But *you* would know, my friend. And that's why you called me."

Jesus, Connor thought. Maybe this guy Crilly had called his house, talked to Katherine about his habits.

That was an absurd thought.

"How did you know?" Connor asked.

"I'm an alk. It all sounds perfectly logical to me."

Connor went back to the sugar bowl, removing the Sweet 'n Low now.

Crilly asked him about his family, about his work. Connor saying he thought family trouble and work pressure had increased his drinking. Crilly said doctors blamed surgery and cops blamed crime and auto workers blamed boredom, concluding, "You drink because you're an alk, that's all."

He finished the banana split, lifting up the bowl and tilting it so he could spoon out the last of the syrup. When he was finished, he asked, "When is the last time you dried out?"

"Dried out?"

"Tell me a little bit about your drinking," he said, wiping his mustache again. "When was the last time you went an extended period without doing anything? Or, let me put it this way: When's the last time you went a full day without a drink?"

Connor thought back. Some days were lighter than others.

"Lent," he finally said. "Not this year, but last year. I went a week for Lent."

"Lent lasts six weeks," Crilly said.

"I drank beer for the rest."

"I'm sure the Lord God took note."

Crilly motioned to the counter girl. He wanted a glass of water.

"Beer is good for Lent," Crilly said. "I liked beer for mowing grass. Anything physical. Morning work. Good for flushing you out, and you still get an ounce of what you need per can."

Then Crilly asked, "So, since then, how much, you figure? Just an average, per day."

"A couple at lunch." Then Connor thought about it. Made a realistic appraisal. "Make that three or four at lunch. Then three or four, or maybe five or six, after work."

"What about home?"

"Sure, after dinner. Some brandy, usually. Maybe two or three, while I read briefs, motions. Stuff like that."

"You go to sleep at night?" Crilly said. "Or do you pass out?"

Connor didn't answer, saying, "But I didn't drink in the morning."

"What about weekends?"

"Well, some Bloody Marys on the weekends."

"What time do you get up, on weekdays?"

"Eight, or eight-thirtyish. I like to be on the bench by nine-thirty."

"And you're at lunch by noon, right?"

"Close to it."

"Well, that's only a few hours after you get up, right?"

"Yeah," Connor said. "So?"

"Well, I'd consider that the morning, wouldn't you?"

When Connor asked where all this was going, Crilly explained that he was probably going to have it pretty rough, the first three days being the worst. He said he drank the same way. Never really getting thoroughly sober. Always staving off a hangover by getting a couple in him early the next day.

"But I wouldn't get drunk," Connor said. "I had to be on the bench."

"Who's talking about getting drunk? I'm talking about feeling normal. Getting back to square one. Maintenance drinking. The French, a lot of

Europeans, are really good at it. Sipping wine all day and night. Never getting too carried away. They're fine, until you take it away from them."

"Then what?"

"We had a guy at the meeting. Came over here with Renault when it merged with Chrysler. His third day into it, two hunters with shotguns and a springer spaniel came trouncing through his bedroom. That's when he realized he had a real problem."

"You mean the DTs?"

Crilly said, "It wasn't hunting season, my friend."

The counter girl brought the water. Connor asked for one too. He drank the entire glass in one gulp, then asked for another.

"You think I'm that bad?" he asked.

"Shit, I don't know. But if you're really having problems, physical problems, mental problems, there's another way to do this, you know."

Crilly wanted to know if he had good health insurance.

"The county gives us a good deal," Connor said.

"Look," Crilly said. "I know some people at Brighton. They've got a nice facility an hour from here. They bring you down easy."

Connor said, "Detox?"

"You'd be there a week, maybe two. I'll take you up there, if you want. I got plenty of wheels."

Connor thought, Nobody is taking me to a detox center. Not Katherine. Not this guy Crilly. But he remained polite.

"Look, you don't have to do anything like that for me."

"I wouldn't be doing it for you. I'd be doing it for me."

"I don't understand."

"Stick around. You will."

Connor thought this guy Jack Crilly was talking in riddles.

"I think I'll just stick with the meetings," Connor said.

He looked at his watch, but didn't leave the stool. He went back to playing with the sugar, breaking a packet open now, making patterns on the counter.

"You work your own program," Crilly said. "I can only make suggestions. But I do suggest you get to that meeting I told you about tonight. Before you drive home."

Crilly added, "You know where it is?"

Connor nodded.

"I can meet you there at six. You'll be out of there by seven."

"I should probably go right home," Connor said.

"Why?"

He was thinking of Katherine. "I've some fences to mend."

Crilly said, "How long, you figure, your wife has been putting up with your drinking?"

Connor didn't answer.

Crilly said, "She can put up with a few more nights. Besides, you're getting sober. You don't have to apologize. Down the road, if she can't understand that, then we'll get you a new wife."

"That's cold," Connor said.

"No, that's first things first."

"I don't get it."

"You put staying sober over everything. Your wife. Your kids. Your job. Your dog. You can't get sober for them, either. You do it for yourself. Or you won't make it. Because if you drink, you'll lose all of them anyway. You follow what I'm saying?"

He saw something ruthless in Crilly's eyes.

Connor looked away, back at the patterns of Sweet 'n Low.

"I just thought it would be a good idea to spend some time with the family."

"Spend it after the meeting. The meeting is your best insurance against taking that first drink."

Connor spun around in the stool and got up, putting out his hand, shaking Crilly's. The used-car salesman smiled, showing a little gold.

"Listen, I appreciate you coming over here," Connor said. "I appreciate everything you're trying to do for me."

"Like I said, it's my pleasure, my friend," Crilly said, getting up himself now.

"And I don't want you to worry," Connor added.

"Oh, I'm not going to worry," Crilly said.

He dropped a two-buck tip. "I'm not the one who has to make that drive."

CHAPTER 10

HE HAD SEVERAL dozen assignments to hand out, indigent defendants needing court-appointed attorneys. Most defendants were poor. Their cases were steady income for criminal attorneys, the assignments handed out by judges in every courtroom.

Barbara kept the assignment case list on her desk. The criminal attorneys Nelson Connor appointed often came in to sign up there.

"Put a stack of tickets to my fundraiser next to the assignment sheet," Connor said. The tickets were fifty apiece, money he'd use to run for reelection in November. "That way they'll get the message when they pick up work."

During the afternoon recess, he disappeared again into his chambers, leaving his robe on this time. He wanted to call Kace. Tell her he'd be home before six tonight.

Reaching for the phone, Lewis buzzed him with an incoming call.

"Who is it?"

Lewis said, "I don't know. I'm covering for Barbara."

"Where's Barbara?"

"The smoke shop, I think."

Connor said, "Just find out who it is, Lewis. Find out what they want."

Lewis buzzed him back, saying it was a Mr. Dali.

He didn't know a Mr. Dali. "Concerning what?"

"He said it's about your Comerica check."

Shit, Connor thought. He'd forgotten to make a deposit, to cover Ozzie's three hundred. Now the bank was calling him, probably giving him a courtesy call before they sent it back. He was used to such favors. In return, he sometimes dispensed a little legal advice.

He picked up the phone. "This is Judge Connor."

"Honor," the voice said. "I have your check here."

"That was quick," Connor said.

The voice said, "Check fifty-two thirty-two, Honor. Pay to the order of James Osborne in the amount of three hundred dollars."

Not "Your Honor." But "Honor." Connor thought that a little odd, but dismissed it.

"I meant to get there this morning to cover it," he said. "But I had a hearing. Can you hold it?"

The voice said, "Oh, I am going to hold it all right, Honor. I'm holding it right here in my hand."

The guy's voice. Maybe in his thirties. Spoke with confidence and clarity, like he had some education. But the tone wasn't right. The connection wasn't good, not like a business line.

"Who is this?"

"They didn't tell you?"

"I didn't get your first name."

"My first name's Salvador, Honor."

Later, Connor would think he should have recognized that name. But he was thinking about banking. He wasn't thinking about modern art.

"You don't work for Comerica."

"No, but I was very big in the surrealistic movement."

"What the hell is this?"

"Well, being up front about it, what I'm looking at here is genuinely surreal. I mean, it's gotta be. Because only surrealism could explain why a man of your stature would write a check to a little deadbeat piece of shit like Jimmy Osborne."

He thought, What did Ozzie do? Pay somebody off with his check?

"I don't understand," Connor said.

The voice said, "I didn't either. At first, I thought, Hey, maybe the piece of shit put in some windows for you. Or maybe you lost bad in a golf game. Or maybe somebody did somebody a favor. But that doesn't make sense, really."

"Who the hell is this?" Connor demanded.

"No, Honor," the caller said. "That's not the way it works. Let's start with who *you* are."

"Me?"

"Yeah, you're the guy who makes it all work."

The caller paused, then said, "Now, let's see. His Honor, Judge Nelson Arlen Connor, born Detroit, Michigan, 1951. Admitted to the bar, 1977, Michigan. Education: Wayne State University, B.S. Cum laude. 1974. Wayne State University J.D., magna cum laude, 1977. Article and book review editor, 1976–77, *Wayne Law Review*. Law clerk, Wayne Circuit Court. Member: State Bar of Michigan. And these sections, Honor: Litigation. Torts. And boards. I'll skip the dates. WDET Radio. Detroit Zoological Society. Zoning Board of Appeals, Northville, Michigan. And let's not forget the governor's task force on drugs. That's good. A lot of my people are grateful for the work you did on that."

He was reading out of Martindale-Hubbell. Connor knew it by the cadence, the way the dates and the positions followed one another in the national law directory. He didn't like the way the guy's voice sounded, all full of himself.

"You can find that out in any library," Connor said, trying to block fear from his own voice, trying to knock him down a notch.

He wanted to hang up, but he didn't.

"Let me interpret further, Honor. Nice house. Turn-of-the-century Victorian. Nice cars. Reatta. Destined to be a collectible. Good road machine. Two-seater. What, maybe thirty thou? Just for you and the old lady, or maybe you got a *thang* on the side. Put the dutiful wife in a Cherokee. Twenty-five or thirty K, but *safe*. No getting stuck in snow there. Good family man, thinking about his family. Nice neighborhood. High taxes, but what the hell, the schools are good. Altogether, a real nice picture, until you add this little check for three hundred. That's when things get a bit hallucinatory, a bit *distorted*. That's when—and I'm sorry, Honor—they begin to look just plain fucking stupid."

"He's just a friend," Connor said. Then he wished he'd kept his mouth shut.

"Oh yes. Hold on, Honor. I forgot. Can't overlook your old *friend*. Jimmy Osborne, pseudo yuppie, former stock broker, branch office type. Closest he ever got to the big board was B roll on Dan Rather. Moved into windows. *Big field*. Was going to make lots of money, join a golf club, selling that vinyl-clad shit to seniors. Lowering their gas bills. Their best interests at heart. Did a little moonlighting, too. With a different crowd, now. Moved a little cocaine, which is a Class A substance, sometimes a little herb. Always had something in stock. Gave credit, too, if you needed it in a pinch. Sold these materials to *old friends*, some in high places."

The voice paused. Then, "Shall I go on?"

Connor could hear sounds on the line. It was a city bus, a diesel, pulling away. He walked over to the window and looked down at Jefferson Avenue, half expecting to see someone at the public phone in Hart Plaza.

He saw no one.

"Go right ahead," Connor said.

"So, this certain two-bit dealer gets a check for three hundred dollars, which by itself might not be a big deal. But Jesus, when you look at the whole picture, like I said, that's where this surrealism comes in. Not only is the check for three yards, but it's written on the same day that one Jimmy Osborne has appeared and received a very favorable sentence. *Nice deal.* Curiously, this is also the very same day Honor has spent the night in the poky. Made a little splash in the paper. Sounds like a bad day altogether. Hell, if it was me, I'd go home and go to bed. No, not Honor. He wants to cover his tab for a few grams of blow. Takes care of his homeboy. That's what I mean by *surreal.* That's fucking *distorted,* Honor. In my book, when you do somebody a favor, they pay you. You don't pay them. It's hard to figure."

"Isn't it?" Connor said. He was looking for a way to end this conversation now.

"But I imagine," the voice said, singsong, "that tenure outfit that watches you boys and girls could probably get it all sorted out."

Connor walked to his chair. Sat down, his robe catching under his rear, pulling back his neck.

"Who are you?" he said. "And what do you want?"

"Let's just say I'm in collections. Not a bad business, really, but tiring. You see, Honor, I got your marker. But guess what? Your paper is no good. Insufficient funds, my man."

Connor looked around his own office, trying to think of a strategy. He looked at the inside wall, where he kept the Michigan Laws Annotated, twenty volumes, green with gold brocade. Katherine bought them, a gift after his last reelection. But there were no answers there, only more problems.

Connor said, "The check will be good by tomorrow."

The voice said, "No, Honor. Let me explain briefly how the collections business works. You see, the collector assumes the debt. Assumes the risks and expenses of collecting for the debtor, then collects what he can, taking a certain percentage for his effort. That way, we make everyone happy."

We, Connor thought.

"Is fucking Ozzie in on this?" he said, angry now.

"The Oz? In a way, yes. You see that's the thing about surrealism, Honor. Things aren't as they appear."

Connor snapped, "That goes for you, too, asshole."

"That tells me something, Honor."

"Is that right?"

"It tells me you need to keep up with your mail."

He quickly buzzed Barbara, asking her if anything had come in. She brought in a manila envelope. It was marked PERSONAL AND CONFIDEN-TIAL. No stamp.

"When did this come in?" he asked, the phone on his ear.

"A runner dropped it off."

"Who?"

"Black guy. Never seen him before."

She stood there looking at him, waiting for him to open it.

"We're ready when you are, Judge," she whispered.

It was nearly four.

"I'm sick," Connor said. "Adjourn everything."

"Until when?" she asked.

"Jesus Christ, I don't know. Have the attorneys call tomorrow."

She spun around, almost slamming the door behind her.

He ripped open the envelope. It was a clean copy. Connor's eyes went to his home address and phone number on the check. He remembered arguing with Kace about that, telling her he didn't want that the last time she reordered. He especially didn't want "The Hon." in front of his name. She'd called him paranoid. He'd stalked out of the house. Got real drunk that night.

"Got it, Honor?" the voice said.

He was furious, so he went with it. Culpability went both ways. "Listen to me, asshole," he said. "You think you can get your hands on some paper, pick up a phone and blackmail a circuit judge? You're the fucking guy with the delusions. I've got a jail cell waiting for your surreal ass."

The line was silent for a couple seconds. Then, "Honor, now that's not the kind of language we've come to expect from our elected officials."

"Fuck you," Connor said, his voice low.

"Now, Honor, I want you to be thinking about making an offer. A good-faith offer, what you think is fair to square up your account."

Connor said, "Fuck you again."

He got up, looking down at the street again. Wishing he could see some son of a bitch out there, looking up at him. Take the elevator down. Even had a line for him: "Let me show you some research you overlooked." Then, beat the guy until he couldn't walk.

The voice said, "I'm going to let that go for now, Honor. I know how it is. They say disbelief comes first. Then anger. Then bargaining. And through bargaining, finally, acceptance. I'm gonna let you work through it, though."

"I'm not going to work through a thing."

There was a pause, then, "Well, suit yourself. But, I gotta caution you, before you get too carried away. It is awfully warm outside. They say the high eighties for the next couple of days."

The guy was all over the place, Connor thought.

"You're talking nonsense."

"Perhaps, but if I was you, I'd still try to keep that sweet little Buick of yours out of the sun."

"What does my car have to do with anything?"

"Well, it's not the car, it's the smell. You get that smell in that Buick's interior, Honor, you're never going to get it out."

HE PILED MOTIONS into his briefcase and walked out, avoiding eye contact with Lewis and Barbara. His bailiff was slumped in his chair with his solitaire. Barbara blew out a lungful of smoke, holding her cigarette at mouth level, saying, "See ya."

As he reached the door, she yelled out, "You gonna call me?"

He didn't answer, and he didn't stop.

He took the private elevators, the ones behind the courtrooms they used to transport prisoners, and sometimes, as a matter of courtesy, a local celebrity entangled in a high-publicity divorce. Two bailiffs from the fifteenth floor stepped on with a guy with a bad goatee and long, unwashed hair. He was in prison greens and belly chains, looking like a surgeon who'd been on skid row for a week.

"Beatin' the rush, Judge?" one bailiff said.

Connor nodded. But the inmate had his attention, staring at him with dead eyes, looking like he didn't give a shit.

Connor looked away. The prisoner turned around slowly, crossing his wrists like it was natural for him to stand that way. Connor behind him, looking at his flimsy pants sagging around his ass now, the crotch way too low. He smelled like bacon and old cigarettes and industrial cleaner. He remembered smelling that when he was taking assignments, instead of giving them. He remembered how claustrophobic he could get, talking to prisoners in the Wayne County jail.

Connor took the elevator all the way to the basement. Pushed past everyone when the doors opened. He walked quickly ahead through an underground loading dock used by police and service vehicles, heading for the light of day.

He climbed the ramp to Congress, but when he got into the sun, he saw photographers and TV cameras on both sides.

A cameraman yelled, "There he is!"

Connor froze momentarily, startled. The media ran down the ramp, but went right past him, getting angles on the perp in the greens.

Later, he wouldn't even remember walking across the street to the parking garage. Didn't have a clue if he waited for the light, or just dodged the cars. He would remember only walking to his trunk, and standing there for maybe a minute. Smelling moldy concrete and hearing cars coming down on the ramps, their tires screeching. He would remember sliding the key in, his hand shaking, the grooves falling into place.

The Cohan loafer. Ozzie's lifeless face.

Then panicking, really. He'd have no other word for it. Driving to the

Anchor Bar, not even thinking about doing anything else. At first he thought everyone was following him, but it was just downtown traffic. A car. A meter reader. A church van.

Later, he would remember pulling up in front of the Pick-Fort Shelby, putting two quarters in the meter. Later, it would strike him odd as to what he would recall, and what he would forget.

He would remember going in, hearing Boy George again on the jukebox. The place not very busy, before the after-work crowd. He would recall going directly to the bar and taking the first two drinks, double Wild Turkey on the rocks.

Sitting with the regulars. Looking up at those eight-by-tens, picking out a couple judges, and the bookie.

All of them looking down at him.

Days later, Nelson Connor would remember all of that.

But the rest of the night would be gone.

CHAPTER 11

"HAVE YOU BEEN associating with any known felons?" the parole officer asked.

"Felons?" Gary asked back.

"Cut the bullshit," the woman said. "You know what I mean."

Lawrence Gary was looking out the window. He could see Tino Dentz waiting for him, the church van idling on Cass Avenue, Tino saying he'd keep the air on.

Gary looked back at the PO with the bad skin and tired eyes. Probably working four hundred files, he thought. Hardly enough time to stack the paperwork and fit in a half dozen cigarette breaks behind the building, let alone check anything out. He had the urge to shoot her picture, but he resisted it.

"I know the rules," he said.

"Have you been seeking work?"

He explained he was heading down to the Center for Creative Studies, as soon as she let him go. Going to check out the board in the placement office for freelance work, he said. Check into student loans, too. Maybe go back to school in the fall.

"I'm looking for leads," he said, lifting one of his cameras up, making sure she got a good look at it.

"What kind of leads?"

His eyes went back to the window. He looked again at the official vehicle of Big Rock Church, the way the purple body and the gold lettering demanded the eye. He decided it looked like something from a theme park, especially among the boarded-up buildings and puke-stained winos that lined the Cass Corridor. The van was no good for the kind of leads he needed right now. And he had serious questions about its driver. The man just couldn't move in certain circles. He thought that Big Rock vehicle had to go.

"Mr. Gary?" the PO said.

He turned, looking.

"You need to get serious. You have more going for you than most people who sit in that chair. You either find work, or we'll help you find it, but I don't think it's going to be in the art field."

"I need a car," he said.

You can't work without a car. You can't get to school, either, he said.

"There's always public transportation," she said.

"You can't freelance on a bus line. That's not how it's done."

"So how is it done, Mr. Gary?" she asked.

He explained you were always taking different gigs in different parts of the city, maybe shooting a magazine spread one day, doing graphic design the next, picking up a check for keylining one week and a photo layout the next.

"What would you need to freelance?" she asked. "Besides a car, that is."

"Like I said, some leads. And some good ideas, some good concepts. My mother's house is a studio, of sorts."

"Oh, really?"

"As for ideas, I'm swimming in them," he added.

"I'll bet you are," she said.

He almost told her about the leather-and-lingerie shop near the airport, but decided that would surely lead to Twenty Questions on how he planned to capitalize the venture, or who his partners might be. He toyed with sanitizing the plan, giving her something she could handle.

But the PO stood up.

"When you come back in two weeks, why don't you bring me a short list of some of your *concepts*?" she said.

"I'll work on it," he said.

She pulled a lighter and pack of smokes from her purse, ready to make a dash for the back exit.

"Mr. Gary," she said. "Do more than *work on it*, okay?"

AFTERWARD, THEY WENT to Jumbo's, not five minutes from the Detroit Metro Parole Office. Dentz pulled into the parking lot, but Gary made him move it, directing him to park the van around the corner on Selden, not saying why.

Dentz complained, "Whatup? Why walk, when we can ride."

Gary said that parking the church van right in the lot of a Cass Corridor bar was pretty stupid, especially considering a rescue mission was located almost directly across the street. Righteous people there could read the Big Rock phone number off the van and drop a dime. Stir shit up. "I don't think you would want to be meeting the Reverend Roy for the first time under those conditions," Gary said. "Or would you?"

"I guess I never looked at it that way," Dentz said.

Inside Jumbo's, there was a couple of regulars at the bar and a half dozen whores sitting alone at tables. The interior was decorated with beer posters, the Busch and Miller girls bearing little resemblance to the hookers who'd spaced themselves around the tables like feeding pigeons instinctively cutting each other's operating room.

Gary sat down at a small, round Formica table, sending Dentz to the bar for drinks. One of the whores started walking over, saying, "Hi, baby." Gary turned his back. He could hear her heels turning around. The rest never got up.

Dentz came back with a Hennessy on the rocks. He pushed a rum-and-coke across the table. Gary stirred it, studying the patterns in the ice cubes, thinking how artists airbrushed those with subliminals in liquor ads.

"Gary, look at me," Dentz said, sitting now, his legs out in the aisle, already looking bored. "What we doing here?"

Gary reached in for the lime and squeezed it. "Bobby Tank used to hang here. Maybe somebody's seen him around."

"They locked Bobby up, man," Dentz said, his voice going higher. "In the county."

"When did you hear that?"

"Waiting to see my PO. Guy sitting next to me told me."

"He knew Bobby?"

"Guys says he's from West Virginia. I tell him I worked with a guy from West Virginia on a few jobs. One thing leads to another. Turns out they were in the same unit at the county."

"How long is he in for?"

"Guy told me Bobby's waiting for some kind of arraignment. His court lawyer was saying to just hold on. Wait until the jail gets crowded, then he can bond him out on a personal bond."

"The guy tell you what Bobby did?"

"Guy says Bobby took a check machine from a scrap yard and bunch of scrap-yard checks. Sounded like it could have been a good thing."

Gary could imagine how it went bad. "Bobby Tank doesn't know how to move paper. That's not one of the man's talents."

Bobby Tank was hard labor, Gary thought. He went into places where nobody wanted to go, did things nobody else wanted to do. Gary always figured that was because his people worked in the coal mines.

Dentz said, "A dog got him, Gary."

"At the yard?"

"Guy at the parole office said Bobby sees the check machine when he sells the scrap dealer a bunch a copper plumbing he took out of one those boarded-up houses. Making halfway decent money doing that, too, keeping his PO off his ass. But after he sees this machine, he starts feeding this Bouvier at the yard Slim Jims every night through the fence. Then he makes his move. Gets in okay. Gets the machine. Gets back to the fence. But then the dog gets him."

"Why did it attack?"

"I don't know. I guess he ran out of Jims."

"The dog hurt him?"

"No, just got part of his pants. He still gets over the fence with the machine and the checks. Had them in a backpack."

"I thought you said the dog got him."

"The dog *did*. They find the dog with Bobby's wallet the next morning. The cops had Bobby by noon."

Gary was thinking he'd heard a hundred stories like that in Jackson. Guys with halfway sound ideas, but no eye for detail. The results always the same.

Gary asked, "So, when did you find out?"

"About Bobby?"

Gary nodded.

"Last week."

"How come you didn't tell me?"

"You never said you were looking."

"Well, I'm looking now."

"You said you never wanted to see that motherfucker again, remember?"

"Yeah, I said it, but the man does follow directions," Gary said. He said it in a way that implied Tino Dentz did not.

Dentz didn't pick up on the slight. "Polite motherfucker, too," Tino added. "Politest criminal motherfucker I think I've ever seen."

"They raise them that way down there," Gary said.

Dentz took a healthy sip of his drink. "But why would you be looking for Bobby?" he asked.

"I think we could use him."

"For what?"

"For the judge."

"Shit," Dentz said, half laughing. He took another drink of the cold cognac, then added, "Gary, that judge of yours ain't ever going to speak to you again. How many times I got to say it, man?"

Gary looked away, in the direction of the whores, without making eye contact.

"Like I told you," Gary said. "He's just away from the office."

"You called again?"

Gary nodded, still looking over the room.

"What they say?"

"They say he's on vacation now," he said, irritated that he had to repeat it. "They say he'll be back."

"How long?"

"They say soon."

"And how many times we been out there now to his crib?"

"We've only driven by. I'd like to get closer."

"We got close enough to see his old lady. Working in her little flower bed. I still say that might be a daughter. Bitch has a real nice ass."

"That's his wife. I saw her picture in one of the papers I pulled up at the library."

"What did you say she do?"

"I don't know what she does."

"Then why was she in the paper?"

"They were at a DIA fundraiser."

"What's a DIA?"

"Detroit Institute of Arts. The museum downtown."

Dentz hit the drink again, finishing it. "Well, that don't matter anyway. Woman working in the yard. Kid's bicycle on the porch, waiting to get ripped. You don't take no vacation, leave that kind of shit around."

"Maybe."

Dentz paused, then said, "Maybe this vacation is just the judge's way of telling you to fuck off, Gary."

Gary was looking around the bar now, thinking maybe one day he'd come back. Do some environmentals with the hookers. Convince the owner to let him put a table and chair in the parking lot. Sit them down there, one at a time, where the light was good. Use some low-grain Pan-atomic X so he'd get all the detail. Pick up the texture of their makeup and the needle tracks. Exhibit the collection in Birmingham, letting those upscale types see the way it really was.

Gary said, "Vacation or no vacation, we still got everything we need."

Dentz leaned forward, lowering his voice. "Look, Gary, you squoze the man, okay? It was a good idea. But the man has come up dry. And face it, we ain't going to go to nobody with that check. I know it. You know it. And he knows it, man. Not with the hang time on a homicide case."

Gary turned to him and said, "And just whose fault is that?"

Dentz crushed an ice cube, then sucked in some air, warming his teeth. "You told me you wanted me to hurt the man if he didn't cooperate. *Hurt the man*, you said. Ain't my fault he thought he was some kind of bad motherfucker."

"You're talking mandatory life," Gary said, quietly.

"Ain't nobody's gonna put nothin' together. Not unless we give them a little help."

Gary hunched forward. "You're talking the kind of time where only the governor can get you out, and that's when you're in that Jacktown nursing home sucking on baby formula through a tube."

"No, *we're* talking, Gary," Dentz said. "Remember, you was there, too."

TINO DENTZ WENT back to the bar for another drink, getting hung up there for a good five minutes, trying to tell the whore that he was not interested, that he got plenty of pussy for free.

When he sat back down, Gary asked, "What's your PO like anyway?"

"Wack, big and black. And he thinks he's pretty bad."

"A *PO?*"

"Used to be a cop. Says he's on his second career."

"He cutting you slack?"

"That's what's good about working for Big Rock. Shit, man, everybody knows the Reverend Roy."

Tino could see Gary's brain going. He always played with his cameras when he was thinking. Gary, always doing things the complicated way. Can't just walk into a 7-Eleven, put a Ruger seven to some pimply motherfucker's head, say, Give me the money. Can't just take the dope dealer's check and put it in his pocket. Shit, Gary had the paper in his hands. No, he gives it back to the gimpy motherfucker, drives over to the guy's house and makes a big production out of it.

"Whatup, Gary?"

"I got a few ideas. If you're interested, that is."

"Maybe."

"Or, maybe you just want to drive your pastor's church bus."

"Hey, they call me *Mister* Dentz."

"Then, Mr. Dentz, you still in on this, or what?"

Tino waited until Gary had his eyes. "Seems right now I'm in, whether I want to be or not. The way I figure, I might as well get something for the risk involved. But mainly I'm thinking somebody's got to keep an eye on your complicated ass."

"And why is that?" Gary asked.

"So you don't do nothin' stupid, chasing after that big score."

"I'm not talking stupid," Gary said. "I'm talking about improving our position. That's why I brought up Bobby."

Tino didn't like that idea. "What the fuck has Bobby done? Why should we cut him in?"

"Don't worry. He'd get a flat rate."

"Besides," Tino reminded him. "He's in the county."

"That's why we need to get him a message. Can you?"

"If I had to."

"Then why don't you tell him where he can find us."

Tino thought about it, then said, "I'm working on some things of my own."

"Things?" Gary said.

He could have told Gary about the guy from fourth tier, how he was fronting him half-Zs of street meth, preweighed and -packed, but he spared him the details.

"Just a little something for those girls at the Maverick," Tino said. "Maybe a little for myself here and there."

"You been back there?"

Tino grinned. "Already culled me a couple out of the herd."

Gary went into a long thing about how he was letting his dick do his thinking, taking risks, especially moving that kind of product to girls working in a place where a lot of people were coming and going. Dealing with a bunch of chatty bitches who could put his name out on the street.

"I'm just doing the girls a few favors," Tino said. "Favors get you the real dance, not something they advertise for twenty bucks. Gonna stop there on the way back, too."

Gary stood up. "You can drop me home first."

"I thought you don't like hanging around there," Tino said.

"I just need to use her car," he said.

Gary pulling his cameras over his shoulders. "So, you going to get the message to Bobby?"

"That could take a couple of days."

"We've got a couple days. You take care of your business. I'll take care of mine."

"Then what?"

Gary started walking. "Man's on vacation, remember? You know how that goes. Coming back from vacation can be a bitch."

CHAPTER 12

HE FIRST SAW the golf hole the day they moved him out of the detox unit, its flag hanging limp a couple hundred yards from the entrance. A hundred patients in Brighton Hospital, but Nelson Connor had yet to see anyone attempt a chip or putt.

He mentioned this to the medical director who examined him on the fourth day, Connor alone in his room in a hospital gown, the physician in a white coat with *Dr. Robb* embroidered on his breast pocket in royal blue. Dr. Robb said the golf hole was a nice touch, that you could see it from the road. Made potential patients think that Brighton Hospital was relaxing.

"But let me ask you, Nelson," he said, looking down at his chart, "do you feel like playing any golf?"

You needed a decent night's sleep to golf, Connor said. "Hallucinations do nothing for the game, either," he added.

Dr. Robb said, "Ten years here, I've never seen anybody in the 300 Club who did."

"Club?" Connor asked, his hands between his legs, palms together. "What goddamn club is that?"

Dr. Robb turned his chart around, holding it up momentarily. "You scored a 3.30—the day we admitted you. Blood-alcohol level. Most mortals are usually comatose at 3.0."

Connor said, "I walked in here, didn't I?" He did remember arriving.

"You were still on your feet, but I don't think you could have gone another round. You did have the good sense to call somebody. The guy who holds the record, he drove himself."

Connor asked, What record?

"The hospital record. A nuclear physicist from the University of Michigan a few years back. He not only drove here, he carried in his own bags. We checked the blood twice, just to make sure. He was hitting 5.0—and it was morning. The guy ran some kind of reactor, too."

"That's kind of frightening."

"That's acquired tolerance. Clinically, he should have been dead."

Dr. Robb listened to his heart, his breathing. Looked in his eyes with a small light, then asked him to lay on his back. He tapped on his abdomen softly with his knuckles.

"Your SGOT levels are pretty high, but I'm not feeling anything hard."

Connor asked, Like?

"Your liver. You do have some liver damage. And that's normal, considering your drinking habits. But the undamaged portions take over. You'll be okay. As long as you don't drink anymore, of course."

After Connor sat back up, Dr. Robb said, "You might shake and quake a little bit for the next few days, but I think you already know the worst is over, at least as far as physical withdrawal goes. Two weeks from now, you won't even remember how bad it was."

"I don't think I'll forget," Connor said. "I don't think I want to go there again."

"Good," Dr. Robb said. "That's a good start."

Dr. Robb said he'd be moving him into the regular hospital population. Start attending classes, lectures, and meetings.

"You'll get a real education," he said.

When he looked like he was ready to leave, Connor pointed at his clipboard.

"Who sees that chart?" he asked.

"We do."

"I mean, after I get out of here. I've been pretty frank with people in here."

"Nobody sees it."

"What about references to drugs? I'd hate to see that find its way back to the county, or even the insurance carrier."

"Nothing goes back," Dr. Robb said. "As for the insurance carrier, they're satisfied with a description of the clinical diagnosis and course of treatment. We don't get into it further than that."

"Which is?"

"Two weeks of inpatient treatment for recovery from alcohol dependency."

"You sure about that?"

"The diagnosis?"

"No, the description."

"Absolutely sure. We're here to solve your problem, Nelson, not create new ones," Dr. Robb said.

THAT NIGHT, HE was the first patient in line when the staff turned on the pay phones after a dinner of chicken and rice he could hardly eat.

Katherine wanted to talk about how he was doing. He wanted to talk about his car.

"Did you leave it downtown like I said?" he asked.

"They brought your car home," she said. "And you've got a couple of parking tickets."

"Who, the police?"

"A coupla guys who said they knew you. It had a flat, so they changed it. They said it would've been towed."

"What guys? Where were they from?"

He tried not to sound so urgent, but, Christ, if somebody changed the tire, somebody was in the trunk.

"I don't know, a car lot or something," she said. "I don't know anything about your friends downtown."

Crilly, he thought. "That's Jack."

"He was very nice" she said. "He dropped the tire off for me at the station."

"How do you know him?" Katherine asked.

"Who?"

"The older man with the mustache."

For days, his mind would race with all the possibilities.

"He's the guy from AA who brought me here," Connor said.

———

"So, HOW ARE you?" she asked a week later.

"Better," he said. He could hold a full cup of coffee without spilling it now.

He offered her a decaf in the patient lounge, but she passed. Outside, she wanted to sit in the gazebo, but he said he didn't like gazebos, feeling like he was on display. They sat at one of the picnic tables, facing each other, under a willow tree. Others sat on park benches or walked the Brighton Hospital grounds with visitors, nobody really talking very loud. Saturday was family day, but this was her first. Last Saturday he'd waited in the pay-phone line for fifteen minutes to tell her not to come, that he wasn't ready for her.

He thought he was ready for her now.

She pointed at the hospital's small chapel behind him, not a hundred feet away, saying, "That's very New England."

Quaint steeple, four pillars in the front.

"People go to that church?" she asked.

"We go to meetings there," he said.

"What kind of meetings?"

AA meetings, he said. Discussion meetings. Open meetings with guest speakers. Lecture meetings with somebody on the medical staff saying things like, It takes at least a year for an alcoholic's brain to repair, a year before the neurotransmitters normalize and put you on an even keel.

"They say you get a lot of mood swings in the first few months," he said.

He'd finished his coffee already. Now he was making patterns with his thumbnail on the rim of his empty Styrofoam cup.

She reached out, took his hand and squeezed it. "I'm so glad you decided to do this."

He didn't think he'd done anything heroic. "I'm glad Jack brought me here," he said. "I'm learning a lot."

He could feel her studying him, looking for more, maybe expecting him to say now that he was never going to drink again. He'd learned in Brighton you don't set yourself up like that. And mainly, he didn't want to get her going, feed her information so she would begin asking a lot of questions. Pretty soon she'd be talking about wanting to share what he was going through. He didn't want to share anything, not right now. But he did have questions. He decided he'd take it like a good cross, gingerly extracting what he needed, trying not to disturb the witness.

"Anybody stop by?"

"Stop by?"

"I mean, looking for me."

"Jehovah's Witnesses last week," she said. "Said they'd talked to you before."

He remembered sucking scotch one Saturday, debating a couple of them in his study for sport, maybe six months ago.

"How's John?"

"John's good," she said.

"Did you tell him?"

"I told him you were at a conference. He doesn't need to know anything more that."

"I'll eventually tell him," he said.

"You think so?"

"If I stay sober, he'll notice anyway," he said.

"*If,*" she said, looking around at the grounds, then back at him. "Connor, look where you are. Are you telling me you haven't had enough?"

He took his hand away, putting the thumbnail back to work on the cup. "It's just a manner of speech," he said. "First thing you learn around here is that there are no sure bets."

He nudged the conversation back to his son, asking how Little League was going.

"It's the last few games. They put him in the outfield."

"The outfield is good."

"He's not really happy about that at all. He says it's boring."

"Punctuated by moments of sheer panic. Every play is a big one."

"Maybe you ought to tell him that," she said.

"I will," he said. When he got out.

"What about the house?" he asked.

"What about it?"

"The monkey, you know."

"No damage—lately."

"I've been thinking, maybe we ought to get rid of it."

"Maybe you should have never bought it."

"That's what I'm saying."

"It's a little late for that now."

"Maybe we can think of something to tell John."

"About you being here?"

"No, the monkey, I mean."

"Maybe *you* can," she said. "I'm not going to lie."

The trial lawyer in him took over, saying, "So, it's okay to lie about me, but not the monkey?"

"That's different," she said.

"Is it?"

He sat down the cup in front of her. He'd decorated it with vertical lines around the top, the edge accented in ruffles.

"That's nice," she said sarcastically, examining it.

"Around here it seems to be the prevailing art form," he said.

When she set it down, he asked, "How's things with the studio?"

She seemed relieved he'd switched the subject. "I got the Northville Downs account. They liked the fact I was local. They want posters. And they're talking about graphics in their lounge."

"I thought you didn't like horses," he said.

"I like horses, I don't like that they make me sneeze. I watched a couple races last week. The Sudafed made me psycho, but also gave me some good ideas."

"Drugs don't enhance creativity. That's a myth."

"Not the Sudafed, dummy," she said. "Going to the track. But it's not going to be easy do that with John at home."

"Why not take him with you?"

"He'll complain about standing around."

"Why don't you job some of your small stuff out?" he suggested.

"I already am."

"You are? You didn't tell me."

"I told you six months ago. You just don't remember. You ought to. You complained enough about the money."

"Well," he said. "It's not a problem now. Hell, we'll save a bundle on my bar tab alone."

Later, he asked, "You locking up at night?"

"Connor," she said. "I can handle the house."

They'd gone through this before. "Lock it, will you?"

"I'll lock it."

"Where's my car parked?"

"Where you always park it."

"Where are the keys?"

"I've got the keys. You want the car in the garage, too?"

"No," he said. He didn't want her near that car.

She was becoming irritated by his questions.

He tried to force the car from his mind.

"What I'm saying is, I don't want people thinking you're home alone."

"Since when did that matter?" she said.

He grabbed the cup again. "It matters to me now."

She nodded, squinting her eyes a little. She was looking at the coffee stains on his gray sweatshirt. He'd asked her to drop off his old sweatsuit with the receptionist the day he got out of detox.

"Do you wear that every day?" she asked.

He said, "Still fits, doesn't it?"

"When's the last time you wore that?"

"Yesterday. Day before. Day before that."

"Obviously. I mean, before here."

"Sparring. At the police gym."

"Isn't it hot? I mean, it *is* August."

She was wearing pressed khaki bermudas and a forest green sport shirt.

He said, "It feels good to sweat."

"Hey, how 'bout I bring you some decent clothes?"

"Well, they say I'm out of here in a couple of days."

"Really?" she said, smiling. "When do you want me to pick you up?"

He didn't want that. "Jack's coming by," he said.

"Jack?"

"Guy from the downtown meeting, the guy with the car lot. Since he brought me here, I figured he ought to pick me up."

"Oh," she said. She seemed hurt.

He added quickly, "I'll be home by dinner."

She didn't react.

"Hey, listen to me," reaching for her hand now. "I'm looking forward to it. I can't wait."

Part of him couldn't wait. Another part was lying, wanting to stay. Stay a month, a year. Stay long enough, and everything might blow over.

"You're going right back to work?" she asked.

"They say here that I should."

"What did the chief judge say?"

"The chief judge is fine with it. One of the retired judges from that Tuesday meeting talked to him, the day after I checked in. I told you that, didn't I?"

"Connor, I don't know," she said. "The way this whole thing has happened so quickly, I'm not sure I really understand what in the hell is going on."

She pulled her hands away, putting them both on the bridge of her nose, closing her eyes.

When she opened them, he saw tears.

She sniffled twice, then said, "You have any Kleenex?"

He pulled a strip of toilet paper from his sweats pocket, handing it to her. His nose had been running all afternoon. It started running during a movie everyone watched on cocaine abuse.

She snatched the tissue and blew, handing it back to him in a ball.

When the tears stopped, she said, "You know we're talking here, but we're not saying anything. You do that, you know. Drunk or sober, you've been doing it for years."

"I don't understand," he said, though he did.

"Is that all you can think about when you see me? Where the car is parked. What my house looks like. Christ, ask me a real question. Or, at least tell me how you *feel* about all this. I feel like I'm talking to a shadow."

He wanted to ask her if she'd seen anything in the paper. Ask her if she'd seen any strange people in the neighborhood. Ask her if she'd received any phone calls from some guy named Dali. But the way she was taking everything, he didn't dare.

"Why don't we talk about all this later," he said. "I'm still trying to get a lot of things sorted out."

She put her hands palms down on the table. "Okay," she said, sounding very logical now. "So, what are the other people like?" she asked.

"What people?"

"In your group."

"The AA group?"

"No, here, at the hospital."

"Oh, there's a couple of Detroit cops. We've got a female firefighter. A carpenter. A gal who owns a couple of beauty shops."

"Do you like them?"

"Do I like them?"

"Yeah, *do you like them?* Or do you want to think about that for a while, too?"

Liking them wasn't the point, he said.

She got up and walked away from the picnic table. When she reached the trunk of the willow, she turned and faced him, leaning back against the tree, her eyes on her feet. He felt sorry for her, in a way he never had before. That was something new: feeling sorry for someone else. He was coming to realize, that was an emotion he'd reserved exclusively for himself.

"Kace," he said. "Look at me, will you?"

When he saw her eyes, he said, "The people in my group are alcoholics. I am an alcoholic. They belong here. I belong here. That's my only point."

"Is it me?" she asked. "Am I why you drink?"

"You have nothing to do with it," he said.

He realized he'd said *that* wrong. "What I'm saying is, I thought there were a lot of reasons. The work. Or, hell, we came from the sixties, everybody was doing drugs. Or, deep down, I felt I didn't belong on the bench. That I rode into office on the old man's name."

He looked at his cup, then back up.

"But in here they say that's all bullshit. You drink simply because that's what alcoholics do best."

"That's for sure."

"It could very well be hereditary. Not that that's an excuse."

She was still looking at him.

"Hey," he said, "You know what they say about why God invented whiskey, don't you?"

"No," she said, wanting to smile. "Why did God invent whiskey?"

"So the Irish wouldn't conquer the world."

WHEN SHE WENT inside to use the bathroom, he stayed at the picnic table. Made himself stay out there and think. He tried to lay it all out logically, look at everything, the way he might decide a complex personal-injury case.

Ozzie was dead. He'd thought about it, and was sure of it, body or no body. At first he tried to tell himself that Ozzie was dead because Ozzie did something stupid, used his check to cop dope. But Ozzie wouldn't put him at risk like that. No, Ozzie must have been blindsided. That's why this guy Dali killed him. Maybe he wouldn't give up what Dali wanted. Ozzie was trying to protect a friend. Or maybe Dali was just sending him a message. Either way, Connor decided, he, himself, was at fault. Because of his negligence, because of his name and his title, his old friend Jimmy Osborne was dead.

When he got out of Brighton Hospital, he should go straight to the Homicide section. Tell them everything, hand out the appropriate punishment for himself. Face the *consequences*. They talked a lot about consequences at the meetings. He tried to think of it as if he were looking beyond the first drink.

So, he thought, go to Homicide. Then it hits the papers and the six o'clock news. The tenure commission takes his seat. The bar pulls his ticket. No law practice to fall back on. Lose the house. Probably lose Kace and his son. Or, even worse, they stay. Go through that kind of humiliation in Northville, not Detroit, where Kace worked, where John has to go to school.

Projecting. Don't do that, somebody at a meeting said.

Connor looked across the lawn, over at the golf hole. Still nobody playing out there. Twelve days there, and he'd yet to see one sorry son of a bitch pull the stick.

He'd told himself that every day: that he wasn't there for golf, or to work the pay phone. He wasn't there to call the police or figure out what had happened to Jimmy's body. Besides, if the police had found the body in his Reatta, they would have already called on him. *First things first.* He'd heard that over and over at the meetings and from counselors. Don't worry about your problems on the outside, they said. That's why you're here. A little vacation from the outside, so you can work on your main problem.

And he'd tried to take their advice.

But now he was getting out in a couple days, and thinking about Ozzie again. Ozzie was messed up. Ozzie was just like him. Christ, he wanted to take Ozzie to an AA meeting. But Ozzie didn't listen. Hell, he hadn't listened either. It took *this* to make him listen. Ozzie was dead, but punishing himself and his family wasn't going to do a damn thing to bring him back.

So, he decided. If this guy Dali was still in the picture, he would have to find him. He had to find out exactly who and what he was dealing with. And for now, Katherine must not know. God knows, he'd already put her through enough. He still had his job and his house and his family. A lot of patients in Brighton didn't have half that waiting for them.

But he did.

And he hadn't gotten sober just to let some punk take it all away.

CHAPTER 13

LAWRENCE GARY DECIDED he was probably looking at one of those private hospitals for rich mentals. The entire place one story. Cozy chapel. Gazebo. The way people walked around, nobody in a hurry, drinking plenty of liquids in Styrofoam cups, probably spiked with Thorazine.

He watched from the car for five minutes, thinking about the implications, thinking how good he was at this. Then he got out of his mother's Ford Escort wagon and strolled onto the grounds like he belonged there. Walked toward the hospital's entrance. Walked right by the judge himself and his little woman at the picnic table, His Honor all suited up for shuffleboard camp.

Inside the lobby, he saw a receptionist, a pixie-looking thing, hardly out of her teens. He walked up to her, drumming his fingertips on her desk.

"I'm interested in some information on the hospital."

"You'd like to speak to someone?" she asked.

"You have any written material? Brochure. Something like that."

"Is this for yourself, or a family member?"

"Do I look insane?" he said, smiling.

She couldn't find the words to answer, so he leaned closer, speaking in a low voice now. "It's my mother. She's the one with the problem."

The receptionist, nodding now, said, "In that case, you really should speak to a counselor. But you'll have to make an appointment during the week. Brighton does offer intervention."

Lawrence Gary wasn't sure what an intervention was, but he liked the way it sounded. A good word, like *proactive*.

"That sounds pretty serious," he said.

She nodded. "That's where we involve the entire family in getting the patient to seek help. It's kind of like giving someone an offer they can't refuse."

"Well, I'm not sure I want to go that far," Gary said, tapping his fingertips together. "Mainly, I'm just interested in the facilities for now."

She slid open a lower file drawer, looking at its contents. "Can I ask the nature of your mother's problem? I've got several things I can give you here."

Gary thought about it a second, then said, "She paints."

The receptionist said she didn't understand.

"She *paints*—too much," he said again, miming a brush and a pallet. "Portraits. Landscapes. Still lifes. Anything. As long as there's paint involved. That's why my father left her. There's nothing in her house but canvas and turpentine and drying paint." He leaned forward, lowering his voice again. "I'm talking about *every room in the house.*"

The receptionist thought about what he'd said for a couple seconds, then pulled out a brochure and several one-sheet handouts. She handed them over as she talked. "Okay, here is some general information on Brighton Hospital. And, this sheet details our various inpatient programs. You'll note we do have outpatient as well. Here's a list of health insurance carriers we work with. And here's a questionnaire. Something you might want your mother to take, but don't be surprised if she refuses. You might want to read it, however."

She looked up. "Does your mother have insurance?"

Gary said, "I'll have to check."

He picked up the materials.

She continued, "I'm sorry, none of these *specifically* addresses your mother's problem. But the same treatment applies. As I said, you might want to consider making an appointment with our counseling staff."

"The number is on here?" he asked, glancing at the sheets, wanting to leave now.

She nodded.

He started to go, but she said, "You know, if you don't mind me saying, that's really pretty amazing about your mother."

"What's that?" he asked, backing up, moving toward the door.

"I thought only kids did inhalants."

"Inhalants?"

"Paint cans. Solvents. We call them inhalants. I hear they're actually doing gasoline now. Can you imagine that?"

Outside, Gary found a tree to lean against. He put on a pair of RayBan's he'd bought with some of the Oz's money. With the shades, he could keep his head down as if he were reading, but with his eyes, he could watch.

He was maybe a hundred feet away.

The way the scene was playing at the picnic table, Gary decided there was some kind of dispute. The little woman was making her points, driving her index finger into the table for emphasis. Not the same gal he'd tailed with the Escort earlier, watching her hustle in and out of Northville shops with a large artist's satchel in her hand. The little woman definitely was not having a very good day.

His eyes went back to the literature, reading about what kind of patients came to Brighton Hospital. He read about how the intervention worked: A counselor met with family members who listed all the problems the drunk or dope fiend caused. Later, they lured the subject into a room under false pretenses and confronted him. They told him in so many words, get your shit together or we're history. The last part was supposed to be the offer he couldn't refuse.

Gary's eyes went back to the picnic table.

He thought: What a very cute little charade His Honor had going. Shit, he gets caught burning some herb, his PO throws his ass back in Jackson. Honor fucks up, and he gets a gazebo and two weeks of Ping-Pong.

"So what do you think?"

Gary turned around. It was the receptionist, a purse over her shoulder. She beamed like someone who'd just gotten off of work.

"About what?" he asked.

"Brighton Hospital."

Gary took off his sunglasses and smiled. "You know," he said. "I think I really can work with this place."

LATER, GARY TOLD Tino Dentz to meet him at a Taco Bell on Jefferson at eight o'clock sharp. He wanted Dentz waiting at least ten minutes. You wait for the man who has got the goods. Made sure of it by cruising by the DIA first. Checked out the art museum's replica of *The Thinker*, Rodin's sculpture from the Gates of Hell reminding him of the way he last saw the judge sitting on the picnic table alone, all hunched over and shit.

Gary didn't go directly to the booth where Tino was sitting. He ordered a Mountain Dew and one soft taco with extra-spicy sauce first. "No beans," he told a young black cashier with acne. He hadn't ordered anything with refried beans since he worked one week in a Taco Bell in high school and pissed into the refried beans his last hour on the night shift.

Dentz was sideways in the booth, leaning back, his legs on the seat. Four or five other people in the Taco Bell, the Saturday rush over.

"Yo," Dentz yelled to no one in particular, shaking a cup full of ice. "I need a refill."

The girl with acne was wiping the counter.

When Gary sat down, Dentz slid out of the booth and walked toward her. "Yo, *girl*. I said I need a refill here."

She looked up, putting a hand on her hip.

"Sign says free refills," Dentz said.

You get your own refills, she told him, pointing to the dispenser at the counter. He handed her the cup anyway.

On his way back, Tino Dentz swayed his hips. Gary decided he looked as if he'd been into the crank again.

"Whatup?" Dentz said, sliding back in, resuming his position.

Gary asked, "Where's your church bus? I didn't see it outside."

"Bitches dropped me off. You're giving me a ride back."

"Bitches?"

"They picked something up. Want a taste? Got some back at my place."

Gary said he didn't want to get high. He wanted to talk. "Look," he said, unwrapping his taco. "I found out something good about our man today."

"You still on *that*?"

"Fine," Gary said, food in his mouth now. "I guess that means you're not interested."

"Not interested in what?"

"In what I got to say."

"Well, that depends," Dentz said, sitting a little more upright. "You finally hook up, or what?"

"Something like that."

Gary took a couple minutes to eat the taco, saying nothing, Dentz waiting.

Wiping his mouth, Gary finally said, "You know what your problem is, Tino?" He took a gulp of Mountain Dew.

"Problem? I don't have a problem. Not so far."

Gary pulled out a Kool, tapping it down. "You want everything handed to you on a fucking silver platter." He lit the smoke. "We fell into this thing, and I'll be the first to say it. We did *fall* into it. And there's been a few complications, I'll also grant you that. But *you* think from that point, it's all just going to happen, or not happen. A few phone calls. A few demands. The man brings over a check, or he doesn't. Just like that. But even if we kept it simple, and we might have, you'd still have missed it, you know why?"

Dentz said, "Give me a cigarette."

Gary held up a Kool, making Tino come out of his slouch to reach for it. "Because I take care of all the *details*, man, that's why."

"What you saying?" Dentz asked.

"I'm saying you're all set up over there with the Reverend Roy. Got you a nice ride. Got yourself a nice little stable of pussy. Got yourself a little party going now. And what am I doing? I'm driving around in my mother's fucking station wagon. Got hardly enough money for new clothes and gas. Working with limited funds. Eating here at Taco fucking Bell. But I'm still taking care of details, Tino. I'm *working*, man."

Gary hit the cigarette, exhaled, and added, "What I'm saying is we have a real fucking opportunity here. But you, Tino, ain't pulling your own weight."

Dentz thought about it for a second or two, then said, "I'm here, ain't I? Why you getting all righteous on me now?"

"Yeah, you're here. You're here 'cause I called you. Called you simply because I understand what loyalty means. By all rights, considering the work I'm doing, considering the conditions I work in, I should just go ahead and hook up with Bobby and do this thing myself from here on in. But no, I come in here to eat my one fucking taco. Because now there's more details that need to be handled."

Gary looked around for an ashtray, but saw none. He flicked the ashes on the floor between his knees. "So, what happens? I meet you here, and all you got to ask me is whether I've hooked up with the man or not. Presumably meaning that if I talked to him and he said he was coming over with the money, I guess that means you're ready to rock. But if there's some more work to do. If this gig requires some more effort, some more attention to *detail*, then you got *other things to do*. You follow what I'm saying now?"

"That ain't what I'm doing," Dentz said. "That's not the way I look at it."

"No, that *is* what you're doing, whether you're looking at it that way or not. And that's no way to treat people. Didn't your mother and that big fucking church she go to, ever teach you that?"

Gary could see Dentz's eyes drooping, the big smile gone now. Crank was fine, Gary thought, but coming down was a bitch.

"Yo, Gary, we just got out," Dentz said. "A man is entitled to party. Build a little posse."

"I need some help here," Gary said, hitting the smoke hard. "I was trying to tell you that the other day when I was talking about Bobby."

"Help for what?"

"Keeping track of these people, for one. That's how the good shit falls right into your hands."

He told him the whole story. Told him how he'd gone out the judge's place, thinking he was going to walk right up to the door and tell her he was from Greenpeace, looking for a donation to save the humpback whale. Instead, he followed her out of her driveway, tailing her to various Northville shops. Saw her carrying the satchel. "And that meant only one thing. The little woman was in the art business." Then, after building up the story with the drive out to Brighton, Gary said, "You were right, Tino, His Honor is not on vacation. The man is at a twitch farm."

Dentz wanted to know what that was.

"Where they dry you out. The man is a stone alcoholic. A fucking drunk. You know what that means?"

Dentz said no, he did not know what that meant.

"It means we can roll this guy easy. Roll him big, maybe for years if we do it right."

GARY STARTED PLAYING with his cameras.

"So how we going to do it?" Tino asked.

"I'll work that out," Gary said. "I may need you to attend to some details first."

Gary, Tino thought. Always wanting to call the shots.

The idea of rolling a drunk got Tino thinking about the windows in the Taco Bell: arched windows on three sides, but no view. Big paper signs taped up on the glass, advertising, Head for the Border! and three tacos for a buck. Nobody sees in. Nobody sees out. Couldn't even see Tula Gary's wagon outside, let alone get a make on the Escort's plate.

Tino looked for cameras—not Gary's; the kind with red lights that blinked. He saw the cashier girl out front now, wiping tables. He saw only one young brother back in the kitchen, stirring beans.

Shit, Tino thought, no wonder these Taco Bells were always getting hit.

"We need some ashtrays," Gary said.

Tino yelled out, "Yo, my man needs an ashtray here."

"We don't have any ashtrays," the girl said.

Tino motioned her over with his finger.

"Every Taco Bell got ashtrays," he said when she arrived.

Gary said, "You know, those little tin ones."

"Actually," the girl said. "You're not supposed to smoke in here. But I didn't say anything since nobody's in the place."

"No smoking?" Gary said.

"All Taco Bells are smoke-free."

"When did that happen?" Tino asked.

"Two years ago."

"No shit," Tino said, looking at Gary now, and adding, "Give me your cigarette, man."

When Gary didn't hand it over, he took the Kool, butting it in his cup of ice.

"How's that?" he said to the girl. "Now give me that towel you got."

She looked like she didn't want to give it up.

"Come on, girl," he said, laughing a little. "Want to show you a little trick."

She handed it over, Gary looking at him now like he also was wondering what he had up his sleeve.

He slid his legs off the bench, facing Gary. Unfolded the towel, holding it up, showing her both sides.

"Nothing there, right?" he asked.

"Right," she said, forcing a smile.

He dropped the towel on his lap. Gary rolled his eyes, looking at him like he was about to show the girl his dick.

Tino Dentz reached into his right pants pocket, pulling out what he had, sliding it under the towel.

When he peeled the towel back, the girl's eyes were on the front sight of a Taurus .38. He preferred a Ruger, but there was only so much available cheap on the street.

"See that?" he asked.

She was all froze up. He could tell Gary could see it, too.

"Now, you want to make it go away?" Dentz asked, smiling.

She nodded.

"Then you go over to your two registers there, and load me up a nice big order to go."

They sped away in the Escort wagon, Gary saying, "Jesus Christ, why didn't you tell me you had a piece?"

Tino Dentz dropped the bag of bills in his lap.

"Just taking care of *details*, man," he said. "So, tell me now, whatup? How we going to do it?"

Gary glanced at the butt of the Taurus poking out of his waistband, then said, "Maybe it's time we do an intervention on our man."

CHAPTER 14

JACK CRILLY PICKED up Connor in a black metal-flake Jaguar. They sped away from Brighton Hospital on a two-lane lined with twisted oaks.

"So, what do you think?" Crilly asked.

Connor said, "I'd be lying if I said I wasn't worried." He was still wearing the old sweatsuit, but one of the staffers had thrown it in the wash for him the night before.

Crilly turned, smiling, his left hand hardly touching the wheel. "I mean the car. Picked this baby up the other day at a DEA auction. Not bad for ten grand. I'll sell it for sixteen in a week."

"No, not bad."

"I've driven a different car every week for the past five years. One of my adventures. That's how you want to think of it. You are about to embark on a great adventure, my friend."

Connor had been thinking about it all morning.

"Speaking of cars, thanks for getting mine," he said.

"You insisted on it, remember? That's the only way I got you to come out here."

No, he didn't remember. "How did you get it back?"

"Me and one of the boys from the lot."

"It was okay?"

"Just a flat," Crilly said, not a hint of deception in his voice.

Connor was at a loss for words. If Crilly didn't find Ozzie, who the hell did?

Crilly said, "Hey, you know that Buick's not bad. I don't know why they ever discontinued that Reatta. If you weren't so new, I'd make you an offer."

"New?"

"Newly sober."

Connor wondered to himself if Jack Crilly talked about *everything* in those terms: drinking, the program, staying sober. But he also knew he needed to be around someone just like Jack Crilly right now.

"What does being new have to do with it?"

"Didn't they tell you that in there?"

"Tell me what?"

"About not making any major changes in the first year. You don't change wives or jobs. Some people carry it farther. Houses. Cars. The point is, you don't want to be making those kind of major decisions."

"That's all I do is make major decisions," Connor said. "Christ, I'm on the bench, Jack."

"That's different. Point is, you don't want to go off half-cocked with your own life just because you got a little sobriety under your belt."

"Believe me, I'm not feeling very half-cocked."

"Well, they have a saying. They have a lot of sayings in the program. You'll get sick of hearing all kinds of happy shit. But one of the real good ones goes: What do you get when you sober up a horse thief?"

"I give," Connor said.

"A sober horse thief."

Connor told him he didn't understand.

"Point is, a sober alk still needs treatment. Needs a sponsor. Needs to work the program. You can take away the booze, but you still got that alk *personality*. Some alks quit drinking and get into one hell of a lot of trouble simply because they're more alert."

Crilly looked over, "They told you about getting a sponsor, didn't they?"

Connor nodded, saying, "But I'm not sure what they do."

"Sponsor is just somebody with some quality sobriety, somebody you can talk to."

"Isn't that what the meetings are for?"

"Some things you don't want to bring to a table. Some things you're better off keeping off the street."

"I thought meetings were confidential."

"Supposed to be. But you know people. And if you start talking about something, shall we say, incriminating, well, you're in a position to address that better than me."

Connor immediately wondered if Crilly knew more than he thought he did. Maybe he'd spilled his guts the night he blacked out. "What are you saying?" he asked.

"I'm saying you're the judge. What does the law say?"

Or maybe he'd spilled nothing.

"Depends on the circumstances. A New York court ruled that a self-help group does not have the same privileges as a therapist, or a priest. That was a murder case."

"So it would depend on the offense?"

"And the state. Here, you can put a shrink on the stand."

He waited for Crilly to say something; when he didn't, he decided to come right out with it.

"Jack, what was I talking about the night I called you?"

"You called me from the bar. Remember, I told you not to do that."

"But you came anyway."

"There were three messages on my machine."

"What was I saying?"

"The usual nonsense. That's why I don't like getting calls from drunks."

"What kind of nonsense?"

" 'I'm finished.' Nonsense like that."

"On the machine?"

"On the ride out."

"So what did I mean?"

"You're asking me? I assumed you were talking about booze. That's how I justified taking you to Brighton." Crilly looked over, chuckling. "You don't remember a damn thing, do you?"

"Is it really that funny?"

"I'm laughing with you, not at you. I've been there, my friend."

"I only remember the first couple," Connor said.

"I used to call my blackouts 'the greatest time I'll never remember.' You talk to Dr. Robb? He knows all about blackouts."

"You mean what causes them?"

"No. He's had quite a few himself."

"Dr. Robb is an alk?"

"You ought to catch his open talk. Tells a story how he saves four people in an emergency room one night. Wakes up the next morning in the doctor's lounge. Everyone back-slapping him, telling him what a great job he did. He kept his bottle in his locker. He didn't remember a goddamn thing."

"Like being on automatic pilot," Connor said.

"Stick around you'll hear a lot of stories. Airline pilots flying across the country, stuff like that. You thank your stars you never woke up one morning to find some poor son of a bitch's body parts imbedded in your grille. I've heard that story at the tables."

Connor was quiet.

They reached the freeway, Crilly running the Jag through the gears, not merging, but shooting into I-275 at ninety.

"You hear anything?" Crilly asked, letting off the gas now.

"Hear what?"

"Rod knocking. Got to watch for those hidden defects. I try to tell the customer about them, though my inclination is not to. Honest car dealer, right? That's what keeps them coming back."

"I didn't hear anything."

"Then neither did I," Crilly said.

Crilly let the Jag cruise.

"You know, Judge, I remember when I got out."

"You were worried?" Connor asked.

"Hell yes. There's something reassuring about being locked up. Meetings every day. Seeing the same people. Three squares. Coming out, it's different. Some can't handle it. Some go right back."

"You went through Brighton?"

"No, Jackson."

"I didn't know they had a treatment center out there."

Crilly glanced over. "State Prison of Southern Michigan. I'm sure you've sent them a lot of business."

"You were in Jackson Prison?"

"Six years in the joint," Crilly said.

The joint. Connor hadn't heard that term in years. He should have guessed. There was something just a little jaily about the guy.

"That's no treatment center," Connor said.

"For me it was. They have meetings. Lot of guys went just to get off the cell block. That's how I got started, just running another con. You go to enough meetings, though, sometimes it takes."

Connor asked, "So what were you in for?"

"Obtaining money under false pretenses. Possession of stolen property. But I should have been in for a hell of lot more than that."

"The car business?" Connor asked, figuring maybe he'd turned back some odometers, bought a couple of hot cars.

"No," Crilly said, turning and smiling. "I got into cars after I got out."

"So what were you?" Connor asked.

Crilly said, "I was a hood, Judge."

"A *hood*?" Connor hadn't heard that term in a while, either.

"The old school. Before people started shooting people just for the hell of it. Don't get me wrong. I'm not saying I was anything special, but at least we had a code."

"Violent crimes?" Connor asked, adding, "If you don't mind me asking."

"Only when the code called for it. But I wasn't into hammering people. You gotta be straight to do that, or you don't live long yourself. I worked with a numbers outfit, before the state lottery killed it. A bunch of Irish guys in Corktown, one generation off the boat. When the numbers died, I moved into the confidence game. You know, inheritance scams, reigning in little old ladies with stories. All the usual crap. But I got sloppy. I was drinking. I made a bad read on a mark."

"How bad?"

"Tried to sell a truck of stolen rabbit to the wrong guy. You know, telling him it was mink."

"A cop?"

"The task-force kind."

Connor said he remembered his old man talking about the old Irish gangs in Corktown.

"Who was your sentencing judge?" he asked.

Crilly turned, smiling. "Don't worry, wasn't your old man. It was Schmanski. But to this day he swears he doesn't remember. He can tell you about blackouts, too."

Connor found himself basking in the irony. Considering the kind of decisions he'd made in the past month, he absolutely deserved it. A circuit judge, being driven home by an ex-con.

Connor asked, "What's it like to do time?"

"The joint?"

"Yeah, Jackson, what's it like?"

"Well, there were the other inmates. Then, there was me. I thought I was different. I was a genius, cleverly disguised as an asshole. I gotta say, though, once I got involved in the group there, it was a real education in the criminal mind. How it works."

"I see it on a daily basis."

Crilly said, "I'm talking about my own."

"I'm impressed," Connor said, meaning it.

"You shouldn't be."

"I'm impressed the way you've pulled yourself together."

"I'm still that guy."

"I don't see it," Connor said.

"I didn't either. I used to think the guy who ended up in Jackson was my evil twin. But it was me. That's why I keep working the program, my friend."

Connor thought about what he was saying, the two of them silent for a couple of miles. He was thinking about his own evil twin and this program Jack Crilly always talked about. Crilly always coming back to that, like it had *all* the answers. But so far, all anyone ever said was, Just don't drink, go to meetings.

When he saw the Northville exit ahead, Connor asked, "Jack, you sponsor anyone?"

"A few," Crilly said. "But I'm no hand-holder. Some guys, they make their pigeons drive them to meetings. Call them every day. Some guys need that. Me, I'm not into that."

"You think you could help me?" Connor asked. He felt strangely embarrassed, like he was asking the guy to marry him or something.

Crilly thought about it for a few seconds, Connor worrying now he was going to say no.

"You sure you don't want a lawyer, or a judge, maybe?" Crilly finally asked. "Old man Schmanski's always on the prowl for pigeons."

"I don't need a lawyer," Connor said. "Not yet, at least."

Crilly looked over, grinning.

"I'd be honored, Judge," he said.

He looked back at the road ahead and added, "As long as my background doesn't bother you."

"Not one bit," Connor said. "Considering what I might be up against, I think you're just the guy I need."

SHE LEAFED THROUGH his portfolio more quickly that he would have liked, then stopped when she got to the bandito.

"You do have a pretty offbeat approach to things," she said. "But *this*, I've to say, is just awfully cute."

He'd drawn the bandito with colored markers.

"I love this potbelly, the way it sticks out between the gun belts," she continued, pointing at it with her finger now. "And the mustache. The hat. Everything so big on top, balancing on those little feet."

She looked up, smiling. "Who did you do this for?"

Lawrence Gary thought, for a guy doing twenty to forty for taking his wife out with an ax. Guy paid him to do it as a birthday card to his mother. Then the con didn't like the concept, didn't like the little feet.

"It was spec," Gary said. "I was thinking of getting into greeting cards, until I got seriously sidetracked into performance art."

She leafed backward, to the front of the book, where he'd placed the résumé he'd put together a couple of days ago in a Wayne State computer lab. Only one lie on it: Gary Liebermann, his name.

Katherine Connor said, "I almost went to CCS. I see you did some internships from there, these underground magazines. But what about recently? There's quite a gap after that."

"Like I was saying," Gary said. "I got sidetracked."

He rested his cheek on his right index finger and added, "And the sad thing is, Mrs. Connor, I've only got one thing to show for it."

"Which is?"

"I've learned that's not what I want to do."

She took a sip of coffee.

His eyes focused on her cup.

"I'm sorry, would you like some coffee?"

"Coffee would be very nice, Mrs. Connor."

"Call me Katherine," she said.

She pulled open a desk drawer and rummaged. Then she stood up, smoothing her short black denim skirt at her thighs. "Let me run in the house and get you a cup. Like I told you yesterday, this place runs on a staff of one."

He sat back in the overstuffed couch, listening to her shoes on the stairs, savoring just exactly where he was and what he was doing. Yeah, he could get used to this. Two light tables. A drawing board. Three draftsman file cabinets. Maybe a thirty-thou remodeling job, counting the equipment. He'd get rid of the skylight, put up some mini blinds. But he liked the way the studio was quiet and high, not low and noisy like his basement, his mother's footsteps always creaking the floorboards. He got up and walked over to a bulletin board, one she was using for snapshots, pinned there with clear pushpins. Looked at his honor, a lot younger in the shot, holding a stringer of perch with a young boy. Next to it, another with his honor dead to the world on a lounge chair. The beach looked like it was in Michigan, someplace north where the water was blue, not sewer gray like Lake Erie. He saw a five-by-seven: Another photo of the Honorable Mr. Nelson Connor at the annual Detroit Institute of Art fundraiser. The little woman in a very sexy white dress, his honor in black tie, a martini in his hand. Man had to have some serious money to be running with that crowd.

He was still at the bulletin board when she came back. He turned around and said, "Your husband?"

She nodded, filling his cup from a carafe on her desk.

"What's he do?"

"He's a circuit judge."

"I didn't see him when I came by yesterday evening," he said, working his way back to the couch.

"No, he's at a conference. I'm expecting him home very soon."

Gary decided he could deal with that, if he had to. "What kind of conference?" he asked.

She hesitated.

"Oh, forget it," Gary said, gesturing at the wrist. "I don't know a thing about the law."

She walked over with the cup. He took a sip, then toasted her. "Thank you, Mrs. Connor. This is *very* good."

She seemed to soak up the compliment. He decided to improvise on that theme, maybe put her even more at ease.

"You know, *I* thought all judges looked like Judge Wapner," he said. "Apparently they don't all have the same hairdresser, do they?"

She chuckled, sitting now, "I don't think he'll ever get gray."

"Well," Gary said, pausing now for effect. "You're husband is a *very* good-looking man."

She smiled. "He's not too shabby."

"I'll just bet he's very proud of your work."

"He doesn't know a thing about it," she said, the smile leaving now. "He's always got his nose in his briefs."

"BVD's or Jockey's," he said, winking.

She laughed again.

"Sorry," he said. "I couldn't resist."

Lawrence Gary was thinking now how he had her pegged. Little woman in her big house, her old man always gone. Getting no feedback. An artist needed feedback. So she kept herself occupied with her little business, working to resist the urge to take it somewhere else.

He took the subject back to business. After all, business was why he was there. Gary Liebermann, free-lance commercial artist, looking for free-lance work.

She said, "Well, I do contract some things out. I really have a pretty good stable of people right now. But I also have to say, the way you just knocked on my door during dinner yesterday, kind of shows me something. I guess it reminds me of when I got out of college. Not too many people pick up leads by hitting the pavement, asking businesses who does their graphics. These new students don't knock on doors."

"You know," Gary said. "That's why I left CCS. Too much theory. Not enough practical training."

"I'm not sure you can teach enterprise anyway. I think that's born in you."

"Oh, I agree," Gary said.

He took another sip of her coffee, looking like he was really enjoying it, but thinking that he really did have that certain talent. Walking right up to the little woman's house, dropping the names of Northville proprietors, saying he'd heard she was looking for help. Sat right down with her in her living room, using all those graphics buzz words like "keylining" and "drop-outs" and "double reliefs." Checking out all those antiques and that pet monkey, while she went into the other room, getting her business card.

She was looking at the portfolio again. "You sign your work with your first name," she said. "That's different."

"That's all I go by; I'd like to have it legally changed," he said. He knew she'd buy it. Artists did weird shit like that.

She was in the back of his book now, into the pictures.

"Photography, too," she said, raising her eyebrows. "You've done a little of everything."

She turned another page. "Oh, look, Old Main. I had classes there."

He'd slipped in some interiors of empty old classrooms at Wayne State and Detroit Zoo shots, hoping to offset the avant-garde ink work at the front of the book. She lingered over the photos, not moving as quickly as she did with his drawings.

"You like horses?" she asked.

"Always wanted to have one."

"I guess I like them. But they also make me sneeze."

When she closed the book, she said, "You know, Gary, can I give you a little advice?"

"I was hoping you would."

"Pick something you're good at, and concentrate on it. That's where I went wrong. Trying to do everything, trying to be all things to all people, that's what gets you into trouble. You're still young enough. Me, I'm kind of stuck here doing this."

"It's a nice studio," he said.

She looked at him, thinking, then handed him back his portfolio.

"You've got equipment—cameras?" she asked.

"Everything I need."

"It's just my opinion, but I think that's where your talent lies. Particularly, the black-and-whites. How can I get a hold of you?"

"I don't have a card," he said. "I can't afford them yet."

She handed him a pad of Post-it Notes. He scratched out a phone number.

"I live with my mother," he said, figuring that would really sell it. "Just say you've got something for Gary. She'll take a message if I'm not there."

He could see she was thinking now.

"I do have this new account," she said, pausing. "The harness racetrack up the road. Northville Downs. You know where it is?"

"Passed it on my way here."

"I'm looking for images. I don't know if I'm going to actually use photos, or just work from them. Maybe drop them out into silhouettes. But I do need pictures. Ideas for the lounge there. Black-and-whites. I think you see more in black and white, don't you?"

"Absolutely," he said.

She hesitated, then said, "How would you feel about spending a couple of days there? Just shooting everything you see."

"How would I feel about it? Peachy. That's how I'd feel."

Then he added, "How soon?"

"Well, we've got a couple weeks. No hurry. Pick a couple a good days. And what the hell, do some night shots, too. The races are well lit. That's where it might get really interesting."

She got up from the desk.

He stayed on the overstuffed sofa, remembering how he'd read in the *The Art of Negotiation* that if you let anything go cheap, it would be perceived that way, no matter how good it was.

He let his eyes tell her he wasn't going to work for free.

"I can pay you seventy-five a day and expenses," she said, almost apologetically. "Plus, film and processing, and keep your receipts. Is that acceptable?"

"I was thinking more like one hundred and twenty-five," he said.

She studied him momentarily.

"Okay, I'll go a hundred, so I can see what you come up with. Then, if I use anything, we can work something more out from there."

"That's very fair," he said.

He added, he wanted special access, saying, "I'd like to be able to go everywhere and anywhere in there."

"I'll call over to the track manager, give them your name. Any problems, you call me." She handed him her card. "The number rings up here, but I'm always checking the machine. My husband doesn't like me to give out our home phone, considering the line of work he's in."

"I don't blame him," Gary said.

He stood up, putting out his hand.

She shook it, softly.

"Mrs. Connor," he said.

"Call me Katherine, damn it," she said, mockingly scolding him. "Or Kace, if you want."

"Katherine, thank you. And I won't disappoint you."

Smiling she said, "Gary, something just tells me you won't."

THE FIRST NIGHT home, he snuck out to the Reatta in his boxers and looked the car over with a Maglite. He checked the trunk and the Buick's interior. He had about eight hours he could not account for, Crilly telling him he'd picked him up at the Anchor near closing. *Eight hours.* That was a long time to sit in one bar, even by his standards. In the car, he'd hoped to find a receipt, a pack of matches, something that might have given him a clue of where he might have gone, what else he might have done.

He closed the door to the house quietly.

"Connor, what are you doing out there?"

Her voice startled him. She was sitting in her undies in the dark living room. He suspected she thought he was sneaking a drink.

"Just checking the car. It was downtown all those days."

"At two in the morning?"

"It must have been all the coffee I drank at the meeting."

He'd hit a Northville meeting that night, just like Crilly had told him to do.

"Plus," he added, "the people at the hospital said I might have trouble sleeping for a while."

"They prescribe car repair in your underwear?"

"Not exactly."

"I got a better idea," she said.

She sat on his lap. He kissed her.

Upstairs, he sat on the edge of the bed. She kissed his shoulders, but when he didn't respond, she fell back on her pillow.

"Maybe I'm not ready yet," he said.

She looked at him curiously. "You?"

He told her they had a class about that at Brighton Hospital, too. And they had. But he wasn't thinking about sex in recovery. He was thinking about the car. Blood. A shoe, perhaps. Some pocket change or Ozzie's keys. Shit, he'd expected to find *something* in that trunk.

She pulled the sheet over her shoulders, turning away.

"Connor," she said. "How long is that supposed to last?"

"I really don't know," he said.

CHAPTER 15

WHEN CONNOR REACHED the parking structure downtown the next morning, saw how dim it was inside, he started going the other way, leaning toward the possibility that maybe his imagination had come into play. Maybe he was detoxing *then*. Maybe he was seeing things that afternoon in the structure. Wouldn't that be a kick in the ass? Going on a bender like that over a goddamn hallucination? He hadn't thought of that.

At the City County Building, he took the back elevators up, not wanting to run into the morning crush, not wanting to make up stories for other judges about a vacation he never had.

When he walked into the clerical office. Lewis and Barbara were at their desks. They both looked up at him like he was a cancer patient.

"What the hell are you two staring at?"

Barbara reached for a cigarette.

"I've got my eye on you both," he said. "Both of you could be next."

Lewis's eyes went back to the computer screen.

"Christ," Barbara said. "I hope this isn't going to be like working with an ex-smoker."

In his chambers he found a homecoming gift, a stainless-steel carafe, filled with hot coffee.

"You trying to send me a message?" he asked, walking back out with it through his chambers door.

"She was convinced you were going to need your own stash," Lewis said.

It felt good to be in the office.

"You're going to need all of that you can drink," Barbara said. She handed him a small stack of pink phone slips.

He stood there, going through them. The usual stuff, attorneys wanting conferences about adjournments, a couple others wanting to contribute to his campaign account, others who'd already contributed, looking for assignments.

The messages from "Mr. Dali" were together at the bottom, stapled.

"This Dali," he said. "What did he want?"

She rolled her eyes. "He's a strange one. How many people you know who call themselves 'mister'? He called three or four times, wouldn't leave a number."

"What did he want?" Connor asked again.

"He just said he'd get back to you. I told him you were on vacation. Who is he, anyway?"

"He's a banker—a bad one."

"He's a pain in the ass."

Connor started walking back to his chambers.

"Barbara, if he calls again, I do not want to talk to him."

"What do I tell him?"

"Tell him," Connor said. "That I've found a new bank."

BY MIDMORNING, LORI Eisenberg, his court aide, was sitting in one of the two leather-and-oak *bergères* arranged in front of his desk. She was a petite woman with hands hardly larger than a young teen's, a stature she used to her advantage, disarming most of the criminals she interviewed with a face that appeared to be permanently cast in an expression of empathy and concern.

"Your vacation was good?" she asked.

He told her the truth for the same reason he'd told Barbara and Lewis the truth from the hospital pay phone. She'd demonstrated her trustworthiness in the six years she'd been on the job.

"I didn't realize you had a problem," she said.

"I didn't either," he said. "But sometimes the guy with the problem is the last to know."

"I'll bet Katherine is happy."

"Relieved, maybe."

"And you're going to meetings now?"

Connor nodded.

"You concerned about that?" she asked.

"Which part?"

"We send a lot of defendants to meetings."

He chuckled. "Maybe I can shake a few of them up."

He waited until they were halfway through a stack of presentencing reports she'd brought in with her. She was summarizing her recommendations rather than having him read all of them, so he could get caught up. She'd just suggested probation on a B&E.

"Speaking of probation," he said, "that defendant I sentenced last month, James Osborne, I guess his attorney is having trouble reaching him. Apparently he hasn't paid his legal bill."

"You want me to check?"

"Could you?"

"I can call his PO."

She pulled out another report, ready to move on.

He pointed at the phone, saying, "Go ahead, use mine."

He rested his chin on his fingers as she dialed, looking out the window at the haze as she talked with a field office, taking a half page of notes.

When she hung up the phone she sighed. "I guess I blew it," she said. "He never reported. Never showed up at the drug clinic, either."

"It happens," Connor said, leaning back in his chair. "I suppose the Department of Corrections wants a bench warrant?"

She tossed a legal pad on his desk. "Old man Kaufmann signed one a week ago. But the PO's already been out to his house. Figured the guy had such a good deal, he ought to haul his butt in himself. Tell him he was blowing it."

She looked upset.

"What he do, skip?" Connor asked.

"No, Detroit Homicide's got him."

"He killed somebody?"

"No, they found his car torched on the southwest side."

"But they didn't find him?"

"Not yet."

Lori Eisenberg got up and walked to the window. Connor knew she hated making bad calls, though with the volume of cases they handled, they were both bound to make bad calls. This one, she just happened to hear the results.

"I try to tell these people to be honest with me," she said. "That it's in their best interest to be honest."

She turned around, her petite frame silhouetted the summer glare outside.

He tried to console her. "That's all any of us can do, Lori."

"I guess he was a dealer, huh?" she said.

Connor nodded, tapping his fingers together. "I wonder who he owed," he said. "Other than his attorney, that is."

IT WAS NEARLY six o'clock when Torino Dentz heard the keys slide into the door of the Reatta, the man running about a half hour later than Gary said he would. When the door shut, he pulled the ski mask over his face and came up with the Taurus, jamming it into the judge's jugular, not making the move as smoothly as he would have liked, all sweaty and stiff from lying in the cargo area behind the coupe's two bucket seats.

"Yo, start the fucking car."

The judge froze. "Where we going?"

"Just start the car and turn on the fucking air."

The judge asked, calmer than Tino expected, "How did you get in here?"

He could have told the judge about the set of keys that Gary had made at the twenty-four-hour Meijer's the night they dumped the dealer, but he'd rather let him wonder.

"I'm here," Dentz said. "That's all that matters now."

As the car started, Dentz could see eyes on him in the rearview mirror.

"Are you the guy?"

"What fucking guy?"

"Dali?"

"No, man. I ain't fucking him."

"Then who are you?"

"I'm the motherfucker who's going to make sure you return your calls."

NELSON CONNOR TOYED with the idea of leaving the five-speed in first, giving the guy wedged behind him a ride down the ramp he'd never forget. Instead, he followed directions. Drove out slowly, the guy telling him to wave to the car jockeys as he lay back down behind the seat.

Outside, on the streets, he barked directions, telling him to drive around Joe Louis Arena, take West Jefferson along the Detroit River.

When he sat back up, he heard him pull the ski mask off, saying, "Fuck this." Connor caught a glimpse of his black skin in the mirror. He saw black hair in tight ringlets, all matted down from the mask.

The guy shouted, "I see your eyes in that motherfucking mirror one more time, I'll blow 'em right out of your head."

Connor drove slowly, like the guy told him, away from Joe Louis, toward the Ambassador Bridge. They passed old truck terminals and warehouses, few of them in operation anymore. Even during rush hour, there was no one on West Jeff.

A cellular phone dropped into the seat next to him.

"Now, motherfucker, it's time to make a call."

Connor picked it up with his right hand.

"Can I pull over?" Connor asked.

"Just dial it."

He punched in the number the guy gave him. He suspected the guy was reading the number from the way he recited it.

Connor recognized the voice that answered.

"Honor, you picked a hell of a time to go on vacation."

"Did I?" he said, coldly.

"Yeah, and you know what they say, don't you?"

"No, what do they say?"

"No man needs a vacation like a man who's just got back from one."

"I think I can handle it."

"I hope so. I hope you can handle it better than your buddy Oz. You see, the man with you right now in that little two-seater of yours, well he's kind of *explosive*. If I was you I wouldn't let him sit back there too long. He has a real aversion to riding in the back."

"I'm not sure I get your point."

"I thought I'd made it pretty clear, before you decided to take off on me, Honor. Let me make it once again. I'm not fucking around, you understand?"

"So sue me. Or, have your pal here shoot me. Frankly, at this point, I really don't give a shit." And he didn't. The proposition seemed painless compared to what he'd gone through in detox two weeks ago.

"Now, is that what I call real sound judgment? From a man on the bench, no less."

"And I'm still on it, Dali. You ought to consider that."

"But what would your family say? I mean, funerals are a bitch."

Connor spat, "You come near my family, my house, I'll kill you, asshole."

He gripped the steering wheel hard, then felt the gun poke hard into his neck. "Yo, slow this motherfucker down."

Connor backed off, but not because of the gun. The guy shoots him, he decided, they had nothing.

Dali said, "You done now? Did that feel better? You just hang in there, Honor. We'll be done soon here. Then you can drop off your passenger and go get yourself a couple drinks."

Stay cool, Connor told himself, and try to get some kind of lead.

"Honor, you still with me? You got a good cell there?"

"I'm here."

"Maybe you ought to pull over."

He let the Reatta coast to a stop in front of a small welding company, sliding the car in park, but leaving the engine idling.

"Good," Dali said. "I want us to have good connection."

"We've got one," Connor said. "Now, what the fuck do you want?"

"Okay, Honor, here's the shot: I want you to get one hundred K in various denominations, but nothing higher than hundreds. You don't want anything less than hundreds anyway. You get into those smaller bills, shit, that's a just a fucking lot of paper to have to carry around."

Connor said, "I don't have any money."

Dali chuckled. It was a high pitch kind of chuckle that sounded like a staccato whimper. "That's a good opener, Honor. *Nothing*. That's a hell of a first offer."

"It's not an offer. It's the truth."

His voice became demanding. "Then, you're going to have to find a way to fucking raise it. Big shot like you, you're credit ought to be real good."

"It's not the way you think. Christ, I work for the government. Look up my salary. It's public record. You know anyone who works for the county running around with that kind of cash?"

"I don't know any government types, Honor, not on a friendly basis at least."

"Maybe I could make a couple introductions," deciding now it was his turn. "I know some people down at 1300 Beaubien who'd love to meet you. Fifth floor. Homicide section. You ever been there, Dali?"

"They'd have to come and pick me up."

"I don't think that's a problem. I've tried enough cases to know you guys trail like wounded slugs."

"You seem to be forgetting something, Honor."

"I'm not forgetting a damn thing."

"No, you're forgetting quite a bit. You need a body to prosecute a homicide, Honor."

Connor hesitated, then decided to hide what he did not know by sticking with what he was willing to do. "You're forgetting the statute. Murder connected with blackmail. That's murder during commission of a felony. That's natural life. You think you're prepared to do that kind of time?"

"Hey, I've seen people do it. The question is, are you?"

"I didn't kill anyone."

"Well, honor, that's the beauty of what I do. It's always subject to different interpretations. Your friends in Homicide could also decide that you killed your pal. Judge—I'm sorry, *corrupt judge*—gets shaken down, so he gets rid of the one guy who could really hurt him. Hey, it works for me."

"Either way, you're *involved*. And who do you think they're going to believe?"

"You know the drill," Dali said confidently. "They're going to believe whoever comes to the window first."

Connor knew he had a point. He'd handled a hundred plea agreements like that himself. Incriminating testimony in exchange for leniency, the deal going to the perpetrator of the lesser crime in order to convict a more powerful figure.

Like a judge.

A man in green workclothes walked out of the welding company. He glanced at Connor's Buick.

Connor stuck with the argument. "So, I guess that makes us about even, doesn't it? So, do something smart. You send me my check, we'll go our separate ways."

He felt the gun in his neck again, the black guy saying, "Pull around and start driving again, motherfucker. I don't like sitting here."

Connor did a U-turn, checking his side mirror, hoping to get a look into the backseat, but seeing only glare and window glass.

Dali said, "Honor, you're moving again."

"Your man told me to move. You want to talk to him?"

Connor turned his head to the right, starting to hand the phone to the back. The guy behind him, yelling now, "Fuck you man! Turn the fuck around!"

Dali voice was coming from the little speaker. "Honor. Honor."

Connor held it up for a few seconds, then put it to his ear again.

"I'm here."

"All right. Now hold on now. Let's everybody calm down." There was a pause, then, "I'll tell you what I'm going to do. I'm going to give you two weeks to raise the hundred."

"I told you, you've got the wrong guy."

"No, I got the right guy," Dali said, his voice in a forced calm. "Or a little package goes in the fucking mail, you understand?"

"Send it," Connor said calmly, bluffing. "I have friends on the tenure commission. They won't give a shit."

Connor heard what sounded like Dali tapping his finger on his mouthpiece.

"I'm sorry, Honor, I think we're having some real phone problems here. I think you have a bad cell."

"The phone's working fine."

"Then you're not paying attention. My little package goes to *Homicide*.

U.S. mail. No waiting in the lobby. No chitchat. No time-consuming personal introductions. Just an offer of proof."

"What proof?" Connor asked.

"The check. Where they can find your pal. You think I'd leave an important detail like that to you? I think I'll throw in a little background note, too, just to help them out." His voice took on a vicious quality. "Like I said, Honor, we're not *fucking around*."

Christ, Connor thought, *they* took Ozzie from his trunk.

Dali continued. "And you know, that's why I'd rather not have a Buick, Honor. Those carpeted luggage departments are luxurious, but man do they leave the fibers. A little help from the crime lab, and they'll be able to put the homeboy right back in your trunk."

The news hit Nelson Connor hard. They were in control of all the evidence. That's why they'd killed Ozzie. Two weeks ago they already were setting him up.

"Honor?"

And what could he tell Homicide? He could see himself sitting in one of the interview rooms at 1300, trying to explain it to one of those no-bullshit Detroit detectives. He could hear himself telling the truth, hearing just exactly how it would sound: *"I'm sorry, I just don't remember."*

"Honor?"

He started to pull the car over, under the approach to the Ambassador Bridge. He could feel the gun in his neck again. "Hey, what the fuck you doing?"

Connor swerved away from the curb, not saying anything.

"Honor, you still with me? Or are you breaking up?"

CHAPTER 16

AFTERWARD, HE DROVE straight to Prestige Motors, the address on Jack Crilly's business card. He walked straight into Crilly's private office and began telling the story, standing near a window that overlooked more than a hundred washed and prepped used cars.

"Go on, my friend," Crilly kept saying, listening from a leather swivel chair.

He told him almost everything: Blowing the coke. Writing the check. The calls from Dali. The homicide investigation. Being shaken down in the car. He did not tell Jack Crilly about seeing Ozzie's body. He'd resolved to tell nobody that. If it ever came down to making a statement to police, he would deny he ever saw it. If he said he saw it, a detective would want to know why he didn't report it. Then he'd have to tell the detective that he didn't remember, and the interview would go downhill from there. And now, if he told Crilly the truth, then Crilly might one day have to lie to police, maybe even a jury. He didn't want to put the man in that position. Worse, if he told Crilly, and Crilly was honest, any minimally competent assistant prosecutor could destroy Connor's credibility simply by putting the car salesman on the stand.

When Connor ran out of words, Jack Crilly got up and walked over to a coffeemaker on a small credenza.

"You ever try these Bunn coffeemakers?" he asked as he poured. "They make great coffee fast. You like it straight up, right?"

"Christ, Jack," Connor said, sitting down, lighting a cigarette. "Is that all you're going to ask?"

Crilly set a Prestige Motors cup on the polished maple in front of him.

"I could ask you why in the hell a smart guy like you would kite a check to your man in the first place," he said. "But I won't."

"I was following your advice."

"What advice?" Crilly said, sitting back down in his chair.

"At the first meeting. You sat next to me, remember?"

"I recall getting you a coffee," Crilly said, stroking his mustache. "I recall you looking like you were in pretty bad shape."

"You also said, 'Take care of old debts.' When you talked, remember?"

Crilly leaned forward. "We have a step where you make amends, take care of old debts, *except* where to do so would harm yourself or others. Did I forget the second part?"

Crilly stood back up.

"Jack, I can't remember half the shit I heard that night," Connor said.

Crilly walked back to the credenza, looking for more sugar for his cup. Connor could see the skin over his white collar turning bright red.

"The exception is very important," Crilly said adamantly, his back still facing him. "Your situation being a case in point."

Connor was seeing pictures on Crilly's desk now. Crilly grinning with a fifty-something bleached blonde in a vintage wood runabout. Crilly grinning with a double-barrel shotgun over his shoulder, holding a handful of broken skeet. Crilly shaking hands and grinning. Hell, Connor thought, with the mayor of Detroit.

"Jack, where was this taken?"

Crilly turned around. "That?"

"Yeah, the mayor."

"Fundraiser I helped put on for a place they dry out street alks. Stay sober, you get better. Things will get better in time."

No, Connor thought, no more AA bullshit. This had nothing to do with AA.

"Jack," Connor said. "I only have two weeks."

"That's two weeks you didn't have before."

"No, I mean they want the money."

Crilly pointed his finger at him. "No, you got one day. You're sober today. Remember, that's what keeps you ahead."

"That's right, but—"

"And you told me. That's also progress. Progress, not perfection, we always say."

"Okay," Connor said, holding up his hands in mock surrender.

Crilly studied him momentarily, then said, "Where did you leave it with these hoods today? Did you tell them you'd give them the money?"

"I never said I'd pay them the hundred in two weeks."

Crilly nodded. "That's a good start."

"But they want five thousand by next Monday. *'An expression of good faith,'* this guy called it."

"He used those words?"

"The guy thinks he's some kind of negotiator."

"The guy in the car, or the guy on the phone?"

"The guy who calls himself Dali. What an asshole. Likes to throw vocabulary around. He might have some education. But he's all air. I've sentenced a hundred like him over the years."

"There's a lot of good reading in the joint."

"I'm thinking they've both done some time. The guy in the car, he's strictly street. I think he listens to the other guy, but only to a point."

Crilly nodded. "One guy figures he's got brains. The other has the balls. They always find each other because neither knows anything about what the other *thinks* he knows."

"I've never heard it put quite that way."

"But that's why you pick the life. To be *totally independent.* But when you get right down to it, everything you're thinking and doing in the life hinges on what everybody else is doing and thinking. So, there's really no independence at all."

Crilly lit a smoke.

"So, what about the five grand?" he asked.

"I told them I'd work on it."

Crilly exhaled, looking at him.

"Jack, at this point, what the hell else can I do?"

"You got the money?"

"Five, yeah. But not much more. Certainly no hundred, by any stretch."

"You know, you pay 'em, then it starts. That's what we used to say. First, you get the money. That's when you know you've set the hook."

Connor had to agree.

Crilly asked, "What about your wife? She know about this?"

"She doesn't know anything. She doesn't deserve this."

"And neither do you. Above all, don't forget that."

"But I got myself into it."

"But now you're taking care of your problem, so forget about all that guilt crap. It won't do you a damn bit of good."

"Things aren't going very well at home," Connor said.

Crilly looked at the Camel, saying, "They often don't. You'd think they'd be happy you're sober, but they're usually goddamn miserable. They don't have somebody to take care of anymore."

"This would finish us off."

"You think these guys would make a move?"

"On Kace?"

Crilly nodded.

"Not as long as they think they got something coming."

Connor got up now, walking to the window, wanting to light another cigarette himself. He saw his Reatta out there. A customer was checking it out, a brunette in black nylons and spikes.

"Well, you got a few days," Crilly said. "I'd use them wisely. I'd think someone in your position does have certain advantages, as long as you stay on your own turf."

"That's what I'm thinking."

"So you're going to go to the cops?"

He turned, looking at Crilly. "I want to find out who these guys are. But I need a place to start."

"What about this Osborne's friends or family? I doubt your college buddy let these hoods walk in off the street."

"I don't know his friends. His folks are dead. Plus, I've got to be careful about talking to anybody. There's a homicide investigation under way."

"You've got a problem."

"No shit," Connor said, looking back out the window. One of the salesmen was on the brunette now, steering her to another car.

Crilly said, "You know, Judge, I don't dispense specific advice. That's not the way it's done. But it seems to me there are two ways you can handle this. The new way or the old way."

"I was afraid you'd say something like that."

"The new way, you try to get honest with yourself and others, but in a way that you can live with the consequences."

"And the old?" he asked, looking at Crilly.

"Everything we do so well: Tell some lies. Cheat a few people. Then dish out a good ass-kicking when the opportunity presents itself."

Connor looked back out the window, his eyes going to the lot again. He scanned the rows of late-model cars with prices in Day-Glo across their windshields. He saw the brunette, bent over now, looking in the door of a Pontiac, the salesman checking out her behind.

No, there *was* someone, he thought.

"So what's it going to be?" Crilly asked.

"Jack," Nelson Connor said, turning. "How much did you say you'd give me for my Buick on a trade?"

LAWRENCE GARY LOOKED up from the label of Korbel Brut, pausing, then saying, "Tino, you're not going to believe who just came walking through the fucking door."

"I'm busy," said Dentz. His eyes were glued on the lap whore with a cowboy hat. She'd straddled him, her breasts inches from his face.

"Trust me," Gary said. "You're not too busy for this."

Dentz peeked around her bare torso, then looked at Gary, panic in his face. "Man, what the fuck is he doing here?"

The dancer started to turn. Gary grabbed her shoulders, aiming her back toward Dentz. "No sidesaddle, honey," he said. "Stay with that western ride."

Gary lit a Kool and watched the Honorable Nelson Connor approach the Maverick's coat check. Watched him talk to the girl there for about a minute, hand her a bill, but not the charcoal suit coat he had slung over his shoulder.

"What's he doing?" Dentz asked.

Gary watched, saying nothing. He watched the judge walk slowly into the lounge, stopping not twenty feet away. He looked at Gary. Their eyes met, but the judge looked away quickly. He was looking around as if he was there to meet someone. Or faking it, Gary decided, so people would not think he was a pervert coming in alone.

"Gary?" Dentz asked again.

"He's sitting down."

"This shit's wack, man. Where?"

"In a booth over there. On the other side of the stage."

"He see you?"

"He saw everybody. And he saw nobody. Question is did he see *you*."

"Me?"

"Yeah, earlier today."

"He didn't see shit."

"Then don't worry."

Dentz pushed the cowgirl dancer off his lap, the song not over, a good minute left on his ride. She grabbed a fringed vest off the table and walked off, her hips moving with an attitude.

"Didn't you pay her?" Gary asked.

"I don't need to." Dentz said. He finished off half a flute of Korbel in one hoist. "She's a customer of mine."

A minute later, they both watched as a brunette approached the judge's table. She stood over him, a tall girl, maybe five-seven, and unbuttoned her top, showing him her goods. The judge made a motion with his hand. Then she snapped her blue sequinned top back together and slid into his booth.

Dentz poured another glass of the Brut. "Gary, what is the man doing in here?"

Gary worked on the Kool, thinking about what he was seeing. He watched the brunette lay her head on the judge's shoulder, getting cozy with her customer, like all the girls did at first.

Gary said. "Just think what the people who elected that man would say."

Dentz said, "Are you going to answer me?"

Gary turned, slightly irritated. "Where were you expecting to see him, in your pastor's church? Like I've told you before, we're dealing with a dirty official here. In fact, I've probably underestimated the extent of all his dirt."

Gary looked back over, studying the girl's body now. He liked the line of her spine, the way her wavy dark hair cascaded onto her wide shoulders. She'd look good in a simple nude, he thought.

He asked Tino, "You know her?"

He shook his head. "I know of her. I hear the bitch is moody."

"Well, maybe you can get her in the mood to come over here afterward. See what His Honor had to say."

Dentz said he didn't like that idea.

Gary didn't push it. He was watching a waitress bring the judge what looked like a gin-and-tonic, the judge smelling it first, then hitting it hard.

"Out of the twitch farm not even a couple of days, and the man is already back at it," Gary said. "Digging himself deeper and deeper."

Dentz poured himself more Korbel. "I don't like it."

"Neither would his little woman."

"No, I mean getting this close."

"Close is good. The more we know, the better."

"And I don't like this thing you're doing with his old lady, Gary. I think you going too far."

"I'm taking it where it needs to be taken."

"Doing business with the man's wife? Why you need to do that? Yo, what the fuck is that supposed to do for us?"

"Trust me. It'll pay off down the road."

"No, I think you're doing it because you like the action."

"Action?" He glanced over to Dentz, then put his eyes back on the judge's table.

"You always been that way. You don't think I know you, but I *know* you, Gary, so don't deny it. All those cameras and shit. All the mind games. Trouble is, you play too hard, we're looking at going away for natural life."

Gary kept his eyes on the judge. "Nobody is going away."

"I was in the car remember? All that talk about going to Homicide. All that legal shit."

"You only heard one side of the conversation."

"I heard enough."

Gary looked at him again. "Look, I'm trying to help you out here. We're playing it this way, because this is the only way there is to play it. We've got to make the man pay for what he wants. Then, when he gets it, he'll feel like he got a deal."

Gary looked back at the judge's booth. "Besides, Tino, look at him. That's not the way he does things. The man is fucked up. Fucked-up people look for fucked-up solutions. That's what makes it all work."

"What if it don't?"

"Maybe you should have thought about that," Gary said, "before you killed the man."

Gary scoped out Nelson Connor for two songs, while Dentz nearly finished off the bottle, bringing the cowgirl back for one dance, but then telling her to get lost again. By the third song, Gary was wondering what the judge's problem was, wondering why the judge bought another round, but never bought a dance.

"Is that all he's gonna do? Just sit there and move his mouth."

"Maybe he's a regular," Dentz said. "Maybe he's a fucking freak."

"Freaky how?" Gary was intrigued.

"Girl was talking about one the other night. One guy comes in two three times a week. Sits for hours. Buys the girl dinner. Buys her drinks. Tips the shit out her. But never buys a dance. Just spends all that money to sit with a girl and *talk*. Doesn't fuck her or anything, man. Happens all the time."

"Well, I don't think His Honor is a very good tipper," Gary said. "Looky here."

The brunette was getting up now, looking upset. She walked quickly to the dressing-room door.

His Honor, alone now, stirring the lime around in his gin.

Dentz said, "Gary, what if the man don't come up with the money?"

"He will," Gary said.

"All of it?"

"He'll show with the five. Guaranteed. The rest, that might take a while."

"What about the drop?"

Gary had been doing some thinking about that. He told Dentz the first thing he was going to check out at his photo shoot at Northville Downs were lockers. They ought to have lockers for the chronic gamblers at the track.

Gary reached over for the Korbel. The bottle was empty.

He was going to say something to Tino Dentz about being a pig, but then he saw the brunette come through the door of the dressing room. She was in jeans and a halter top now, a small costume bag over her shoulder.

Gary watched her reach for Nelson Connor's hand.

"Check this out," Gary said.

They watched them walk out together, the Honorable Nelson Connor holding the door open for the lap whore. Gary motioned for the waitress, wanting some champagne for himself.

"I told you, Tino," he said. "The guy is dirty. I'm talking totally corrupt."

CHAPTER 17

THE GIRL WAS driving over the limit, passing a car in the left-turn lane, rolling through a right turn on a red, not making legal stops.

Following the blue Camaro, Nelson Connor was thinking the black Pontiac Grand Am handled okay, but it wasn't the Reatta. With the Reatta he'd have been right on her bumper. Instead, he trailed nine or ten car lengths back. He was glad Crilly had insisted he drive the Pontiac for a week, before he made up his mind.

"Stay out of wet places," people at the tables always said.

But he had a good reason to be in the three topless bars he'd visited that night, looking for a girl named Taylor—or Kelly Johns, the name in the presentence report. The search had cost him nearly fifty bucks. There was no way around the valet parking, not to mention the drinks at the Maverick. At five bucks a pop, he thought, the club soda with lime was just a little overpriced.

Chasing the girl, he was concerned about lying to Katherine. She wasn't happy when he called her, saying he and Crilly were going out for dinner, that he'd be home late. He thought about calling her again, but the Grand Am didn't have the horsepower to catch the Camaro, so he could tell the girl to pull over at a pay phone. And he'd be damned if he'd call her from the dancer's place.

The blue Camaro pulled into a two-story apartment complex in Westland. It was just past eleven o'clock. She was waiting for him at the front door, jingling her keys. He followed her inside.

Kelly Johns tossed her costume bag on the couch and headed straight for the bathroom, saying, "There's beer and wine in the fridge."

He sat on the couch and stayed there. Listened to the shower running as he looked around, trying to get a read on the woman who inspired Ozzie to leave his wife, then sell drugs to an undercover cop. The apartment was not what he expected. She was into white monochrome—the couch, the chairs, the coffee table, and the modern prints on the walls—everything in various shades of white. There was a white bookcase with hardcover titles, mostly poetry, anthologies, and complete works. *Cosmopolitan* was on the coffee table. He saw no pictures anywhere. Nothing of her with Ozzie. No family snapshots either.

She emerged toweling her hair, wearing red plaid boxers and a white sleeveless men's undershirt. The fabric was damp, clinging to her nipples. The white room put coal-like highlights in her hair and accented the freckles on her nose and chest. He found her more striking this way than when she showed him her breasts at the Maverick, thinking he was just another dance.

Nelson Connor tried to remind himself why he'd followed her home. She walked into the kitchen.

"So," he heard her say. "You think they're gonna find Jimmy?"

"I don't know."

She came out with a glass of zinfandel. "Want some?"

He shook his head.

She walked to the other end of the couch and sat down.

"He's probably dead," she said.

"I thought you said you didn't know what he was doing."

"No, I said I told him that I needed some space, and he'd been giving me some *reluctantly*." She sipped the wine.

"So what makes you think something happened?" Connor asked.

"Look, Jimmy wouldn't let anybody near that car of his. Jimmy wouldn't let anybody touch anything he *thought* he owned. That's why we started having problems, in fact."

"What kind of problems?"

"Well, at first, as you know, he was married. And you get hit on by a lot of married guys in my line. But he was different. You could talk to Jimmy. He wasn't as superficial as he appeared. He also had *great* dope." She paused, bringing her dark eyebrows together, thinking.

Connor said, "You were saying he was married."

"Right," she said, nodding. "I figured no strings. You wouldn't believe how the single guys I meet turn into lapdogs. Hey, I'm twenty-eight. I've got things I want to do. Well, that's what I liked about Jimmy. He had a life, until one day he tells me he's getting a divorce. Next thing I know, he's telling me he doesn't like me dancing. I kept telling him, Jimmy, they're only customers. Only the people I care about get the real goods."

"That's an important distinction."

She sipped the wine again and winked. "It works for me."

Connor was thinking this Kelly didn't seem too broken up, not the way she was at the bar when he told her the police had found the Firebird torched. He wondered how close they really were. He wondered what her story was.

"I see you like poetry," he said, looking at the bookcase.

"I *love* poetry. That's what I like to do when I'm buzzed."

"You write it?"

She shook her head. "Two more years of this, I figure, then I'm going to go to school. I was thinking Wayne."

"How did you start dancing?"

"Congratulations," she said. "You've got the record."

"Record?"

"Yeah, most guys ask that in the first five minutes. Took you nearly two hours. That's a record."

Connor shrugged. "I'm just curious."

"I've been dancing since I was five. Not this bullshit, real dancing. Ballet, jazz, you know. Things started going downhill in high school."

"Downhill in what way?"

"There's not much of a future for a C-cup in legit dance."

"What about your parents?"

"What about 'em?"

"What do they do?"

"My father is an asshole. My mother left me with these." She cupped her hands under her breasts.

"But you got the dance lessons."

"My grandmother paid for them. My grandmother introduced me to Robert Frost."

Connor told her he knew something about poets. He'd loaded up on lit classes during prelaw. They talked about the writers they liked. She liked Frost, was working on Yeats and was enthralled with cummings. He remembered liking Ginsberg and T. S. Eliot. She seemed to be genuinely interested in the stuff.

"I tried to read that long one by him," she said.

"*The Wasteland.*"

"I didn't understand it."

"That's okay," he said. "Neither does anybody else."

"That's why I like cummings," she said. "He's easy to understand."

"They brought him to Detroit years ago," he said. "This poetry club I was in at Wayne."

"You wrote poetry?"

"I drank wine and tried to pick up girls there. But they did bring in cummings."

Her eyes widened. "You mean, e. e. cummings himself?"

He nodded. "They brought cummings in to judge it. The winner got to spend the afternoon with him."

She seemed to bounce on the cushion. "Did you win it?"

"Like I said, I never wrote anything. Cummings supposedly picked out this poem by a girl, not a very good poet, really, but very attractive. She was pretty excited, until she spent the afternoon fending him off in an empty lit class."

They both laughed.

"I wish you wouldn't have told me that," she said, "but I guess it fits, doesn't it?"

He could see why Ozzie liked her. She was beautiful and unabashed, in almost an adolescent kind of way. She also seemed intelligent. No wonder Ozzie wanted to get her out of the topless bars.

"Kelly," he said, his eyes meeting hers, and holding there for a couple seconds. "That's a good Irish name."

"Black Irish."

"Me too."

"Jimmy told me all about you," she said, "but he never said a thing about the way you looked."

He was a little surprised when she scooted over next to him, saying, "All right, just hold on one minute, buster."

Now she was playing with his hair, inspecting his roots.

"What the hell are you doing?"

"Looking for gray hairs."

He could smell the zinfandel from her mouth, and the freshly washed skin of her chest.

She explained. "My grandmother told me that's how you can tell pure black Irish. Black Irish stay dark until they're at least fifty, and you don't look a day over forty."

"I've never heard of such a thing."

"It's true," she said.

She stopped searching, their eyes meeting again.

"I guess you must be the real thing," she said.

He fought the urge to reach for her. Take his dead friend's woman right there on the couch. Something inside was talking to him, telling him to put himself in total jeopardy. Then, the effort required to deliver himself would have to be total. Deliver himself or go down big. Either way, no longer some chump going down for a lousy three-hundred-dollar check.

He stood up. "You think I could get something to drink?"

"Like I was saying," she said. "Help yourself."

In the kitchen he opened the fridge and saw the bottle of zinfandel and a half a six-pack from an obscure microbrewery. He took an old orange juice he saw, condensation clinging to the half-filled glass.

When he came back, he stood near a window. She was sitting on the edge of the couch now, over a small mirror on the table.

She was chopping with a razor blade.

"Kelly," he began. "Like I was saying at the club, the reason I wanted to talk to you was, I'd like to help find out what happened to Jimmy."

"So talk," she said, never taking her eyes off the cocaine.

"Well, there are some things I'd like to do. I know a lot of people. But I can't stress enough, that if anyone ever found out we had any kind of relationship, there could be no end to the trouble for both of us."

She looked up. "I see my customers and their wives all the time in malls. I just keep walking."

"I'm talking about Jimmy and me, but yes, that goes for us, too. I believe Jimmy trusted you. So, I'm going to assume we can continue that kind of trust, even if the police question you."

"Why would police want to talk to me?"

"They probably see him as just another dead dope dealer. They'll give it a week and if nothing turns up, nobody raises hell, his paperwork will be filed away in a drawer."

"That's unfair."

"That's why I want to get involved—but from afar. You can understand that, can't you?"

"Like I was saying," she said, "Jimmy told me all about you."

Connor continued. "I don't believe this is some random thing."

"I still don't see why I'd be talking to the police."

"Well, your name is in his probation report."

"It is?"

"And Jimmy told me himself you're the one who introduced him to the undercover cop."

Connor looked at the mirror. She'd laid out four lines, was hitting one of them now with a short plastic straw colored like a candy cane.

"*That,*" she said, lifting her head, her hair falling over one eye. "That fucking cop set us up."

"That's generally the way they do it."

"No, I mean he was a freak. He spent a month trying to jump my bones. Then, right after he busted Jimmy he came straight out with it. Said if I fucked him on a regular basis, he'd make the case go away. That's all he wanted. Didn't Jimmy tell you?"

"He never mentioned it."

"Jimmy told me to not even think about it. He said he knew some people. I guess that's where you came in, huh?"

She did the other line, then put her head back, closing her eyes. Frozen.

"Kelly?" Connor asked. "You okay?"

She opened up her eyes, flicking away a tear from one as fast as it came. "Jimmy was possessive. But he'd do anything for his friends."

"I believe he would," Connor said.

She laughed, wiping away one more tear. "You know, he never tried to jump my bones? I had to. Jimmy's the only guy who ever did that."

Connor walked over and sat down next to her, looking in her eyes again.

"Jimmy told me you helped him, too," he said.

"Only when he gave me the chance."

Nelson Connor decided it was time. "Kelly, Jimmy told me you took his phone book when he was arrested."

"Well, like I was saying about this cop, you think he would have hit his house, looking for more shit. But he never did." She paused, looking at him quizzically. "What are you looking for, anyway?"

"I'm looking for any people he owed money," Connor said. "The people he bought his drugs from would probably be a good start."

"You think that's what happened?"

"I don't know. But if I had some names, I could get them to the right people, without involving you, of course."

"I stayed out of his business," she said matter-of-factly. "Besides, he said he was always flush."

"Always?" Connor asked again.

She pushed the mirror closer to him. He kept his eyes on her.

"Well, there was one guy he talked about. But that was from years ago. I only remember because he told me this story about the guy's name."

"What was it?"

She thought for a couple seconds. "Larry, I think. Actually, it wasn't Larry, but that's what Jimmy called him. We were laughing about this guy's name one night. We got really goofy. You know, you ever start laughing at something and can't stop?"

Connor nodded. "Happened to my wife and I once during a symphony. We had to leave."

She was still remembering. "I guess the guy was a little weird. I think that's how it came up, now that I think about it. Jimmy owed him some money and he was saying he was glad that the guy had dropped out of sight."

Connor asked, "So what's so funny about Larry?"

"*Lawrence*," she said, excited. "*That* was his name. Because he *hated* to be called Larry. That's what we were laughing about."

"I still don't get it."

"Something to do with his last name. The way it rhymed. And we kept saying it over and over. That's why we were laughing. We were pretty stoned that night."

"You can't remember the last name?"

She thought about it, still holding the straw between her fingers.

"Berry? Larry Berry?"

He could see she wasn't sure.

"Terry? Larry Terry? Something like that. God, it's right on the tip of my tongue."

"Do you still have Jimmy's phone book?" Connor asked.

She leaned back into the couch, still holding the straw in front of her as if she were about to write something with it in the air. "Jimmy told me to toss it. Why?"

"The guy's name is probably in there. For that matter, so is mine. I'd hate to see that get around."

She put her head back again, closing her eyes and sighing, her nipples pushing at the flimsy fabric. Her hand with the straw dropped, her fingers touching his knee.

"Judge, your secret's safe with me." She said it in a seductive girlish whisper.

"Good girl," he said.

Her eyes opened. "Gary. That's it. Larry Gary. That was the guy's name."

She sat back up, took his hand and closed it around the straw.

"Those lines are for you," she said.

He glanced at the cocaine, then her breasts, his eyes with a will of their own.

CHAPTER 18

GARY SPENT THE entire morning in the stables, but he never photographed a complete horse. He shot parts. A leg. An eye. A nose profile, trying to get the way the bridle came over the top, the contrasting textures of the leather and hide. Everything was just like the little woman said it would be at Northville Downs. He could go anywhere. Shoot anything he wanted.

He wanted to shoot the lockers, but when he got to the concourse, he found a worker removing them, one guy taking down the wall behind them, part of the refurbishing project for the track.

He took some pictures anyway, until the guy with serious biceps and a leather tool belt walked up to him with a crowbar.

"What those pictures for?" he asked.

"I'm here on assignment," he said.

"What kind of assignment?" The guy said, his lower lip pushed out with Skoal.

"I'm doing some artwork for the lounge."

"Do I look like a model?"

"No," Gary said. "But in the right circles you could wreck a few homes."

He put the tip of the crowbar on Gary's chest. "This ain't your fucking circle, asshole." Then he walked away.

A few minutes later, he called Tino Dentz from a pay phone, asking about Bobby Tank.

"He's coming out Friday," Dentz said. "That's what the vent say."

Gary knew the vent was the way inmates relayed messages through the heating ducts in the county jail.

"Did you get him the message?" Gary asked.

"The vent says he got it."

"Good," Gary said.

He lingered at the phone for a few moments, thinking. He wasn't sold on the locker, anyway. It wasn't very creative. He needed a way to pick up the money, minimize any chance of police surveillance and keep Tino Dentz out of the loop. Dentz was getting too pressured, putting too much of that crank up his nose. With Bobby, he could just tell the West Virginian to pick up a package.

But where?

Gary looked over at the worker, swinging the crowbar into the wall. Then he reached into his camera bag and pulled out Katherine Connor's business card.

AT THE END of the hall, attorneys were waiting for the doors of his courtroom to open. Attorneys with motions. Attorneys wanting assignments. Attorneys seeking continuances. Attorneys looking for guidance, lawyers savvy enough to test his receptiveness to a particular maneuver they'd hatched, trying to win brownie points by dry-running it on a theoretical basis in his chambers, instead of surprising him with it in court.

Today, Barbara was opening the gates to the pen.

Nelson Connor kept walking toward them. Waved one hand over his head like a captain signaling from his cabin cruiser, then ducked into his office entrance.

He gave Lewis the name.

Lewis asked, "How about a Department of Corrections ID?"

"Don't have one," Connor said.

Connor glanced down the new hit parade, the *Weekly Docket Status Report*. Two weeks off, he was still near the top of the charts, just down one notch to third.

"What about a DOB?" Lewis asked.

"Don't have one of those, either."

"Known aliases?"

"No."

"How about a Social Security?"

"Nope."

"Jurisdiction he was sentenced?"

"Don't have that, either."

"You know what the people in corrections are going to say when I give them just a name?"

Connor tossed the hit parade in the trash. "Lewis, if I had all that, I wouldn't need to run the goddamn name, would I? Just run the fricking thing. Tell 'em a guy in his twenties, maybe early thirties."

They were always running names, helping attorneys locate missing witnesses, giving process-servers leads. The people at the computers were always bitching, wanting more information than anybody had.

Barbara walked in from the courtroom, carrying a solid six inches of files and paperwork. "The chief judge wants to see you. He called yesterday right after you left."

"Did he say what he wanted?"

"He wants to know how you're doing."

"What did you tell him?"

"I told him you were doing fine."

Jack Crilly was wrong, he decided. Sometimes staying sober had nothing to do with time, but distance. Last night, he'd told himself he only had to get up and walk twenty feet, and he was safely out of Kelly Johns' apartment door.

He was feeling good about that.

Barbara dropped the materials on her desk with a thud.

"What does the rest of the week look like?" Connor asked.

She separated about three inches of paperwork off the top of the pile and tried to hand it to him. "Lori sent these up. More sentencings."

He was watching Lewis now, on the phone now with the Department of Corrections, spelling out the name, G–A–R–R–Y, then asking them to also try G–A–R–Y.

Connor looked back at his clerk and said, "What about all those attorneys outside?"

"They've come to see the czar."

"All of 'em?"

"Either the czar or Monty Hall."

"Today?"

"I took the liberty of booking Thursday and Friday. So we can get caught up."

Two solid days of looking at runners and dealers and shooters and stabbers, Connor thought. His jury box packed. Most of them pulled from their bunks before breakfast so they could get them over from the jail, the lint from bedding still in their hair. He'd offer most of them the chance to plea out. Tell them what their sentence would be if their presentence investigation checked out, warning them not to lie to him right there in open court. And, on the day of sentencing, they reserved the right to withdraw their pleas. Or, they could go right ahead and ask for that bench trial, or a jury if they insisted, but they were taking their chances. A beer truck driver he'd sentenced complained once, "That's not fair, Your Honor. You're asking me to pay for my right to a trial by jury." He'd beaten his wife to death. Connor told him something he hadn't heard on Court TV: "No, sir, you're simply paying for the rental of the hall."

Connor told Barbara, "From now on, if we get jammed up, let's spread the manure throughout the week."

"I would have," she said, "but we've got Labor Day next week."

"Already?" he said. "Where did the summer go?"

He looked back over at Lewis; he wrote something on a legal pad, then hung up.

"Guy was released from Jackson last month," he said, handing him the sheet. "If it's the same one."

Connor saw the date and location of his original sentence. Lawrence Gary was sentenced in the Third Circuit.

He turned to Barbara. "I'll trade you."

"For what?"

He handed her Lewis's notes. "I'll take those presentence reports, you get me everything the clerk's got on this case. Call Lori and get that presentence report, too, if it's not in the file."

He picked up the stack of probation reports and headed for his chambers.

"What about the chief judge?" Barbara asked.

"Tell him I'm buried. Tell him I'll drop by when I get a chance."

"What about the lineup outside?" she asked.

"Give me ten minutes," he said. "Then start sending them in."

He opened the door to his chambers.

"By the way," Barbara said, following him in. "Darryl Lensley was in here again yesterday. He's looking for assignments."

"You gotta be kidding me."

"He bought four tickets to your fundraiser."

"He can buy eight," Connor said, turning around. "I wouldn't assign Charlie Manson to the man."

AT NOON, HE walked over in the sky tunnels that connected the CCB to the Millender Center, then made his way through another city gerbil tube across Jefferson to the Renaissance Center. Kace was angry. He knew that when he got to the breakfast nook in the morning and saw the note saying she was already in her studio. When she called him at 11: 50 A.M. from a downtown printer that did her color separations, wanting to know whose black Pontiac that was in their driveway this morning, he suggested lunch.

"We need to talk, not eat," she told him.

"We will," he told her. "But I think we'll do so in a much more civil manner if we're in a public place."

She was waiting for him at a Chinese restaurant tucked between the cavernous building's concrete support pillars, the table brightly lit by a glass roof overhead. They spent the first five minutes figuring out what they were going to order, him going for a cup of coffee and the almond chicken; her, just a plate of shrimp fried rice.

The Pontiac did not come up. Other things did.

"John's last Little League game is Friday. You going to make it?"

"I'll be there," he said. "I've got a whole block of time free after work now."

She said she believed he wasn't drinking, and that was good.

"I'm glad you trust me," he said. "I used to hide it pretty well."

"The bedroom didn't smell like a distillery this morning," she said. "That's how I know."

A minute later, she was using words he'd expect from *Oprah*. She was saying he was "distant" and "preoccupied" and "not in touch with his feelings." He listened. But the waitress interrupted her three times, offering him a refill before he could get halfway through the cup.

The almond chicken came.

Katherine looked at her rice, then him, and said, "I guess what I'm asking, Connor, is when are you going to tell me just what in the hell is going on with you?"

He looked up from his plate. "Look, Kace, about last night, I was with Jack. We got to talking and just lost track of the time."

"You drink coffee through straws now?"

He said he didn't understand.

"I found a straw in your shirt pocket. What was that for?"

Jesus, he thought. She was checking over his clothes.

"Just something to chew on. I'm trying to cut down on the smokes."

She stabbed one of the tiny shrimps with her fork.

"Look," she said. "I'm not really talking about last night. I'm not talking about anything specific. I'm talking about the way you're acting in general."

"I'm making some changes. That's all."

"Changes?"

"Yeah, like the car. I was going to tell you last night. I traded in the Reatta."

"For another used car? You said you'd never buy a used car."

"Like I said, I traded it."

"What does a car have to do with your drinking?"

"I did more drinking in that Buick than you realize."

"You're not listening to me. I realized all too well."

"They say in the program I've got to put my sobriety first."

"What about your family? Or are we supposed to just look for clues, then put it all together. Do we get consulted, or is this some big secret solo thing?"

"They say if I don't take care of staying sober, I'll lose everything I care about. That's you. That's John."

And he meant that.

"Everything okay here?" the waitress said, standing over them, coffeepot in hand.

He glared up at her, wanting to say no, everything isn't okay. It isn't okay because I'm in the middle of a goddamn serious discussion with my wife. And while I appreciate the prompt service, maybe you ought to open your eyes and ears and see what the hell is going on before you interrupt again.

He said only, "Fine."

The waitress left.

He remembered something Crilly told him, something that might get Kace off his back. "You know, Kace, they have a program for you. It's called Al-Anon. They have meetings, too."

"Nelson, there's nothing wrong with me."

He pushed his plate away. "That's not what they say. They say you have to make adjustments, too. You've been trying to help me all these years. Now, the way the program is, I've got to help myself. That kind of leaves you out of it, but that's the way it works."

She said she wanted nothing to do with it, and she wasn't happy with the implication that she was damaged goods.

"Look," he said. "I wasn't implying this was your problem."

He reached for her hand, but got empty table.

"Connor," she said, "for once, would you just tell me how you feel?"

He lit a cigarette.

"I feel good," he said, exhaling. "Damn good."

A surly kind of good, he told himself. He felt good when he was fighting something. He was feeling good about plowing through a dozen attorneys in one morning, a personal record. He was feeling good about the name Kelly Johns had given him. He was *doing something*, making headway. He was feeling good he hadn't screwed the girl, that he'd gone the entire morning without one single urge to drink.

Katherine said, "Nelson, listen to me."

He butted the smoke, remembering what he'd said about the straw.

"I understand this is not easy for you," she continued. "And I can only imagine what you're going through. But if you think I'm going to sit around and play the dutiful-wife routine while you completely shut me out of your life, you're making a serious miscalculation."

"You didn't seem to care when I was drinking."

"At least then you *talked*. Half of what you said made no sense, but you *talked*."

"I'm talking."

"No, you're just saying words. What did you do, meet somebody in there, in that hospital?"

"Meet who?"

"I think you know what I mean."

"You've got to be kidding."

Christ, he thought.

He took both her hands, told her that she was his wife and that he loved her. Told her she had to give him some time, that's all.

"Look, Kace, I'll tell you what. I've got a short day. Let me cut out of there early. I'll meet you at home, and let's go do something. We can hit some antique stores in Saline."

She looked at her watch. "I've got to meet somebody at the racetrack."

"Cancel it," he said.

"I can't. I have no way to reach him. It's a photographer on the new job." She thought about it for a second. "Why don't you join us? You can meet us in the lounge there."

Connor thought about the circuit file he'd requested. Besides, he didn't belong in a racetrack bar, tagging along with his wife. "I just realized tonight's the CCB meeting. But I'll be home by seven-thirty, guaranteed."

She seemed to appreciate the gesture. She reached out across the table, squeezing his hand.

"Kace," he said, "I need you to hang in there. Just a little longer. I promise, things will get better. It just takes time."

She leaned across the table and kissed him on the forehead. No passion, just a signal she was calling a truce.

"I gotta go," she said.

When they stood, she said, "Black Pontiac, huh?"

"Yeah, what do you think? I can still take it back."

"You're lucky it's not red or you'd be in deep trouble."

"Why's that?" he said, smiling, somewhat miffed.

"They said on *Oprah* when a guy your age goes out and buys a red sports car, you can bet the house he's got a girl."

FIFTEEN MINUTES LATER, Nelson Connor knew he had something going for him when he saw a section called "Offender's Personal History," two pages inside Lawrence Gary's presentence report, stamped in large red letters:

CONFIDENTIAL FILE.
NO PAPERS TO BE REMOVED OR COPIED WITHOUT CONSENT OF
CIRCUIT JUDGE.

Dali.

He knew it when he read Lawrence Gary was a Center for Creative Studies dropout, then a lot of crap Gary had fed a court aide under "Evaluation and Plan," how he planned to continue his education in prison and secure employment in the art field upon his release. Twenty-eight years old. Product of a broken home. This guy Gary feeding the aide more bullshit about how things might have turned out better for him had his father not left his mother, who was the source of "much emotional ambivalence." The aide writing it up like she bought it: "The offender seems to be a thoughtful, intelligent young man with positive potential. . . ."

The aide apparently ignored Lawrence Gary's CCS academic transcript, full of Incompletes. The aide also overlooked comments from a CCS guidance counselor, who said, "While Mr. Gary has rather grandiose notions about his own talent, instructors reported his work mediocre and cliché-ridden at best."

The sentencing judge was Nicholas Kaufmann. Nelson Connor decided he was on a lucky streak. Kaufmann routinely ordered psychological evaluations on potentially violent offenders at the Recorder's Court clinic. Connor found the report buried deep in the probation jacket, stamped with more confidential warnings. He read about Gary's "manipulative personality" and "narcissistic worldview," tempered by, the in-house shrink wrote, "pronounced voyeuristic tendencies and latent homosexual tendencies."

Connor read:

While this offender may act out his pathology in and around certain criminal endeavors, he is not likely to engage directly in violent acts himself, leaving what he might consider the "dirty work" to others, while at the same time fulfilling his voyeuristic needs and manipulative tendencies. Both his narcissism and voyeurism may be a direct response to his rather low opinion of his own physical stature. In fact, when confronted directly, alone, he would have to rely on his limited physical and psychological defenses and, in the opinion of the writer, would flee rather than choose violence or other high-risk solutions. This, therefore, fuels the offender's need to constantly surround himself with individuals who will not only shore up his personal limitations, but feed his narcissistic feelings of superiority as well.

At the end of the report was the clinic's Axis II diagnosis from the DSM-III: "Antisocial personality disorder."

"You psychopathic little shit," Connor muttered to himself.

He searched the file for a picture, but found none. In the back of the presentence report, under "Investigator's Description of the Offense," he did find in detail what had earned Lawrence Gary three years in prison. There he also found the names of Torino Dentz, a black male, and a white male named Bobby Tank.

"Barbara," he said into his intercom. "There's two more files I'm going to need you to get."

He gave her the numbers.

He was chuckling about the threesome's ill-fated robbery of the FOP party, the poetic justice of it, when Barbara walked in seconds later, dropping folders on his desk.

"That was quick."

"I figured you'd want them," she said. "One of them we already had."

"Here?"

"Possession of stolen property. Uttering and publishing. He's set for a calendar conference Thursday—*again*."

"Tomorrow?"

"It's already been adjourned twice. Isn't that why you wanted these?"

"Right," he said.

She dropped *State of Michigan v. Bobby Tank* on his desk.

He opened the file, glancing at the arraignment, speed-reading the details about the cash-checking machine. The attorney was from the public defender's office, a stable of sharp young lawyers paid by the county for indigent work.

"Barbara, why isn't this PD getting with the program?" Connor asked.

"He's right with it," she said. "It's not a czar case. The PD is looking for personal bond. And he's picked his week."

"They're crowded over there?" he asked. When the jail was overcrowded, pressure came from the Sheriff's Department to release the least violent offenders.

"Court administrator has sent two memos this week."

Connor pushed Tank's file aside, opening the one for Torino Dentz. He riffled through the paperwork, hoping for a mug shot. The Sheriff's Department photo was impaled by the two file fasteners at the back of the jacket.

He recognized the hair. It had to be the same guy.

"You done with these?" Barbara asked, eyeing a stack of sentencings on his desk.

Connor started laughing: about Bobby Tank and Torino Dentz, about Lawrence Gary's little crew.

Barbara took the sentencings anyway, asking, "So, what's so funny?"

"Just more geniuses, cleverly disguised as assholes," he said.

She shook her head, walking out, leaving his door open.

He looked at the names again. Lawrence Gary. Bobby Tank. *Torino Dentz*. Reminded him of Denseley.

"Hey, Barbara," he said, reaching for one of the files. "Get Darryl Lensley on the phone, will you?"

"What in the world for?" she said, appearing at the door again, a look of astonishment on her face.

"Tell him I want him here first thing in the morning. Then see if you can get the PD on the phone, the one for this Friday's calendar conference on the Tank file."

"What do you want me to tell Denseley?" she said, still miffed.

Connor smiled. "Tell him I want to assign him a good case."

CHAPTER 19

AFTER THEY TOOK care of business, giving her his input about what he thought could be done with the lounge, Katherine asked, "You ever been married, Gary?"

Lawrence Gary smiled. "Can't say I have."

"How about a serious relationship?"

He studied her eyes, wanting to give her something, just to prime the pump. "There was one person. In art school. But her parents didn't approve. They were from the Pointes. I didn't have money. You know how that goes."

He took a sip of his iced tea, leaning closer across the lounge booth. "You're looking at me like you want to tell me something," he said.

It was a momentary cry, then a little laugh, one coming right after another.

"I'm sorry," she said, her hand quickly going to her eye.

"It's all right," he said. "We all need someone to talk to sometime."

"I don't even know you," she said, embarrassed now.

He squeezed her hand, saying, "Sometimes strangers are the best people. After all, how much does the average person know about his shrink?"

She laughed. "You've got a point there."

"But, Katherine," he said, "I think a vivacious woman like yourself would have a ton of friends."

She shook her head. "You know, I'm just beginning to realize how isolated I've let myself get."

"Art can be isolating."

"It's not that," she said. She looked him in the eyes. "I think I've just spent too many years worrying about my husband."

It didn't take long for the little woman to lay out the whole sad story. Gary primed her again, saying, "My dad was an alcoholic. That's why my mother left him."

"Did he ever go to those meetings?" she asked.

Gary came up with another lie. "No. One night he drove into a tree."

"I'm sorry," she said.

When she ran out of words, Gary asked, "So, is he drinking?"

Katherine Connor shook her head. "He says I should be going to meetings, too."

Gary tapped her glass of iced tea. "You don't look like you have a problem."

"Meetings for family members."

Gary saw another opportunity for a story. "My mother went to those," he said. "You know, they really help."

They talked for a good half hour, Gary going with the general theme that she just needed to cut the man a lot of space. He liked her this way, her not knowing about the other sinkhole the man was in.

"Maybe he's just under a lot of pressure," Gary finally concluded. "Does he have anything big coming up down the road?"

"He's up for re-election this year," she said.

"That must take a lot of money."

"I don't think that's it," she said. "I'm sure plenty of attorneys are contributing to his campaign account."

"Really? What do they use the money for?"

"Ads on the radio, usually. Close to the election."

"That must be difficult. Not knowing if you're going to have a job every four years."

"The bench has its own pressures."

"Maybe you both just need a vacation," Gary said.

They talked for another fifteen minutes about the cottage the Connors had in the north.

———

HE TOLD JACK Crilly he didn't want to go to the City-County meeting. He said he felt uncomfortable around all those lawyers, which wasn't true. He felt uncomfortable around Michael Cooney, but he didn't tell Crilly that.

"I've got a better idea," Crilly said.

Crilly gave him an address on Vernor, said the place was over a store on the southwest side.

"A meeting?" Connor asked.

"Not quite."

When Connor opened the door with the sign, Southwest Detroit Alano Club, he saw a half dozen people sitting at a bar rail inside. The place dimly lit, a jukebox going. A dozen tables scattered around.

Crilly's voice came from behind a curtain of light cast by a lamp at the pool table. "Get yourself a drink, Judge, then come over here and grab yourself a stick."

It looked like a bar, Connor decided, but it didn't sound like one. People weren't shouting over the music. People were speaking reasonably, not making wild gestures the way they did in bars.

The woman behind the rail had a ten-year token around her neck. Coke, Vernors ginger ale, or Sprite, she said. "And there's coffee over there. Just help yourself."

Connor carried a Vernors over to the pool table.

"Thought you'd walked into trouble, didn't you?" Crilly said, grinning.

"For a second, I thought you were already there."

"They have clubs like this all over. They're not officially affiliated with AA. But program people keep them going. They're not for everyone. But you ought to know they're around."

Crilly gathered balls from the velvet. "You can handle a stick, can't you?"

"Where I grew up, pool was a contact sport," Connor said.

"Then you're breaking."

Crilly was racking, but Connor could wait no longer.

"Jack," he said, "I got a line on these guys."

He took several minutes to tell him everything he'd found out about Lawrence Gary, how Gary appeared to be working with a black convicted felon named Torino Dentz; he'd told them about the police party they'd tried to hold up three years ago.

Crilly listened, leaning on his cue stick. Then he centered the rack.

"Tell me about the shade," he said.

Another term Connor hadn't heard in years.

"Just the one felony arrest, for both of them. Surprising, really, considering both these guys. I mean, you ever go to an FOP party, Jack?"

"Can't say I have."

Connor fired the cue ball, sinking two balls on the break.

"Cops from three out-county departments at the one they hit. A lot of them carrying off-duty. Five and six deep at the bar. The probation report said they thought they were going to take down a wedding. But, *damn*, how do you misread a situation like that?"

"Takes special talent," Crilly said.

Connor laughed, Crilly with him, but not from the gut, the way Connor felt it.

"*It*" was that feeling. The feeling that he was on top of the situation now. Connor told Crilly he had four days to deal with these ex-cons before Monday, when Dali said he'd be calling him with directions. Connor would slap them up with the system, using an invisible hand.

"You're sure about that?" Crilly asked.

"That's just the way it is," Connor said. "People do favors for you."

That's why you ran for the bench and kept that "Incumbent" designation next to your name on the ballot. That's why you fought like hell for it when somebody tried to take it away.

"But what about the shade?" Crilly asked again.

Connor tried to sink the ten in the corner, but missed.

"Well, I've seen better presentence reports. But there was some information about his mother. She apparently got a sizable wrongful-death lawsuit from the city years ago; one of her kids killed by a city bus. This guy Dentz complaining she spends all her money on some church."

"That's it?"

"No, the usual shit. A bunch of lies they all tell the court aides, trying to get sympathy. Apparently he did have some problems as a juvenile."

"What kind of problems?"

"I don't know. By statute, they keep a tight lid on those files. I'd have to formally request his file from the Juvenile Court. What I've done so far is totally informal. I'd like to keep it that way."

Crilly tried to run the nine down the rail, but ran it too close to the bumper.

"Sound like you're all set," he said. "Now all you do is call somebody at police headquarters. Guy like you, sounds to me like you could start with the chief."

Connor walked closer, not even looking for a shot now. "I'm not going to the police, Jack."

"Okay, you want to start at that outfit that regulates you guys, I can help you with that."

Crilly wasn't hearing what he was saying. "The tenure commission? How can you help me?—presuming I even would want to do that."

"You've got friends, Judge. Friends in the program. You got one of the top guys in Schmanski's meeting. I'm on very good terms with the man."

"Michael Cooney?"

Crilly nodded, leaning on his stick.

"You don't sponsor Cooney, do you?"

Crilly grinned.

"You been talking to him about my situation?"

"I don't talk about nobody's business. I told you that."

Connor took a meaningless shot at the table, the four on a double bank, never expecting to make it.

Crilly circled, looking. "I saw Cooney reach out for a lawyer we had come in a couple years ago. Guy was about to lose everything. Cooney stepped in. Made a few calls. Asked the proper authorities to cut the guy some slack."

"That's the state bar. Goddamn Cooney *is* the proper authority, Jack."

"I'm sure he'd be discreet."

"But he's running for the Supreme Court. I might as well announce it on the Capitol steps."

Connor thought about it some more, then said, "No, Jack. I'm not going to 1300. I'm not going to the commission. And I'm particularly not going to Mike Cooney. No fucking way."

Crilly, leaning on his pool stick, looked disappointed. But Jack Crilly, Connor thought, didn't have everything Connor had on the line.

"Well, I can see I'm not going to change your mind," Crilly said, looking over the balls on the table again. "So what you going to do?"

Connor said, "I look at felons all day long. You give a felon a choice, present it in just the right way, they'll usually take the path of least resistance."

"Like I told you, you don't want to play in their world."

"I don't plan to."

"So, where does the con come in?"

"Con? I wouldn't call it that."

"What else would you call what you're doing?"

"I'd call it using the confidence people have in my position. And I'm trying to take it day by day, like you said."

"That's called the short con. But that's only going to work with legit people, not these guys."

"What are you trying to tell me, Jack?"

Crilly lit a smoke, setting it on the edge of the table.

"Most people don't understand the game. They think it's like that movie—what was that one about the game?—with George C. Scott?"

The Flim-Flam Man.

"Right, the movie kept saying you can't cheat an honest man. Greed made the whole thing work. That's true, but it's not the whole story."

"So what is?" Connor asked.

Crilly started circling the table, looking.

"The best cons, the party doing the make, has put himself at risk. The mark has to think your ass is way out on the line. That's why you can sell bad Jap watches from a coat. That's the inducement. That way, the mark feels more comfortable joining you out there on the plank.

"I think I've got that department covered."

"My point, exactly. You know it. They know it. You've got no operating room, my friend."

Crilly sunk the seven, then said, "That's why I wanted to know about the shade."

"What does he have to do with it?"

"You need a handle. You're going to need a handle on the shade if you want to make him go away."

Crilly sunk the five.

"Then, you go to work on the other guy. Preferably, you do both at the same time."

Crilly ran the table, sinking the eight on a combination in the side pocket, then sat down on the edge. "Like I was saying, I need to know more about the shade, presuming you want some direction on this."

Connor could swear he detected enthusiasm in his voice.

"I thought you didn't give out advice."

"I don't," Crilly said, leaning forward, butting a cigarette. The light from the overhead lamp chiseled his face with shadows. "But that doesn't mean that, in certain areas, I can't provide a little expertise."

THEY DROVE AROUND the town of Romulus, near Detroit Metropolitan Airport, Gary wanting to get out on Main Street and "scout locations," as he put it. Tino Dentz following Gary three blocks, Gary walking fast, but stopping twice to look in the windows of empty storefronts. Tino pointed out a place called The Landing Strip, a topless club.

"I told you this area was hot," Gary said.

Then Gary said he wanted to get back to the van, saying something about an old gas station for sale he'd seen on their way in. Saying it was not something called "*art deco*," like he preferred, but they could work with it.

"We could call it The Station," Gary said.

They started walking back to the van, hardly anybody on the street, most of the shops in the small town closed.

"I thought we came out here to look at the lockers in the airport," Tino said.

"We drove by it, didn't we?" Gary said.

"I thought we were coming out here to check out the drop."

"It costs too much to park," Gary said.

Besides, Gary said, he decided he wasn't going to use a locker now. He'd figured out a way for the judge's wife to pick up the money, then deliver the money to him.

Tino wanted him to explain.

Gary stopped, putting one boot up on a bench, using his hands like he was telling the story from a stage. "Okay, Tino, picture this: Several times a week, the woman picks up her color separations from this place downtown."

"Colored what?"

"They're films they make from photographs for the designer, for the printer's use."

"I don't understand."

"You don't need to. Point is, people pick these separations up night and day at this place."

"How many?"

"Hundreds a week. So, I have the judge deliver the money in a package, the name I gave her on it, of course. Then I tell her, Hey, I've got a separation waiting for me there, could she pick it up?"

"Then what?"

"We send Bobby to pick it up from her."

"What if she looks inside?"

"People in that business don't mess with other people's stuff."

"But then the judge got the name you using."

"Like I've told you, the man and his wife don't talk."

"But I don't see what it gets you."

Gary said, "We'll be watching. On the outside chance he's got the drop wired, we get to see the cops bust his wife."

They started walking again, Tino thinking about it, all the ramifications.

"You been into the E, Gary?"

"Why?"

" 'Cause you fucking crazy, that's why."

All huffy, Gary said, "No, like you said earlier, you just don't understand."

Tino Dentz thought Gary was starting to get a real mouth on him, especially for somebody who hadn't produced shit since the day they came out of Jackson.

He said, "You get paid for those racetrack pictures yet?"

Gary said he had to do something with them in his darkroom.

"Wait until she sees them," Tino said.

"What makes you say that?"

" 'Cause you never done something like that before."

"She likes me."

"She *likes* you? What makes you say that? You do her?"

Dentz knew he hadn't.

"I *talked* to her. Talked to her for a good hour in the bar there. Little woman was all touchy and feely. She even picked up the tab."

Tino pictured the scene. Put it next to another he already had in his mind, the day they saw her bending over the flower beds. Then, he thought of Gary, not knowing what to do with it, wanting always to take his pictures.

"Yo, talking don't mean liking," Tino said, starting to walk, now leading the way. "Fucking means liking."

"I could, if I wanted," Gary said. "She's not happy."

"I'd fuck her."

"Her old man's put her through a lot of shit."

"You finally find some, Gary, and now all of a sudden you going soft?"

"No, what I'm saying, what she's been telling me is *helpful.*"

"What she say?"

"She told me to choose what I did, and who I did it with, carefully. Use your head, she said."

"I'm asking, What did she say about the man?"

"Well, they got money, despite what that motherfucker says. Got a place up north. Summer house up near the bridge."

"What bridge?"

"Mackinaw Bridge. She was talking all about it. How they usually go up there in August, but not this year. Said everything was too fucked up."

"She said 'fucked up'?"

"No, she said 'up in the air.' "

"You sure he hasn't told her?"

"No way. She was talking about that, how the man has been acting *distant.*"

"Distant?"

"Yeah."

Gary stopped across from the van and flicked his cigarette into the middle of the street. He looked both ways and said, "And I must say, if I was sitting where His Honor was, I'd be acting pretty distant myself."

CHAPTER 20

"I THINK I'M evolving into a new understanding," Nelson Connor said. "I'm beginning to believe we're not doing anything for drug offenders unless they face some serious negative consequences."

"Even possession cases?" Lori Eisenberg asked.

They were in his chambers, first thing in the morning.

"Especially possession cases."

Her mouth dropped open. "I wouldn't call that evolution," his court aide said. "I'd call that an about-face."

He sipped his coffee, feeling reflective, looking judicial. "And I'm thinking the only way to do it, is to serve up a little time."

She thought about his words, then said, "Trouble is, Judge Connor, there's just not much help in the system."

"There is for those who want it." Then he slipped the matter in, making it sound routine. "Speaking of doing time, seems we've got a little neighborhood problem."

"Your neighborhood?"

"My wife. She likes that show *Cops*. And she's got this studio that looks out over the street. To make a long story short, she started noticing this car back when I was in Brighton. Same guys always together. A black guy and a white guy. Thinks they're casing the street."

"You want me to run the plate?"

"I already did. I did a little digging, figuring I'd ease her mind. Plus, there *was* a B and E recently on the street. And that's got some old people in the neighborhood scared half to death."

Connor paused.

"And?" the court aide asked.

Connor shook his head. "Well, I gotta say, Katherine must have instincts. They're felons all right. Sentenced by the bench a few years back. Got to be pretty stupid, planning something in my neck of the woods."

"On parole, I take it?"

"Sure, when you consider their sentencing dates. I've pulled their case files. They both had firearms felonies. I'd sure like to see their terms."

She looked at her watch. "I can call Metro. Have them faxed over to me before noon."

"I could pass them on to local police," Connor said.

She nodded, looking concerned for the seniors, Connor guessed. "Judge, I can do better than that," she said.

He knew she could. Parole and probation were both Michigan Department of Corrections. But he wanted her to suggest it.

"What did you have in mind?" he asked.

"It wouldn't take much. Their POs can put them on a leash. One thing about parole officers, give them the green light, most jump at the chance to get out of the office, so to speak."

Connor protested. "*That* could be precarious. Katherine, quite frankly, is frightened. Especially since I took on this czar thing. These cons find out I passed along her information, I'm not sure she'd be able to sleep at night."

Lori Eisenberg stood up. "I'll just say I have it on good authority that they're on the job again, that it comes from a high authority on the circuit bench. In fact, I'll tell them when I call for the reports."

"Then what?" Connor asked.

"Tell your wife not to worry. The POs will do the rest."

A HALF HOUR later, she delivered Gary's and Dentz's parole files. They had everything Jack Crilly said he might need.

At lunch, he drove out the Jeffries, which trenched through some of Detroit's toughest neighborhoods, to the Southfield freeway, then north past Rosedale Park with its grand old city homes. Then the real estate decreased in value, the big colonials and Tudors giving way to tract bungalows built and bought after World War II with GI loans.

The small homes reminded him of his old neighborhood near Mc-Kenzie. His father never was enamored with real estate, dying of a heart attack in the same small brick house where Connor grew up. His county salary and simple interest put Connor through law school and left his mother with some pretty prosperous years in West Palm before she passed. Connor failed to see the wisdom of it when he was younger. Later, he guessed the neighborhood had motivated him. It wasn't easy being white and a judge's son in a "changing neighborhood." It wasn't that the punks were out to bust his balls simply because he was white and his father was on the bench. But among those who busted everybody's, with Nelson Connor they just had two more excuses.

He took the Eight Mile Road exit, heading west a few blocks, then south. The address he was looking for was only a quarter mile inside the Detroit city limits, a neighborhood that changed not after the '67 riot, but a few years later, when a federal judge began busing white students into black schools throughout Detroit.

Connor slowed to a crawl as he passed the home of Tula Gary. He saw a white Plymouth with a Michigan Department of Corrections seal parked out front.

Lori Eisenberg worked quickly, he thought.

He went around the block, coming back again, taking a closer look. All the curtains drawn. The sash trim needing paint. An Escort wagon in the driveway. Security bars on all the windows. On a nearby corner, he saw a couple of teens in Fila sweats and Air Jordans.

Lawrence Gary, Nelson Connor thought. Twenty-eight and still living with his mother. Wise guy in a little house, with great big plans of his own.

He took Eight Mile east to Woodward, heading south, back toward downtown. He parked along the curb across from the church. He recalled the building as being a Protestant cathedral years ago. The entire complex—the sanctuary, the school, the rectory—took up nearly a city block. The church was a modified Gothic in cut stone, full of rib vaults and pointed arches and stained glass. Connor stared at the sign out front: Big Rock Church. The Bishop H. Roy Butler, Pastor.

He knew the name from somewhere.

He knew that van, the purple van pulling up.

HEAVEN
MAKE YOUR RESERVATION

He remembered seeing that slogan pass him as he pulled up to the Anchor Bar weeks ago, before he started slamming bourbon, before he blacked out. He remembered because he thought that it was a strange thing to see, considering the cargo in his trunk that night.

Torino Dentz getting out now, strutting into the entrance of the Big Rock Church.

Connor thought they'd followed him, watched him all night.

But now, he was watching them.

THE PO WITH the bad skin was sitting at the Formica-and-stainless table in his mother's kitchen, Gary not inviting her any deeper into the house because he'd have to move too many paintings in the living room, just to let her sit on the sheet of Visquine that covered the couch.

Lawrence Gary was still half asleep.

"*These*, Mr. Gary, are for urine drops," she was saying, pulling a small box out of a big canvas bag. "Do you know what a urine drop is?"

He heard his mother's voice. "Larry, who are you talking to out there?"

"It's my parole officer," he shouted back.

He waited for her footsteps, but didn't hear any. He didn't want his mother getting into this.

"You mean samples of my urine?" he said to the PO.

"Exactly."

She opened the box, pulling out the plastic container and labels inside, doing it like it was a show-and-tell.

"First, you use this for your business." She had the plastic cup in her hand, some pretty sophisticated Tupperware. "Then you put the lid on, of course. Then you attach this label to the cup. Then, this self-addressed label to the box. Then just drop it in the mail for the lab."

She reached into the bag, pulling out three more.

"I want one a week for the next three weeks, Mr. Gary," she said coldly.

"But there's four there," he pointed out.

"That first one is today's. I'm taking it with me as a control sample, so don't get any ideas about having somebody else pissing in these other three."

A minute later, he was standing in the john, wondering what he'd done to bring all this on.

He asked her when he got back. "Why you hassling me?"

He tried to hand the sample to her, wanting her to feel how warm it was in her hand.

She directed him to set it on the table, ignoring his question.

"Now," she said. "Let's see this darkroom of yours."

She followed him down the steps, Gary's mind racing now, wondering what he'd left hanging in there on his drying wire.

He stopped at the door. "Don't you need a warrant to do this?" he asked.

"Mr. Gary, because you are on parole, you remain, by statute, and in the opinion of the Michigan Supreme Court, in the custody of the Michigan Department of Corrections. This entire domicile, ostensibly, is no different than your jail cell."

Bitch, he thought.

"Open it," she said.

He unlocked the clasp, then swung the door open, turning on only the safe light.

She pulled a chain for an overhead bulb.

He quickly scanned the five-by-sevens clipped and hanging from the wire.

She snatched the last one in the line, a shot of Jimmy Osborne burning a joint.

"Very creative," she said. "You know, I could violate you right here and now for this."

She tossed the photo on the enlarger table.

"I'm doing a job," Gary said. "My first big freelance job."

"Where is it?" she asked, studying other things.

"I haven't printed it yet."

"How long will that take?"

"A couple of days."

She turned around and walked out.

He followed her to the foot of the stairs.

"Mr. Gary," she said, walking up, not looking back at him. "I want to see your *job* on my desk on Monday, or I'm going to violate you, is that clear?"

"Why are you doing this to me?"

"I'm your parole officer. I'm looking out for your best interests."

"But I'm not supposed to report until next Friday."

She stopped at the top, turning around. She pulled a pack of cigarettes out of her canvas bag, then glared down at him. "No, you're reporting Monday and Friday," she said. "*Every* Monday and Friday from now on."

BACK AT THE CCB, Connor asked Barbara, "The Reverend H. Roy Butler, where do I know that name from?"

She finished chewing a bite of pastrami, then wiped her hands carefully on a napkin. "He's a contributor," she said.

"To what?"

"Your campaign."

"He bought tickets to the fundraiser?"

She held out her fingers, wanting a cigarette. He handed her one, but didn't take one for himself.

"No, he just sent a check," she said, exhaling. "From what I hear, he gave everybody who is up a couple hundred. He's called a couple times."

"He's got one hell of a church up on Woodward. Why didn't I take his call?"

She rolled her eyes. "That was before your—vacation. I can give you a list of the people you told to buzz off, if you want."

He'd always thought he'd been pretty accessible. Lately, he was learning he was wrong about a lot of things he'd thought.

"Barbara," he said. "What did the man want?"

"He wants our business."

"Business?"

"Probation referrals. He's putting together some kind of work-release program. Wanted to talk to you about what he was doing, until you blew him off."

"Reverend H. Roy Butler," Connor said. "Have I read about him somewhere?"

Barbara snuffed the half-burnt cigarette. When she looked up, he saw the corner of her mouth wry with sarcasm. "You want me to prepare a detailed report for you about the last five years of your life?"

He didn't say anything.

She started sorting motions, saying, "Butler knows a few pols. He's been helpful in the mayor's church machine. And yes, he's been in the paper."

Nelson Connor went into his chambers, closing the door behind him. When he reached Prestige Motors, Jack Crilly said he'd been waiting for his call.

AN HOUR LATER, Nelson Connor asked Darryl Lensley, "Darryl, why do you always wear a blue suit?"

Lensley shifted a little in the *bergère*. "So, you've noticed?"

Connor, his fingertips together below his chin, nodded. "For years, Darryl. For years."

"Actually, it works for me."

"Works?"

The lawyer everyone called Densely hunched forward, lowering his voice. "Actually, I read it in one of those 'Dress for Success' books after I got out of law school. Blue inspires trust, did you know that?"

"No, I did not."

Densely leaned back in the chair, mirroring Connor's posture now, trying to look astute. "In fact," he continued, "green is actually the most trustworthy color. A deep forest green. Not that bright green you see all those idiots wearing on Saint Paddy's Day." Densely paused. "Say, you're not Irish are you, Judge Connor?"

"Not professionally," Connor said.

Densely seemed satisfied with the answer. "Well, as I was saying, these colors evoke trust. With the defendant. With the jury. With some judges, perhaps. Of course, green would not be an appropriate attire to wear in open court."

"Of course not," Connor said, though he'd give a hundred to see it. In the bright green, particularly.

"So, I always go with blue."

"I see."

Connor got up, walked over to his law books, running his fingers over the gold titles. He still had his robe on from hearing miscellaneous matters. He knew a little bit about wardrobe, as well.

Connor asked, "So, I take it you've had time to read the file that Barbara gave you on this defendant Bobby Tank?"

Densely nodded. "Sure did. But I'd be less than honest if I didn't warn you up front. I'd go straight to trial, Your Honor."

It was a dead loser. Densely had to be famished for work.

"We have a calendar conference set for Thursday," Connor said.

"And I'm sure Mr. Tank is looking forward to bail," Densely said, adding, "So he can better assist me in the preparation of his defense, of course."

Connor sat down on the edge of his desk, saying, "Darryl, that's where we might have a problem."

"Why's that? There was no weapon involved."

Connor pointed out that Bobby Tank had at least one conviction involving a firearm. "And Darryl, as you know, I'm up this term for reelection. I cut him loose and he hurts somebody, makes the six o'clock news, you can see how that could blow up in my face."

Densely shifted in his chair.

"On the other hand," Connor continued, "I don't have time to try it. I'm swamped with this czar program right now."

"So what did you have in mind, Judge?"

Now, Connor knew he was starving. "If I give you the case, I'd like to forgo a decision on bond. Then have the case reassigned to another court. In fact, under the czar program, you could even pick your judge for a bench trial."

"Who would you suggest?"

"How about Leonard Talbot?" Connor asked.

Leonard Talbot decorated his chamber bookshelves with a miniature collection of medieval punishment devices—a guillotine, a gallows, and rack. Connor was hoping Densely was unaware the items reflected his basic sentencing philosophy.

"Isn't Talbot a bit *harsh* on repeat offenders?" Densely asked.

"Oh, you don't believe his press, do you? He was always very fair with me, when I was walking in your shoes."

Darryl Lensley thought about it for a couple seconds.

But only a couple.

"Works for me," he said, standing up. "Have you talked with the public defender originally assigned to this case?"

"Not yet."

"What are you going to tell him."

"Oh," Connor said. "Let me handle that."

Densely started to turn to go, but then hesitated. "Judge, what if Mr. Tank doesn't go for it?"

Connor slipped off the desk, back into his chair.

"Well, Darryl, that's where your best blue suit comes in."

AFTER THE ATTORNEY left, he buzzed Barbara.

She answered on the intercom.

"That Reverend H. Roy Butler," Connor asked. "You still have his phone number?"

"Somewhere."

"Find it, will you?"

Connor swiveled his chair around and opened his chamber safe. He could see trial evidence and an envelope of cash, a couple thousand in donations for his fundraiser. For the balance, he decided, he'd tap the slim margin left in his home equity account.

He saw Lewis's gun belt. Take it along, he told himself. Slip it in the small duffle bag with his sweats. Take the bag. Put the Colt .45 right in the son of a bitch's face if something went wrong. He thought, Then what? Pull the trigger if the guy made a move? Blood everywhere, like the crime-scene photos he'd seen on the bench. What then, clean it up? No, burn the van. Then go hunt that guy Gary down.

That's what he wanted to do. That would *feel good.*

Then, he could see himself up on the fifth floor again at 1300, trying to explain, how complicated *that* would get. He found himself thinking on two levels. One, what he wanted to do. The other, the jurist in him, seeing it play out on the stand. He could hear the assistant prosecutor's cross: "So, let me get this straight, Judge Connor. You were taking five thousand dollars in unmarked bills to your extortionists, but you were not agreeing to the blackmail?"

Connor closed the safe. He knew Lewis would leave the Colt there during lunch. Jack Crilly was right. He was still a horse thief, a damn good one. But then again, so was Jack Crilly, though Crilly never mentioned taking a gun.

The intercom buzzed.

"I've got the number," Barbara said. "You want me to bring it in?"

"No," Connor said. "I want you to get the reverend on the phone."

CHAPTER 21

TINO DENTZ'S DAY had started all wrong, his PO, the black ex-cop, banging on his door at seven in the morning, the lap whore hearing it before he did, then passing back out. The PO pushing right past him at the front door, walking right into his bedroom, saying he was doing a "spot check." The lap whore still asleep, Tino complaining, "You can't just walk in here, man."

The PO grabbing him by his pecs and throwing him up against the wall, saying, "What you call this place you live in?"

Tino saying, "A carriage house."

The PO saying, "That's where you're wrong, nigger. This is your prison cell."

Then, the PO telling him he was to report three times a week from now and observe a nine o'clock evening curfew until further notice.

"Yo, for what? I didn't violate *nothin'*."

The PO saying, "This is just to make sure you don't."

Then, the Reverend Roy himself calling him, pulling him off the road just after he'd copped. The pastor having a real attitude. Saying that he wanted somebody picked up downtown at exactly noon, which was no big deal, until he added that he didn't give a holy damn how much his mother donated, that if he didn't keep his shit together on this assignment, he was going to find his black ass out on Woodward Avenue before dinnertime.

Tino Dentz pulled the van into the traffic circle on the Congress side of the City County Building at 11:50 A.M., ten minutes to spare. He reached into his shirt pocket for the item the rag at the party store had sold him. "They call it bullet—good item," the rag had said, showing him how to screw it on top of a vial.

Now, Tino turned his vial over, like the rag showed him, so the crank filled the little channel in the clear plastic bullet, then turned it back right-side-up, making a half turn on the item, opening the channel at the top.

He hit one side, then repeated the procedure for the other.

It was exceptional street meth. He liked the way it stuck with him for an hour or two, not taking him up and down every thirty minutes the way coke did. He liked blowing it right there in front of the county building, pulling it off with the rag's "good item" by cupping it in his hand and making a casual gesture to his face.

Two minutes later, he had his eyes on some butt, and some painted lips biting into an apple from a vendor's fruit cart. He wasn't thinking about the PO or the Reverend Roy's holy black ass anymore.

The air was running, and all was right with the world.

The knock on his window startled him.

Seeing the man startled him again, the guy right there. Standing outside looking in at him, a duffle bag in his hand. Then walking around to the panel door now, opening it up and, man, fucking getting right in.

"You can go now," Nelson Connor said. "There's nobody else coming on the tour."

Tino pulled out into Congress, the nice ride from the crank turning on him now. He felt himself shaking, but when he looked at his hands, they were still.

The judge in the back talking now. "You know, if I was you, I wouldn't take the freeway. There's a lot of construction. You might be better off on Woodward."

"Yes sir," Tino said, not able to think of anything else to say.

He turned at the light, made his way around the old Hudson's building. Stopped at a red light at Woodward. He wanted to bolt out of the car. Call Gary.

Just be cool, he told himself.

"What's your name, young man?" the judge asked.

"Torino, sir." Hardly getting it out.

"Torino what?"

"Dentz?"

"I'm Nelson Connor. Judge Nelson Connor, with the Third Judicial Circuit. Most people know it as the Wayne County Circuit Court."

"You got business with the pastor?"

"You might say that. But lately, I've been having some real problems with my car. It was awful nice of him to send you over. He said you were part of his parolee program. Is that true?"

Tino nodded, saying nothing. He avoided the rearview.

A couple blocks later, the judge said, "Torino Dentz. Is that with an S–E, or a Z?"

"A Z, sir."

"Good thing, too, huh?"

He looked in the mirror now, the man's eyes smiling, theirs meeting.

"Why's that, sir?"

He felt the judge's hand slap him on the shoulder.

"Either way, really, I'll bet you sure took your share of shit growing up in school."

NELSON CONNOR WALKED through the oak cathedral doors of the Big Rock Church, carrying the gym bag, Torino Dentz trailing ten or fifteen feet behind. The Reverend H. Roy Butler approached rapidly from the altar, his one-inch leather heels echoing in the high vaulted ceiling. He was in his forties, a slim six feet, his hair natural and short, a neatly trimmed full mustache angling downward under his narrow nose. The charcoal suit looked custom-tailored, the work and fabric from Hong Kong.

"Nelson Connor," he said, putting his hand out. "So nice to finally meet you in person."

His grip was firm and friendly.

"The honor is mine, Reverend Butler."

"Can I take that for you?" he asked, looking at the bag.

"No, it's fine. I'm going to work out on the way back."

"Call me Reverend Roy. Everyone does. May I call you—"

" 'Judge' is fine."

"Then you've introduced yourself to Mr. Dentz."

Torino Dentz was lingering near the pews, his hands behind his back, leaning against a bench. He hardly looked in his twenties, but much older in his eyes.

"We had a nice chat," Connor said.

The minister narrowed his eyes at Dentz, who responded by joining them, the Reverend Roy putting his arm around the ex-con's shoulder.

"Mr. Dentz is one of our success stories," Reverend Roy said, starting to walk now, his hand now on the back of his neck.

"Really?" Connor said, walking with them.

"You see," the Reverend Roy said, winding into his pitch, "my philosophy here with many of these men, is that if you put a roof over their heads, take care of their basic needs, then put them in a position of trust, they'll respond appropriately."

Connor stopped. "How has Mr. Dentz responded *inappropriately*? In the past, that is."

The Reverend Roy said, "Torino?"

"I was paroled from Jackson," Dentz said sheepishly. "The reverend here is helping me get on my feet."

"What were you sentenced to prison for?" Connor asked.

"—Robbery."

"I'm sorry," Connor said. "My hearing is a little bad. An old sports injury."

"Armed robbery," Dentz said again.

Connor nodded. "Who was your arresting officer?"

Dentz seemed incapable of answering.

"What I mean is, quite a few officers come through my courtroom. Maybe I know him."

Dentz mumbled, "I was booked by the county."

Connor smiled. "I know most of the Sheriff's Department as well."

Dentz gave up a name. Connor didn't recognize it, but he continued along the same theme, saying, "Well, then, you've both moved on to bigger and better things, haven't you?"

He turned to the Reverend Roy, who was smiling patiently, but looking a little perplexed. Connor said, "His arresting officer is with the county executive now."

The Reverend Roy nodding now.

Connor continued. "Part of the exec's personal detail, in fact. You know the executive, don't you, Reverend?"

"I've met the man," the Reverend Roy said. "But I must confess I've not sat down and talked with him at length."

"Well," Connor said. "You should."

"You know the executive well?"

Connor nodded. "They say it's a nonpartisan office. But, realistically, on the bench you get around. The mayor. The governor. You count on the support of those people. Have you met the governor?"

"Quite honestly, I have not."

Connor said. "We'll have to see what we can do about changing that."

The Reverend Roy's lids widened, making room for all the state dollar signs Connor could see running across his eyes.

"Well," the minister said, holding out his hand, "why don't we step out of the sanctuary? I'm eager to show you the rest of the Big Rock."

"That's why I'm here," Connor said.

Nelson Connor turned to Torino Dentz and winked.

AN HOUR LATER, Tino was feeling like he'd survived the situation. He'd kept cool as the Reverend Roy showed the judge the church movie theater, the preschool, and his TV and radio studios. The hardest part was when he started coming down from the crank, the three of them standing around for thirty fucking minutes in the building the Reverend Roy said he wanted to fill with desks and computers so he could teach word processing and spread sheets, or some bullshit like that.

The hardest part was listening to the names. The judge and the Reverend Roy talking about who they knew, how they knew them and what they could all do for each other, like some kind of name gang bang. He kept thinking of Gary, the motherfucker so sure the judge had one foot with the winos on Michigan Avenue and the other in the courthouse. As far as he could tell, the man was *together*. The Reverend Roy sure thought so, the way he was kissing his ivory ass all the way out the door.

On the way back to the CCB, Tino kept waiting for the judge to say something. But he was silent, sitting back there with that bag next to him. When the judge didn't ask to be dropped off at a gym, Tino started to wonder what was really in the bag, why he even brought it. He was tempted to ask about the workout, but he kept his mouth shut. Took care of his business at the wheel.

They passed a little theater on Woodward. The judge asked him if he remembered when it was a burlesque house, before it started showing hardcore porn.

Tino did. He'd snuck in there when he was ten. But he also remembered what the Reverend Roy said about staying straight.

"Can't say I do, sir," he said.

It was just a crazy coincidence, Tino Dentz decided. The Reverend Roy knew a lot of people. The judge knew a lot of people. Now, they knew each other. That's all.

He could hardly wait to tell Gary about it.

Tino pulled into the traffic circle at the CCB, parking in the same spot where he'd picked the judge up ninety minutes ago.

"Mr. Dentz," the judge said.

Dentz slipped the van into park, looking back at him in the mirror.

"Yes sir."

"Or do you prefer 'Torino'?"

"Tino, actually, sir."

Dentz heard the gym bag unzip.

"Tino, turn around and look at me."

Tino did not want to turn around. He looked at the judge's eyes in the mirror.

"Why's that, sir?"

"*Turn around.* I have something for you."

He didn't like the way the judge was saying it, talking like a guy sitting back there ready to take him out, wanting him to see it coming. Another part of his brain told him, Just turn slowly. Stay fresh, man. Then make your move.

His eyes went to the bag first. Then the judge, sitting there in his pinstripes, his legs slightly apart. In his lap, right over his johnson, he saw a manila envelope.

"What's that, sir?"

"It's for you. Or, maybe it's for Larry."

"Larry?"

"Yeah, five thousand dollars for you *and* Larry Gary, your pal. Or, maybe it's 'Mr. Larry' to you. Maybe Mr. Larry is just going to give you a couple hundred, for being his toady."

Tino didn't know what to say. He ended up saying, "Toady? What's that, sir?"

"A toady is like what you do for the Reverend Roy. Gopher. They used to call it house nigger, but in your case, I think that would be politically incorrect. Basically, Tino, a toady is someone his employer thinks is stupid, but is real good at saying 'Yes sir.' And I have to say, I think you've already demonstrated you're pretty good at that."

"Why would you want to give me five thousand dollars?" Tino said, trying to stay with it.

"Because Mr. Larry wants it. You know, I figured you'd be the one he'd send. Put your ass on the line. You always send the toady to do the shit work."

Dentz was looking at the envelope.

"Go ahead, Tino," the judge said. "Take it."

No, he wanted to pick up the car phone. Call Gary, ask him why the fuck he had set this all up without telling him. Then he thought, No, the judge is bluffing.

Shit, he couldn't call anyone.

"Maybe you want me to count it?" the judge said.

He started sliding hundreds out, one by one.

"No, sir," Tino said, glancing out the windows. Looking for unmarked Chevrolets, wondering now if the judge was wearing a wire. "I don't know what you are talking about."

The judge slid the money back in, leaving the envelope on his lap.

"I think you do. You see, I know about everything there is to know about you. And that goes for Mr. Larry, too. I've gotta say. First a cop party. Now a judge. I say both of you have a peculiar way of getting involved with law enforcement."

Tino turned back around, saying, "I ain't involved in nothin'."

His mouth was so dry his tongue was sticking to his teeth.

"Let's start with murder. You being the toady, I know you did Ozzie. Hell, Larry himself told me that on your phone."

Tino blinked, his eyes glancing at the cellular. Later he would tell himself he should have just told the motherfucker to get out of the van, that he was goddamn crazy, but he didn't do that.

He sat there and listened.

"Now," the judge continued, "I've tried an awful lot of cases, both as an attorney and as a sitting judge. And while the law doesn't differentiate between someone who actually commits homicide, and the one who orders it—they're both supposed to be treated equally in a murder case—juries have a real difficult time with that concept, you follow what I'm saying?"

Tino glanced at the judge's eyes in the mirror.

"Yes, I can see you do. Plus, everyday people, the kind of people who serve on juries, they want to put away the guy who actually did the deed. And often, the other individual, the one who has the toady, is manipulative. Makes a good witness for himself. Is able to convince a jury that he had no intentions of killing anyone. 'That was the toady's idea. The toady went off on a nut.' "

The judge chuckled. "Hell, I've successfully argued that myself. But my clients could pay for a good lawyer. In your case, I think you'd be looking at court-appointed counsel, especially after your old lady found out. You know about those kind of lawyers, don't you, Tino? Tell me, how much time did your last one spend putting together your case?"

Tino Dentz was scared now. More scared than if the man had pulled a gun. He could handle that. He was scared the way the judge had it all worked out—except one thing. The judge was wrong about Gary. Gary would probably flip, sell him out to the prosecutor, before they ever got to court.

The envelope landed on the seat next to him.

"Go ahead," the judge said. "Take it."

Tino got out of the van, wanting to bolt down Congress. Instead, he walked around and slid open the back panel door. Trying to stay cool. Trying to stay with it.

He handed the judge the envelope. "I can't take tips on this job," he said.

The judge dropped it back into the gym bag, never taking his eyes off of him.

The judge said, "You tell Mr. Larry not to send his toady next time. Tell Mr. Larry if he wants his money, he's going to have to come and get it himself."

CHAPTER 22

THE DARKROOM DOOR flew open, the light wiping out the image on the print in the tray of Dektol. Gary turned, pointing a set of tongs at Tino Dentz. "This is a *darkroom*, man. That means you got to keep the room *dark*."

Gary walked out, pushing past Dentz, closing the door behind him. Not that it made any difference, all his meticulous dodging and burning now wasted. He went directly to the sink and began washing, calmly saying, "Tino, sometimes you just don't think."

Gary saw his hands jettison the stream of water, feeling his body coming away from the sink as one unit.

Dentz slammed him hard into the darkroom door.

"You call the fucking man today?"

"What man?" Gary hardly had the air to say it.

"The judge man."

Gary saw Dentz's eyes. His highbeams were on.

"I been down here all day."

"Then he *knows*, man!"

"Who '*knows*'?"

Dentz blinked a couple times.

"You mean, the judge?"

Dentz nodded, gripping his shirt harder.

"Knows what?"

"That I took out his homey."

Gary tried to chuckle, saying, "Tino, I think you're way too bumped. How would *you know* what the judge knows?"

Dentz gathered another inch or two of his French infantry shirt, then slammed him hard again into the door.

"Because he just told me you told him, that's *how*."

"Larry?" Tula Gary called. "What are you doing down there?"

They looked and saw her sandals and the bottom of her smock on one of the upper stairs, the rest of her body above the floor joists.

"Larry, what have I told you about you and your little friends? *I am working*."

"I'm working, too," Gary said between breaths. "I dropped a box of chemicals. That's all."

Her feet stood motionless for a few moments, then they turned, going back up the stairs.

"Tino, listen to me," Gary said. "You got to chill, man, and tell me what the fuck is going on."

IT TOOK HIM a while to talk Tino Dentz down, eventually working him into the darkroom, taking a folding chair inside where he could sit with the safe light on, Gary hoping the warm red amber lighting would help. Gary tried going about his own business calmly, hoping that might also have a soothing effect as Dentz told his story about the judge and the Reverend Roy. Besides, technically he had to have a couple dozen prints done by next week.

When he got to the part about the money, Dentz was blowing crank straight from a Ziploc. An eight ball, with at least two or three grams gone.

Gary removed the negative he was working on—the horse's nose—from the enlarger.

"So where is it?" Gary asked, turning from the Bogen.

"Where's what?"

"The money."

"I wasn't taking anything. I wasn't giving nothing up."

Gary shrugged. "Wise move, considering your predicament."

Dentz powdered his right nostril, then looked up from his chair. "He says, you want the money, you got to get it yourself."

"Me?"

"Yeah, *you*, Gary. He asked for you."

"He say my name?"

"He said '*Larry*.' "

"He say my last name?"

"He said it earlier. Like I said, he *knows*."

Lawrence Gary didn't like it, but in the back of his mind, he'd always knew this development was a possibility, and now he was prepared to accept it, then deal with it.

"So, he *knows*," Gary said, saying it calmly.

Dentz stood up. "So whatup, Gary?" He gestured with the Ziploc. "I want to know exactly what the fuck you gonna do."

"Tino," Gary said. "You need to sit down. And you need to sit real still. You're looking at about a couple grand of equipment in here."

He lowered Dentz into the chair.

"I wonder how he put it all together?" Gary asked.

Dentz was dipping into the Ziploc again, his knee going up and down like a sewing machine.

Gary thought about the Oz's house, how they'd gone back that night and wiped everything down. That was after they looked for a phone book, but didn't find one, the place real easy to search, the Oz's old lady having cleaned him out.

"You tell him, Tino?" Gary asked gently.

"Tell him what?" Dentz's eyes were still on the bag of crank.

"You give the man my name?"

Dentz looked up, perplexed.

"I would understand if you did," Gary said. "You had to be real pressured, spending the time you did with the man."

The whites of Dentz's eyes glowed red in the safe light. "Like I told you, I didn't tell him shit."

"Maybe he saw you in the car that day."

"So what if he did? You see my fucking name tattooed across my head?"

Dentz had a point.

"How about those Maverick whores? You been talking to them?"

Dentz asked, "Talking about what?"

"Talking that you got something big coming your way."

"They for fuckin', not talkin'. What you telling me?"

"I'm telling you the man was in the place, remember?"

Gary could see it. Dentz cranked up, shooting off his mouth. One lap whore tells another. Pretty soon the judge hears the story while he's smoking a cigarette in bed.

Dentz rolled up the Ziploc, sliding it into his pocket. "Yo, Gary," he said. "What makes you so fucking sure it was me?"

Gary turned back to the enlarger table, checking the F-stop on the lens. "It don't matter anyway. The man is a judge. The man has access to records. He gets one of us, it don't take much to get us both."

"Maybe his old lady gave him a name," Dentz said. "You ever think of that?"

"No way."

"No, not 'no way.' Like I been telling you all along, you been getting way too close."

Gary turned around. "I told you, the man doesn't tell her anything."

"Maybe the little woman is slow-walking you, Gary. That thought ever cross your mind?"

"The man got lucky," Gary said. "That's all."

"Is that what you think he's got going, Gary?" Dentz said. "Fucking luck?"

No, it was more than luck, Gary thought. The whole situation reminded him of CCS, the way it worked for all those preps who came out of Cranbrook and Detroit Country Day. Sons of auto execs, sons of doctors and *judges*. Luck had nothing to do with it. They had all the advantages because they had the money. They fucked with him back then. Now he had one fucking with him now.

"So he's made a move," Gary said. "Like I said, so what?"

Gary leafed through a stack of negative sheets, sliding out a five-frame strip. He placed it in the enlarger, then projected the image onto the easel, framing it.

"So, Gary, whatup?" Dentz demanded again.

He knew exactly. "I'm going to make a print," he said. "So stay away from that door."

He took out a sheet of Polycontrast Rapid paper, number two, sliding it into the easel. Set the timer for a 15 seconds at F 5.6, giving him some time to dodge the grainy image. You got a lot of grain when you pushed Tri-X to its limit.

"You going to answer my question, Gary?"

"I'm going to answer your question. Just hold on. I need to do this first."

Gary waited for the timer. When the enlarger light went off, he pulled the eight-by-ten from the easel and dropped it into a tray of Dektol.

"You know, he's probably looking to make a counteroffer," Gary said, gently rocking the tray. "It's part of the process."

"You not listening, man. The only *process* he talkin' about was the kind that can send us both away."

"Can he?" Gary said, agitating the print some with his tongs.

"Man, you didn't hear him. All the cops he knows."

"Look, Tino, think about it. What's really changed? So, he knows now who is putting the squeeze on him. But that doesn't change the fact that he's being squoze."

Dentz said, "Gary, this motherfucker even knows the deputy that took us down on that wedding. Guy's a bodyguard or something now. You should have heard him talking with Reverend Roy."

"He says he knows the guy that wrote up our case?" Gary asked, looking back at him over his shoulder.

Dentz nodded rapidly, licking his dry lips.

Gary pulled the print out of the developer, sliding it into the stop bath for a couple seconds, then removing it and sliding it into the fixer tray.

"Man, he was just fucking with you. Can't you see that? Look at the way he set you up."

"And he can set us up with the police now, too."

Gary turned from the fixer tray, letting the chemical do its work. "He always could have, Tino," he said matter-of-factly. "But he *hasn't*."

"What makes you so sure?"

"If he had, they would have taken you down right there in the van."

"And what makes you so sure he won't?"

"We still got what he wants."

"Then why is he fucking with us?"

"He's trying to set himself up."

"For what?"

"To make a counteroffer, like I said."

"You trying to tell me the man is negotiating?"

"Sure," Gary said. "In his line of work, it's in his nature to deal."

Dentz took the Ziploc out again, as if the bag had all the answers. It made Gary feel good about his resolution to stay out of the dope game. A line here and there. A few all-nighters. Pretty soon you're rolling eights and quarters, the shit just reaching out and grabbing you. Then a hassle hits, and there you are bumped out of your gourd, unable to think.

Gary pointed to the door, saying, "You can open that now."

He took the print to the sink where he had a wash bath, Dentz following him halfway there. He slid the print into the water, trying to calmly explain the central theme to *The Art of Negotiation.*

"Tino, nobody is happy when somebody accepts the first offer. If you think about what's going on here, this whole thing is as simple as that."

"Simple?"

He could feel Dentz pacing behind him. He watched the print oscillate in the wash bath. "Yeah, they had a pretty simple example in the book. About this guy selling a sailboat."

"What the fuck does a sailboat got to do with this deal?"

Gary turned around. "If you will listen, I'm going to tell you."

"I've been listening since I walked in the door, but I ain't heard nothing yet that I fucking like."

Gary leaned back on the utility sink, reaching into his pocket for a smoke. He wanted to take his time with it. Make sure Tino Dentz got the point, presenting what he had in mind with a certain dramatic flair.

"Okay, this guy is selling a sailboat, right? Puts a picture and price on the bulletin board in his country club. Wants ninety thousand dollars, okay? So, this other member who happens to be in the market for a boat sees it. Likes this particular model. In fact, it's just what he wants. He thinks it's a fair price. So he calls the guy and says, Sure, he'll give him the ninety grand. So the guy writes a check, but guess what? A couple days later, both of them are pissed off. Now, why do you think that is?"

Dentz was still now, glaring.

Gary blew out smoke in a long, measured stream. "Well, after he pays the money, the guy selling it is thinking, Shit, I didn't ask enough. I could have sold it for a hundred thou. Meanwhile, the guy who bought the boat is thinking, Man, I paid too much. I should have offered him eighty. The guy took my money too quick. So you see, nobody is happy."

Gary hit the cigarette again. "See, that's why you got to *negotiate*. When you gotta work for it, it makes everybody feel like they got a fair price."

Dentz said, "The man tried to give me the money."

"Tino, you're not listening. You gotta apply what I just told you. This is about the hundred. I told him I wanted a hundred. But he's yet to counter."

"He didn't talk about that."

"No, he offered you the five because he knew you would not take it. That's why he wants to take care of business face-to-face. He thinks he's got some leverage to negotiate now."

"So, you going to see him?"

Gary asked, "What about Bobby? He call you yet?"

"Fuck Bobby," Dentz said. "I got to stay away from people with sheets right now."

Gary asked, "Your PO talk to you?"

"I wouldn't call it talking," Dentz said. "What, you get a visit, too?"

Gary shook his head, thinking it might be prudent to lie, considering Tino Dentz's agitated state.

Dentz stepped closer. "No, they rousting you, too, aren't they?"

Gary turned around, checking the print wash.

"So, *whatup*, Gary? I'm asking you for the last fucking time."

Gary turned around, dropping his Kool on the floor between them, stepping on it. "I'm thinking maybe the time has come to apply some leverage of our own."

Dentz said, "You fucking wack, man. Crazy, too."

Gary reached into the bath, pulling the print out, but Dentz already was moving rapidly toward the stairs.

Gary followed, saying, "Yo, Tino, you need to check out this photo."

"Show it to that little woman of yours."

Gary stopped at the foot of the stairs, looking down at the print. Pretty grainy, he thought, but it worked.

Dentz, two steps up, spun around.

"Mr. Larry ain't negotiating with fucking nobody," Dentz said, his voice different now.

"Mr. Larry?" Gary said.

Gary heard the hammer lock back, then looked up as the Taurus revolver touched his nose.

"Larry," Tula Gary called from upstairs. "Is that you?"

CHAPTER 23

DURING LUNCH FRIDAY at the police gym, he worked out first on the body sack, then moved to the speed bag. He was surprised how easily the rhythm came after, what, a dozen years? He thought about Torino Dentz, then Bobby Tank in his courtroom. The way the guy sulked over from the jury box and stood before him with a dazed look. The guy with hair so dirty it separated at his scalp in clumps. Standing next to Tank, Darryl Lensley looked like F. Lee Bailey.

Nelson Connor thought about Lawrence Gary, and the black bag became faceless. He hit it one more time, hard, and hoped Jack Crilly was right. He'd probably never hear from the man again.

When he returned from the gym a message was waiting. The slip said: "Kelly. See her today at the club."

"Who's Kelly?" Barbara asked, raising her eyebrows.

"A friend of a friend," Connor said.

He put off thinking about Kelly Johns, concentrating on miscellaneous matters in his courtroom that afternoon. He sentenced four defendants, one of them the beer-truck driver who'd beat his wife to death with his bare hands. The guy had agreed to forgo trial and plea, Connor promising him thirty years for manslaughter—meaning he'd serve ten to twenty with good time—if his probation report checked out.

It didn't.

"Sir, I'm sentencing you to one hundred years," Connor said.

If the guy took it, which he wouldn't, Connor fully expected to be overturned by the Court of Appeals for exceeding the sentencing guidelines established by the Michigan Supreme Court.

His lawyer, a general practitioner from one of the western suburbs, asked to approach. The attorney was hardly thirty. They both knew he wasn't ready to take a murder case to trial.

"What gives, Your Honor?" he whispered.

"You got the probation report. Your client lied to me. He said there was no history of violence between him and his wife. The presentence report showed Dearborn police had been called to his address *twenty-six times* in three years. You can't say he wasn't warned when he pled, Counsel. I'll put it on the record, if you wish."

The attorney sighed. "I don't think that's going to be necessary."

The driver was waiting back at the lectern, smoldering. He was still in belly chains, Connor making a point earlier to Lewis to leave them on. Connor's eyes never left him as his attorney walked back. The attorney said something in his client's ear, then the defendant shook his head, saying something back.

The attorney said, "Your Honor, in light of the sentence, my client now wishes to recall his guilty plea to manslaughter and ask for a jury trial on the evidence."

"That is his option," Connor said. "I'll send the case back up to the assignment clerk." He looked at the defendant, saying, "Sir, considering the nature of the offense, I'm still ordering you held without bond."

Maybe he'd get lucky, Connor thought, draw Leonard Talbot on a blind assignment. Or, he could call the assignment clerk himself, ask for a favor. Steer the case to Leonard. No, that would be pushing it, and he was already pushing on other fronts. Pushing the justice system, which really wasn't a system at all. It was a conglomeration of systems, each judge operating his own model of something called justice. It was that way because it had to be. Without it, the lawyers would bury them in paper, and the defendants would be lined up down Jefferson Avenue three miles to Belle Isle.

"All rise," Barbara said.

In chambers, he hung up his robe and sat for a while, just thinking, his feet on the corner of the desk.

Lewis came in, putting away his Colt.

"They don't learn, do they, Judge?" Lewis said.

"What's that?" asked Connor.

"The truck driver. Lying like that when he pled."

"He was just trying to cover his ass. I guess we showed him what that gets you in here, didn't we?"

"Sure did," Lewis said, at the door now. "Good night, Judge."

"Good night, Lewis," Connor said.

Connor eyes focused on his robe. He thought about other lies. Not just one, but a bunch. To Katherine. To his court aide. To Barbara. To Lewis. Lying to people he cared about, not to leave out those he didn't. To Densely. To the public defender he jerked from the Bobby Tank case, telling him in chambers he wasn't adequately representing his client. To the Reverend Roy, the guy trying to do something decent, and Connor just greasing the man. Hell, to Torino Dentz. He could lie to them. But he punished those who lied to him? No, he told himself, that was because he was wearing the robe. The robe was the institution. They were lying to the robe, not him.

He felt uncomfortable being a liar. Particularly such a damn good one at that.

His phone rang; no one in the office now to pick it up.

Lawrence Gary, he thought.

"This is Judge Connor."

He could hear music in the background.

"Hey, this is Kelly," she said. "You coming to see me, or what?"

THIRTY MINUTES LATER, he walked into the Maverick. He could smell the place this time. Beer. Liquor. Perfume. He could smell the crystal blocks in the urinals when he stopped to splash a little water on his face.

She slid into the booth next to him, calling the waitress over, ordering a Virgin Mary. He didn't want anything. Not anything that went with his program, at least.

"You have to order something," the waitress said. "House rules."

"One of those five-dollar cups of coffee," he said.

The waitress disappeared into the crowd.

"Do we have to meet here?" Connor asked. She'd insisted they not talk on the phone.

"I haven't been spending much time at home," she said. She readjusted the strap on her top. "The guy came and talked to me."

"What guy?" Connor asked.

"The cop who busted Jimmy. You know, the guy who was trying to get in my pants. He's got Jimmy's case."

Christ, he thought. He got busy trying to remember exactly what story he'd told her, so he could get another set of lies in line.

"Jesus, he asked me all kinds of questions," she continued.

"What kind?"

"Same kind you did. Who Jimmy knew. All that."

Connor looked in her eyes.

"Don't worry, I didn't say anything about you. But I was wondering if somebody should tell him about that Larry guy."

The waitress interrupted, bringing the drinks.

When she walked off, Connor said, "Well, I passed the name along. But I'm not sure it checked out."

"Well, that's the other thing I wanted to tell you," she said, a look of intrigue on her face. "The freaking guy was here. Can you believe it? He comes in here once in a while with this other dude who's been dealing meth to some of the girls."

"Larry?"

She nodded.

"You said you never saw the guy," he asked. "How did you know it was him?"

"One of the other girls called me to their table. This guy that this Larry was with, wanted a two-on-one. So one introduction leads to another, and boom. It's him. I thought you'd want to know about it. And the cop, too."

"Black guy?" Connor asked. "The guy he was with."

"Right," she said. "How did you know?"

He hesitated, then said, "I've heard a few things from the cops."

"Funny, the cop didn't mention it."

"They play it close to their chest," he said.

She nodded, sipping on her drink with a straw, looking at him with a certain innocence.

Connor asked, "The cop come in here, too?"

She shook her head, still sipping.

"He take you downtown?" Connor asked.

"He came right to my apartment. Stayed nearly a freaking hour, telling me all about Jimmy's body. Not a pleasant way to wake up."

"What do you mean, his body? They found him?"

"You didn't know that?"

Connor shook his head. "I haven't talked to anyone in a couple of days."

"They found him yesterday," she said.

"Where?"

"Someplace downriver. In some old warehouse or something. The cop was really gross. Telling me how the rats had gotten to Jimmy and all this shit."

"What did you tell him?"

"I told him the same thing I told you, except about Larry. That's why I wanted to talk to you. I thought somebody should tell him where he can find this Larry guy."

Connor sipped the coffee. It was burnt and bitter. He asked, "What do you think? You think this Larry is involved?"

"The guy is definitely weird. He carries these cameras, like he's shooting for Vogue or something. Then both these guys try to get me to leave with them. I said no thanks. I wanted to say 'in your dreams,' but I didn't like the vibes."

"From which one?"

"From both of them," she said.

She looked him in the eyes, then looked at his coffee.

"Say," she said. "You on the wagon or something?"

Connor was glad she changed the subject. "Something like that," he said.

"How long?"

Connor thought about it momentarily. "Next week, I believe, it'll be a month."

"I've been trying to quit myself."

"Drinking?" he asked.

"Everything," she said.

"Why?" he asked.

"This thing with Jimmy. Now this cop again. It's all getting too crazy. Trouble is, it's not easy working in this place straight."

He looked in her eyes, saw a look he knew firsthand. He knew what he was supposed to do. He knew what the program said. He was supposed to carry the message now. That's what everyone at the meetings called it. Tell her about the meetings. Tell her his own story, how he hit his bottom. Lay it all out.

But he couldn't do that, not without lying.

"Try AA," was all he said. "It works."

But she wasn't looking at him anymore. She was looking over his shoulder. He started to turn, then he saw her abruptly reach behind her back and drop her top.

"Don't move," she said.

Just like that she was on him, straddling her legs across his lap. Her hips began moving with the music. She pressed her breasts together with her palms and touched them to his face.

"Kelly," he said, looking up. "What are you doing?"

She dropped her head, her long dark hair cascading into his face, the smell of her shampoo hitting his nostrils, then the inner caverns of his head.

"Shhh," she said insistently in his ear. "Grab hold of my ass."

When he didn't, she placed his hands there for him.

"Just pretend like you're enjoying this."

He was, instantly, but he didn't want to.

"Hmm, Your Honor," she whispered feeling him beneath her now. "I guess you don't have to pretend."

"Kelly," he said. "I didn't come here for this."

"I know," she said, staying close, smothering him with her body. He could hear AC/DC belting out "All Night Long." But he couldn't see anything but the stage strobe, breaking through the thick strands of her dark hair.

He lifted his head slightly, his mouth near her ear. "Kelly, you are a beautiful woman, but I really do have to get home."

"Not yet," she said, staying close. "Maybe the creep will leave after a couple of songs—if he sees I'm occupied."

"Who will leave?"

"The cop I was telling you about," she said. "He's standing over there by the door."

HE THOUGHT ABOUT the homicide detective for five miles, wondering what he'd seen and what he hadn't. Then his thoughts turned to Katherine, the story Ozzie told him about lying to his wife about the dancer. He thought about getting the click, the way the click kept you from doing so much thinking. And that's when he remembered.

Tonight was his son's final game.

He arrived in the sixth inning, walking directly to the first-base side, taking a position on the chain-link fence next to a couple of other fathers. He waved to Kace, who was sitting in the small set of bleachers with other spectators. She waved back enthusiastically, smiling, not giving a hint that he was late. She'd always been so perfectly good at covering for him. He didn't like her doing that for him anymore.

He could see John on the bench, his team at bat. He thought about going over, saying hello and good luck, then decided against it. He'd made only the first game that year. If he went over now, he'd only put the pressure on.

He found himself not watching the game, but looking at the expanse of grass and the amber sun, heading for the treetops beyond left field. He could smell the grass, and it smelled good. And then he realized he couldn't remember the last time he'd smelled it, though, Christ, he'd sure played his share of golf over the years, and golf courses were certainly grassy.

It had been happening a lot lately, even with the mess he was in. Noticing buildings downtown for the first time, wondering when they'd been remodeled. Noticing new employees at the CCB, only to learn they'd been working there for years. People, places, and things *looked* different. People acted differently than he remembered them acting. Actually, if he was honest about it, he didn't really remember how they acted when he was drinking. Sometimes, he felt like Rip Van Winkle, coming out of a long sleep.

He saw John walking into the on-deck circle.

"How many out?" he asked no one in particular.

A guy in shorts and a rugby shirt spoke up. "One, but we could be in trouble."

"We're behind?" Connor asked.

"Two runs," the guy said. "But the kid on deck can't hit."

Connor couldn't think of anything to say.

He looked back over at John, his boy was watching the pitcher, the bat on his shoulder. Between pitches, he'd take a couple of swings. He was gangly, more gangly than he remembered his son being, his legs and arms a little long for his torso. He remembered how he was that way at his age, how it made him awkward, until someone showed him what you could do with a reach like that at the Kronk.

Connor told himself, Go show him. But what would the people in the bleachers think? You show up at one game, and now you're a fricking coach. When he was drinking, he wouldn't give a damn about the bleachers. But now he did.

So fuck 'em, he told himself.

Connor knelt down at the fence behind the on-deck circle.

"John," he said quietly, the boy looking.

"Get your timing down. See the ball."

His son looked at him with puzzlement. Connor wasn't sure if he was puzzled that he was there, or just didn't understand what he meant.

Connor made a batting motion with his fists. "When the pitcher throws to the batter, you watch the ball and swing as if you were at the plate. *See* the ball. Watch it all the way in. That way you'll have him down when you're at bat."

John nodded, then took a swing.

Connor walked slowly back to first, feeling the eyes from the bleachers on him, but not looking.

Back at the fence, he studied the action at the plate, the teenage ump signaling two-and-one. The kid at bat was slightly bull-legged and moved like an athlete, one of those who seemed to be born with it.

The bull-legged kid fouled another off.

He looked back at his son, his legs spread now in the circle, concentrating now, swinging with awkward determination as the bull-legged kid confidently watched his third ball sail by.

Nelson Connor felt something deep and dark, something that mixed pity and guilt and anxiety all together and came at him like a wave of nausea. His boy, out there all summer. Out there this week. Tonight.

And where was he?

Dealing with bottom feeders. And maybe now, a cop.

The pitcher walked the bull-legged kid. Bases loaded.

John walked to the plate.

Everyone was quiet around him now, the word probably spreading who he was among the fathers along the fence.

"C'mon, son," one of them finally yelled. "You can do it."

The bleachers chimed in with encouragement.

"See the ball, big John," Connor yelled.

That and nothing else. He could see himself. Only guy there in a suit, diamond dust all over his oxfords. Showing up late.

He looked over at John, cocked and ready.

Even before his only son struck out, Nelson Connor already had decided. He was going to have to change the way he'd been doing things.

Either that, or drink.

CHAPTER 24

"DID I EVER tell you the story about the red dress and the blue dress?" Jack Crilly asked.

A Greek waiter lit the three plates of saganaki at a nearby table, yelling, "Oopah!" as the cheese burst into flames. They were in Pegasus, the winged horse on the restaurant's menus.

"I don't believe you did," Nelson Connor said.

Crilly buttered his bread. "Story goes: Alk and his wife have a big formal event that night. Alk leaving in the morning for work. Wife says, 'Honey, would you pick up my red dress from the cleaners?' He says, sure. But he has a tough day. Halfway home, he realizes he's forgotten about the dress, and now he hasn't time to stop. So all the way home, he's thinking, Shit, she's going to be pissed. There's going to be an argument. She's going to say I'm an inconsiderate son of a bitch. I'll tell her to fuck off. The night is ruined. So, by the time the alk walks into his own house, he's pretty pissed himself. She's standing there. He shouts, 'You know, that goddamn red dress of yours, well, I fucking forgot it.'"

Crilly paused. "And you know what she says?"

Connor's eyes asked.

"She shrugs and says, 'That's okay. I'll wear the blue one instead.'"

Crilly laughed. Connor smiled, but he was still worried.

Crilly took a bite of the bread and said, "I've lost a few years of my life worrying about that dress."

Connor said, "I'm sorry I involved you in all this."

Crilly waved the bread. "I can't say I haven't enjoyed it. Still, it's always been your ass on the line, not mine." He looked past Connor, then said, "Here he comes."

Connor didn't turn around. He waited for Michael Cooney, who shook his hand vigorously, then slid into the seat across from him. Cooney reached for a menu and turned to their sponsor, saying, "Jack, you crusty son of a bitch, how are ya?"

Before he could answer, he turned back to Connor. "Jack's a good man, Nelson. He's saved my ass more than once. I presume he's now in the process of saving yours."

When they ordered, Connor watched him, asking himself what was it about the man that got under his skin. He was dressed in khakis and a polo shirt, his wavy red hair slightly disheveled. He'd always been easygoing. He'd always been glib and irreverent, qualities Connor generally admired in others. In fact, there was really nothing about Michael Cooney that Nelson Connor hadn't always wanted for himself.

"The fried squid," Connor told the waiter. "And bring us a plate of the saganaki as well."

Crilly didn't perpetuate the small talk. "Mike, Nelson here is alooking for a little guidance. He's got some sobriety going for him now, and I told him you might be able to help him out."

Cooney waited for Connor to say something. When he didn't, he asked, "A problem on the bench?"

Connor nodded.

The waiter brought the saganaki, lighting it, then dousing it with lemon juice. When he left, Connor could not find the words to begin.

"That bad?" Cooney asked.

Connor nodded.

"I'll tell you what," Cooney said. "Take it from a theoretical perspective. The county prosecutor has yet to find a way to charge obstruction for an academic exercise."

Connor looked at Crilly, who gave him an encouraging nod. Then he began in third person. "Let's say a jurist found himself in the position where, against his better judgment, he'd sentenced a defendant with whom he'd had a long-standing personal relationship."

It took several minutes to lay out the details. He detailed what he saw as his culpability: The meeting at the bar. The cocaine and the marker. The failure to disclose at sentencing. The sentence itself. Then, he moved into what he considered the second level of impropriety: His retaliation. The use of court resources. Dodging the cop circling the case. He included everything but the body. That was going to the grave with him. Besides, police had already found what was left of Jimmy Osborne.

The body was a moot point now.

Cooney was into a plate of moussaka when he finished. "What about mitigating circumstances?" he asked. "That's always in the mix."

"Let's say the jurist isn't making any excuses for himself. As far as he's concerned, he did what he did."

"Still, from the standpoint of a tenure commission investigation, you can't discount the relevancy."

"Relevant to what?"

"The sentence, for example. Did the drug dealer's sentence conform to the presentence report and his sentencing practices at the time?"

Connor nodded. "The sentence exceeded his court aide's recommendations. As for his prevailing sentencing philosophy, that's changed somewhat since then."

Cooney asked, "What about the jurist's commitment to his own rehabilitation? Presuming, of course, he would approach the proper authorities in a spirit of full disclosure."

"That's why he would be disclosing in the first place."

"And there would be other mitigating factors to consider."

"Such as?"

"It certainly would be helpful if the jurist went to the appropriate police agency and revealed what he knew. After all, there is a serious felony involved."

"The jurist realizes that fully," Connor said. "After disclosing to the tenure commission, that would be his next stop."

Crilly interrupted. "You people ever talk English?"

Neither one of them answered.

Michael Cooney set his fork down, then broke the silence. "Jesus Christ, Nelson," he said. "This is pretty goddamn ugly."

Connor was surprised. Mike Cooney, no longer the *State Bar Review* poster boy, or the official with his future in his hands. Mike Cooney, his chin between his knuckles now, looked as if the situation was his problem as well.

He leaned forward, lowering his voice. "Nelson, speaking from one alk to another, the program is pretty specific about a situation like this. The program wants you to get honest, but not to the point where you have to build and carry your cross, as well as stage your own public crucifixion. The idea is to get rid of the goddamn cross, you follow what I'm saying?"

"That's what I'm trying to do," Connor said.

"He needs to stay sober, Mike," Crilly said.

Cooney put his hands on the table, switching back into academic mode. "Does the jurist have any friends at 1300?"

"Depends whether he's booted their cases or not," Connor said.

Cooney nodded, thinking. "I could be of some help there. I know the new inspector in Homicide. He could get the dirty cop out of the picture."

"That's a start," Connor said.

"Still, any investigation, as you well know, will result in statements, arrest, testimony. I don't see any way that you—that the jurist—can avoid having this go public. That's what I mean about ugly."

Connor looked at the squid he'd ordered but hadn't touched. He began cutting some of the tentacles. "He'd have to ride that out, if his family was willing. It might help if he knew what was waiting for him at the end of the line."

"Like what?" Cooney asked.

"What's the range?"

"We do several hundred private admonishments a year. You know the drill. Letters that warn judges about their misconduct."

"What kind of misconduct?" Connor asked.

"You want examples?"

Connor nodded.

"Unjustifiably jailing a lawyer for contempt. Creating an appearance of preferential treatment. We had a district judge who arraigned a friend's brother. Another heard a motion after being disqualified from a case. That kind of thing. Their names are not made public, even though in some cases, their misconduct did receive news coverage."

"Is that really an admonishment?" Connor asked.

"If a judge reforms, the commission feels there's no need to perpetuate his troubles. Then, of course, there's public admonishment, which is self-explanatory."

Connor said, "And I've seen you guys pull somebody's ticket."

"All out banishment, yes. That usually involves assigning another jurist to do a full investigation, then having him prepare a full report for the commission to consider. That's done in extreme cases." Cooney paused. "Is your jurist worried about that?"

Connor said, "He's worried about supporting his family. He wants to be able to practice law."

Michael Cooney wiped his mouth, thinking. "If this somehow can be handled without the rockets' red glare, that would help."

"What if it isn't?" Connor asked.

"I'd worry more about the voters of Wayne County than the commission. Nobody padded somebody's wallet. That's a sure-bet banishment. I would be thinking admonishment. Possibly private. At the worst, a public one."

"How?" Connor said. His situation seemed worse.

Cooney smiled and said, "That's where your friends and those mitigating circumstances come in."

AFTER COONEY LEFT, Jack Crilly ordered baklava.

"Feel better?" he asked.

Connor nodded.

"I hope you didn't hold anything back."

"What makes you say that?" Connor asked.

"A thing you hear around the program."

"What *thing*?"

"You're only as sick as your secrets," Crilly said.

THAT EVENING, HE spent the time with Kace and John. Really spent it, not just in the house, with his mind off somewhere else. He sat in the living room, playing with the squirrel monkey, of all things. The animal had never been fond of him, but tonight it seemed to be warming up. It started when the monkey scampered into the living room, Connor's car keys in his hands. When he called, the animal jumped on his lap and handed them over, looking around, making no eye contact, like it was trying to distance itself from the act of stealing them.

His son was eating popcorn on the couch with Kace, watching the double episode of *Cops* they ran on Saturday nights. He called, "Squirrelly."

John handed the monkey a popcorn kernel, but rather than consuming it, the animal shot like a bullet back to Connor's lap, offered it, again looking around.

It went on for several minutes, the monkey shuttling the popcorn over a kernel at a time. Connor began sending it back to John and Kace with deliveries of his own, dollar bills, credit cards, his State Bar of Michigan card.

They became hysterical. It was the animal's demeanor, the way it rocketed back and forth, crossing the living room as if it were running a gauntlet. The animal unable to laugh as they laughed harder, until their sides hurt.

That night, Kace took longer than usual in the bathroom as he lay waiting. He heard the shower running as he half watched *Saturday Night Live,* thinking about how to tell her, what to say. When she came out, she wore only a short terrycloth robe. She lay down next to him, flipping her hair behind her ear. She kissed him, then reached for the remote, flipping off the TV.

"You sure you want to do that?" he asked.

They'd used the TV to camouflage their lovemaking for years.

"John's asleep," she said. "I want to *hear* you."

He found himself trembling, like some kind of high-school kid. He looked at her, thinking, Who is this woman? Certainly no high-school girl. Or a dancer. But a woman. Then he wondered, Had he ever made love to her totally sober? He couldn't remember making love to any woman without *something*. Wine. A couple beers. Or a joint, Van Morrison, and at least 40 watts of stereo power back in college.

He couldn't shut off his mind, until he felt her fingers spread into the back of his hair, pulling at the roots gently.

Then his thoughts slipped away.

And he let go.

Afterward, after he didn't reach for his cigarettes on the night-stand, he lay on his back, listening to her breathing, his arms behind his head.

"Kace, I'm being blackmailed," said.

She rolled over on her side, putting her head in her hand. She grinned, as if he had just made some kind of joke. When he didn't break the silence, she said, "What are you talking about?"

He was looking at the ceiling. "I messed up. On the bench. Didn't disqualify myself from a case. Some people found out about it. Now they want money."

"Who? What case?"

"You remember Ozzie."

She squinted her eyes. "Ozzie from school?"

"He got busted. His case landed in my court."

"You dismissed it?"

No, he said. He'd sentenced him and he knew him. The way the rules were, that was enough.

"What kind of blackmail?" she asked.

"They want a hundred thousand dollars."

She laughed nervously. "You've got to be kidding me."

"I wish I was."

"Who are these people?"

"A couple of ex-cons. People who knew Ozzie. People who know the system. They got lucky. They stumbled into it."

"What are their names?

He turned on his side, looking at her. He could see a hundred questions in her eyes.

"That's not important," he said.

"It's not?"

He told her what was important was what he wanted to do next. "I'm thinking about going to the police," he said. "But that could mean trouble for all of us, especially if the papers get hold of this."

She lay her head on his chest. "How long has this been going on?" she asked.

"Since before I went to Brighton."

"Why didn't you tell me?"

"I—"

Her fingers quickly came up, touching his mouth. "No," she said. "You don't have to answer."

She seemed to know his answer. He could tell by the way she was holding him now, the way her cheek was soft and warm on his chest.

They lay that way for a while. He was glad she stopped him. He didn't want to get into the body, the details he feared would probably scare her half to death.

When she spoke, she said, "I went to one of those meetings."

"What meeting?" he asked.

"Al-Anon, for people who love people like you." She put her chin on his chest, looking him in the eyes. "I do, you know."

"I love you, too."

They didn't say anything for a while, just feeling it.

Then he asked, "What do they do at those meetings?"

"They said that I was the one who had to change now. They said people like us get all tangled up in the person with the problem. Then when the problem goes away, we're kind of left out in the cold. They call it co-dependency."

"Sounds like some kind of cough medicine, doesn't it?"

"Sounds like that guy on *Saturday Night Live*."

"Maybe we should be talking to ourselves in a mirror," Connor said. They laughed.

Then Kace asked, "What do you want to do?"

He'd been thinking about it all afternoon. He said the police might arrest the extortionists outright. Or, they might want to set up some kind of meeting, have him wear a wire, and get evidence on tape. Either way, he said, he'd prefer she was out of town.

"We've got Labor Day," he said. "Why don't you and John go to the cottage? When it's over, I'll drive up. God knows by then, we'll need a break."

She frowned. "He's going to Cedar Point with one of his teammates this weekend. When you didn't say anything about the north, I told him to go ahead."

"Can't he cancel?"

"He's been talking about riding those new coasters they've got all week."

Connor asked, "How long they going?"

"They won't be back until Monday. They've got a cottage on Johnson's Island, right across the water from the amusement park."

He began scratching her back. "Well, isn't that fortuitous?"

"What?"

"That means we can be up there alone."

"We could just drive up together," she said.

"I'd rather you go early."

She didn't say anything for a few moments. He could tell she didn't want to do it.

"Is it going to be dangerous?" she asked.

"Not with the right people involved."

She looked up, into his eyes. "You sure you want to do this alone?"

"I've got to, Kace," he said.

He stroked her hair for a while.

"All the shit I've put you through," he said. "Now this. And in some ways this is worse."

She looked up at him again. "Hey, I knew what I was getting into."

"You did?"

"Sure, I asked you about that when we first met, remember?"

He searched his mind, coming up with nothing.

"Oh, come on," she said. "How do you get an attorney out of a tree?"

"Cut the rope," Nelson Connor said.

CHAPTER 25

THE NEXT WEEK, Lawrence Gary went proactive. He drove his mother's Escort to the CCB, took the elevator to the seventeenth floor and sat down in Nelson Connor's courtroom, the benches teeming with witnesses and attorneys and families of defendants. They never made eye contact, the judge busy laying down the law to a customer, Gary checking out the architectural detail that told the big lie. He eyed the white recessed dome in the ceiling, illuminated with baffled lights, as if the man below was enshrined. He saw a wall of solid Italian marble behind him. On the rose-and-white stone, he saw the 3-D stainless-steel type: The True Administration of Justice Is the Finest Pillar of Good Government.

Moving, Lawrence Gary thought. He was so moved he got up and left.

In the hallway, something else caught his eye, just beyond the people sitting on benches. He saw a door and a short hall leading to an office behind Nelson Connor's courtroom. The door was open and attorneys were there. They had to be attorneys, with their large leather briefcases and white shirts and summer-weight wool suits. But it wasn't the accessories that stopped him. It was a hundred-dollar bill one lawyer carried between his two fingers, impatiently tapping it against his leg as he waited in the line.

Gary moved into the little hall, leaning against the wall, looking bored. He could see into the office now, a secretary sitting at a desk. There, he could see one of the attorneys leaning over, signing something, then counting out to the gal ten twenties. The gal gave him two blue tickets. The gal smiled and said, "Hope to see you there."

He recognized her voice.

Next, please.

The next attorney pulled out a checkbook in black pebbled leather and started writing. The gal handed him six of the blue tickets as he ripped the check from the book.

Gary stepped into the line, only two others in front of him now.

When he reached the desk, the gal looked up. "Can I help you?"

He looked at the ashtray on her desk, thinking about all the No Smoking signs he'd seen in the building. "How much for the tickets?" he asked, smiling.

"Are you an attorney?"

"I'm with *Detroit Legal News*," he said.

"Oh, I'm sorry, hon," she said, satisfied now. "The tickets to the fundraiser are one hundred dollars. We're holding it this year at Trapper's Alley. There'll be hors d'oeuvres and a cash bar. Weekend after Labor Day."

"Band?" Gary asked.

"Pardon?" she asked.

"Are you going to have a band?"

"There'll be music, hon. Probably a deejay."

"So, for a hundred bucks I get to listen to some records, eat those little meatballs and buy myself a drink?" Gary asked.

She leaned forward. "It's a *fundraiser*, hon," she said, no smile anymore. "Break it down into two words."

"For what?" Gary asked.

Her eyes went back the desk. "His reelection fund," she said, saying it routinely, then looking back up, curiously. "Do I know you?"

"Not likely," he said.

Suddenly, there he was, in his robe, stopping at her desk. His Honor, looking him right in the eyes, nodding, smiling, then saying, "Nice to see you."

The big lie continuing, Gary decided, as Nelson Connor dropped two files on her desk and said, "Barbara, I'm going to need these moved to next week."

And he was gone, through a door, the robe flowing just a little behind him.

The gal looked back up, impatience on her face. Gary could feel attorneys behind him now, a new line forming.

"Do you want a ticket, or don't you?" she asked.

Gary smiled. "I think I'll wait and see how he does in the election, *hon.*"

Afterward, he drove to the main branch of the Detroit Public Library and worked with the microfilm. They didn't have an index for the *Detroit Legal News*, but he found what he was looking for on the third spool. Took November, December, and January and just went back four years. Four years ago the county election commission reported what every candidate for the bench raised.

Later, he drove to downtown Royal Oak and walked the streets, thinking, getting into a slow burn, not fighting it. He thought, You lay it out like it is, give the man the opportunity to negotiate in good faith, offering reasonable terms. And the man fucks with you, all the while running his little shakedown. They didn't even do that in Jackson, where everyone was looking for an angle. In Jacktown, that got you killed.

As he walked, the coffeeshops and outdoor cafes he passed began to irritate Lawrence Gary, the places filled with people sucking on lattes, reading the *Times*, trying to look like they were really into it. He thought, You are in *Dee-troit*, assholes; reading about New York is not going to change that fact.

Gary stopped in front of Noir Leather, checking out the window treatment, the blond manikin in a leather bikini, dog collar and storm trooper boots. He walked inside, ignoring the girl who asked if she could show him anything. He spent a minute looking in the display cabinet filled with masks, gags, and other S&M regalia. Then the thought suddenly popped into his head. He wished he had a piece on him. Take out a big blue Ruger Redhawk, grab the bitch from behind the counter and stick it in her mouth. Make her put on a bunch of merchandise. Leave her there with a dog muzzle on, cuffed and chained, clearing out the register on his way out.

Leather and lace, he thought. It could work.

But not now. Not here.

He got back in the Escort and drove to Record Time, a Detroit record store jammed with bins of imports and vintage Detroit techno, plus some newer acid-house sides. All first-rate hard house, none of that CD shit they sell in shopping malls. He was looking at Kraftwerk and Orbital when the deejay with the buzz cut handed him a card, saying his 'jay name was Skinbracer, that his day gig was clerking the store, but he was spinning raves at night. The invite was on the card for Thursday night, ten until dawn. It didn't give the location, just had an address on Gratiot Avenue, "The map point," the guy explained. "You go to the map point and buy your ticket there. They give you directions to the rave."

"No shit?" Gary said. He knew the ritual, the promoters coming up with mystery like that to build exclusivity and intrigue. He was doing raves before they started filling up with tourists, old hippies checking out the scene, and teenagers from Grosse Pointe fucked up on meth.

The deejay said, "We're trying to be real discreet because cops are saying we need to be taking out insurance policies for liability and all this other shit."

"So where is the event?" Gary asked.

"You got to buy the ticket, man."

Gary had a camera with him. "Maybe I'd like to cover it. Maybe do a little photo essay for the underground."

"You a photographer?"

"No, I'm an ex-convict, newly released from the State Prison of Southern Michigan. I just carry this around for conversation."

The deejay grinned, then asked, "*Orbit* mag?"

Gary started leafing through the imports again, ignoring him entirely.

"Why you want to know?" he persisted. "Most people like the mystery."

"Maybe I'm busy with other jobs. Maybe I don't want to spend Thursday night driving the ghetto looking for some fucking hole in the wall."

The deejay leaned closer. "This no hole, man."

"Tell me about it."

"It's 1315 Broadway. Nice."

"Downtown?" Gary asked.

"Only a couple blocks from police headquarters."

"I thought you were worried about cops."

"They come with helmets and sticks."

"So why make it close?"

"Being close, that's what makes it a rave."

Back in his car, he started thinking about the envelope of prints he had with him for his appointment with his PO. Mail the PO six ounces of piss and take his chances, he decided. Get Tino Dentz's vibrator going. Get him straightened out with the whole story. Then drop in on Katherine Connor with the prints of the racetrack.

The time has come, he decided, to get fucking paid.

WEDNESDAY EVENING, AS he walked with her to the Grand Cherokee, Connor was thinking of how good a four days it had been. On Sunday, they'd gone to some antique shops in Saline, Kace buying an old french-fry press, saying her mother had one just like it. They'd peel potatoes and make bowls of fries at the cottage, fry them in lard. Maybe take a couple days off their life span, but it was worth it, she said. He hit noon meetings, leaving his nights free. Being with her was like he remembered it back in law school. He came home with motions, but didn't go into the study. She sat next to him, reading a biography of Margaret Thatcher, while he worked on the briefs, breaking to make wisecracks with John about the hair on the news anchors on TV.

He half expected Lawrence Gary to make one more run at him. In fact, he wished he had. It may have forced him to take care of it *now*. Instead, he procrastinated. He told himself, If Gary hasn't called, what's the rush? He kept thinking if he gave it time, it might just all go away. But then the voice inside would tell him he was fooling himself. When he listened to the voice, he always reached the same conclusion. It came down to justice.

Ozzie was dead. Somebody had to pay for that.

Katherine, her pillow under her arm, talked about the squirrel monkey as he looked over the suitcases in the back of the Jeep. When it had to be fed. How it needed to spend its evenings out of his cage. Where he had to take it.

"I've reserved the boarding at the vet for the weekend," she said. "You can take him in Thursday if you get home in time. They're open to seven. Or, you can take him in Friday morning. For God's sake, don't forget."

"I'll remember."

"No, I better call you and remind you."

"You think I'm going to leave him here? Let him rot in his cage all weekend?"

She tossed the pillow in the luggage department. "No, I think you've got a lot of stuff on your mind."

He closed the hatch.

"Connor," she said. "When are you going to do it?"

"I've given everyone Friday off," he said. "I'll get an early start. I ought to hit Mackinaw sometime in the early afternoon."

She reached out and adjusted the collar on his golf shirt, then fastened his bottom button, looking at him with curious eyes.

He asked, "You sure you want to make this drive tonight? Five hours. You'll be doing at least half of it in the dark."

"But no traffic," she said. "And that's not what I'm asking."

"You mean the police?" he asked.

She nodded.

"I'm going to set the meeting up for Friday morning."

"With these people?" She looked worried.

"No, with the department." He almost said "Homicide."

"Maybe I shouldn't be going. Maybe I should be here."

His son was in the car now, waiting.

He rubbed her shoulders. "I'd feel more comfortable with you away."

"These people are violent?"

"That's not what I meant. I haven't heard anything in over a week. Once I tell the police, they'll simply pick them up and it will be over. This part of it, at least."

"Then why do you want me to leave?"

"So I don't have to clean the cottage," he said, grinning.

She punched him in the arm.

He hugged her, then steered her toward the driver's door. Then he walked over to his son's window on the passenger side.

"Remember," he said, rubbing his red hair. "Scream on your way down. Like fighter pilots do. It keeps the blood from rushing out of your brain."

His son nodded, smiling. Excited.

Behind the wheel, she looked over at him. "Connor," she said. "Why are you waiting?"

"Waiting for what?"

She glanced at their son, then back. "Until the end of the week for the meeting."

"It's all a matter of timing."

"What kind of timing?"

"If this goes public, I figure I'll have about twenty-four hours to get out of town."

TINO DENTZ ARRIVED at the address on Grand River at ten-thirty Thursday, just as Gary told him. Fuck the curfew. He'd already violated two nights this week anyway, not wanting to hang around the carriage house, going to the Maverick instead. PO didn't leave the police department, he figured, just to start working nights now. Still, he didn't like it. And he didn't like not having a handle on Gary. All week, noticing full-size Chevrolets with plain wheel covers. Saw one at the Maverick and two parked on Woodward near the church. He didn't know if it was the narc squad or Homicide. So he didn't move any powder, didn't go see the guy from Eleven Block. He just hung at the bar. Stuck with the Hennessy. Bought a bunch of dances from the big-titted gal one night, the lap whore they saw with the judge. Almost blew his load in his Calvin Kleins, figuring he needed one more song. But she ran off to the dressing room, saying it was time for her break.

He put a twenty on the counter for the Arab girl, saying, Yo, he needed a ticket.

"A ticket for what?"

"I'm not talking the lottery," he said.

She took the money and reached under the counter and handed him a three-by-five card. It had a yellow smiley face and an address: 1315 Broadway. He hadn't hit a rave since before he did his three-to-five. All the bullshit they put you through, just to party. He wished Gary could keep it simple. Just meet him somewhere and talk.

Five minutes later, he found a parking spot on Brush Street near Greektown and walked toward the Broadway address. It was hot, no breeze, and he could feel the silk sticking to his back. He hadn't seen any Chevys all night, except the bunch that were already parked outside 1300, a block from where he put the van.

Closer, he heard very low bass notes, not the kind from a band or a hop jay, something deeper. But there was nothing moving outside of 1315 Broadway. A storefront with five stories, but the business inside gone, its windows and doors covered with accordion gates. But he heard the sounds, like punch presses were stamping out parts for those Chevys inside.

He saw a couple of teenage girls cross the street, go around the corner. He followed, catching up to them as they turned into the alley, slowing to watch their tight little butts pump with the building's sounds.

Ahead, they disappeared through a black alley door marked 1315 Broadway, on both sides two very large brothers in black T-shirts with YOU ARE UNDERGROUND across their chests.

At the door, one brother put a hand on Tino's shoulder, the other dude coming up behind him, patting him down. He'd left the Taurus under the seat, figuring it was coming.

"Where you going, holmes?" one asked.

"Who's askin'?"

"Record company pays us to make sure nothing goes down."

Tino removed the brother's hand from his shoulder and slapped the smiley-face card in his palm. "You have a nice day, motherfucker," he said.

Inside it was loud, louder than he remembered it. Speakers across an entire wall of a big room, ductwork and pipes hanging from the ceiling. Bass notes coming at you so large they rattled your guts. Deejay spinning that high-tech shit. Lasers. Smoke machines. Strobes. Sixties shit projected on the walls. People standing and sitting, looking fucked-up. A couple hundred of them. Some dancing, but it was more like standing. Standing with their legs apart, moving their elbows and their arms and their head to the tech tune, but nothing else.

Tino walked up to a white kid in a T-shirt and shades, the guy's head and hands moving like the others.

He leaned in close, saying, "Yo, man, where the chill-out room?"

He felt his lips move, but he couldn't hear his own voice; the kid either, off in the zone somewhere.

He grabbed the kid by the shirt and marched him around the speaker stacks. The kid fighting him at first, then going with it.

"Where the fucking chill-out room?" he asked, shouting now.

The kid pointed to a freight elevator, then ran back onto the dance floor, his head going up and down again.

It was different when he stepped off the elevator, the music upstairs real laid-back. Slow tunes with flutes and electronic tones and soft congas. The room upstairs was smaller, about the size of a couple of Mickey-D's. Everything in flat black, the floor covered with black foam padding, the people wearing black, the people sitting and lying everywhere.

Gary had said to go to the smart bar. It was lit overhead with black lights. A guy with a beard and thin face, maybe in his forties, was running a blender, mixing up drinks, another five or six lined up on the counter. They were in clear tumblers. The liquid in the glass glowed bright orange and yellow.

"What these?" Tino asked.

"Smart drinks," the man said. "Protein and vitamins, mainly. Five bucks." He put out his hand for the money.

Tino asked a question. "You seen a guy? Short and thin. Hair like that actor. Real white skin."

"What actor?"

"Motherfucker who got killed in a sports car. What's his name?"

"James Dean."

"Yeah. You seen him?"

"He's buried in Indiana." The guy smiled.

Tino didn't smile back, the guy finally asking, "What's his name?"

"Gary."

"You Tino?"

He nodded.

"He told me to tell you he's back there," he said, pointing. "By the tank."

Shit, Tino thought. "A guy named Bobby with him, too?"

The guy pointed. "By the *tanks*. The nitrous tanks, back there by the wall."

Tino drew a line with his eyes through the people on the floor, made the decision he wasn't tiptoeing around those motherfuckers, even the ones in clusters, their arms around each other, stroking each other's hair and shit. Just keep walking and they'll get the message after he stepped on a few hands, then they can go back to tripping on disco biscuits and E.

The floor opened up in front of him.

Ahead, on the other side of the people, he saw two cylinders of nitrous, one guy sitting cross-legged with a long hose, filling up balloons and handing them off to people on the floor. Another hundred balloons around, filled and tied off, glowing in the black light. Some balloons lying on the floor, others being bounced around by the tripping people.

Gary wasn't near the two tanks. He was in a corner, running a tank of his own. Laying on a bare mattress, his head against the wall. A long hose, the nozzle and hand valve draped across his shoulder. Three E-bunnies on the mattress with him. All fine and young and tight.

Closer, Tino saw Gary had the lips of a balloon between his fingers. He was feeding the nitrous into a bunny's open mouth, making the balloon squeal. She was sitting on top of him, grinding a little, her head back, eyes closed. The other two bunnies stroking him, one his legs, the other his face.

He stopped at the foot of the mattress, his arms folded, waiting to be noticed.

Gary didn't look at him. He kept his eyes on the bunny's mouth and said, "Yo, Tino, how things lookin'?"

"Got to admit," Tino said. "They lookin' fresh so far."

CHAPTER **26**

FRIDAY MORNING, AS he shaved, Nelson Connor had the feeling that something was different. He'd been downstairs to turn on the coffee-maker. Found the kitchen exactly as he left it the night before, his packed suitcase near the breakfast nook, the address for the vet on the table.

Still.

He was listening to WJR on the bathroom radio, the guy doing the road report saying the traffic heading north was already starting to build. He reached over and lowered the volume, listening. Then he turned the radio off.

Heard silence.

That's what was different. Not only Kace and John not there, there was something more.

He turned off the water.

The monkey. In the morning, the squirrel monkey always rattled his cage.

Connor wiped the remnants of shave cream from his face with his bath towel, then wrapped it around him, tucking the corner in at his waist.

On the stairs, a morning breeze swelled the white curtains on the landing window. He stopped there momentarily, looking out at the drive-way, seeing the Grand Am parked where he left it. Then he continued down.

Kace kept the cage in the living room, saying it was better for the animal's temperament if he was around family activity, even when he wasn't free. When Connor turned the corner, his eyes went there, but it was empty, the door open, his first thought being, Shit, the damn thing had run off. Now it was outside.

He looked at his watch. He had an hour until his meeting with the Homicide inspector at 1300. He didn't have time to search the neighborhood for the goddamn thing.

He caught the monkey's profile first, out of the corner of his eye. He turned and saw its nose and mouth, sticking out just beyond the sides of his leather chair. He chuckled with relief, the damn thing sitting there like it was reading the morning *Free Press*.

But it wasn't reading. It wasn't moving. As he walked around the chair he saw its swollen tongue jutting out of the corner of its mouth.

The monkey. Dead. Propped up in his chair, his eyes open, riveted on a set of curtains he'd violated a couple months before.

The monkey clutched a manila envelope in his hands. But closer now, Connor saw he wasn't really holding it. It had been stapled to his palms, a trickle of blood dripping down one edge.

And more red. Stamped on the front: PHOTOS, DO NOT BEND.

Later, he wouldn't remember opening the envelope. He'd remember sitting on the footstool, holding the photographs in his hands, looking at them one by one.

The first: His Reatta under an overhead light, the grain so thick it seemed to be raining. The back of a figure, his hand on the side of the trunk, as if he was leaning on it, trying to get his balance.

The second: *His face*, looking up.

The third: His arms under Ozzie's armpits, pulling him out.

The fourth: Him on his knees, over the body.

The fifth: The Reatta driving off, Ozzie's body a lump near a pile of broken bricks.

The evidence right in front of him. Lawrence Gary and Torino Dentz had not dumped Jimmy Osborne's body.

He had.

HE HAD NO IDEA how long he sat there. Five minutes. Maybe fifteen.

When the phone rang, he answered it, picking up a living-room extension, an antique pedestal with a dial in the base.

Katherine said, "I called to remind you about the monkey."

"Yes," he said.

"And don't forget to close the landing window. In fact, you might want to check them all."

He didn't answer.

"You running late?" she asked.

"No."

"You'll be up here by dinner?"

"I—"

"There's somebody I want you to meet."

He heard her say to someone, "Good, so you're staying nearby."

Christ, he didn't want to meet anybody. He didn't even know if he could go. Not now.

"Meet who?" he asked.

"Here," she said. "He says he wants to introduce himself."

He heard her voice trail off, the phone passing hands.

The voice said, "You know one of these days we're going to meet in person, Honor. You and me. Seems like all we ever do is talk on the telephone."

LAWRENCE GARY TURNED to Katherine Connor. She was sitting at the varnished-pine picnic table in the cottage kitchen, three cups of steaming coffee served up. Thoughtful, Gary said earlier, especially considering they'd driven all night. She was holding a Danish, but stopped chewing suddenly when Torino Dentz went to the window and pulled out the Taurus, using it to push aside the cherrywood miniblinds.

Gary covered the mouthpiece, the judge having trouble finding the right words to say.

"Where's the boy?" Gary asked.

"Ohio," she said, setting down the Danish.

"Too bad," Gary said. "I was looking forward to meeting the young man."

Gary slid onto the table next to her, putting his feet on the bench, his mouth back on the phone. "Now you listen to me, Honor. I'm going to make it simple. You get all the cash you can together and hit the road. See how much your main squeeze is worth to you. And, the photos. Hell, if the price is right, I might even throw those in, too."

"I told you," the judge said. "I don't have the money you think I do."

Gary shrugged. "Maybe I'm asking the wrong person."

He grabbed a handful of her hair and pulled Katherine Connor over hard. He slammed her face into the table, her cheek on the Danish.

She screamed.

Gary liked that, figuring that the judge heard it, too.

"Mrs. Connor," he announced. He said it loud, holding the phone at arm's length. "Time for a little civics quiz. What happens every four years?"

He put the phone to her mouth. "Connor," she whimpered.

Gary pulled the phone back with his left hand, taking another inch or two of her hair with the right. "I'm sorry," he said. "In the State of Michigan, what happens in *November* every four years for every incumbent circuit judge?"

He put the phone back to her lips. "He runs," she said, hardly getting it out.

"Runs for what?"

"He runs for reelection."

Gary brought the phone back up. "He runs for reelection. Did you get that, Honor?"

He held the phone out again, saying, "And how does a judge run? Doesn't that take *money?* How much *money* does that take, Mrs. Connor?"

Crying now, she said, "I don't know."

Back to the phone now. "She doesn't know, Honor. How about you? You know how much fucking money it takes to run a campaign these days?"

He was shouting, "Leave her alone, goddamn you."

"Well, since nobody seems to know fucking anything around here, I took the liberty of checking myself. How about forty-five thou? That's what the Honorable Nelson Connor spent four years ago. And what's the source, you say? *Detroit Legal News*. You read the *Detroit Legal News*, Honor? Damn, I mean, you should."

He put the phone back to the little woman's mouth. "Connor," she said, hardly getting it out.

"She says, 'Connor.' You hear that, Honor? Does she sound like she's having a very good fucking vacation?"

He was shouting. "I'll get the money."

Gary waited until he could hear Nelson Connor breathing hard on the other end.

"That's right, Honor," Gary said, calmly now. "You get the money. No more fucking around."

"Let me talk to her."

"There'll be time for that."

"Let me talk to her now."

"You bring the money, you can talk all you want."

"You'll be there?"

"You just mix yourself a drink for the deck. I'll be in touch."

"When?"

"And no more fucking games. Or, the next time you see her, it won't be to talk."

Then he hung up.

GARY RELAXED HIS grip, feeling the silkiness of her hair as he slowly removed his hand. She lay there for a second, her eyes closed. Then she sat up, wiping some of the Danish from her cheek, using her fingers. Doing it with a certain dignity. Gary decided he had to give her some style points for that.

He sipped her coffee. "This is very good, Mrs. Connor."

She didn't say *"Call me Katherine"* this time.

He set the mug down. "You know, there's something about getting away from the city. Kind of frees up the mind, don't you think?"

He could see she was running over all her options. He could practically read them going across her eyes like a light-scroll sign. Maybe thinking, Make a run for it now. Or, more likely, Try later. Maybe they had a piece somewhere in the house, but he doubted it, considering the judge's liberal leanings.

Gary said, "You just keep going with the performance, hon, and everything will work out just fine."

He handed her a napkin, saying, "Say, you missed a spot there on your cheek."

She wiping with her hand instead. Gary seeing a little anger now.

"I tried to help you," she said.

"But, Mrs. Connor," Lawrence Gary said. "You did."

TINO DENTZ TURNED away from the window. "Maybe we should split. What if the man calls the police?"

Gary lit a cigarette, exhaling. "He won't call anybody. Not now."

Tino saw the Danish on the table and reached for it. He scarfed it down, putting the .38 in his pants. "Where's this big fucking bridge you said was up here?" he asked, his mouth still full of sweet roll.

Gary said, "I tried to wake you up when we crossed. That crank will do that to you. For days after you kick."

Tino was looking around now, checking out the log walls and the peaked ceiling, beams running across. One big room basically, with some small bedrooms and a john at one end. The pine table, sink, and cupboards on one side. On the other, a plaid couch and two easy chairs arranged around a fieldstone fireplace, a nearby bookshelf filled with old *National Geographics* and old hardcover books, no dust jackets.

He walked over to the small table near the south window, the view facing the straits. He wanted to run his fingers across the long telescope lying there.

"Hey, Gary," he said, turning. "This motherfucker is gold."

"That's brass."

"What's this for?" Tino asked, looking at the judge's wife. "There ain't no people on that beach out there."

When she didn't answer, he walked over. He lifted her chin with the nose of the .38. "I said, baby, What the fuck that telescope for?"

"We like to watch the ships," she said, quietly.

He turned, walking back to the window. He picked up the scope and looked, the scope pretty heavy. Saw nothing but hazy blue. All blurry.

"There ain't no ships out there," he said. "How do you hold this motherfucker?"

"There's a tripod in the closet," she said. "I'll get it if you want."

Gary said, "You just sit tight, Mrs. Connor. We're almost done here." Gary, looking like he was really into the cigarette and coffee now, watching the smoke stream out of his mouth.

Tino felt restless. He checked the window again, looking at the driveway, then past the trees at the highway, looking for blue Fords with single red flashers, or cars with stars on the side.

"So, he bringing the fucking money or what?"

Gary turned to the woman. "Mrs. Connor? what do you think? You think he'll bring the money? Or you think he'll trade up for a new model?"

"He's not like that," she said.

Gary smiled. "Well, I gotta say in all honesty, I've had my doubts. In fact, you really should have your doubts, too."

"He's my husband," she said. "What would you know?"

Gary looked at Tino, saying, "Why don't you go out to the van and bring Mrs. Connor the housewarming gift we picked up?" Then he looked at the woman, asking, "Me, I believe you always bring a gift, don't you?"

Gary giving orders again, Tino thought. He just had to deal with it a little longer.

"Now?" Tino asked. "What you thinking?"

"I'm thinking she's not going to be happy. Better she work that out here than a motel with a lot of people around."

Tino hesitated, then walked out the door, doing it only because Gary had a point. He let the screen door slam behind him.

When he came back two minutes later, Gary was sitting next to the woman, his arm around her.

Tino pushed the lap whore into the center of the room, the duct tape still across her face.

"Mrs. Connor, say hello to Taylor," Gary said. "Or is it Kelly? I'm never sure."

DRIVING DOWNTOWN, THE first thing he wanted was a drink. A bar or a party store. Get some travelers. Where and how didn't matter. Only when and what. But it didn't stick with him, not like it used to. It was only an option now, not an internal demand.

The second option was the police. But Detroit Homicide was out of the question now, for different reasons. Detroit police couldn't help him. He was dealing with different laws, different jurisdictions. He'd have to go to the county sheriff in the Upper Peninsula, or the Michigan State Police post. But he had to get there first. He'd be damned if he'd turn the situation over to a bunch of cops he didn't know over the phone.

An hour later, he was in his chambers, alone with the open safe, his law books, and two piles of cash, the halls quiet outside. He'd counted out one pile of worn twenties and fifties and hundreds, Barbara already having put the bill wraps on some. The other pile was crisp twenties. He had nearly eight thousand in miscellaneous cash, all donations for the fundraiser. The other pile was the line-of-credit money he'd taken out a week ago.

Thirteen thousand dollars.

The rest was in the bank, but he couldn't get it out. He wanted to tell Gary that, but Gary never gave him the goddamn chance. Only Barbara could write checks. Barbara paid for the newspaper ads and radio spots. Barbara was his campaign manager, to preserve the appearance of propriety, of all things. And now she was gone. Someplace up north, like half the goddamn people in the state.

Thirteen thousand lousy dollars for his wife. The hell with the photos. That didn't matter now.

He beat himself up pretty good. He'd been foolish not to see it coming. Not to suspect that Lawrence Gary would worm his way in with the art connection. It seemed so obvious to him now. It also seemed obvious that he would have tried to dump Ozzie's body. Hell, that's all he'd been doing for weeks, trying to save face.

And now Gary had Katherine.

Nelson Connor picked up the phone. He should have picked up the phone an hour ago.

The voice that answered was young.

"Jack Crilly around?" he asked.

"He's gone for the day."

"You know where I can reach him?"

"Who is this?"

"Judge Connor. A friend."

"Hey, Judge. Say, what's the story on that Reatta of yours?"

"Talk to Jack about it." Connor took a breath. "So, is he at home?"

"Right about now he ought to be on Lake St. Clair. He was heading out to his boat."

"You know when he'll be back?"

"He's taking the weekend off, but I think he's sticking around town." The salesman paused, then said, "I don't want to bug you, Judge, but what is going on with that Buick? I had somebody real hot for it today."

"Jack didn't tell you to sell it?"

"We just got the new title, but Jack said no. He's convinced you're going to change your mind. So, how's that Pontiac treatin' ya?"

"It runs fine."

"So you're going to keep it?"

Thinking now, Connor asked, "What do you mean by a new title?" Maybe he could get it back and sell it. Raise another quick fifteen or twenty. Or sign it over to Gary.

"Dealer title. Technically we own it, but if you want it back, you just fill in your name, send it to Lansing. We still have your plate, too. You probably ought to pick up your tag. Take care of the paperwork on the Poncho."

"Don't sell it, I'm coming right over," Connor said.

He hung up and reached below his desk, pulling out his gym bag. He dropped the cash on his old sweats, then tossed in the presentence report on Gary. He saw Dentz's and Bobby Tank's nearby. Dentz had to be there, he thought. Gary wouldn't be alone. He tossed in Dentz's paperwork, but left Bobby Tank's on the desk.

He looked over at his law books. A part of him wanted to take the statutes on extortion and kidnapping and homicide. Refresh his memory. Maybe call the local prosecutor when he got up there. He could see the county seat in his mind, a small tourist town, a tiny courthouse, a couple of attorneys with shingles out. He remembered the police, reading about them in the local paper. They busted up beach parties and wrote tickets for ten over on the state highway. He could see the family cottage surrounded by cars. A couple cops with deer rifles. An elected sheriff with a bullhorn.

That was the system there. It was different. Different cops, different judges, different personalities. Only one thing was the same everywhere. Once you put the system into motion, you couldn't stop it. You couldn't stop the paperwork or the people who pushed it, and when it was over, you had to live with the results.

The system was no help to him now.

He reached into the safe and pulled Lewis's Colt .45 out of the safe, squeezing its pearl handle in his hand.

Thirteen thousand and a car.

He had to make Lawrence Gary go for that.

Connor dropped the pistol into the bag, just in case he didn't.

CHAPTER 27

GARY WALKED TO the small convenience store across U.S.-2 and came back to the motel, room 21, with cigarettes, a bottle of Amadeus rosé and a fifth of Hennessy.

Tino Dentz asked, "You get ice?" He was sitting on the bed, his shirt off, watching *Starsky and Hutch*, it also being *Starsky and Hutch* week on the USA channel, Gary heard the announcer say.

Gary set down the grocery bag, thinking the man didn't belong there on the bed, he belonged in the adjacent room with the two women. "You never been in a motel before?" he asked. "You want ice, they've got a machine outside."

"You pressured, or what?" Dentz said.

"I'm solid. But you're too solid. What if one of those bitches makes a run?"

Dentz aimed the revolver at the door that connected the rooms. He had a clean view of the entrance to room 20. "Yo, I told 'em try it," he said. "Just like at the arcade."

Gary shook his head. Dentz got up and went out the door with the ice bucket.

The rooms weren't bad for thirty-five per, two doubles in each. Gary wanted an efficiency, figuring since they had Visa and Mastercard and American Express now, they ought to have a stove and fridge. Maybe have the little woman cook for them, keep her busy. But the old guy in the office said the only place like that was another fifteen miles down U.S.-2. The Brevort Motel was already a half hour west of the bridge and twenty-five miles west of the judge's cabin. Not crowded at all, like the

mile of new motels they saw in St. Ignace, the town packed with people
catching ferries to Mackinaw Island or gambling at a casino run by the
Sault Chippewa tribe. Gary liked the rear parking, places for the Reverend Roy's van and the Jeep Grand Cherokee. He liked the view of
Lake Michigan, the way it funneled there into the Mackinaw Straits.
Earlier, he'd shot the sunset, but he had only a short lens, hardly picking
up a sailboat in the glare.

Gary opened the wine, checking out the perm on Starsky, the bell-
bottoms on Hutch. Dentz came back through the door, filled a plastic
cup with ice, and resumed his slouch on the bed.

"So whatup, Gary?"

Gary lay back against the headboard. "We wait. Keep the girls en-
tertained."

Dentz said, "Maybe we ought to check out that casino."

"After we score, we're not hangin' around."

"I'm not talking after. I'm talking before."

Gary shook his head. "What, take the bitches along?"

"I wonder if it's any good, like Vegas."

"You been to Las Vegas?"

"Never been to a casino."

"Then how do you know the ones in Vegas are good?"

Dentz hit the Hennessy. "All I'm saying is I'd like to check it out.
Vegas casino. Or, casino run by Indians. Might even be better. I wonder
if they dress up and shit."

"It's not like that," Gary said.

"How you know?"

"I was talking to the guy across the street. He says they got blackjack
and slots, some crap tables. But he says you don't see any Indians in
the place. They hire people to do the dealing, run the tables."

"Where the Indians?"

"They're in the back, counting the money," Gary said. "And they're
counting it *twenty-four hours a day*."

Dentz drained the cognac, swirling the ice around in the glass. "What
time he say he'd be here?"

"The judge?"

Dentz nodded.

"I didn't give him a time. I just told him to come, that's all."

"What about Bobby?"

"What about him?"

"You think he gonna call?"

"He called my mother's, didn't he?"

"You left another message with the number he gave her?"

Gary nodded, drinking the Amadeus from the bottle, watching Starsky and Hutch taking a corner in their red Ford Torino.

"Who he with, anyway?"

"I don't know," Gary said.

"Then how'd you leave a message?"

"It's a machine."

"Bobby at a place with a machine? That don't figure."

Gary said, "Hey, you can pick 'em up at Kmart now for twenty bucks."

"So," Dentz said, "you give him the number here."

Gary looked over, shooting him a look. "No, I fucking gave him the number at the phone across the street. We listen for it, then you're going to run your ass across that highway. So you better keep your pants on tonight."

"Just asking," Dentz said.

"You ask a lot. Maybe you're the one that's pressured."

"I'm okay with it."

"You weren't okay in my fucking basement."

"I was amped."

"You were more than that."

"I forgot about the pictures. That's all."

"I need you straight-up here," Gary said.

"I told you in Detroit. I'm not rollin' bump no more. And if I was, I wouldn't be driving around with it. Not a whole lot of brothers driving around up here."

"Brothers go to that casino. That's what the guy across the street was saying. They have bus charters right out of Detroit."

Dentz asked. "You going to ask Bobby to get on a bus? If he calls?"

Gary put his finger to his lips. "Down, man. I don't want the bitches hearing what's going on." He took another sip of the Amadeus, then added, "Guy across the street says they got a bus station in town."

"Maybe Bobby can watch the bitches," Dentz said.

"Why? That's not what I had in mind."

"So I can try to take some of the money from those Indians."

Gary wished he'd drop it. He turned to Dentz. "Tino, man, we didn't come up here to play fucking cards."

A LITTLE LATER, after Tino had a couple drinks, he asked Gary, "When we gonna call the judge?"

"Let him sleep on it. I want him thinking about the photos. I told you those shots would give him a new attitude."

Tino said, "Man, you got his woman."

"You think that's it?" Gary asked.

Tino, looked at him, seeing he meant it. "You take any motherfucker's woman, you're gonna get his attention. Wait until he finds out we took them both."

"I say it's the pictures," Gary said.

He couldn't see it, the judge hanging with the woman all those years. "How you figure?" Tino asked.

Gary said, "Simple. He loses the women but gets the negatives, he still gets to be a judge. I keep the negatives, but he takes the women, he loses both his job *and* the bitches."

"I still don't see it."

"Those photos are time—three to five, maybe. Those bitches aren't gonna hang with him while he's in Jacktown. See what I'm saying?"

"Yeah, I see," Tino said, looking at him, but he really didn't.

"So," Gary continued, "That's why the new attitude. It was my mistake, fucking around with him. Hey, I'm man enough to admit it. I should have used the photos from the get-go. Then we wouldn't be sitting here, three hundred miles from home."

Tino's eyes went back to the TV, Starsky kicking the shit out of a guy with an afro. He thought the judge's attitude may be new, but the basic circumstances hadn't changed.

He figured no sense telling Gary that.

Gary asked, "When you think the Reverend Roy will miss his van?"

"No Bible school this weekend. He'll give it a day. Then he'll call my mother."

"Then what?"

"She'll tell him what I told her. That will give us until Monday, but he'll be good and pissed off."

"Can you deal with it?"

"Yeah," Tino said. He'd deal with it with the phone number the con from Eleven Block gave him. A guy in Tampa, the con saying, if you had the stomach for that kind of work, they took real good care of you down there.

But, he figured, no sense telling Gary that.

They both watched the TV commercial, a guy standing in a furniture store, talking about a sale, one arm making a gesture, the other stiff at his side.

Tino put the Taurus on the pitch man and asked, "What if the judge try to pull some shit?"

"He won't."

"What if he do?"

Gary grabbed the bottle of wine. "That's why we got both bitches. That's why I left the message for Bobby."

"You want to send Bobby for the money?"

"I'm thinking along those lines."

"Yo, what if Bobby takes the money?"

"I'm thinking we'll stay close. I'm not worried."

Tino wasn't worried, either. Shit, it would never get that far.

And he definitely wasn't going to tell Gary that.

KATHERINE CONNOR WAS in a chair under a pedestal light, sketching. The lap whore was on the bed, her knees up near her chin, her arms around her legs. Her eyes were on her toenails, not on *Close Encounters* playing on HBO.

Gary stood in the doorway, saying, "So, they got cable up here."

The little woman said, "They've got a police department, too."

He held out a pack of Kools. "Cigarettes, ladies?"

The lap whore looked up, glaring. "Who the fuck you think you are, anyway?"

Gary lit one for himself.

"Now, Taylor," he said, exhaling. "Is that any way to treat a potential customer?"

"It's Kelly. Since you're not paying."

"All right, *Kelly*. I presume you've gotten to know Mrs. Connor, also known as Katherine, or sometimes, Kace. *Kelly and Kace.* I kind of like that. That's got a nice ring to it, don't you think?"

Neither answered. Gary walked over to the sink, unwrapping two plastic cups, filling them with the rose, the cigarette hanging from his lip. He placed a glass next to the little woman, glancing at her sketch. The Mackinaw Bridge on motel stationery. She was working from memory.

"Not bad," he said.

He walked over to the lap whore, setting a glass for her on the nightstand. She glanced at the wine, hesitated, then picked it up and guzzled it, holding out the glass for more.

Gary poured again, saying, "So, Kelly, have you explained to Kace here your role in our little deal?"

"So I know the guy," Kelly said. "So fucking what?"

"Know?"

"Yeah, *know.* And for the life of me, *asshole*, I can't figure out how that gives you permission to pull me off the street and drag me all the way up here."

"Is *knowing* the same as servicing?"

"Servicing? What are you talking about?"

Gary walked over to the doorway and leaned against the jamb. He sighed, looking at the little woman. "I was trying to be nice. Kelly here has been *fucking* your husband, Kace."

The little woman glanced at the lap whore, then went right back to the sketch with her pencil.

"Is that why you're doing this?" the lap whore asked. "You think I'm fucking her husband?" Trying to sell it.

The little woman looked up again, eyeing them both.

Gary looked at her, saying, "She wouldn't tell you." He looked back at the lap whore. "Don't you have some kind of code?"

"Is it true?" the little woman asked.

Gary answered for her. "It presented a problem, Kace. I thought, What if we get up here, ready to do this deal, and His Honor says something like, 'Hey, I don't give a shit about the old lady, I'm getting plenty on the side.' "

The little woman checking the lap whore real good now, seeing her painted toes and the nipples poking against her Maverick T-shirt. Checking out her air-conditioned jeans, the fashionable rips in strategic locations on the inside of her thighs.

Gary answered his own question. "So, I decided we needed you both. Let His Honor decide where his priorities lie. I mean, I can't do it for the man. Plus, you throw the photos into the negotiation process, then it really gets complicated."

Gary could see the little woman's eyes watering up.

"Photos," she said. "What photos?"

The lap whore slammed down an empty cup on the nightstand, saying, "I am not involved with the guy." She stood up and put a finger in Gary's face and yelled, "You, asshole, are insane."

Gary used a backhand, the lap whore's head turning, but she stayed on her feet.

Tino Dentz walked in, the gun in his waistband. "These girls getting cranky? Maybe they're hungry."

Katherine Connor stood up, saying, "Yes, are you going to feed us? Or are you just going to slap us around all night?"

Then the telephone in room 21 rang.

CHAPTER 28

GARY WAS STANDING at the foot of his bed. "I'm going to get Bobby," he said. "You like chocolate doughnuts?"

Tino Dentz rubbed his eyes and slid back to the headboard, not ready yet to think about food. He looked at the digital clock on the TV. It was almost noon.

He took the .38 from Gary, asking, "What about the bitches?"

Gary said, "One's in the shower. The other's still crashed in the bed."

He watched Gary go out the door. Lay there for a minute holding the Taurus in one hand, using the other to make a nice tepee with the sheet just below his waist. He was thinking about forty-five thousand dollars, not half of that, but forty-five thousand—that's what Gary said—and that not being a whole lot, considering he was the one at risk. He was thinking about Cherry Hill. How much was taking a run right by that cemetery worth?

Today, he thought. He'd wait to hear what Gary had to say. Wait for the right situation to present itself. Then he'd make his move.

He heard the shower running.

A minute later, he was sitting on the dresser at the foot of Katherine Connor's bed, eating something the little woman called a pasty, kind of a meat pie. Not too bad cold, he thought, but better warm, the way they were when Gary came back with a bag of them the night before.

Tino studied Katherine Connor's shape, the little woman facedown, his eyes penetrating the motel sheet. He liked the way her knee was up a little, making her ass round in a way he'd seen once in a nude painting, the time Gary took him to the museum. He looked down at his black Calvin Klein briefs. He saw a shape down there, too, but it wasn't round.

He picked up the glass of warm cognac he'd brought in from the other room and washed down the pasty, then walked over to the side of the bed.

"Yo, mama," he said, softly. He wiped his mouth.

Her eyes twitched a little, her cheek facedown on the pillow. Faking it, he figured. If he was in her situation, he wouldn't be sleeping. But he'd be faking it, too.

He sat down next to her. "Mama. I know you listening to me. What you say you come over to my side? Check out the executive suite."

He set down the cognac on the nightstand, then put the muzzle of the revolver under her strawberry hair, lifting it away from her face, curling it behind her ear.

"C'mon now, time to rise and shine."

He wanted her last night, but Gary kept saying he had to sleep, so he could stay up and watch today. So now he'd slept. And Gary couldn't say shit, even if he was there.

"I know you can hear me, mama."

When Tino heard the bathroom door open behind him, he turned quickly with the Taurus .38, ready.

The lap whore, naked.

Walking over to him now.

She picked up his Hennessy and drained it.

"Hey," he said. "That mine."

She handed him the empty cup and said, "Where's your asshole friend?"

"He's gone to town." He looked up. He liked the view.

The lap whore said, "So what's with you, anyway?"

"With me?" He was checking it all out now, no G-string like in the Maverick.

"Yeah, *with you*, Paco. I figured by now you would have finished what we started at the bar."

LAWRENCE GARY SWUNG by the cottage, spotting the Reatta parked in the driveway, then drove to the Kewadin Casino, going through downtown St. Ignace, following the signs that took him five miles north of town. The casino, pretty much out in the middle of nowhere, except for a nearby subdivision of bungalows, subsidized housing for Indians. Gary wondered if the tribe was pulling in so much gambling money, how come the Indians still lived like that. Hell, he'd have a place on the beach, not live in a shack with old cars and a rusty Kmart barbecue outside.

The Kewadin Casino was one building the size of a Red Lobster, with a big white tent attached to that, the tent the size of four barns. He could see a footing being poured for another addition. The casino parking lot was as big as ten football fields, nearly full. Rather than walk, he parked just across the road, where a guy in a John Deere hat was charging ten bucks a car.

Inside the tent, Gary saw at least a thousand slots, a lot of old ladies feeding nickels and quarters, plastic buckets in their laps. He worked his way through the crowd into the main building. There he saw black-jack and roulette and craps tables. He saw a couple of bars, and more machines, most of them the dollar variety. He liked the themes, back-lit color panels with artwork and names like *Treasure Island* and *Shangri-La*. He liked the sound of the place, the sound of money dropping into the stainless-steel bins.

People were dressed casual. They wore sweatshirts and T-shirts, jeans and khakis, and a lot of shorts. Nobody all duded out like he imagined Vegas would be. No sign of lowlife, either. He saw a few Indians, guys in black slacks and mismatched shirts, guys with their eyes on the peo-ple, not the games. Just all-American fun, he thought, the Indians trading the worthless pieces of colored plastic to the white man, the white man throwing his fucking money away *this* time.

He liked the casino, the big crowd mainly. In the casino, he could keep his eye on Bobby Tank at close range. If the judge was setting him up, he'd see it coming. He liked the idea of money changing hands in that environment. Send Bobby in with the lap whore first, just to make sure everything was straight-up. Leave the little woman tied up in the motel room. Maybe give the judge the photos and the lap whore with the keys to room 20, then split with the little woman for insurance. Or leave the lap whore with the keys and take the photos.

He'd decide in time.

A half hour later, he was back in downtown St. Ignace, sitting on a park bench eating a Hostess chocolate doughnut from the box. The business district followed the bay, one street with not a stoplight on it, lined with gift shops and fudge shops for tourists—"fudgies" the guy at the convenience store called them, because they bought so much fudge. Gary watched a white ferry steaming toward Mackinaw Island, the stern throwing a small rooster tail. The water looked bluer than any water he'd ever seen, not a light blue, but a deep blue, almost navy.

A seagull landed on the sidewalk. He broke off a small piece of the doughnut and lured it over, the bird cautious but eager. He teased it for a while, faking it out with a couple balks. Then he fired the piece at the bird, the gull chasing down the morsel and flying off with it over the blue.

Lawrence Gary felt good.

Shit, he decided, it was turning out to be a very good day.

THE BUS PULLED to the curb in front of the small two-story hotel that also served as the local Greyhound station, the coach groaning, then its air brakes hissing. Gary was thinking about the statement Bobby Tank signed on the K of C case. Maybe he could find a way to work in a little payback, too.

Bobby Tank, the last one out, walked across the street, a shopping bag in his left hand. He was wearing a flannel shirt and yellowed jeans. His sandy hair hung to his jaw in thick strands, unwashed.

Bobby put out his hand. Gary rose and put his arms around him, hugging him, patting him on the back, trying not to smell him, but saying, "Bobby, my man."

He stepped back and handed Bobby a doughnut.

"Where to?" Bobby asked.

Gary said, "First thing, we got to get you some decent clothes."

They went into a little tourist shop called the Deerskin Coral. The store smelled like pine and leather and was stocked with moccasins and sweatshirts with silkscreens of the Mackinaw Bridge and white-tail deer. Bobby Tank spotted a pair of knee-high boots, soft cowhide, laces all the way up the front, leather fringe on top. Bobby said they reminded him of Davy Crockett.

"He from West Virginia?" Gary asked.

"State of Tennessee," Bobby said, saying it like it was a country all its own.

Gary waited while he laced the boots, the teenage girl waiting on them saying, "Believe it or not, we still get quite a demand for those."

They shopped for an hour. Gary bought him a gray sweatshirt. Picked out one with the Mackinaw Bridge across the chest. They walked to Sam's department store, where he bought Bobby a pair of Levi's, Bobby insisting that the pants be tucked *into* the knee-high boots. They stopped in a drugstore. Gary bought a *St. Ignace News* and hair scissors, figuring that later he'd trim up Bobby a little. They even hit a fudge shop for a pound of chocolate walnut and green pistachio. He put everything on Visa, nobody asking for ID, or even running the cards for approval, the shops making their final run before they rolled up the street after Labor Day.

Gary spotted an army surplus store, an .80-caliber machine gun in the window. They walked over and read signs and bumper stickers behind the glass, the store selling them. Clever words like: THIS PROPERTY PROTECTED BY SMITH & WESSON. And, Gary's favorite: TED KENNEDY'S CAR HAS KILLED MORE PEOPLE THAN MY GUN. Gary went inside and bought a desert hat with a neck shield, the kind the troops wore in the Charge of the Light Brigade. He paid cash, not Visa, considering the vibes he was getting from the display.

In the Jeep, Gary asked, "So, tell me how you walked out of the county."

He handed Bobby a Kool.

Bobby declined, pulling out a can of Skoal, green long-cut. "Judge let me out."

Gary pulled the Grand Cherokee from the curb, heading back toward U.S.-2. He checked his mirror, but he hadn't seen a street cop or a cruiser since they crossed the bridge.

"I already figured a judge let you out," he said, settling in behind the wheel, "He set bail, or what?"

"I couldn't make no sense of it," Bobby said.

"Let me try, Bobby."

"The lawyers." He said "lawyers," but it sounded like *"liars"* with his accent.

"What about him?"

"I just know in two days I had two lawyers and two judges. Figure that."

"What did the judge say?"

"Which one?"

"The first."

Bobby picked an empty McDonald's cup off the floor and spit in it. "First one says he's giving me a new lawyer 'cause the guy he says ain't doing me right."

"That's the second lawyer, then?"

"Right. Pretty slick dude."

"Then what?"

"This new lawyer picks a new judge. Says we're goin' to trial, which is cool with me, long as I get out of the county. But on Monday, I'm back in the courthouse again, and the new lawyer and the new judge, they start talking about bail."

"So, what doesn't make sense about that?" Gary asked.

"Well, jail is really crowded. But this motherfucker starts arguing why I shouldn't be let out."

"Some judges are like that."

Bobby spit again. "No, the motherfucking lawyer. He's arguing I should stay in. Figure that."

Gary was thinking: Probably one of those attorneys he saw buying tickets.

Bobby continued, "So this second judge says to the second lawyer that if he's going to be arguing that way, then he's got to look out for me. *'Represent my interest,'* he says. Gave me a personal. Represented my ass right out the door."

Bobby spit again, saying, "Now, does that make sense to you?"

Gary said, "What was the first judge's name?"

"Judge Connor," Bobby said.

"Makes perfect sense to me, Bobby. And I wouldn't complain."

On U.S.-2 now, he set the cruise control at fifty-five. Bobby didn't ask him about Jackson. He didn't ask him about Gus Harrison Regional.

Gary figured Bobby was thinking if he asked him about Jackson, then that would lead back to the statement. If he was Bobby, he wouldn't want to talk about that.

"So, Gary," Bobby finally asked. "Tell me a little more about this thousand I'm going to make."

"I told you, we're just collecting a marker."

"From who?"

"From a lame."

"Up here, man?"

"People I do business with get around."

"Marker from when?"

"From when I was rolling powder."

"That's a long time ago."

"Marker is a marker," Gary said. "As far as I'm concerned, time don't change a fucking thing but the amount."

Bobby asked, "So, what am I doin'?"

"Picking it up."

"We going to hurt the man?"

"You don't have to hurt anybody."

"But I get a grand?"

"Plus I bought you some threads, Bobby. Room and board. Don't forget that, too."

"What if I don't like it?"

"Where we're staying? It's pretty nice."

"No, the job."

"Like I said, it's simple."

"What if I don't think it's simple?"

"All you got to do is walk in. Pick it up. Walk out. That's simple, ain't it?"

"You coming? Tino?"

"We'll be nearby."

"What if I don't like goin' in somewhere alone?"

"Don't worry. There's going to be plenty of people around."

Bobby Tank sat there for a while, working the dip, spitting when he needed to, checking out the scenery, U.S.-2 following the Lake Michigan shore.

"This kinda like home," he said finally.

"There's no water like that in West Virginia," Gary said.

"The trees," Bobby said, pointing to the national forest on his right. "We got trees like this. Far as the eye can see."

Gary thought, Such a simple son of a bitch. But that had a plus side, too. Keep it simple, and Bobby Tank did what you wanted. That was how they probably got the statement. They kept it simple. Gave him a simple offer and he took it. Bobby Tank was simple, but he wasn't a fucking fool.

Bobby let the wad of Skoal drop into the cup, pulled out the can again and reloaded, pushing the pinch deeper into his upper lip this time.

"How much longer?" he asked, spitting again.

"Until we do the thing?"

"Until we get there."

"The motel?"

Bobby nodded.

"Just up this road a ways," Gary said.

Bobby leaned over, rummaging around in the shopping bag at his feet, and saying, "We doing the thing tonight?"

"Probably," Gary said.

When he heard a slide rack, Gary turned. He saw Bobby holding a compact semiautomatic. Gary saying, "What the fuck is that?"

"Star Model PD," Bobby said. "Smallest .45 made." Bobby did know his guns.

"Still blow a hole in somebody," Gary said.

"But not through them, like a .357. That way you're not wasting people who just happen to be standing around. Shit, a .45 be good for this job."

Gary said, "You're not going to need that."

Bobby Tank leaned over, spitting, the cup now in the console. "If I'm going in alone, I am."

TINO DENTZ WISHED he had Gary's camera now. Wanted to have a picture of Gary's face in the doorway, the way he was looking at him, Tino in the bed, the lap whore sitting on his ass, giving him a back massage. He wanted a picture of Bobby Tank, walking in, looking like Buffalo Bill.

The lap whore pulled the sheet around her, dragging it with her to the other room. She looked at Gary, then Bobby as he sat on the dresser, watching her go by.

Gary, still standing, said, "Now you're beyond solid, Tino. You're approaching stupid."

"She fine," Tino said, getting out of bed now, hopping from one foot to the other as he pulled up his pants. He walked over to Bobby, putting up five.

Bobby pulled up his sweatshirt first, pulling out a nice little semiauto, setting it on the dresser. Then he gave him his hand.

Tino grinned. "Yo, Bobby, you armed and dangerous, motherfucker."

"Just like old times," Bobby said.

Bobby pulled out a bag, began rolling up some bud.

Tino turned to Gary, dropping the smile now, and saying, "You got it wrong, man."

"About what?"

"About the man and this girl."

"I got nothing wrong."

"No, you got it very wrong."

Bobby was watching them, his head going back and forth as he rolled the Zig-Zag, getting ready to smoke down.

Tino continued, "She not fucking the judge. That night he left with her, man, he was looking for us."

Bobby lit the stick.

Gary tossed a newspaper on the bed, flopping down next to it. "Looking? Now why would he be looking with her? Tino, that just don't make sense."

Tino walked over to the TV, pouring the last of his Hennessy, making Gary wait. He finally said, "She was fucking the man with the marker, Gary. That's why the judge looked her up. Your homey dealer just another one of her fucking tricks."

"Then why did she leave with him?"

"She had the Ozzie guy's book with the judge's name in it, back from a time when they got cracked by the narc squad. She was thinking about shooting a move of her own."

Bobby handed Tino the joint. He hit it, then was going to hand it to Gary, but Gary was looking past him now.

Tino turned around, saw Katherine Connor standing there.

"What you lookin' at, mama?" he asked.

When she didn't answer, he held out the bud, offering it to her.

She didn't take it. She said, "It's almost five o'clock. We haven't eaten all day."

Gary tossed a box of fudge, the woman catching it.

Bobby Tank blew out a lungful of smoke he'd been holding for a good minute, asking in a hoarse voice, "Who the fuck she?"

"She's going to help collect the marker," Gary said.

The lap whore walked into the room, jeans and T-shirt on. She took the bud out of Tino's hand. Hit it hard and deep, Tino liking the way she looked, her back arched, holding her breath, her lungs nice and full.

Bobby scratched his goatee with the Star .45, and asked, "So who's this one?"

Gary started to answer, but Tino cut him off. "She's with me," he said. He glared at Gary, letting him know that's the way it was going to be.

"You grab her?" Bobby asked, motioning with the Star at Katherine Connor.

"Something like that," Gary said. He tossed a military hat to the lap whore, saying, "Try this on."

She put it on the TV, refusing.

"Goddamn," Bobby said, reaching for the joint. "This don't look like no thousand-dollar job to me."

THEY SENT BOBBY out for smoked fish and beer and homemade beef jerky. When he came back, Tino Dentz walked over to the convenience store for more cognac, Gary following him, demanding to know what the fuck was going on.

Gary said, "She's playing you, man."

"Maybe she is," Dentz said, walking. "Maybe she ain't."

"Then what you doing? We need her at the casino with Bobby."

"Why that so important?"

"On the remote possibility the judge has got the drop wired, police are going to grab Bobby and the lap whore, thinking the lap whore is the judge's wife."

"That's what that hat for?"

Gary nodded, puffing on a cigarette. "Cover her hair. Keep cops guessing if they're looking for a hair color."

"Judge not going to like that," Dentz said, stopping at the highway.

"If he wants the little woman, he's got to give Bobby the money."

"Then what?"

"The lap whore vouches for the fact that his wife is alive and well. She gives him the keys to the motel, where we leave the little woman. Or, maybe we have the little woman in the Jeep."

"What about Bobby?"

"I'm still working on that."

"What about us?"

"By then, we'll be on the road heading north."

"Where we going?"

"Place called Sault Ste. Marie. Canadian side. We ride sixty miles up the old highway that runs in front of the casino. Hang there for a few days."

They crossed U.S.-2, Dentz stopping again in the convenience-store lot. "What about the pictures?" he asked.

"That's what buys us the ride," Gary said.

Tino Dentz nodded, looking impressed with the plan. "Gary, lap whore don't mean nothing to me," he said.

"Then why hang with her so tight?" Gary asked.

Dentz said, "Because I'm the only motherfucker here who can get her to walk into the casino with that hat on her head."

IT TOOK LAWRENCE Gary until almost ten to work it all out, the principles of *The Art of Negotiation* coming into play. Bobby driving a hard bargain. Bobby, well into a six of Stroh's, getting a little weepy, talking about some town called Matewan where coal miners were gunned down trying to get a decent wage.

Gary told him they were getting fifteen total, figuring Bobby wouldn't have time to count it when he got it. Then he tried to hold Bobby below a third.

"It's my fucking marker, Bobby." He said it several times.

A couple times he looked for help from Tino Dentz, the lap whore next to him, whispering in his ear, Tino whispering back, then backing him up.

"I'm down with you, Gary," Tino said.

All of them partying, except Gary—wanting to keep his head straight—and the little woman, watching more cable in the other room.

Five thousand, Bobby kept saying. Sticking with it.

Then the lap whore got into it, saying she wasn't into charity work. If they wanted the performance, they'd have to pay for it.

When Gary finally agreed to Bobby's terms, Dentz said, "Don't worry, baby, I'll split my share with you. We'll spend it together."

"That'll work, Paco," she said.

Dentz looked at Gary. "So, when are we going to make the call?"

"Two in the morning when the bars close," Gary said. "Cops will be busy by two-thirty with the drunks. Then we do the deal."

Dentz got up, the lap whore with him.

"Where you going?" Gary asked.

"To the casino," he said, sliding the .38 into his pocket. "Maybe play some cards for just a little while."

Gary looked at him, telling him with his eyes he didn't like it.

Dentz winked. "You fill in, Bobby. She wants to see the place first."

Gary thought Tino Dentz was working with him, not against him, for a change. "Check out a slot called *Treasure Island*, by the blackjack tables. Then report back. I'm thinking we could do it there. And don't be late."

After they left, Gary thought, Shit, he should have told him to take his cellular phone.

CHAPTER 29

THE NIGHT BEFORE, he'd driven the strip for three hours, looking for the Grand Cherokee or the purple church van. He checked the Best Western, the Quality Inn, and a dozen other new hotels near the new strip north of town, then methodically canvased the lots of the small ma-and-pa, one-story motels in town and on U.S.-2, places with names like Straits Breeze and Bridge View. He checked in the KOA campground, then worked the grid of residential streets on the hill above the shopping district, looking at every house in a town of five thousand. He checked the houses by the Coast Guard station, surveying the streets near the old car-ferry dock they used before the bridge was built.

On his way back, Nelson Connor took the shoreline route below U.S.-2, heading down a road marked, Bridge View Access, just past the I-75 freeway entrance to the span. The two-lane sloped downward and came to a dead end at the Mackinaw Straits, the bridge a quarter mile to the left, its tollbooths glowing in the night.

The parking lot was empty. He walked over to the dime telescopes. He sat on the ground, his back against the pedestal, his eyes going to the lit towers and the white caps frothing with the moon.

He knew all about the Mighty Mac, as people called it. Anybody who spent time near the straits did. For years, it was a bigger attraction than the UP itself. Six men died building the bridge, his father used to say, "going into the hole," as the iron workers called it. It was as high as the Golden Gate, the towers 552 feet above the water, but two miles longer, five miles across.

Nelson Connor remembered being under it one time. He was with his old man in the family runabout when the straits came up fast and high, a front blowing in off Lake Michigan. He was twelve, and little help. It was the only time he'd seen fear in his father's face. The old man made a run between the towers, shooting an angle for the shoreline. But under the span, the boat stopped moving, the prop still churning. Later one of the local fishermen explained it. Said the straits ran in one direction on the top, but had another equally powerful current just below the surface, Lake Huron flowing in to Lake Michigan. Connor remembered how the old man poured on the power, taking six-footers over the bow, but getting them home. After that, he never took the runabout under the bridge again.

He sat there for maybe two hours, watching the waves crash on the other side of the guard rail at the end of the road.

Thinking one thing.

Christ, they had Kace. He was still thinking it, and now he couldn't even look for her. Spending the entire day at the cottage, waiting for a goddamn phone call. All he could do was call Jack Crilly and listen to the message on his machine. He tried to remember things Crilly said. *He was not drinking*. He had that going for him. It was nothing, and it was everything. Don't drink, Crilly always said, and you've always got a fighting chance.

When the sun set, he went to the refrigerator. *Halt*. Don't get too *hungry* or *angry* or *lonely* or *tired*—Crilly also said that. That would lead to a drink. At the fridge, he could do something about at least one of them. He saw a snapshot of his boy and him, stuck with a magnet on the door, both of them holding a stringer of perch.

Inside the refrigerator, everything was new. New Dijon mustard and new stacks of thinly sliced Swiss and hard salami and bags of new produce. A new bag of coffee, Jamaican Blue Mountain, with a note attached, Katherine's handwriting: *Connor, this ought to make the wax run out of your ears.*

He fell to his knees and cried.

LATER, NELSON CONNOR was in one of the overstuffed chairs, looking out at the dark straits through the sliding window, the breeze coming through the screen, one desk lamp on.

Someone knocked on the door.

It was not a hard knock, like a man's. It was a small, precise knock, like the knuckles of a woman or a child.

Kace, he thought. But probably not alone.

He reached for Lewis's Colt .45, on the table in front of him, next to the telescope, and stood, sliding the revolver into his jeans under his hooded sweatshirt.

He walked to the window, peeked out, saw nothing but a dark driveway. He wished there was a window in the heavy spruce door. He reached for the handle, thinking, Just open it. Find out what the story is before you make any kind of a move.

She was standing behind the screen, her raven hair picking up the highlights of the moon.

"Kelly?" he said, the sight of her not connecting with anything.

"You gonna just stand there, Judge?" she said. She was smiling, sucking on a candy. "Or you going to let me in?"

He flipped the hook on the screen, pushing it open.

She walked right past him, practically skipping in, Connor saying, "What in the hell are you doing here?"

When he turned to follow her, he heard the click and felt something hard jam into the skin behind his ear.

"Yo, motherfucker," the voice said. "Who be the toady now?"

Tino Dentz's hand came around to the front of his sweatshirt. He reached in, ripping the Colt out of his jeans, the sight tearing at his stomach.

"Well, looky here," Dentz said. "Man expecting somebody." Then he barked, "Turn the fuck around."

He slammed the door behind him. Dentz, with a gun in each hand now.

Kelly, looking around, saying, "Shit, Paco. Why we in that fucking little motel? We ought to be staying here."

She was bopping around. Looked high. He'd never seen her that way. Screw her, he thought. He didn't have time to figure that out now.

Connor said, "Where's Gary?"

Dentz said, "He not here."

"He's coming?"

"He's out of the picture."

"What picture?"

"My picture."

"What about my wife?"

Dentz shrugged. "Shit, man. That's between you and him."

Dentz walked two steps closer. "Where's the fuckin' money?"

"We had a deal."

"You and Gary had a deal. Me, I decided it was time I become a little more independent."

Connor glanced at Kelly Johns. She was at the fridge, the door open, her back to him, her hand patting out a rhythm with her right hand on the door.

She turned around and said, "This is empty. What the fuck, Judge. Didn't you promise me the next you saw me, you were gonna buy me a great big drink?"

He wanted to slap her.

"Fuck that," Dentz said. "This man probably drank it all up."

But now Connor was thinking about what Kelly Johns said. He remembered what they talked about the last time he saw her at the bar.

"Where's my wife?"

"She cool. You're a lucky man."

"Lucky?"

"Yeah, lucky I ain't stayin' another night."

"Hey, you got a telescope!" Kelly said, now darting over to the table, Connor's eyes following her. She pulled it off the table, walking over to the sliding-glass window. She propped it up, looking out, her arms flexing, her hands gripping the brass. Firmly, the way she gripped the brass stage pole at the bar.

"You can't see nothin'," Dentz said.

"There's a moon, Paco," she said, still looking. "Look how clear it is up here."

"No, it's blurry."

She looked away from the eyepiece, saying, "You have to focus."

She went back to the eyepiece.

Dentz glanced over, but when he looked back, Nelson Connor let him catch his eyes on the gym bag, on the table.

"Move over there," Dentz said, motioning toward the fireplace.

Connor walked over, slowly.

Dentz went to the table, setting down the Colt, their eyes locked. Kelly Johns on his right, still working on the moon.

Dentz spread open the bag with his fingers, looking in.

Connor saw it all coming. Kelly Johns, letting the length of brass tube slide through her fingers to a baseball grip, then swinging with an uppercut, putting her hips into it, right across Tino Dentz's eyes and the bridge of his nose.

Dentz going down, taking the table with him, the Colt going somewhere, the revolver leaving his hand, Connor making a dive for it.

Had it.

Dentz back on his feet now, his eyes full of blood.

Connor turned.

But so did Tino Dentz. He crashed through the screen, running.

Nelson Connor saw Kelly Johns sitting on the floor, her legs flat and spread. She tossed the telescope away from her with both hands and began to sob.

Connor hesitated for a couple seconds, his heart pounding. Then he ran to the cabin door, throwing it open. He saw Dentz's shape running up the drive toward the highway, then the lights of a van strobing through the pines as it took off.

Later, he wouldn't even remember getting in the Reatta, or starting it. But within minutes, he was doing ninety on U.S.-2, the revolver in the passenger's seat, the nose of the Buick right on the back of the purple van.

Three miles down the highway, a chorus of voices started in his head. What are you going to do when you catch him? Kill him?

Yes.

No, another voice said. You make him take you to Kace.

Connor saw the sign ahead on the highway: I-75 SOUTH. LOWER PENINSULA.

A hundred feet before the freeway entrance, the van suddenly turned right, kicking up gravel on the corner. Dentz had turned on the two-lane, by the smaller sign: BRIDGE VIEW ACCESS.

Connor glanced down at the revolver, thinking maybe Dentz had another gun with him. He was leading him down to the water, the parking lot. He thought Dentz was taking him there to make a stand.

They reached nearly a hundred down the long slope, the bridge twinkling ahead in the distance. Then Connor let up on the gas. He let up first because he thought, What the hell would a shoot-out accomplish? Then he touched his foot to the brake, because he knew there was one hell of a turn waiting ahead. Or the bridge-view parking lot with the dime scopes.

The Reatta was coasting when he saw it.

The church van, doing at least ninety. It crashed through the guardrail. Airborne, landing a good hundred feet out into the Straits of Mackinaw.

Nelson Connor pulled up, getting out of the car, leaving it running. He walked to the boulders, the waves lapping at them. In the moonlight, he could see the glow of the letters.

HEAVEN!
MAKE YOUR RESERVATION.

The exclamation mark pointing up. The van going down.

Then nothing.

All the way back to the cottage, Nelson Connor wondered why Torino Dentz never saw the sign.

CHAPTER 30

AFTER HE TRIMMED Bobby's goatee, Lawrence Gary slouched on the bed with the *St. Ignace News*, looking at the top story on the front page:

FIFTY THOUSAND EXPECTED FOR ANNUAL BRIDGE WALK.
Mighty Mac Draws Governor, Mighty Crowd.

He read about the walk, how a former governor had started the Labor Day tradition almost forty years ago. Now it was so big, they used the National Guard for crowd control. It started at seven in the morning and lasted until almost noon, beginning on the Upper Peninsula side. For a buck-fifty you could park in Mackinaw City and take a bus back to St. Ignace, so you could finish on the side with your car. Gary almost wished they were staying. He wouldn't mind shooting a wide angle of the mob pouring through those cables, the towers reaching for the sky.

Inside, next to a feature about a guy with the largest collection of lawn art in the UP, Gary found a column simply called "Police Activity Log." Entries were printed by day and time:

• Thursday, 2:22 A.M.: Two Detroit residents were detained following a scuffle outside the State Bar and charged with being drunk and disorderly.

• Friday, 5:36 P.M.: State Police were dispatched when a deer bolted into the tollbooth area of the Mackinaw Bridge, after eluding capture by Mackinaw County Sheriff's Deputies. The deer was shot with a trooper's service revolver.

• Sunday, 11:33 P.M.: A local resident was ticketed for urinating on a public sidewalk outside the True Value Hardware.

Gary giggled, then tossed the newspaper onto Tino Dentz's bed, next to Bobby, nodded out. In room 20, he found Katherine Connor, sitting in the chair near the light, working on another sketch.

She looked up and said, "Will this be over soon?"

He didn't answer. He held out his hand, saying, "Let me see."

She hesitated, then handed him the artwork.

It was a profile view of Bobby Tank, his head slumped over a little, his hair hanging forward, covering most of his cheek and his jaw.

Gary saw a pile of hotel stationery on the dresser, the pile much smaller than he remembered it. He walked over and squatted down, pulling open the top dresser drawer. Saw a Gideon Bible and a phone book. He opened the phone book where he saw a narrow split in the yellow pages.

Standing up now, he went through them. Front views and side views, just like "America's Most Wanted." Sketches of Tino Dentz and Bobby Tank. Sketches of himself. Not close composites. Good likenesses.

Gary said, "I think you have a new future in front of you."

He folded the sheets and slid them into his jeans. She didn't seem upset, or disappointed. Gary figured, living with His Honor, she was probably used to things not working out like she planned.

She asked, "How much money is my husband going to pay you?"

"How much is enough?" he asked back, sitting on the edge of the bed.

"I heard fifteen thousand dollars."

"Something like that."

"But I also heard forty-five on the phone."

Gary glanced at the doorway, Bobby Tank, still crashed out on Tino's bed.

Katherine Connor asked, "Are you straight with anybody?"

"Straight as I have to be."

"Doesn't it bother you?"

"Working things to my advantage?"

"That's not what I'm asking."

Gary liked that she was taking an interest. "I don't understand," he said.

"I'm asking, Doesn't all this take a lot of time, a lot of energy? Always looking for an angle."

"Everybody does. Ask your husband."

"But what if you took that persistence and did something with it? Something legitimate. Don't you think that would be easier?"

Gary winked. "But not nearly as creative."

She looked in his eyes now. "It isn't the money, is it?"

Gary didn't say anything at first. Then he said, "Everybody needs that, too."

"So, how long has he been paying?"

"Didn't he tell you?"

"He doesn't tell me anything. I've told you that from the start."

"When did you find out?"

"After you came to the cottage."

Gary asked, "So why do you hang with him?"

"You said it."

"I did?"

"The alternative is not nearly as creative," she said.

Gary thought about it, but he wasn't sure what she was saying. He looked her over, sitting there in a pair of baggy chinos. Quiet, never rattled, but that mind of hers going. The little woman, looking for another way in, he decided. Just like those composites she was doing. Going to ask him a bunch of questions. Most of them innocuous. Then slip in, *"Where you going to spend the money?"* And later, *"Where you going?"*

Gary stood up, her eyes following him. He looked at the clock on the TV.

It was nearly one A.M..

He wondered if in the Upper Peninsula, he'd be able to page Tino Dentz.

NELSON CONNOR TALKED to Kelly Johns for nearly an hour, first asking about Katherine, then everything he could glean about the Brevort Motel. He made them a pot of Jamaican Blue Mountain, the two of them sitting at the table. He wondered to himself at first how Bobby Tank got past Judge Leonard Talbot. He came up with only one answer. He'd

involved Darryl Lensley. That's all he needed to know. When he heard
Tank had a gun, he abandoned any thought of going to the motel. He'd
seen Tank's glazed eyes in his courtroom. You didn't corner a man like
that. You didn't give him the moment of glory he'd been chasing for most
of his life.

"What's he like—Gary?" he asked her.

"He hit me," she said.

Connor noticed the swelling in the corner of her mouth. "Did he hit
Katherine?"

"I think so. But not in front of me."

But that's not what he was looking for. "What else does this Gary
like?"

"He likes to think big. Likes keeping things complicated."

"You mean grandiose?"

"That's a good word."

"Tell me more about what he wanted to do with the casino."

"I thought I told you everything."

"But why there? Shit, why not just come here? Get the money, like
the other guy did."

"That's what I mean about complicated. Plus, I think he likes the idea
of a big crowd. The more people, the better, he said."

"And he asked you to help them?"

"No. I just found myself involved."

"He didn't suspect you?"

"The guy, Gary, yeah, I think so. But one thing about him, face-to-
face, the guy backs down, unless you're a woman. In that case, you just
get slapped around."

Connor thought about Kace again, but he forced her out of his mind.
"So, you were saying you were involved."

"I didn't get all of it. But the other guy—"

"Dentz?"

She nodded. "He was saying I was going to have to wear this hat."

"A hat? What kind of hat?"

"Like some Foreign Legion thing. So my hair was covered."

"And you were going to go with this guy Bobby?"

She nodded, sipping her coffee.

"And Dentz and Gary, where were they going to be?"

"I think they were going. All that Tino told me was that I'd have to go into the casino with this Bobby. Tell you your wife was okay. Have to sell it. Then he and I would hook up later."

"What were you going to do?"

"I told Tino I was leaving with him."

"But, really, what were you going to do?"

"I was looking for an opportunity. I got one sooner that I thought."

"But what about Katherine? Were they going to take her to the casino?"

"They never decided about that."

Connor thought the way they had it set up, he'd probably never see Kace again. He was glad he hadn't involved the police. Lawrence Gary, he decided, always liked to hold something back.

He said, "But you and this guy Tino never went to the casino."

"No, Tino said we were going to Florida with the money, after we dropped in on you."

He reached out and touched her hand. "I owe you a lot," he said. "That took guts. Damn sneaky, too."

"It felt good. I'd been waiting."

"You're a real good actress."

"That's all I've been doing. Five days a week. I'm sick of it."

"I'll pay you back."

"You don't have to."

"No, when I get back. There's someplace I want to take you."

"A place?"

"You still want to go to a meeting?"

"You mean AA?"

"If you want."

She nodded, yes, she'd like that.

He added, "They cater to people with acting problems, too."

She looked him in the eyes, asking, "What about you?"

He got up, walked over to the window, looking out at the straits. Beyond a point of land to his left, he could see the southern approach of the bridge, the lights twinkling.

"Are you going to call the police?" she asked.

"I can't."

"Is it the thing with Jimmy?"

"I don't think so. Not anymore."

"Then why?"

"If I call the police, then I lose all control."

"I understand."

He turned around. "You do?"

Kelly Johns said, "Of course. That's where all the acting comes in."

CONNOR WAITED UNTIL one-thirty, long enough to get Lawrence Gary rattled, but not too long, he decided. If he waited too long, Gary might come looking for him. He'd gotten lucky once already at the cottage. Odds were, he wouldn't get another gift like that tonight.

Sitting at the table, he dialed the number from the local directory. He asked for room 20, not room 21.

He didn't hear a ring. Just the phone picked up fast, Kace's voice. He figured he'd have only a second.

"Just go with it," he said. "Whatever Gary tells you to do."

He heard the phone pulled from her hands.

Gary's voice. "Tino, where the fuck are you, man?"

Connor gave it a solid two or three seconds, then said, "You might want to check at the foot of the bridge. They ought to be pulling that van of his out with a winch right about now."

"*Connor?*"

Not "*Honor.*" He felt ahead already.

He continued, making sure to say "*Gary,*" not "*Larry.*" "But Gary, you want to be careful. There's a couple of county cruisers down there, too."

"You called the police? You must want this woman dead pretty bad."

"Don't get excited. Just a tip from a concerned motorist. Somebody who saw him go in."

"You saw him?"

"Yeah, he came over. He was way ahead of you. He wanted the money. Said he needed it to get to Florida."

"Where is it?"

"It's not here. Just in case you're thinking about it. I wouldn't make the same mistake he did."

"How did you find me?"

"Your guy told me. But he suggested I shoot my way in."

"Where's the girl?"

"*Who?*" Connor asked, glancing at Kelly.

"Your lap gal. He had her with him."

"I didn't see any girl. But I didn't see inside his van, either. I never got that close."

Gary dropped it. "Then what happened?"

"He got sloppy. One thing just led to another and he ran. But he wasn't very observant behind the wheel."

"And you could be full of shit."

Connor could hear the change in his voice now, Gary trying to get back in the game again. He liked to play. That's why he wouldn't stay down for long.

"Call the sheriff, check it out," Connor said.

The line was silent.

"Gary, I want those pictures, and my wife," Connor said.

He wanted Gary to think the photos were just as important. Gary would make a deal, but no doubt renege. Hold something back. Connor wanted him holding back the negatives.

"You got the money?"

"Forty-five thousand, just like you said. You bring the negatives? I want this over."

"Somehow I knew you'd get around to that."

"You get to keep all the money now, Gary. And I want you out of my life."

"That's a whole different negotiation, entirely."

"Then how about the Reatta?"

"Your car?"

Connor thought he detected a hint of interest. "You know what a dealer title is, Gary? You just sign your name, and it's yours."

"Maybe I don't need a car."

"You can sell it. You can keep it. It's up to you."

Gary paused, Connor listening. Then, "How do I know you're not setting me up?"

"Think about it. Brevort Motel. Nice little place about twenty miles west of here. If I wanted you, right about now you'd be looking at about a half dozen cars with flashing lights out there on U.S.-2."

Connor paused, then said it again. "I want this over."

Gary said, "You know where the casino is?"

Connor took a breath. He didn't want it on Gary's turf. "Not there," he said. "Too many cops there. Look, you're bringing those photos, I don't want to see law enforcement people any more than you do."

Gary said, "I didn't see any police."

"They're all under," Connor said. "The tribe has its own force. It's their jurisdiction. They're all over that goddamn place."

"How do you know?"

"I've been thrown out of the place a few times." Connor paused. "But the casino's a good start. I like the idea of a lot of people around. Just so you don't pull something. And I want to see her, before I give you the money."

"You'll see her."

"And the people?"

"What, in this town?"

Nelson Connor wanted plenty of potential witnesses. And he wanted someplace Gary wouldn't have the opportunity to thoroughly scope out. He wouldn't be very mobile for the next twenty-four hours, not with Dentz gone.

He needed something grandiose.

"How about on one of the ferries?" Connor asked. "People coming back from the island."

"No good," Gary said.

"There'll be a lot of people. It's Labor Day weekend."

"I don't like boats."

"How about the island, the Grand Hotel? There's thousands of people on that porch."

Christ, come on, Connor thought.

"How about the bridge?" Gary asked.

Don't take it, Connor told himself. Not yet.

"There's no walkway for pedestrians," Connor said. "They don't let people out there."

Lawrence Gary said, "The day after tomorrow they will."

THE NEXT DAY, Nelson Connor was glad he had one day to work out the details. He bought a local newspaper, gleaning all the information he could about the annual walk. Then he drove across the bridge to Mackinaw City with Kelly Johns. He'd crossed it a hundred times and walked it on Labor Day a few years ago, but this time, he looked at it in a different way. At dawn, authorities would close two lanes for the walk, leaving the other two open for traffic. He saw only two emergency turn-offs. They were on top the enormous blocks of reinforced concrete that anchored the suspension cables, three miles apart. Between them were the two main towers, four lanes, and a four-foot guardrail on both sides. No place to hide, or stop. The bridge had drawn only a handful of suicides over the years, and they had to abandon their cars on the span to jump. He told Kelly about the bridge's most famous fatality, a woman a few years back. She was behind the wheel of a Yugo when a November gale wind blew the subcompact over the railing. One medical examiner theorized she died of heart failure on the two-hundred-foot ride down.

They drove twenty miles south of Mackinaw City to the old Pellston Air Force Base, now the Pellston Airport. It was a large airstrip with one little terminal, one car-rental company and a small parking lot. He bought Kelly Johns a ticket to Detroit Metro.

"I can stay," she said.

"You need to stay safe," he said.

"That's not in my nature."

He kissed her cheek, then handed her Jack Crilly's card. "If this doesn't work out, if something happens to me, I want you to call this man. Tell him what happened. Then tell him to do what he has to do to balance the scales."

"He'll know what that means?" she asked.

Connor nodded. "Better than I do," he said.

He stood outside behind a chain-link fence, watching her climb the steps of the boarding platform. Then he watched the commuter until it was gone.

He drove another twenty miles to Petoskey and found a K-Mart. Saw the manager in his office, flashing him his State Bar of Michigan card. Told him he and a hundred other people connected with Detroit law enforcement were on a golf outing at one of the nearby premiere golf courses and were running out of singles for this three-day, buck-a-hole game they had every year. And damn, tomorrow was a holiday. No bank open.

The guy asking, "How many singles you need?"

Connor said, "That depends on how many singles you've got."

On the way back across the bridge, he was thinking he needed just to get close. Give Gary the money, the keys, and the car title. Then get Kace out of there, disappear into the crowd. When she was safe, he'd find a cop.

Then he remembered. The paper said there would be no police. Only National Guardsmen. They would direct the start of the walk and be posted along the railings every couple hundred yards.

He got to thinking: Why not make sure the cops would be there? There, but looking for something different. He was dealing with two ex-convicts on parole. That gave him a lot to work with.

Still, he was missing key details. He'd been unable to pin Gary down to an exact location. He was supposed to leave the Reatta on the Mackinaw City side. They were to meet somewhere on the bridge between seven and noon for the exchange. Gary said he'd call at dawn with a specific time and place.

Waiting in line at the tollbooth, Connor reached for the newspaper, speed-reading.

Hell, he thought, he didn't need a specific time.

It would work because they all had to walk one way, south to Mackinaw City. The guardsman would not let you double back, even if you could buck a river of fifty thousand excited tourists.

Nelson Connor liked it.

Lawrence Gary, he decided, would have to go with the flow this time.

CHAPTER 31

NOT A BAD morning for a payday, Lawrence Gary decided, though he would have preferred a different crowd. He didn't like the looks of all those fudgies in the large field they were using as a parking lot. RVs with little satellite antennas and station wagons and hatchbacks packed to the dome lights with luggage and coolers and pillows. Brats running around, and fat fucks standing around with their bellies hanging over their shorts, shooting pictures of the bridge, using a goddamn flash at twilight, as if you could light it from more than a mile away.

Everybody moving toward the bridge.

Gary turned to the little woman in the backseat, sitting there with Bobby Tank, the child locks on. "You ever do this?"

"A few times."

"How long does it take?"

"It's five miles."

"That's not what I asked."

"It depends how fast you walk."

He looked at Bobby Tank. Bobby pulled out the Star .45, the little woman glancing at it. "The man is asking you a question, ma'am."

Gary said, "This is not the time for that, Katherine. Shit, you're almost home."

She said, "Most people walk about three miles an hour."

"Fuck, man," Bobby said. "It looks cold out there. Ain't this summer?"

"It's the straits," Katherine Connor said. "It should warm up later."

Gary noticed she had on a wool sweater, the little woman all prepared. He had his infantry shirt, but he figured he'd warm up, once he got walking. He was prepared in another way. He'd checked with the county sheriff, just like His Honor told him. Said, Yeah, he was calling because he'd seen that purple van go into the water. A little chitchat, the deputy on the phone saying they'd fished out one body, not two. The lap whore probably gave him a pretty good briefing, Gary decided, the man thinking now that he knew exactly what was coming. The man, trying to be clever. It was just His Honor's nature, and he was going with it.

Lawrence Gary had to admire the man for that.

Gary checked his camera bag. Saw Tino Dentz's cellular. Two canon bodies and two lenses. He was glad he'd come north with just his Pulitzer kit, traveling light. He could use the bag for the money. And something else.

He turned around. "Bobby, when we leave I'm going to need that."

"Need what?"

Gary's eyes went to the semiautomatic.

"You?"

Gary nodded.

"Fuck that, I ain't goin' naked."

"All you got to do is meet the man. Bring him to me."

"I don't know if I remember him."

"You were in his courtroom."

"I wasn't looking."

"You'll know him. I'll work that out when I call him."

"Where you going to be?"

He turned to the little woman, smiling. "I'm going to be with Katherine, enjoying our bridge walk."

"What if it's fucked up?"

"It won't be. As a matter of fact, Bobby, unless you are carrying, what could they take you down you for? Walking across the bridge? If he's got it wired, I'm the one with all the exposure on this gig."

Bobby Tank thought about it, then nodded. He could see the point.

"Guns, Gary," he said. "That's not like you."

"Hey," Gary said, lighting a cigarette. "Sometimes an artist has to take risks."

A SHORT TIME later, the phone rang in the cottage. Nelson Connor listened to the instructions. The first tower. On the Upper Peninsula side. Go there and wait. At nine o'clock.

Gary asked, What was he wearing?

"What does it matter?" Connor asked.

"Honor," Gary said. "After all, we have never met."

"Gray sweats," Connor said. "I'll be carrying a gym bag."

"Man of your stature, I'd think you'd be a little more fashionable than that."

"Cut the bullshit," Connor said. "You know nobody can stop walking very long."

"Just look like you're enjoying the view," Gary said.

He wanted to ask him about Kace, but Gary hung up. Then the phone rang again.

"Gary, goddamn you."

There was silence, then, "You sound like you need a meeting, my friend."

Jack Crilly.

"Jesus, I've been trying to reach you."

"I headed for the water for a few days. Finally checked my machine. I should have told you, but it was one of those last-minute things."

Connor didn't know where to start. Now he didn't have time.

Crilly said, "I checked the papers, so I figure you're sober."

"What does that have to do with anything?"

"If you weren't, I figured you'd be making headlines by now."

It began pouring out of him. Fragments of what had happened.

Crilly interrupted, "You've got the police involved in this, I hope?"

"Not yet," he said.

"Jesus Christ."

"You're meeting them?"

"Yes."

"With money?"

"Some."

"Where?"

"This bridge walk they have up here."

"That Mackinaw bridge walk?"

He wasn't going to give Crilly the chance to talk him out of it. "Jack, I've got less than two hours to meet them at a tower nearly three miles out in the fucking water. When it's over, I'll call you."

As he pulled the phone from his ear, he heard Crilly shouting that he wanted to help him.

He thought, *Help?* He was three hundred miles away.

THE NATIONAL GUARD had already staged a substantial crowd at the foot of the bridge, maybe twenty-five thousand, Gary guessed. As they walked closer, he could see two hundred yards of those fudgies lined up, two lanes wide, backed up where the freeway sloped down to the toll-booths. He was on the high ground now, with a pretty good view.

As they walked closer, a guardsman in camo was saying on a bullhorn: ". . . No dogs. No bicycles. No Rollerblades. No wagons, or similar vehicles. Baby strollers and wheelchairs are allowed. No racing or playing tag is permitted. Walkers must stay away from bridge railings. No dogs. No bicycles. . . ."

At the front of the mob, Gary noticed athletes in running shorts and T-shirts, some covered with sleeveless jerseys, large black numbers on paper squares, pinned on their backs and chests.

He turned to Katherine Connor, walking between him and Bobby, saying, "I thought there was no running."

"Those are walkers," she said. "They have some kind of event. You know, Olympic style."

"Exciting," Gary said, sarcastically. But he was excited, in a different way, over different things.

Behind the athletes, Gary saw two or three TV lights go on, a cluster forming. "That must be the governor," he said. "He come every year?"

"Usually. In an election year, everybody does. It's a good place to be seen."

"Fascinating," Gary said.

They were still coming down the hill when a starter's pistol went off. It was 7:00 A.M. The crowd gave up a cheer. The men and women in athletic gear lunged forward, their arms pumping, hips swaying in that fast chicken-walk, the crowd streaming around the cluster of politicians.

Bobby Tank said, "Damn, you-all take this holiday serious up here."

Five minutes later, they reached the bridge approach, moving to the back of the crowd. Gary looked at his watch, then the ribbon of concrete ahead of them, the green railings and suspension cables, the white towers in the distance, bisecting the morning blue.

He reached out and took the little woman's hand, squeezing. It was limp at first. Then he felt her reposition it, sliding her fingers between his.

"Please," she said. "Don't do anything stupid. There's a lot of children."

Gary said, "Stupid?"

She nodded. He saw a tear, but figured it was the wind.

He said, "I think you're talking to the wrong guy."

IMMEDIATELY NELSON CONNOR ran into problems.

Traffic backed up a mile on U.S.-2 because of the bridge lane closure. He'd never intended to leave the Reatta in Mackinaw City, or take a shuttle bus back to the north side. He'd only planned to hand Gary the keys and the title, tell him where the car was located.

That wasn't the problem. The problem was he couldn't even get to the bridge parking area now.

Connor did a U-turn, speeding back to a two-lane that cut along the edge of the national forest into St. Ignace. He remembered they used to have shuttle buses to the bridge walk there.

He found a yellow school bus parked at one of the ferry-service parking lots, a line of people outside its door, another bus pulling behind it. He saw three pay phones near the ticket office. He paid ten dollars for the island parking and jogged over to the telephones, the gym bag in his hand.

He dialed the local post of the Michigan State Police. A desk sergeant answered. He had a tip, he said. Two Detroiters, ex-cons, were planning to do a major drug deal at the foot of the south tower during the bridge walk sometime after nine o'clock.

"Is nothing sacred?" the sergeant asked.

Connor didn't like the tone of his voice. He gave him names anyway.

A description of Bobby Tank. Said the other might be carrying a gym bag. Warned them they were both armed.

"And who is this?" the sergeant asked.

"Somebody directly involved."

The sergeant paused, then said, "You need to talk to one of our detectives about this."

Connor's eyes were on the school bus. It was pulling away, the one behind it pulling up. The sergeant had covered the phone. Connor could hear him saying something inaudible to somebody in muffled tones.

When he heard the hand come off the receiver, Connor asked, "Can you put a detective on?"

"You're going to have to call back tomorrow," the sergeant said. "They're off today."

"You can't do anything now?"

"I can only pass it along."

Ten minutes later, he was sitting three seats back in the school bus, on the aisle, next to a fidgeting six-year-old, the kid up on his knees a lot, talking to his parents in the seat behind.

As the bus rocked back and forth in an access lane created for the shuttles, Connor took a mental inventory of the gym bag: The keys. The car title and thirteen thousand dollars that looked like forty-five with the twenties and hundreds sandwiched around the singles with rubber bands. At least he thought it looked like forty-five. He had no idea what forty-five thousand dollars looked like. But he was hoping Gary didn't, either. The last thing he figured Gary would do was stand on the bridge and count it.

On top of the money was the Colt, the revolver filled with six rounds. It was something he'd debated all night, then went with it, especially after Jack Crilly called. He remembered what Crilly told him about cons, that the best cons worked because the con man made himself vulnerable. Giving Gary the gun would sell the deal, he figured, sell the short money. He'd tell him it was a bonus, his way of acknowledging he had the edge. What difference did it make? Bobby Tank would already be armed. He couldn't imagine either of them drawing weapons in that crowd, in that situation, especially once they had the money. When the state police collared them at the south tower, they wouldn't find drugs, but the guns, arrest them both on a parole violation. Then they'd get his call.

At least that's the way it was supposed to work. Now he didn't know about the state police.

The bus pulled to a stop at the foot of the Mackinaw Bridge, the driver reaching for the handle on the door.

LAWRENCE GARY WAS cold, as cold as he'd ever been in his life. He walked with his hands in his pockets, his camera bag strapped across his chest. They had to walk slow to time it just right, hundreds of people going around them, as if the three of them were a rock in the middle of a brook.

He felt better when they reached the spot where the suspension cables started, the sun now higher in the sky. It penetrated his shirt nearly as much as the wind coming off the straits. Below his feet he could see waves of blue water through the steel grid roadway. On the right, he saw Lake Michigan, the coastlines of both peninsulas. On his left he saw Lake Huron and the long white porch of the Grand Hotel on Mackinaw Island, even though it was a good three or four miles away.

They had to be nearly two hundred feet up now.

He remembered an old Cagney movie he saw once, that Cagney line, *"Top of the world, Ma."* He loved the line and that final scene, Cagney standing high on top of an oil tank, shouting it defiantly, surrounded by cops.

Then Lawrence Gary got a chill again, remembering Cagney said it just before the tank blew up.

NELSON CONNOR JOGGED most of the approach. He was running late, but it felt good to sweat. He jogged until one of the guardsman about a quarter mile from the north tower came off the railing, saying, "Sir, you'll have to walk."

He walked fast, zigzagging through the crowd. Going by couples holding hands and parents with young children and pairs of middle-aged women side by side, the women talking and walking in that exercise mode.

A couple hundred feet from the tower, his eyes searched ahead, instantly capturing body shapes and hairstyles, then discarding them when he didn't see her strawberry hair or the figure Kace had kept for more than twenty years.

At the tower he slowed, still looking, lowering the gym bag to his side. He walked backward. Then stopped and turned back around. Almost bumping into a guy.

Shit, Bobby Tank standing in his boots, MIGHTY MAC across his chest. Not like he remembered him, but like he'd been put together with spare body parts taken from the cast of felons in his courtroom and the people sitting on the shuttle bus.

"Judge?"

Connor nodded. "Where's Gary? My wife?"

Tank started walking, Connor with him.

"You got the money?" Tank asked, his eyes straight ahead.

"First my wife. My deal's with Gary."

Tank looked down at the gym bag, saying, "That it?"

Connor held his tongue.

"Gary says I got to check it first. Make sure it's there."

He reached for the bag. Connor let it go.

Tank, carrying the bag on his belly now, unzipping it, then saying, "Well, I'll be goddamned."

Bobby Tank slowed, people going around him. Connor looked back to see it. Bobby Tank, pulling out the Colt .45 and sliding it real quick into his own jeans, pulling his sweatshirt down.

Connor felt a hole in his stomach.

When Tank caught back up, he gave him back the bag. Then he reached into his jeans and pulled out a can of Skoal. He packed his lower front lip so thick he almost drooled.

After he spit, he said, "So, you planning something big, Your Honor?" Still looking straight ahead.

"It was part of the deal—for Gary," Connor said.

"He don't appreciate a good firearm," Tank said.

They passed a guardsman, the soldier leaning against the rail, smoking a cigarette. Connor strained his eyes, he couldn't see any more soldiers ahead.

"You're taking me to my wife? Gary?"

Tank nodded, leaning over, spitting again. A woman with wire-rims, jogging shoes, and a long skirt walked around him, looking back in disgust. Tank didn't give her the satisfaction of his eyes.

"Where are they?" Connor asked, looking ahead now too, walking, mirroring Bobby Tank's gait.

"Nice day, ain't it?"

Then Nelson Connor saw people swerving ahead. And he caught a glimpse of Kace's hair. Then her arm. Saw her holding the guy's hand, walking slow.

They were almost to the crown at midspan.

SOME PEOPLE HAD stopped, lingering at the highest point of the bridge. Some took pictures. Others stood pointing out sights along the shore. No Guardsman nearby to keep people moving.

Lawrence Gary stopped, let go of Katherine Connor's hand and slung one camera from the bag around his neck. He framed Bobby Tank and the Honorable Nelson Connor in the viewfinder and let the motor drive do the work for six frames.

The man. Looked pretty ragged in the jogging suit.

Just like he remembered him at the twitch farm.

CONNOR SAW HIM holding Kace's hand again, but didn't look at it directly. It was odd seeing him now, not at all like he expected. A guy with hair out of the fifties. A shirt from the sixties. His pants, the seventies. And the black grunge band boots. He was being blackmailed, his wife kidnapped, by a guy who looked like he was auditioning for MTV.

He forced himself not to look at Kace.

Connor handed over the gym bag. "Here's what you want."

Gary opened it, looked inside, but then closed it, handing it to Bobby Tank.

"Now," Connor said, "where are the negatives?"

Still not looking at Kace, ignoring her, selling it.

"Hey, move over," somebody shouted, walking by.

Gary backed up to the edge of the lane, still gripping Kace with his right hand, the camera bag on his right. The camera bag flap was open. The bridge railing was about three feet away.

Nelson Connor realized he didn't know where Tank was. He was somewhere behind him.

He kept his eyes on Gary.

"The fucking negatives, Gary," Connor said. "That was the deal."

Gary said, "What about the little woman? I was hoping for a big tearful reunion. Take a few snaps. Maybe send you a couple of prints."

He took two steps closer.

"The photos," he said. "That was the deal."

Gary sighed. "Well, I guess it's just going to be one of those difficult new choices, Honor. Is it family or a career?"

Bobby Tank, coming around to his right now, the gym bag in his hand, saying, "Gary, this motherfucker looks short."

He reached for Kace first, but missed her, Lawrence Gary pulling her aside. But she grabbed him by the camera-bag strap, and swung him around, toward Connor. He saw a camera body and lenses spill out onto the pavement—and a gun.

Gary still holding her, but his jaw momentarily up and out, trying to maintain his balance.

The first left jab released Kace's hand, the second drove Gary back to the bridge railing. Then he went once hard to the body with another left, just below the Canon at his sternum. The right uppercut seemed to start at his own feet and end somewhere in the sky above.

They both had a snapshot: Connor, trying to reach for him, Lawrence Gary going over backward, over the railing, his hands reaching for something, but getting only the Canon motor drive hanging around his own neck.

Connor started to lean over the railing, but heard people screaming. When he spun around, he saw fringe boots and the sweatshirt. People scattering, leaving Bobby Tank alone on the steel grid.

Tank leaned forward at the waist, the Colt .45 aimed right at Connor.

He turned his head to the side, spitting, as if he was about to say something.

Connor was frozen, his eyes looking for Kace.

One shot.

Then two more.

Bobby Tank looked momentarily confused, then he collapsed on the roadway.

Only then did Nelson Connor see Jack Crilly standing not ten feet behind Bobby Tank, still taking dead aim, a small semiautomatic in his hand.

CHAPTER 32

IN THE SMALL lobby at the state police post, Kace leaned over, saying, "He followed?"

Connor said, "Must have. I must have told him where."

"He followed you all the way from Detroit, and you didn't know it?"

Connor, his elbows on his knees, shook his head. "He told me on the bridge he came up with Mike Cooney. Cooney wanted some company. Hell, he's been up here two days."

"The circuit judge who's running?"

Connor nodded, looking straight ahead. "He came up to campaign, shake hands on the bridge."

"How are they friends?"

"Jack gets around."

"I mean, how does he know him so well?"

He turned, saw a bemused look on her face. "It's a long story," Connor said.

They were sitting on a wood bench, the trooper at the desk offering them coffee earlier, then saying, Folks, it would be just a few minutes. The trooper on the phone now, Jack Crilly in the back somewhere, no doubt being grilled by the detective brought in off holiday leave. They'd brought them over in separate scout cars. The TV crews were with the governor at a Moose Lodge breakfast, the trooper said. But Connor knew they would eventually catch up with the shooting story. But for now, they were alone.

Kace said, "They won't charge him, will they?"

"Jack?" Connor said quietly.

She nodded.

"It can get complicated. Depends on what he says."

Connor was thinking they had probably already run Jack Crilly and his DOB on the post computer, and now the detective was probably working from a page or two of arrests and convictions that came off the LEIN machine. The police had Crilly, Crilly's sheet, and probably some sketchy accounts from hysterical tourists. Connor had the keys and title to his Reatta in his sweats. They had the bag of money, and maybe the anonymous tip he'd left earlier with the sergeant from the midnight shift.

Connor leaned over, hugging Kace with one arm. "I take that back," he said.

"What?"

"About Jack. It doesn't depend on him."

"It doesn't?"

He put his elbows back on his knees, leaning forward.

"Actually, it depends on me."

THE DETECTIVE CAME out, asking Connor to step through the swinging door with him. Katherine got up from the bench, but the detective said, "Ma'am, if you don't mind, I'd like to talk to your husband alone."

He did not see Jack Crilly. He did not see him in the narrow hall with fluorescent lights as he followed the detective. He didn't see him in the offices they passed.

The interview room was very small, a table and two chairs taking nearly all the space. The detective apologized for the size, saying the other room they had was in use.

The detective offered him coffee, or water if he wanted it.

"I'm not thirsty," Nelson Connor said.

The detective was wearing jeans, a tan shirt, and a coarse woven tie with a hasty knot. He had a full mustache and deeply receding hair. Maybe forty-five, but a flat belly. He had a half dozen sheets of paper in front of him, apparently notes taken by troopers dispatched to the bridge.

So," he began, "I understand you're Judge Connor's son, the cottage down on U.S.-2. Must run in the family, hey?"

Connor nodded. "You knew him?"

"My old man was on the road for thirty-five years with the county. He used to keep an eye on the place in the winter for your dad."

The detective leaned back in the chair, folding his hands in front of him on the table. "From the witness statements we have, you've had one hell of day. How's your wife?"

"She's pretty resilient," Connor said.

"She in law enforcement?"

"Only married to me."

Connor waited two seconds, then asked, "What about the guy that went over?"

"We've got a good dive team up here. But then again, you're dealing with that current. The water at midspan is damn near three hundred feet."

"You figure there's no chance?"

"When I was on the road, I worked a jumper we had some years back. The medical examiner said his hip bones were driven all the way into his rib cage. And he went in feet first."

"I didn't think I hit him that hard."

The detective glanced at the paperwork. "Says here he was holding on to your wife. Hell, Judge, I'd hit him hard, too."

Then the detective sat looking at him, his thumbs circling, saying nothing, but not trying to shake something loose, Connor thought.

"What are you waiting for?" Connor asked.

"We've got one stolen gun, but nothing on the shooter's. That Colt's old. But the guy had a sheet. I was thinking, maybe I'll just take a quick statement from you. Judge, you've already had enough excitement for one day." The detective grinned with private amusement, shaking his head. "You've got to hand it to some of these cons, they are creative."

Connor folded his hands on the table, leaned forward and said it as if he were on the bench.

"You don't need a registration on the gun, Detective."

The grin left the cop's face. "I don't?"

"That Colt .45 with the pearl handle belongs to my deputy in Detroit."

Then Nelson Connor told him everything he could remember, starting at the Anchor Bar.

THE NEXT DAY, both Detroit papers went with the same story. They had front-page headlines about a shooting on the bridge, but played up a feature angle, going with the irony of a reformed ex-con saving a Detroit judge and his wife who apparently stumbled onto a drug rip-off gone bad. Reporters found the midnight desk sergeant who had taken the anonymous tip, apparently figuring they had the inside story when the detective Nelson Connor talked to had no comment on the case. Then they interviewed Jack Crilly when he walked out of the state police post. That sold it.

There was a sidebar, the headline: BRIDGE WALK: IS IT SAFE?

Connor asked him later, "But, Jack, why didn't you tell them you knew me?"

"They would have asked how."

"So?"

"So the program says we're supposed to always remain anonymous on the level of print, radio, and TV. Always remember, it's Alcoholics *Anonymous*, my friend."

Nelson Connor arrived at the CCB early Wednesday. In the morning paper, read a short in "Names and Faces" about the owner of the Anchor Bar. The *Free Press* column reported he was leaving the old Pick-Fort Shelby for cleaner, brighter haunts closer to the Detroit River, but still a good three to four blocks away.

Connor set up a meeting with an investigator for the Judicial Tenure Commission at four, then phoned Homicide. By noon, he'd heard back from the inspector at 1300 Beaubien. He said they'd found photographs of James Osborne in Lawrence Gary's darkroom. They didn't need a warrant, he said. They took his parole officer. There would be no public record, but he couldn't guarantee anything, saying detectives sometimes shot off their mouths at a backgammon game they had going with a night-shift reporter in the police beat on the third floor.

"I'll be in touch," he said. "If we need anything more to close it."

The night before, Nelson Connor had put the photographs Lawrence Gary gave him in a drawer in his study.

"Why you keeping those?" Katherine asked.

"I need to," Connor said. "To remember."

"Remember what?"

"What drinking was like."

At the midafternoon break, Barbara came in to bum a smoke. He was still in his robes, sitting behind his desk. She dropped a ruling in front of him, saying "This just came over from the Court of Appeals."

It was a decision on a request for emergency leave, the case of the defendant who had raped the old woman, the case handled by Densely. His new attorney wanted the sentence vacated, saying it exceeded state sentencing guidelines. Nelson Connor had given him sixty to one hundred years. The appellate decision included a portion of the transcript at sentencing. Connor eyed his exchange with the rapist right before giving him the sentence. It was the day after he was released out of Brighton Hospital.

THE COURT: Did you tell my deputy, "I don't care what Connor gives me. I'll be out in ten years and fuck some more"?

THE DEFENDANT: I remember my lawyer saying something about ten years.

Connor leafed past the summary, his eyes scanning the Courier type. He was prepared, thinking it wouldn't be the first time he'd been overturned by the higher court.

Barbara plopped into one of the chairs, lighting her cigarette.

Nelson Connor saw the words: "In light of the facts of this case, and the attitude of the defendant, it's the opinion of the panel that Third Circuit Judge Nelson A. Connor's punishment was entirely adequate and appropriate."

Barbara said, "Well, Your Honor?"

"It sounds pretty good," Nelson Connor said.